PENGUI

ENTWINED

Titles by Sylvia Day

The Crossfire Novels

Bared to You
Reflected in You
Entwined with You

Seven Years to Sin
The Stranger I Married
Scandalous Liaisons
Ask for It
Passion for the Game
A Passion for Him
Don't Tempt Me
Pride and Pleasure
In the Flesh

Entwined with You

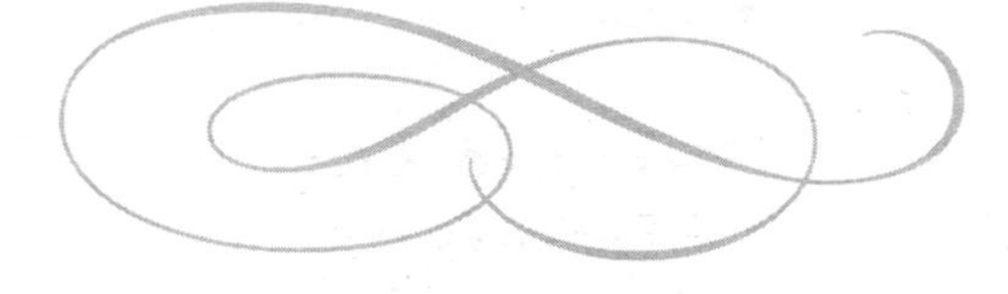

Sylvia Day

PENGUIN BOOKS

PENGUIN BOOKS

Published by the Penguin Group
Penguin Books Ltd, 80 Strand, London WC2R 0RL, England
Penguin Group (USA) Inc., 375 Hudson Street, New York, New York 10014, USA
Penguin Group (Canada), 90 Eglinton Avenue East, Suite 700, Toronto, Ontario, Canada M4P 2Y3
(a division of Pearson Penguin Canada Inc.)
Penguin Ireland, 25 St Stephen's Green, Dublin 2, Ireland (a division of Penguin Books Ltd)
Penguin Group (Australia), 707 Collins Street, Melbourne, Victoria 3008, Australia
(a division of Pearson Australia Group Pty Ltd)
Penguin Books India Pvt Ltd, 11 Community Centre, Panchsheel Park, New Delhi – 110 017, India
Penguin Group (NZ), 67 Apollo Drive, Rosedale, Auckland 0632, New Zealand
(a division of Pearson New Zealand Ltd)
Penguin Books (South Africa) (Pty) Ltd, Block D, Rosebank Office Park,
181 Jan Smuts Avenue, Parktown North, Gauteng 2193, South Africa

Penguin Books Ltd, Registered Offices: 80 Strand, London WC2R 0RL, England

www.penguin.com

First published in the United States of America by The Berkley Publishing Group,
an imprint of Penguin Group (USA) Inc. 2013
First published in Great Britain by Penguin Books 2013

005

Printed in Great Britain by Clays Ltd, St Ives plc

A CIP catalogue record for this book is available from the British Library

ISBN: 978-1-405-91027-9

www.greenpenguin.co.uk

Penguin Books is committed to a sustainable
future for our business, our readers and our planet.
This book is made from Forest Stewardship
Council™ certified paper.

ALWAYS LEARNING

PEARSON

ACKNOWLEDGMENTS

My gratitude to editor Hilary Sares for all her hard work on *Entwined with You* and the previous two books in the Crossfire series. Without her, there would be some rambling, many Latinate words, brief lapses into historical jargon, and other offenses that would distract readers from the beauty of Gideon's love for Eva. Thank you so much, Hilary!

Huge thanks to my agent, Kimberly Whalen, and my editor, Cindy Hwang, for helping me recapture the magic of Gideon and Eva when writing this story. When I needed help, they were there for me. Thank you, Kim and Cindy!

Thank you to my publicist, Gregg Sullivan, for keeping me organized and being a big help in managing my schedule.

Thanks to my agent, Jon Cassir at CAA, for all his hard work and patience in answering my questions.

I'm grateful to all of my international publishers, who've been so tremendously supportive and enthusiastic about the Crossfire series.

And to my readers, I cannot thank you enough for your patience and support. I'm grateful to be sharing Gideon and Eva's continuing journey with you.

1

NEW YORK CABBIES were a unique breed. Fearless to a fault, they sped and swerved through crowded streets with unnatural calm. To save my sanity, I'd learned to focus on the screen of my smartphone instead of the cars rushing by only inches away. Whenever I made the mistake of paying attention, I'd find my right foot pushing hard into the floorboard, my body instinctively trying to hit the brakes.

But for once, I didn't need any distractions. I was sticky with sweat from an intense Krav Maga class, and my mind was spinning with thoughts of what the man I loved had done.

Gideon Cross. Just thinking of his name sent a heated flare of longing through my tightly strung body. From the moment I first saw him—saw through his stunning and impossibly gorgeous exterior to the dark and dangerous man inside—I'd felt the pull that came from finding the other half of myself. I needed him like I needed my heart to beat, and he'd put himself in great jeopardy, risking *everything*—for me.

The blare of a horn snapped me back to the present.

Through the windshield, I saw my roommate's million-dollar smile flashing at me from the billboard on the side of a bus. Cary Taylor's lips had a come-hither curve and his long, lean frame was blocking the intersection. The taxi driver was hitting his horn repeatedly, as if that would clear the way.

Not a chance. Cary wasn't moving and neither was I. He lounged on his side, bare-chested and barefooted, his jeans unbuttoned to show both the waistband of his underwear and the sleek lines of his ripped abs. His dark brown hair was sexily mussed and his emerald eyes were bright with mischief.

I was suddenly struck with the knowledge that I would have to keep a dreadful secret from my best friend.

Cary was my touchstone, my voice of reason, my favorite shoulder to lean on—and a brother to me in every way that mattered. I hated the thought of having to hold back what Gideon had done for me.

I wanted desperately to talk about it, to get help working it out in my head, but I'd never be able to tell anyone. Even our therapist could be ethically and legally bound to break our confidence.

A burly, neon-vested traffic cop appeared and urged the bus into its lane with an authoritative white-gloved hand and a holler that meant business. He waved us through the intersection just before the light changed. I sat back, my arms around my waist, rocking.

The ride from Gideon's Fifth Avenue penthouse to my apartment on the Upper West Side was a short one, but somehow it felt like an eternity. The information that NYPD detective Shelley Graves had shared with me just a few hours earlier had changed my life.

It had also forced me to abandon the one person I *needed* to be with.

I'd left Gideon alone because I couldn't trust Graves's motives. I couldn't take the chance that she'd told me her suspicions just to see if I'd run to him and prove that his breakup with me was a well-crafted lie.

God. The riot of emotions I felt had my heart racing. Gideon needed me now—as much as, if not more than, I needed him—yet I'd walked away.

The desolation in his eyes as the doors to his private elevator separated us had ripped me open inside.

Gideon.

The cab turned the corner and pulled up in front of my apartment building. The night doorman opened the car door before I could tell the driver to turn around and take me back, and the sticky August air rushed in to chase the air-conditioning away.

"Good evening, Miss Tramell." The doorman accompanied the greeting with a tap of his fingers to the brim of his hat and waited patiently while I swiped my debit card. When I'd finished paying, I accepted his help out of the back of the cab and felt his gaze slide discreetly over my tearstained face.

Smiling as if everything were okay in my world, I rushed into the lobby and headed straight for the elevator, with a brief wave at the front desk staff.

"Eva!"

Turning my head, I discovered a svelte brunette in a stylish skirt-and-blouse ensemble rising to her feet in the lobby seating area. Her dark hair fell in thick waves around her shoulders, and her smile graced full lips that were a glossy pink. I frowned, not recognizing her.

"Yes?" I replied, suddenly wary. There was an avid gleam in her dark eyes that got my back up. Despite how battered I felt and probably looked, I squared my shoulders and faced her directly.

"Deanna Johnson," she said, thrusting out a well-manicured hand. "Freelance reporter."

I arched a brow. "Hello."

She laughed. "You don't have to be so suspicious. I'd just like to chat with you a few minutes. I've got a story I'm working on, and I could use your help."

"No offense, but I can't think of anything I want to talk to a reporter about."

"Not even Gideon Cross?"

The hairs on my nape prickled. "Especially not him."

As one of the twenty-five richest men in the world, with a New York real estate portfolio so extensive it boggled the mind, Gideon was always news. But it was also news that he'd dumped me and gotten back together with his ex-fiancée.

Deanna crossed her arms, a move that accentuated her cleavage, something I took note of only because I was eyeing her again with more care.

"Come on," she coaxed. "I can keep your name out of it, Eva. I won't use anything that identifies you. This is your chance to get a bit of your own back."

A rock settled in the bottom of my stomach. She was so exactly Gideon's type—tall, slender, dark-haired, and golden-skinned. So very unlike me.

"Are you sure you want to go down this road?" I asked quietly, intuitively certain she'd fucked my man at some point in the past. "He isn't someone I'd want to cross."

"Are you afraid of him?" she shot back. "I'm not. His money doesn't give him the right to do whatever the hell he wants."

I took a slow, deep breath and remembered when Dr. Terrence Lucas—someone else who was at odds with Gideon—had said something similar to me. Now that I knew what Gideon was capable of, how far he would go to protect me, I could *still* answer honestly and without reservation, "No, I'm not afraid. But I've learned to pick my battles. Moving on is the best revenge."

Her chin lifted. "Not all of us have rock stars waiting in the wings."

"Whatever." I sighed inwardly at her mention of my ex, Brett Kline, who was front man for a band on the rise and one of the sexiest men I'd ever met. Like Gideon, he radiated sex appeal like a heat wave. Unlike

Gideon, he wasn't the love of my life. I was never going to wade in that pool again.

"Listen"—Deanna pulled a business card out of a pocket of her skirt—"pretty soon you're going to figure out that Gideon Cross was using you to get Corinne Giroux jealous enough to come back to him. When you smell the coffee, call me. I'll be waiting."

I accepted the card. "Why do you think I know anything worth sharing?"

Her lush mouth thinned. "Because whatever Cross's motivation was for hooking up with you, you got to him. The iceman thawed a bit for you."

"Maybe he did, but it's over."

"That doesn't mean you don't know something, Eva. I can help you figure out what's newsworthy."

"What's your angle?" I'd be damned if I would sit back while someone took aim at Gideon. If she was determined to be a threat to him, I was determined to head her off at the pass.

"That man has a dark side."

"Don't we all?" What had she seen of Gideon? What had he revealed in the course of their . . . association? *If* they'd had one.

I wasn't sure I'd ever get to the point where thinking of Gideon being intimate with another woman didn't trigger ferocious jealousy.

"Why don't we go somewhere and talk?" she cajoled.

I shot a glance at the staffer at the front desk, who made a good show of politely ignoring us. I was too emotionally raw to deal with Deanna, and was still reeling from the conversation with Detective Graves.

"Maybe some other time," I said, leaving the option open because I intended to keep tabs on her.

As if he sensed my uneasiness, Chad, one of the night crew at the front desk, approached.

"Ms. Johnson was just leaving," I told him, consciously relaxing. If

Detective Graves hadn't been able to pin anything on Gideon, a nosy freelance reporter wasn't going to do better.

Too bad I knew what kind of information could be leaked from the police, and how easily and often it was done. My father, Victor Reyes, was a cop, and I'd heard plenty on that subject.

I turned toward the elevators. "Good night, Deanna."

"I'll be around," she called after me.

I stepped into the elevator and hit the button for my floor. As the doors slid shut, I sagged into the handrail. I needed to warn Gideon, but there was no way for me to contact him that couldn't be traced.

The ache in my chest intensified. Our relationship was so fucked up. We couldn't even talk to each other.

I exited on my floor and let myself into my apartment, crossing the spacious living room to dump my purse on one of the kitchen bar stools. The view of Manhattan showcased through my living room's floor-to-ceiling windows failed to stir me. I was too agitated to care where I was. The only thing that mattered was that I wasn't with Gideon.

As I headed down the hallway toward my bedroom, the sound of muted music floated outward from Cary's. Did he have company over? If so, who was it? My best friend had decided to try juggling two relationships—one with a woman who accepted him the way he was and one with a man who hated that Cary was involved with someone else.

I shed my clothes across the bathroom floor en route to the shower. While I lathered, it was impossible not to think of the times I'd showered with Gideon, occasions when our lust for one another had fueled starkly erotic encounters. I missed him so much. I needed his touch, his desire, his love. My craving for those things was a gnawing hunger, making me restless and edgy. I had no idea how I was supposed to fall asleep when I didn't know when I'd get a chance to talk to Gideon again. There was so much that had to be said.

Wrapping a towel around me, I left the bathroom—

Gideon stood just inside my closed bedroom door. The sight of him spurred a reaction so abrupt it was like a physical blow. My breath caught and my heart lurched into an excited rhythm, my entire being responding to the sight of him with a potent rush of yearning. It felt like years since I'd last been with him, instead of a mere hour.

I'd given him a key, but he owned the building. Getting to me without leaving a trail that could be followed was possible with that advantage . . . just as he'd been able to get to Nathan.

"It's dangerous for you to be here," I pointed out. That didn't stop me from being thrilled that he was. My gaze drank him in, roaming avidly over his lean, broad-shouldered frame.

He wore black sweats and a well-loved Columbia sweatshirt, a combination that made him look like the twenty-eight-year-old man he was and not the billionaire mogul the rest of the world knew. A Yankees ball cap was pulled low over his brow, but the shadow cast by its brim did nothing to diminish the striking blue of his eyes. They stared at me fiercely, his sensual lips drawn into a grim line. "I couldn't stay away."

Gideon Cross was an impossibly gorgeous man, so beautiful that people stopped and stared when he walked by. I'd once thought of him as a sex god, and his frequent—and enthusiastic—displays of prowess constantly proved me right, but I also knew he was all too human. Like me, he'd been broken.

The odds were against our making it.

My chest expanded on a deep breath, my body responding to the proximity of his. Even though he stood several feet away, I could feel the heady attraction, the magnetic pull of being near the other half of my soul. It'd been that way with us from the very first meeting, both of us inexorably drawn together. We'd mistaken our ferocious mutual captivation for lust until we realized we couldn't breathe without each other.

I fought the urge to run into his arms, the place where I so desperately wanted to be. But he was too still, too tightly reined. I waited in exquisite anticipation for his cue.

God, I loved him so much.

His hands fisted at his sides. "I need you."

My core tightened in response to the roughness of his voice, the rasp of it warm and luxurious.

"You don't have to sound so happy about it," I teased breathlessly, trying to lighten his mood before he got me beneath him.

I loved him wild, and I loved him tender. I'd take him any way I could get him, but it'd been so long . . . My skin was already tingling and tightening expectantly, craving the greedy reverence of his touch. I feared what would happen if he came at me full force when I was so starved for his body. We might tear each other apart.

"It's killing me," he said gruffly. "Being without you. Missing you. I feel like my fucking sanity depends on you, Eva, and you want me to be *happy* about that?"

My tongue darted out to wet my dry lips and he growled, sending a shiver through me. "Well . . . *I'm* happy about it."

The tension in his posture visibly eased. He must've been so worried about how I would react to what he'd done for me. To be honest, *I'd* been worried. Did my gratitude mean I was more twisted than I realized?

Then I remembered my stepbrother's hands all over me . . . his weight pressing me into the mattress . . . the tearing pain between my legs as he rammed into me over and over . . .

I trembled with renewed fury. If being glad the fucker was dead made me twisted, so be it.

Gideon took a deep breath. His hand reached up to his chest and rubbed at the area over his heart as if it hurt him.

"I love you," I told him, my eyes stinging with fresh tears. "I love you so much."

"Angel." He reached me with quick strides, dropping his keys on the floor and shoving both hands into my damp hair. He was shaking, and I cried, overwhelmed by the knowledge of how much he needed me.

Tilting my head to the angle he wanted, Gideon took my mouth with searing possession, tasting me with slow, deep licks. His passion and hunger exploded across my senses, and I whimpered, my hands tangling in his sweatshirt. His answering groan vibrated through me, tightening my nipples and sending goose bumps racing across my skin.

I melted into him, my hands pushing the cap from his head so that my fingers could sink into the silky black mane of his hair. I fell into the kiss, swept away by the lush carnality of it. A sob escaped me.

"Don't," he breathed, pulling back to cradle my jaw. He looked into my eyes. "It shreds me when you cry."

"It's too much." I trembled.

His beautiful eyes looked as weary as mine. He nodded grimly. "What I did—"

"Not that. How I feel about you."

He rubbed the tip of his nose against me, his hands sliding reverently along my bare arms—hands with proverbial blood on them, which only made me love his touch all the more.

"Thank you," I whispered.

His eyes closed. "God, when you left tonight . . . I didn't know if you'd come back . . . if I'd lost you—"

"I need you, too, Gideon."

"I won't apologize. I'd do it again." His grip tightened on me. "The options were restraining orders, increased security, vigilance . . . for the rest of your life. There was no guarantee you'd be safe unless Nathan was dead."

"You cut me off. Shut me out. You and me—"

"Forever." His fingertips pressed against my parted lips. "It's over, Eva. Don't argue about something that's too late to change."

I brushed his hand away. "*Is* it over? Can we be together now, or are we still hiding our relationship from the police? Are we even *in* a relationship?"

Gideon held my gaze, hiding nothing, letting me see his pain and fear. "That's what I'm here to ask you."

"If it's up to me, I'll never let you go," I said vehemently. "Never."

Gideon's hands slid down my throat to my shoulders, blazing a hot trail across my skin. "I need that to be true," he said softly. "I was afraid you'd run . . . that you'd be afraid. Of *me*."

"Gideon, no—"

"I would never hurt you."

I caught the waistband of his sweats and tugged, even though I couldn't budge him. "I *know* that."

And physically, I had no doubts; he'd always been careful with me, always cautious. But emotionally, my love had been used against me with meticulous precision. I was struggling with reconciling the absolute trust I had in Gideon's awareness of my needs and the wariness that came from a shattered heart still healing.

"Do you?" He searched my face, as attuned as always to what wasn't said. "Letting you go would kill me, but I wouldn't hurt you to keep you."

"I don't want to go anywhere."

He exhaled audibly. "My lawyers will be talking to the police tomorrow, to get a feel for where things stand."

Tilting my head back, I pressed my lips gently to his. We were colluding to hide a crime, and I'd be lying if I said that didn't seriously bother me—I was the daughter of a police officer, after all—but the alternative was too awful to consider.

"I have to know that you can live with what I've done," he said softly, wrapping my hair around his finger.

"I think so. Can you?"

His mouth found mine again. "I can survive anything if I have you."

I reached under his sweatshirt, seeking and finding his warm, golden skin. His muscles were hard and ridged beneath my palms, his body a seductive and virile work of art. I licked his lips, my teeth catching the full curve along the bottom and biting gently. Gideon groaned. The sound of his pleasure slid over me like a caress.

"Touch me." The words were an order, but his tone was a plea.

"I am."

Reaching behind him, he grabbed my wrist and pulled my hand around. He thrust his cock shamelessly into my palm, grinding. My fingers curled around the thick, heavy length, my pulse quickening at the realization that he was commando beneath his sweats.

"God," I breathed. "You make me so hot."

His blue eyes were fierce on my face; his cheeks flushed and his sculpted lips parted. He never tried to hide the effect I had on him, never pretended that he had any more control over his response to me than I had to him. It made his dominance in the bedroom all the more exciting, knowing that he was similarly as helpless to the attraction between us.

My chest tightened. I still couldn't believe that he was mine, that I got to see him this way, so open and hungry and sexy as hell . . .

Gideon tugged my towel open. He inhaled sharply when it hit the floor and I stood before him completely naked. "Ah, Eva."

His voice throbbed with emotion, making my eyes sting. He yanked his shirt up and over his head, tossing it aside. Then he reached for me, stepping carefully into me, prolonging the moment when our bare skin would touch.

He gripped my hips, his fingers flexing restlessly, his breathing quick and harsh. The tips of my breasts touched him first, sending a sudden rush of sensation through my body. I gasped. He crushed me to him with a growl, lifting my feet from the floor and carrying me backward toward the bed.

2

MY THIGHS HIT the mattress and I landed on my butt, falling to my back with Gideon leaning over me. He hitched me up with an arm banded around my back, centering me on the bed before he settled atop me. His mouth was on my breast before I knew it, his lips soft and warm, the suction fast and greedy. He plumped the heavy weight in his hand, kneading possessively.

"Christ, I've missed you," he groaned. His skin was hot against my cool flesh, his weight so welcome after the long nights without him.

I hooked my legs around his calves and shoved my hands beneath his waistband to grip his taut, hard ass. I tugged him into me, arching my hips to feel his cock through the cotton that separated us. Wanting him inside me, so that I'd know for certain he was mine again.

"Say it," I coaxed, needing the words he swore were inadequate.

He pushed up and looked down at me, gently brushing my hair back from my forehead. He swallowed hard.

Rearing, I caught his beautifully etched mouth in a kiss. "I'll say it first: I love you."

He closed his eyes and quivered. Wrapping his arms around me, Gideon squeezed so tight I almost couldn't breathe.

"I love you," he whispered. "Too much."

His fervent declaration reverberated through me. I buried my face in his shoulder and cried.

"Angel." His fist clenched in my hair.

Lifting my head, I took his mouth, our kiss flavored with the salt of my tears. My lips moved desperately over his, as if he'd be gone at any second and I had no time to get my fill of him.

"Eva. Let me . . ." He cupped my face, licking deep into my mouth. "Let me love you."

"Please," I whispered, my fingers linking behind his neck to capture him. His erection lay hot and heavy against the lips of my sex, the weight of him the perfect pressure on my throbbing clit. "Don't stop."

"Never. I can't."

His hand cupped my buttock, lifting me into a deft roll of his hips. I gasped as the pleasure radiated through me, my nipples beading hard and tight against his chest. The light dusting of crisp hair was an unbearable stimulation. My core ached, begging for the hard-driving thrust of his cock.

My nails raked his back from shoulder to hips. He arched into the rough caress with a low growl, his head thrown back in deliciously erotic abandon.

"Again," he ordered gruffly, his face flushed and lips parted.

Surging upward, I sank my teeth into his pectoral, just over his heart. Gideon hissed, quivering, and took it.

I couldn't contain the ferocious swell of emotion that needed release—the love and need, the anger and fear. And the pain. God, the pain. I still felt it keenly. I wanted to tear into him. To punish as well as pleasure. To make him experience some small measure of what I had when he'd pushed me away.

My tongue stroked over the slight indentations left by my teeth and his hips rocked into me, his cock sliding through the parted lips of my sex.

"My turn," he whispered darkly. Leaning on one arm, the biceps thick and beautifully defined, he squeezed my breast in his other hand. His head lowered and his lips surrounded the taut point of my nipple. His mouth was scorching hot, his tongue a rough velvet lash against my tender flesh. When his teeth bit into the furled tip, I cried out, my body jerking as sharp need arrowed to my core.

I clutched at his hair, too impassioned to be gentle. My legs wrapped around him, tightening, echoing my need to claim him. Possess him. Make him mine again.

"Gideon," I moaned. My temples were wet from the trails of my tears, my throat tight and hurting.

"I'm here, angel," he breathed, nibbling across my cleavage to my other breast. His diabolical fingers tugged at the wet nipple he'd left behind, pinching it gently until I pushed up and into his hand. "Don't fight me. Let me love you."

I realized then that I was pulling at his hair, trying to urge him away even as I fought to get closer. Gideon had me under siege, seducing me with his stunning male perfection and intimate expertise with my body. And I was surrendering. My breasts were heavy, my sex wet and swollen. My hands roamed restlessly as my legs caged him.

Still, he slipped farther away from me, his mouth whispering temptation across my stomach. *Missed you so much . . . need you . . . have to have you . . .* I felt a hot wetness slide over my skin and looked down to see that he was crying, too, his gorgeous face ravaged by the same surfeit of emotion flooding me.

With shaking fingers, I touched his cheek, trying to smooth away the wetness that only returned the instant it was wiped away. He nuzzled into my touch with a soft, plaintive moan, and I couldn't bear it. His pain was harder for me to deal with than my own.

"I love you," I told him.

"Eva." He slid back onto his knees and rose, his thighs spread between mine, his cock thick and hard and bobbing under its weight.

Everything in me tightened with ravenous greed. His big body was carved with rock-hard slabs of tautly defined muscle, his tanned skin sheened with perspiration. He was so powerfully elegant, except for his penis, which was bluntly primal with its thick coursing veins and wide root. His sac, too, hung large and heavy. He would make a statue as beautiful as Michelangelo's *David*, but with a flagrantly erotic edge.

Honestly, Gideon Cross had been designed to fuck a woman right out of her mind.

"Mine," I said harshly, pushing up and scrambling gracelessly into him, pressing my torso tightly into his. "You're mine."

"Angel." He took my mouth in a rough, lust-fueled kiss. Lifting me, he moved, turning us so that his back was to the headboard and I was spread over him. Our flesh slid against each other, slickened by sweat.

His hands were everywhere, his muscled body straining upward as mine had done. I cupped his face, licking fast into his mouth, trying to satisfy my thirst for him.

He reached between my legs, his fingers delving reverently into my cleft. The roughened pads stroked over my clit and skirted the trembling opening to my sex. With my lips pressed to his, I moaned, my hips circling. He fingered me leisurely, building my need, his kiss gentling into a slow, deep fucking of my mouth.

I couldn't breathe for the pleasure, my entire body quivering as he cupped me in his hand and his long middle finger slid lazily into me. His palm rubbed against my clit, his fingertip stroking over delicate tissues. His other hand gripped my hip, holding me in place, restraining me.

Gideon's control seemed absolute, his seduction wickedly precise, but he was trembling harder than I was and his chest was heaving more forcefully. The sounds spilling from him were tinged with remorse and entreaty.

Pulling back, I reached for his cock with both hands, gripping him firmly. I knew his body well, too, knew what he needed and desired. I pumped him from root to tip, drawing a thick bead of pre-ejaculate to the wide crest. He pushed back against the headboard with a groan, his finger curving inside me. I watched, riveted, as the thick drop rolled to one side of his glans, then slid down the length of him to pool at the top of my fist.

"Don't," he panted. "Too close."

I stroked him again, my mouth watering as a gush of pre-cum streamed out of him. I was wildly aroused by his pleasure and the knowledge that I had such a profound effect on such a blatantly sexual creature.

As he cursed, his fingers left me. He grabbed my hips, dislodging my grip on him. He yanked me forward, then down, his hips bucking upward, his raging cock driving into me.

I cried out and gripped his shoulders, my sex clenching against the thick penetration.

"Eva." His jaw and neck taut with strain, he started coming, spurting hot and hard inside me.

The gush of lubrication opened me, my sex sliding down his pulsing erection until he filled me too full. My nails dug into his unyielding muscles, my mouth opened to draw in desperate breaths of air.

"Take it," he bit out, angling my descent to gain that last little part of me that let him to sink in to the root. "Take me."

I moaned, welcoming the familiar soreness of having him so deep. The orgasm took me by surprise, my back bowing as the heated pleasure tore through me.

Instinct took over, my hips moving of their own volition, my thighs clenching and releasing as I focused only on the moment, the reclaiming of my man. My heart.

Gideon yielded to my demands.

"That's it, angel," he encouraged hoarsely, his erection still as hard as if he hadn't just had a teeth-grinding climax.

His arms fell to his sides. His hands fisted in the comforter. His biceps clenched and flexed with his movements. His abs tightened every time I took him to the hilt, the rigid lacing of muscles glistening with sweat. His body was a well-oiled machine and I was taking it to its limits.

He let me. Gave himself to me.

Undulating my hips, I took my pleasure, moaning his name. My core clenched rhythmically, another orgasm rushing up too quickly. I faltered, my senses overwhelmed.

"Please," I gasped. "Gideon, please."

He caught me by the nape and waist, and slid down until we were flat on the bed. Pinning me tightly, he held me immobile, thrusting upward . . . over and over . . . shafting my sex with fast, powerful lunges. The friction of his thick penis rubbing and surging was too much. I jolted violently and came again, my fingers clawing into his sides.

Shuddering, Gideon followed me over, his arms tightening until I could barely breathe. His harsh exhalations were the air that filled my burning lungs. I was utterly possessed, completely defenseless.

"God, Eva." He buried his face in my throat. "Need you. I need you so much."

"Baby." I held him close. Still afraid to let go.

BLINKING up at the ceiling, I realized I'd fallen asleep. Then the panic hit, the horrible inevitability of waking from a blissful dream into a nightmare reality. I surged up, gulping air into a chest that was too tight.

Gideon.

I nearly sobbed when I found him sprawled next to me, his lips barely parted with his deep, even breathing. The lover my heart had broken for, returned to me.

God . . .

Sinking back against the headboard, I forced myself to relax, to savor the rare pleasure of watching him sleep. His face was transformed when he was unguarded, reminding me of how young he really was. That was easy to forget when he was awake and radiating the powerful force of will that had literally knocked me on my ass when I'd first met him.

With reverent fingers, I brushed the inky strands of hair away from his cheek, noting the new lines around his eyes and mouth. I'd also noted that he'd grown leaner. Our separation had taken a toll on him, but he'd hidden it so well. Or maybe I viewed him as flawless and inviolate.

I hadn't been able to hide my devastation at all. I'd believed we were over and it showed to everyone who'd looked at me, which Gideon had counted on all along. *Plausible deniability*, he'd called it. I called it hell, and until we could stop pretending we'd broken up, I'd still be living in it.

Shifting carefully, I propped my head on my hand and studied the decadent man who graced my bed. His arms were wrapped around his pillow, showing off chiseled biceps and a muscular back adorned with scratches and crescent marks from my nails. I'd gripped his ass, too, insanely turned on by the feel of it clenching and releasing as he fucked me tirelessly, stroking his long, thick cock deep inside me.

Again and again . . .

My legs shifted restlessly, my body stirring with renewed hunger. For all his polished urbanity, Gideon was an untamed animal behind closed doors, a lover who bared me to the soul every time he made love to me. I had no defenses against him when he was touching me, helpless to resist the drugging pleasure of spreading my thighs for such a virile, passionate male—

His eyes opened, stunning me with those vivid blue irises. He gave me a lazily seductive once-over that made my heart skip a beat. "Hmm . . . You're wearing the fuck-me look," he drawled.

"And that would be because you're so extremely fuckable," I shot back. "Waking up to you is like . . . presents on Christmas morning."

His mouth curved. "For your convenience, I'm already unwrapped. Batteries not required."

My chest tightened with terrible yearning. I loved him too much. I was constantly worried that I wouldn't be able to hold on to him. He was lightning in a bottle, a dream I tried to hold in my hands.

I let out a shaky breath. "You're a delicious extravagance for a woman, you know. A luscious, mouthwatering—"

"Shut up." He rolled over and dragged me under him before I knew his intent. "I'm filthy rich, but you just want me for my body."

I looked up at him, admiring the way his dark hair framed that extraordinary face. "I want the heart inside the body."

"You have it." His arms tucked against my sides and his legs tangled with mine, the coarse hair on his calves stimulating my hypersensitive skin.

I was restrained. Possessed. His warm, hard body felt so good against mine. I sighed, feeling some of the fearful hesitation easing.

"I shouldn't have fallen asleep," he said quietly.

I stroked his hair, knowing he was right, that his nightmares and atypical sexual parasomnia made sleeping with him dangerous. He sometimes lashed out in his sleep, and if I was too close, I took the brunt of the simmering rage inside him. "I'm glad you did, though."

He caught my wrist and pulled my fingers to his mouth for a kiss. "We need time together when we aren't looking over our shoulders."

"Oh, God. I almost forgot. Deanna Johnson was here tonight." The moment the words left my mouth I regretted the wall they put up between us.

Gideon blinked, and in that split second, the warmth in his eyes was gone. "Stay away from her. She's a reporter."

My arms slid around him. "She's going for blood."

"She'll have to get in line."

"Why is she so interested? She's a freelancer. No one assigned her to you."

"Drop it, Eva."

His dismissal of the subject irked me. "I know you fucked her."

"No, you don't. And what you should be focused on is the fact that I'm about to fuck *you*."

Certainty settled in my gut. I released him, pulling away. "You lied."

He reared back as if I'd slapped him. "I have never lied to you."

"You told me you've had more sex since you met me than you've had in the last two years combined, but you told Dr. Petersen you've been getting laid twice a week. Which is it?"

Rolling to his back, he scowled at the ceiling. "Do we have to do this now? Tonight?"

His body language was so tight and defensive that my irritation with his evasiveness left me in a rush. I didn't want to fight with him, especially over the past. What mattered was now and the future. I had to trust that he'd be faithful.

"No, we don't," I said softly, turning onto my side and reaching over to place my hand on his chest. Once the sun came up, we'd be right back to pretending we weren't together. I had no idea how long we'd have to keep up the charade or when I'd get to be with him again. "I just wanted to warn you that she's digging. Watch out for her."

"Dr. Petersen asked about sexual encounters, Eva," he said flatly, "which isn't necessarily fucking, as far as I'm concerned. I didn't think that distinction would be appreciated when answering the question. So let me be clear: I took women to the hotel, but I didn't always nail them. It was the exception when I did."

I thought of his fuck pad, a stocked-with-sexual-paraphernalia suite reserved in one of his many hospitality properties. He'd given it up, thank God, but I'd never forget it. "Maybe it's better I don't hear any more."

"You opened this door," he snapped. "We're walking through it."

I sighed. "Fair enough."

"There were times when I couldn't stand to be alone with myself, but I didn't want to talk. I didn't want to even *think*, let alone feel anything. I needed the distraction of focusing on someone else, and using my dick was too much involvement. Can you understand that?"

Sadly, I could, recalling times when I'd dropped to my knees for a guy just to shut off my brain for a while. Encounters like those had never been about foreplay or sex.

"So is she one of the girls you screwed or not?" I hated asking the question, but we had to get it out of the way.

He turned his head to look at me. "Once."

"Must've been some lay for her to be so bent out of shape over it."

"I couldn't say," he muttered. "I don't remember."

"Were you drunk?"

"No. Jesus." He scrubbed at his face. "What the hell did she tell you?"

"Nothing personal. She did mention you having a 'dark side.' I'm assuming that's a sexual reference, but I didn't ask her for details. She was playing it like we had an affinity because we'd both been thrown over by you. The 'Dumped by Gideon Sisterhood.'"

He glanced at me with cold eyes. "Don't be catty. It doesn't suit you."

"Hey." I frowned. "I'm sorry. I wasn't trying to be a total bitch. Just a little one. I think I'm entitled, all things considered."

"What the hell was I supposed to do, Eva? I didn't know you existed." Gideon's voice deepened, roughened. "If I'd known you were out there, I would've hunted you down. I wouldn't have waited a second to find you. But I didn't know, and I settled for less. So did you. We both wasted ourselves on the wrong people."

"Yeah, we did. Dumbasses."

There was a pause. "Are you pissed?"

"No, I'm good."

He stared.

I laughed. "You were getting ready to fight, weren't you? We can play it that way if you want. Personally, I was hoping to get laid again."

Gideon slid over me. The look on his face, the melding of relief and gratitude, caused a sharp pain in my chest. I was reminded of how important it was for him to be trusted to share the truth.

"You're different," he said, touching my face.

Of course I was. The man I loved had killed for me. A lot of things became inconsequential after a sacrifice like that.

3

"ANGEL."

I smelled the coffee before I opened my eyes. "Gideon?"

"Hmm?"

"If it's not at least seven o'clock, I'm going to kick your ass."

His soft laugh made my toes curl. "It's early, but we need to talk."

"Yeah?" I opened one eye, then the other, so I could fully admire his three-piece suit. He looked so edible, I wanted to take it off him—with my teeth.

He settled on the edge of my bed, the embodiment of temptation. "I want to make sure we're solid before I leave."

I sat up and leaned against the headboard, making no effort to cover my breasts because we were going to end up talking about his ex-fiancée. I played dirty when warranted. "I'll need that coffee for this conversation."

Gideon handed me the mug, then stroked the pad of his thumb over my nipple. “So beautiful,” he murmured. “Every inch of you.”

“Are you trying to distract me?”

“You’re distracting me. Very effectively.”

Could he possibly be as infatuated with my looks and body as I was with his? The thought made me smile.

“I missed your smile, angel.”

“I know the feeling.” Every time I’d seen him and he hadn’t gifted me with his smile had been another cut to my heart until I’d been bleeding nonstop. I couldn’t even think of those occasions without feeling echoes of the pain. “Where did you hide the suit, ace? I know it wasn’t in your pocket.”

With a change of clothes, he’d transformed himself into a powerful, successful businessman. The suit was bespoke, and his shirt and tie were immaculately matched. Even his cuff links gleamed with understated elegance. Still, the fall of dark hair that skimmed his collar warned others he was far from tamed.

“That’s one of the things we need to talk about.” He straightened, but the warmth in his gaze remained. “I took over the apartment next door. We’ll have to make our reconciliation seem suitably gradual, so I’ll keep up the appearance of using my penthouse for the most part, but I’ll be spending as much time as possible as your new neighbor.”

“Is it safe?”

“I’m not a suspect, Eva. I’m not even a person of interest. My alibi is airtight, and I have no known motive. We’re just showing the detectives some respect by not insulting their intelligence. We’re making it easy for them to justify their conclusion that they’re at a dead end.”

I took a sip of coffee, giving me time to contemplate what he’d said. The danger might not be immediate, but it was inherent in his guilt. I felt the pressure of it, no matter how he tried to reassure me.

But we were working our way back to each other, and I sensed his need for reassurance that we were going to recover from the strain and separation of the last few weeks.

I deliberately took a light tone when I replied, "So my former boyfriend will be on Fifth Avenue, but I've got a hunky new neighbor to play with? This could be interesting."

One of his brows arched. "You want to role-play, angel?"

"I want to keep you satisfied," I admitted with brutal honesty. "I want to be everything you ever found in the other women you've been with." Women he'd taken to a fuck pad with toys.

His irises were cool blue fire, but his voice came smooth and even. "I can't keep my hands off you. That should be enough to tell you I don't need more."

I watched him stand. He took my mug and set it on the nightstand, then caught the edge of the sheet and threw it deftly aside, exposing me completely.

"Scoot down," he ordered. "Spread your legs."

My pulse quickened as I obeyed him, sliding to my back and allowing my thighs to fall open. There was an instinctive urge to cover myself—the feeling of vulnerability under that piercing gaze was so intense—but I resisted it. I'd be dishonest if I didn't admit that it was wildly exciting to be totally naked while he was irresistibly clothed in one of his sexy-as-hell suits. It created an instantaneous power advantage for him that was a serious turn-on.

He stroked a finger through the lips of my sex, gliding teasingly over my clit. "This beautiful cunt is mine."

My belly quivered at the rasp in his voice.

Cupping me in his palm, he met my gaze. "I'm a very possessive man, Eva, as I'm sure you've noticed by now."

I shivered as the tip of his finger circled the clenching opening. "Yes."

"Role-play, restraints, modes of transportation, and varied locations . . . I look forward to exploring all of that with you." Eyes glittering, he slid a finger oh-so-slowly inside me. He made a low purring noise and caught his lower lip between his teeth, a purely erotic look that told me he felt his semen inside me.

Being penetrated and so gently pleasured left me unable to speak for a moment.

"You like that," he said softly.

"Umm."

His finger went deeper. "I'll be damned if plastic, glass, metal, or leather will make you come. B.O.B. and his friends will have to find other amusements."

Heat swept over my skin like fever. He understood.

Bending over me, Gideon placed one hand on the mattress and lowered his mouth to mine. His thumb pressed against my clit and rubbed expertly, massaging me inside and out. The pleasure of his touch spread, tightening my stomach and hardening my nipples. I clutched my bare breasts in my hands, squeezing as they swelled. His touch and desire were magic. How had I ever lived without him?

"I ache for you," he said hoarsely. "Crave you constantly. Snap your fingers and I'm hard." He traced my lower lip with his tongue, inhaling my panting breaths. "When I come, I come for you. Because of you and your mouth, hands, and insatiable little cunt. And it'll be that way for you in reverse. My tongue, my fingers, my cum inside you. Just you and me, Eva. Intimate and raw."

I had no doubt I was the focal point of his world when he was touching me, the only thing he saw or thought of. But we couldn't have that physical connection all the time. Somehow, I had to learn to believe in what I *couldn't* see between us.

Shameless, my body writhed as I rode his plunging finger. He added another and I dug in my heels, arching up to meet his thrusts. "Please."

"When your eyes turn soft and dreamy, *I'll* be the one who put that look on you, not a toy." He nibbled my jaw, then moved to my chest, nudging my hands aside with his lips. He claimed my nipple in a gentle bite, his mouth surrounding the tender peak and sucking softly. The ache he created was needle-sharp, my hunger spurred by the sense that there was a lingering gulf between us, something that hadn't yet been recognized and resolved.

"More," I gasped, needing his pleasure as much as my own.

"Always," he murmured, his mouth curving in a wicked smile against my skin.

I groaned in frustration. "I want your cock inside me."

"As you should." His tongue curled around my other nipple, flickering teasingly over it until it ached for suction. "Your craving should be for *me*, angel, not an orgasm. For *my* body, *my* hands. Eventually, you won't be able to come without my skin touching yours."

I nodded frantically, my mouth too dry to speak. Need was coiled like a spring in my core, tightening with every circle of Gideon's thumb on my clit and every thrust of his fingers. I thought of B.O.B., my trusty Battery-Operated Boyfriend, and knew that if Gideon were to stop touching me now, nothing would get me off. My passion *was* for him, my desire inflamed by his desire for me.

My thighs quivered. "I'm g-going to come."

His mouth covered mine, his beautiful lips soft and coaxing. It was the love in his kiss that pushed me over. I cried out and shuddered through a quick, hard orgasm. My moan was long and broken, my body quivering violently. I pushed my hands under his jacket to grip his back, holding him close, my mouth claiming his until the wracking pleasure eased.

Licking the taste of me from his fingers, he murmured, "Tell me what you're thinking."

I consciously tried to slow my racing heart. "I'm not thinking. I just want to look at you."

"You don't always. Sometimes you close your eyes."

"That's because you're a talker in bed and your voice is so sexy." I swallowed hard with remembered pain. "I love to hear you, Gideon. I need to know that I'm making you feel as good as you make me feel."

"Suck me off now," he whispered. "Make me come for you."

I slid from the bed in a breathless rush, my hands reaching eagerly for his fly. He was hard and thick, his erection straining. Lifting his shirttail and pushing down his boxer briefs, I freed him. He fell heavily into my hands, the thick length already glistening at the tip. I licked the evidence of his excitement away, loving his control, the way he reined in his own hungers to satisfy mine.

My eyes were on him as my open mouth slid over the plush head. I watched his lips part on a sharply indrawn breath and his eyelids grow heavy, as if the pleasure were intoxicating.

"Eva." His hooded gaze was hot on my face. "Ah . . . Yes. Like that. Christ, I love your mouth."

His praise spurred me on. I took him as deep as I could. I loved doing this to him, loved the uniquely masculine taste and smell of him. I ran my lips down the length of him, suckling gently. Worshipfully. And I didn't feel wrong for adoring his virility—I deserved it.

"You love this," he said gruffly, pushing his fingers into my hair to cup my head. "As much as I do."

"More. I want to do this for hours. Make you come over and over again."

A growl rumbled in his chest. "I would. I can't get enough."

The tip of my tongue traced a pulsing vein up to the head, and then I took him in my mouth again, my neck arching back as I lowered to sit on my heels, my hands on my knees, offering myself to him.

Gideon looked down with eyes that glittered with lust and tenderness.

"Don't stop." He widened his stance. He slid his cock to the back of my throat, then pulled back out, coating my tongue with a trail of creamy pre-ejaculate. I swallowed, savoring the rich flavor of him.

He groaned, his hands cupping my jaw. "Don't stop, angel. Suck me dry."

My cheeks hollowed as we found a rhythm, *our* rhythm, the syncing of our hearts and breaths and drive to pleasure. We had no problem overthinking our way into trouble, but our bodies never got it wrong. When we had our hands on each other, we both knew we were in the one place we needed to be, with the one person we needed to be with.

"So fucking good." His teeth ground audibly. "Ah, God, you're making me come."

His cock swelled in my mouth. His hand fisted in my hair, pulling, his body shuddering as he came hard.

Gideon cursed as I swallowed. He emptied himself in thick, hot bursts, flooding my mouth as if he hadn't come all night. By the time he finished, I was gasping and trembling. He pulled me to my feet and stumbled to the bed, settling heavily with me tucked into his side. His lungs labored, his hands rough as he pulled me closer.

"This wasn't what I had in mind when I brought you coffee." He pressed a quick, rough kiss to my forehead. "Not that I have any complaints."

I curled into him, beyond grateful to have him in my arms again. "Let's play hooky and make up for lost time."

His laugh was husky from his orgasm. He held me for a while, his fingers sifting through my hair and gliding gently down my arm.

"It ripped me apart," he said quietly. "Seeing how hurt and angry you were. Knowing I was causing you pain and that you were pulling away from me . . . It was hell for us both, but I couldn't take the risk that you might become a suspect."

I stiffened. I hadn't thought of that possibility. It could be argued that I was Gideon's motive to kill. And it could be assumed that I was aware of the crime as well. My complete and utter ignorance hadn't been my only protection; he'd made sure I had an alibi, too. Always protecting me—whatever the cost.

He pulled back. "I put a burner phone in your purse. It's preprogrammed with a number that will put you in touch with Angus. If you need me for anything, you can reach me that way."

My hands clenched into fists—I had to reach my boyfriend through his chauffeur. "I hate this."

"So do I. Clearing my way back to you is my number one priority."

"Isn't it dangerous for Angus to be put in the middle?"

"He's former MI6. Clandestine phone calls are child's play for him." He paused, then said, "Full disclosure, Eva: I can track you through the phone and I will."

"What?" I slid out of bed and stood. My thoughts bounced back and forth between MI6—British secret service!—to geotracking my cell, unsure of what to latch on to first. "No way."

He stood, too. "If I can't be with you or talk to you, I at least need to know where you are."

"Don't be this way, Gideon."

His face was composed. "I didn't have to tell you."

"Seriously?" I stalked to the closet to grab a robe. "And you said warning someone about ridiculous behavior isn't an excuse for it."

"Cut me some slack."

Glaring at him, I shoved my hands into the sleeves of a red silk dressing gown and yanked the belt into a knot. "No. I think you're a control freak who likes having me followed."

He crossed his arms. "I like keeping you alive."

I froze. After a moment, my brain rewound to look at the events of the last few weeks again—with the addition of Nathan in the picture. Abruptly, everything made sense: the way Gideon had freaked out when I'd tried to walk to work one morning, why Angus had shadowed me around the city every day, Gideon's fury when he commandeered the elevator I was riding . . .

All those times I'd almost hated him for being an asshole, he'd been thinking about keeping me safe from Nathan.

My knees weakened, and I sank inelegantly to the floor.

"Eva."

"Give me a minute." I'd figured out a lot of it already during the time we'd been apart. I'd realized Gideon would never allow Nathan to simply stroll into his office with photos of me being abused and violated, then just stroll back out again. Brett Kline had only *kissed* me and Gideon had beaten him up. Nathan had *raped* me repeatedly for years and documented it with pictures and video. Gideon's reaction to meeting Nathan the first time had to have been violent.

Nathan must have visited the Crossfire Building the day I'd found Gideon freshly showered with a crimson stain on the cuff of his shirt. What I'd originally suspected was lipstick was Nathan's blood. The sofa and sofa pillows in Gideon's office had been skewed from a fight, not from a lunch quickie with Corinne.

Scowling fiercely, he crouched in front of me. "Damn it. Do you think I *want* to micromanage you? There have been extenuating circumstances. Give me credit for trying to balance your independence with keeping you safe."

Wow. Hindsight didn't just make things crystal clear; it smacked me upside the head and knocked some sense into me. "I get it."

"I don't think you do. This"—he gestured impatiently at himself—"is just a fucking shell. *You're* what drives me, Eva. Can you understand that? You're my heart and soul. If something ever happened to you, it would kill me, too. Keeping you safe is goddamned self-preservation! Tolerate it for me, if you won't do it for yourself."

I surged into him, knocking him off-balance and onto his back. I kissed him hard, my heart pounding and blood roaring in my ears.

"I hate to freak you out," I muttered between desperate kisses, "but you've got it real bad for me."

Groaning, he squeezed me tightly. "So we're okay?"

I wrinkled my nose. "Maybe not about the burner phone. The cell stalking is nuts. Seriously. Not cool at all."

"It's temporary."

"I know, but—"

He put a hand over my mouth. "I put directions on how to track *my* phone in your purse."

That news left me speechless.

Gideon smirked. "Not such a bad idea on the flip side."

"Shut up." I slid off him and smacked his shoulder. "We are totally dysfunctional."

"I prefer 'selectively deviant.' But we'll keep that to ourselves."

The warmth I'd felt bled away, replaced by a flare of panic at the reminder that we were hiding our relationship. How long would it be before I saw him again? Days? I couldn't repeat the last few weeks of my life. Even thinking about going without him for any length of time made me feel sick.

I had to swallow past a painful lump to ask, "When can we be together again?"

"Tonight. *Eva.*" His beautiful eyes were haunted. "I can't bear that look on your face."

"Just be with me," I whispered, my eyes stinging all over again. "I need you."

Gideon's fingertips glided softly down my cheek. "You were with me. The whole time. There wasn't a second that passed when you weren't on my mind. You own me, Eva. Wherever I am, whatever I'm doing, I belong to you."

I leaned into his touch, letting it soak into me and chase the chill away. "No more Corinne. I can't stand it."

"No more," he agreed, startling me. "I've told her already. I'd hoped we could be friends, but she wants what she and I used to have, and I want you."

"The night that Nathan died . . . she was your alibi." I couldn't say more. It hurt to think of how he might have filled the hours with her.

"No, the kitchen fire was my alibi. It took most of the night dealing with the FDNY, the insurance company, and making emergency arrangements for food service. Corinne stuck around for some of that, and when she left, I had plenty of staff on hand to vouch for my whereabouts."

The surge of relief I felt must have shown on my face, because Gideon's gaze softened and filled with the regret I'd seen so many times now.

He stood and held his hand out to help me up. "Your new neighbor would like to invite you over for a late dinner. Let's say eight o'clock. You'll find the key—and the key to the penthouse—on your keychain."

I accepted his hand up and tried to lighten the mood with a teasing reply. "He's seriously hot. I wonder if he puts out on the first date?"

His returning smile was so wicked it revved me up a notch. "I think your odds of getting laid are pretty good."

I gave a dramatic sigh. "How romantic!"

"I'll give you romance." Pulling me into him, Gideon dipped me with consummate ease.

Pressed against him from hip to ankle and bowed backward in a yielding curve, I felt my robe slide apart, exposing my breast. He deepened my arch, until my tender sex hugged his hard thigh and I couldn't help but be hyperaware of the power of his body as he supported my weight and his.

That quickly, he seduced me. Despite hours of pleasure and a very recent orgasm, I was primed for him in that moment, aroused by his skill and strength and self-assurance, his command of himself and of me.

I rode his leg with a slow slide, licking my lips. He growled and surrounded my nipple with the wet heat of his mouth, his tongue worrying the hardened point. Effortlessly he held me, aroused me, possessed me.

I closed my eyes and moaned my surrender.

BECAUSE of the heat and humidity, I chose a lightweight linen sheath dress and pulled my blond hair back in a ponytail. I accessorized with a small pair of gold hoop earrings and kept my makeup light.

Everything had changed. Gideon and I were back together. I was now living in a world without Nathan Barker in it. I was never going to turn a corner and run into him. He was never going to appear on my doorstep out of the blue. I no longer had to worry that Gideon would learn things about my past that would drive a wedge between us. He knew it all and wanted me anyway.

But the budding peace that came with that new reality was accompanied by fear for Gideon—I needed to know that he was safe from prosecution. How could he definitively be proven innocent of a crime he actually *did* commit? Were we going to have to live with the perpetual fear that his actions would come back to haunt us? And how had this changed *us*? Because there was no way we could be what we'd been before. Not after something so profound.

Leaving my room, I headed out for work, looking forward to the hours of distraction I'd find at my job with Waters Field & Leaman, one of the leading advertising firms in the country. When I went to grab my purse off the breakfast bar, I found Cary in the kitchen. He'd clearly been as Busy with a capital *B* as I had.

He was leaning back into the counter, his hands gripping the edge as his boyfriend, Trey, cupped his face and kissed him passionately. Trey was fully dressed in jeans and a T-shirt, while Cary wore only gray sweats that hung low and sexy on his lean hips. They both had their eyes closed and were too lost in each other to realize they were no longer alone.

It was rude to look, but I couldn't help it. For one, I'd always found it fascinating to watch two hot men make out. And two, I found Cary's pose very telling. While his handsome face was markedly vulnerable, the fact that he was holding on to the counter instead of the man he loved betrayed his lingering distance.

I picked up my purse and backed out as quietly as I could, tiptoeing from the apartment.

Because I didn't want to be totally melted by the time I got to work, I hailed a cab instead of walking. From the backseat, I watched Gideon's Crossfire Building come into view. The gleaming and distinctive sapphire spire was home to both Cross Industries and Waters Field & Leaman.

My job as assistant to junior account manager Mark Garrity was a dream come true. While some—namely my stepfather, megafinancier Richard Stanton—couldn't understand why I'd take an entry-level position considering my connections and assets, I was really proud to be working my way up. Mark was a great boss, both hands-on and hands-off, which meant I was learning a lot both by instruction and from doing it myself.

The cab turned a corner and pulled up behind a black Bentley SUV I knew all too well. My heart skipped a beat at the sight of it, knowing that Gideon was nearby.

I paid the cabdriver and climbed out of the cool interior into the steamy early-morning air. My eyes were riveted to the Bentley in the hope that I might catch a glimpse of Gideon. It was crazy how excited I was by the idea, especially after a night spent rolling around with him in all his naked glory.

Smiling wryly, I spun through the Crossfire's copper-framed revolving doors and entered the vast lobby. If a building could embody a man, the Crossfire did for Gideon. The marble floors and walls conveyed an aura of power and affluence, while the cobalt glass exterior was as striking as one of Gideon's suits. Altogether, the Crossfire was sleek and sexy, dark and dangerous—just like the man who'd created it. I loved working there.

I passed through the security turnstiles and took the elevator up to the twentieth floor. When I exited the car, I spotted Megumi—the receptionist—at her desk. She buzzed me through the glass security doors and stood as I approached.

"Hey," she greeted me, looking chic in black slacks and a gold silk shell. Her dark sloe eyes sparkled with excitement, and her pretty mouth was stained a daring crimson. "I wanted to ask you what you're doing on Saturday night."

"Oh . . ." I wanted to spend the time with Gideon, but there was no guarantee that would happen. "I don't know. I don't have plans yet. Why?"

"One of Michael's friends is getting married and they're having a bachelor party on Saturday. If I stay home, I'll go nuts."

"Michael's the blind date?" I asked, knowing she'd been seeing a guy her roommate had set her up with.

"Yeah." Megumi's face lit up for a second, then fell. "I really like him and I think he likes me, too, but . . ."

"Go on," I prompted.

She lifted one shoulder in an awkward shrug and her gaze skittered away. "He's a commitment-phobe. I know he's into me, but he keeps saying it's not serious and we're just having fun. But we spend a lot of time together," she argued. "He's definitely rearranged his life to be with me more often. And not just physically."

My mouth twisted ruefully, knowing the type. Those kinds of relationships were tough to quit. The mixed signals kept the drama and adrenaline high, and the possibility of awesomeness if the guy would just accept the risk was hard to let go of. What girl didn't want to attain the unattainable?

"I'm game for Saturday," I said, wanting to be there for her. "What did you have in mind?"

"Drinking, dancing, getting wild." Megumi's grin came back. "Maybe we'll find you a hot rebound guy."

"Uh . . ." Yikes. Awkward. "I'm doing pretty good, actually."

She arched a brow at me. "You look tired."

I spent the entire night getting nailed to my bed by Gideon Cross . . . "I had a tough Krav Maga class yesterday."

"What? Never mind. In any case, it won't hurt to check out the scenery, right?"

I shifted the straps of my bag on my shoulder. "No rebound guys," I insisted.

"Hey." She set her hands on her trim hips. "I'm just suggesting you be open to the possibility of meeting someone. I know Gideon Cross has got to be a hard act to follow, but trust me, moving on is the best revenge."

That made me smile. "I'll keep an open mind," I compromised.

The phone on her desk rang and I waved good-bye as I headed down the hallway to my cubicle. I needed a little time to think about the logistics of playing the role of a single woman when I was very much taken. If I owned Gideon, he possessed me. I couldn't imagine belonging to anyone else.

I was just starting to play with how to bring up Saturday night to Gideon when Megumi called after me. I turned back around.

"I've got a call on hold to send your way," she said. "And I hope it's personal, because holy hell is his voice smokin' hot. He sounds like S-E-X rolled in chocolate and covered in whipped cream."

Nervous excitement raised the hairs on my nape. "Did he give his name?"

"Yep. Brett Kline."

4

I REACHED MY desk and dropped into my chair. My palms were damp just thinking about talking to Brett, and I was steeling myself for the little charge I'd get from hearing his voice and the guilt that would follow it. It wasn't that I wanted him back or wanted to be with him. It was just that we had history and a sexual attraction that was purely hormonal. I couldn't shut it off, but I had absolutely no desire to act on it.

I dropped my purse and the bag holding my walking shoes into a desk drawer, my eyes caressing the framed collage of photos of Gideon and me together. He'd given it to me so he would always be on my mind—as if he ever left it. I even dreamed of him.

My phone rang. The rerouted call from reception. Brett hadn't given up. Determined to keep it businesslike to remind him that I was at work and not available for inappropriately personal conversations, I answered, "Mark Garrity's office, Eva Tramell speaking."

"Eva. There you are. It's Brett."

My eyes closed as I absorbed that S-E-X-rolled-in-chocolate voice. It sounded even more decadently sexual than when he was singing, which had helped to propel his band, Six-Ninths, to the brink of stardom. He was signed with Vidal Records now, the music company run by Gideon's stepfather, Christopher Vidal Sr.—a company Gideon inexplicably had majority control over.

Talk about a small world.

"Hi," I greeted him. "How's the tour coming along?"

"It's unreal. I'm still trying to get a grip on it all."

"You've wanted this a long time and you deserve it. Enjoy it."

"Thanks." He fell silent for a minute, and in that space of time, I pictured him in my mind. He'd looked amazing when I saw him last, his hair spiked and tipped with platinum, his emerald eyes dark and hot from wanting me. He was tall and muscular without being too bulky, his body ripped from constant activity and the demands of being a rock star. His golden skin was sleeved in tattoos, and he had piercings in his nipples that I'd learned to suck on when I wanted to feel his cock harden inside me . . .

But he couldn't hold a candle to Gideon. I could admire Brett just like any other red-blooded woman, but Gideon was in a class by himself.

"Listen," Brett said, "I know you're working, so I don't want to hold you up. I'm coming back to New York and I'd like to see you."

I crossed my ankles under my desk. "I'm thinking that's not a good idea."

"We're going to debut the music video for 'Golden' in Times Square," he went on. "I want you there with me."

"There with— Wow." I massaged my forehead. Momentarily thrown by his request, I chose to think about how my mom would bitch at me for rubbing at my face, which she swore caused wrinkles. "I'm really flattered you asked, but I have to know—are you cool with just being friends?"

"Hell, no." He laughed. "You're single, golden girl. Cross's loss is my gain."

Oh, crap. It'd been almost three weeks since the first pictures of Gideon and Corinne's staged reunion had hit the gossip blogs. Apparently, everyone had decided it was time for me to move on with another guy. "It's not that simple. I'm not ready for another relationship, Brett."

"I asked you out on a date, not for a lifetime commitment."

"Brett, really—"

"You have to be there, Eva." His voice lowered to the seductive timbre that had always made me drop my panties for him. "It's your song. I'm not taking no for an answer."

"You have to."

"You'll hurt me bad if you don't go," he said quietly. "And that's not bullshit. We'll go as friends, if that's what it takes, but I need you there."

I sighed heavily, my head bowing over my desk. "I don't want to lead you on." *Or piss Gideon off . . .*

"I promise to consider it a favor from one friend to another."

As fucking *if.* I didn't answer.

He didn't give up. He might never give up. "Okay?" he prodded.

A cup of coffee appeared at my elbow and I looked up to see Mark standing behind me. "Okay," I agreed, mostly so I could get to work.

"Yesss." There was a note of triumph in his voice that sounded like it was accompanied by a fist pump. "Could be either Thursday or Friday night; I'm not sure yet. Give me your cell number, so I can text you when I know for sure."

I rattled the number off in a hurry. "Got it? I've got to run."

"Have a great day at work," he said, making me feel bad for being rushed and unfriendly. He'd always been a nice guy, and could have been a great friend, but I blew that chance when I kissed him.

"Thanks. Brett . . . I'm really happy for you. Bye." I returned the handset to its cradle and smiled at Mark. "Good morning."

"Everything all right?" he asked, his brown eyes capped with a slight frown. He was dressed in a navy suit with a deep purple tie that did great things for his dark skin.

"Yes. Thank you for the coffee."

"You're welcome. Ready to get to work?"

I grinned. "Always."

IT didn't take long for me to realize something wasn't right with Mark. He was distracted and moody, which was very unlike him. We were working on a campaign for foreign-language-learning software, but he wasn't into it at all. I suggested we talk a bit about the whole-foods locavore campaign, but that didn't help.

"Is everything okay?" I asked finally, sliding uncomfortably into friend territory, where we both made an effort not to go during work.

We put work aside every other week when he invited me along to lunch with his partner, Steven, but we were careful about maintaining our roles as boss and subordinate. I appreciated that a lot, considering Mark knew my stepfather was rich. I didn't want people giving me considerations I hadn't earned.

"What?" He glanced up at me, then ran a hand over his close-cut hair. "Sorry."

I laid my tablet flat in my lap. "Seems like you've got something weighing on your mind."

He shrugged, swiveling away and back again in his Aeron chair. "Sunday is my seventh anniversary with Steven."

"That's awesome." I smiled. Out of all the couples I'd seen over the course of my life, Mark and Steven were the most stable and loving. "Congratulations."

"Thanks." He managed a weak smile.

"Are you going out? Do you have reservations or do you want me to handle that?"

He shook his head. "Haven't decided. I don't know what would be best."

"Let's brainstorm. I haven't had many anniversaries myself, I'm sad to say, but my mom is spectacular with them. I've picked up a thing or two."

After playing hostess to three wealthy husbands, Monica Tramell Barker Mitchell Stanton could've been a professional event planner if she ever had to work for a living.

"Do you want something private," I suggested, "with just the two of you? Or a party with friends and family? Do you exchange gifts?"

"I want to get married!" he snapped.

"Oh. Okay." I sat back in my chair. "As far as romance goes, I can't top that."

Mark barked out a humorless laugh and followed it with a miserable look at me. "It should be romantic. God knows when Steven asked me a few years ago, it was hearts and flowers to the max. You know drama is his middle name. He went all out."

Startled, I blinked at him. "You said no?"

"I said not yet. I was just starting to get my legs under me here at the agency, he was starting to get some really lucrative referrals, and we were picking up the pieces after a painful breakup. It seemed like the wrong time and I wasn't sure he wanted to marry for the right reasons."

"No one ever knows that for sure," I said softly, as much to myself as to him.

"But I didn't want him to think I had doubts about us," Mark went on, as if I hadn't spoken, "so I blamed my refusal on the institution of marriage, like a total ass."

I suppressed a smile. "You're not an ass."

"Over the last couple years, he's made more than a few comments about how right I was to say no."

"But you didn't say no. You said not yet, right?"

"I don't know. Jesus, I don't know what I said." He leaned forward, resting his elbows on the desktop and dropping his face into his hands. His voice came low and muffled. "I panicked. I was twenty-four. Maybe some people are up for that kind of commitment then, but I . . . I wasn't."

"And now you're twenty-eight and ready?" The same age as Gideon. And thinking of that made me quiver, in part because I was the same age Mark had been when he'd said not yet and I could relate.

"Yes." Lifting his head, Mark met my gaze. "I'm beyond ready. It's like some timer is counting down the minutes, and I'm getting more impatient by the hour. But I'm afraid he's going to say no. Maybe his time was four years ago and now he's over it."

"I hate to sound trite, but you won't know unless you ask." I offered him a reassuring smile. "He loves you. A lot. I think your odds of hearing yes are pretty darn good."

He smiled, revealing charmingly crooked teeth. "Thank you."

"Let me know about those reservations."

"I appreciate that." His expression sobered. "I'm sorry to bring this up when you're going through a tough breakup."

"Don't worry about me. I'm fine."

Mark studied me a minute, then nodded.

"YOU up for lunch?"

I glanced up into Will Granger's earnest face. Will was the newest assistant at Waters Field & Leaman and I'd been helping him settle in. He wore sideburns and square-framed black glasses that gave him a slightly retro beatnik look, which worked for him. He was super laid-back and I liked him. "Sure. Whatcha feelin' like?"

"Pasta and bread. And cake. Maybe a baked potato."

My brows rose. "All right. But if I end up passed out and drooling on my desk from a carbohydrate coma, you'd better get me out of trouble with Mark."

"You're a saint, Eva. Natalie's on some low-carb kick and I can't go another day without starch and sugar. I'm wasting away. Look at me."

Will and his high school sweetheart, Natalie, seemed to have it together, from the stories he told. I never doubted he'd walk on hot coals for her, and she seemed to look after him as well, although he grumbled good-naturedly about her fussing.

"You got it," I said, suddenly feeling wistful. Being separated from Gideon was torture. Especially when surrounded by friends who were invested in relationships of their own.

Noon rolled around and while I waited for Will, I sent a quick text to Shawna—Mark's almost-sister-in-law—asking if she was available for a girls' night out on Saturday. I'd just hit the send button when my desk phone rang.

I answered briskly, "Mark Garrity's office—"

"Eva."

My toes flexed at the sound of Gideon's low, raspy voice. "Hi, ace."

"Tell me we're okay."

I bit my lower lip, my heart twisting in my chest. He had to be feeling the same unsettling rift between us that was troubling me. "We are. Don't you think so? Is something wrong?"

"No." He paused. "I just had to hear it again."

"I didn't make it clear last night?" *When I was clawing at your back . . .* "Or this morning?" *When I was on my knees . . .*

"I needed to hear you say it when you're not looking at me." Gideon's voice caressed my senses. I turned hot with embarrassment.

"I'm sorry," I whispered, feeling awkward. "I know you get annoyed with women objectifying you. You shouldn't have to put up with it from me."

"I would never complain about being what you want, Eva. Christ." His voice turned gruff. "I'm damned glad you like what you see, because God knows I fucking love looking at you."

I closed my eyes against a surge of longing. To know what I did now—how important he thought I was to him—made it so much harder to stay away. "I miss you so much. And it's weird because everyone thinks we're broken up and I need to move on—"

"No!" The one word exploded across the line between us, sharp enough to make me jump. "Goddamn it. Wait for me, Eva. I waited my whole life for you."

I swallowed hard, opening my eyes in time to see Will walking toward me. I lowered my voice. "I'd wait forever for you, as long as you're mine."

"It won't be forever. I'm doing everything I can. Trust me."

"I do."

In the background, another phone beeped for his attention. "I'll see you at eight sharp," Gideon said briskly.

"Yes."

The line clicked off in my ear, and I instantly felt lonely.

"Ready to chow down?" Will asked, rubbing his hands together with anticipation. Megumi was having lunch with her commitmentphobe, so she'd taken a rain check. It was Will, me, and all the pasta he could eat within an hour.

Thinking a carbohydrate-induced stupor might be just what I needed, I stood and said, "Hell yeah."

I picked up a zero-carb energy drink at a Duane Reade drugstore on the way back from lunch. By the time five o'clock rolled around, I knew I was hitting a treadmill after work.

I had a membership at Equinox, but I really wanted to go to a CrossTrainer gym. I was feeling the gulf between Gideon and me keenly. Spending time in a place where we had good memories would help lessen it. Plus, I felt a sense of loyalty. Gideon was my man. I was going to do everything I could to spend the rest of my life with him. To me that meant supporting him in everything he did.

I walked back to my place, no longer caring if I wilted since I was going to get messy at the gym anyway. When the elevator in my apartment building let me out on my floor, I found my gaze drifting to the door next to mine. My fingers toyed with the key Gideon had given me. The idea of letting myself in to check out his apartment was intriguing. Would it be similar to his Fifth Avenue place? Or totally different?

Gideon's penthouse was stunning, with prewar architecture and old-world charm. It was a space that exuded affluence, while still remaining warm and inviting. I could as easily picture children in the space as I could foreign dignitaries.

What would his temporary digs be like? Scarce furniture, nonexistent art, and a bare kitchen? How settled in was he?

Pausing outside my apartment, I stared at his door and debated with myself. In the end, I resisted the temptation. I wanted him to walk me inside.

I stepped into my living room to the sound of female laughter. I wasn't surprised to find a long-legged blonde curled up next to Cary on my white couch, her hand in his lap, stroking him through his sweats. He was still shirtless, his arm tossed around Tatiana Cherlin's shoulders, his fingers idly stroking her biceps.

"Hey, baby girl," he greeted me with a grin. "How was work?"

"Same old. Hi, Tatiana."

Her reply was a chin jerk. She was striking, which was to be expected since she was a model. Looks aside, I hadn't really liked her all that much the first few times I met her, and I still didn't. But looking at Cary, I had to admit she might be good for him for now.

His bruises were gone, but he was still recovering from a brutal beating, an ambush by Nathan that had set in motion the events separating me from Gideon now.

"I'm going to change and head out to the gym," I said, moving toward the hallway.

Behind me, I heard Cary tell Tatiana, "Hang on a sec, I've got to talk to my girl."

I entered my room and tossed my purse on my bed. I was digging in my dresser when Cary came to lounge in my doorway. "How are you feeling?" I asked him.

"Better." His green eyes glittered wickedly. "How 'bout you?"

"Better."

He crossed his arms over his bare chest. "Is that thanks to whoever was knocking boots with you last night?"

Closing the drawer with my hip, I shot back, "Seriously? I can't hear you in your room. How come you can hear me in mine?"

He tapped his temple. "Sex radar. I has it."

"What does that mean? That I don't have sex radar?"

"More like Cross blew your circuits during one of his sexathons. Still can't get over that man's stamina. Wish he'd swing my way and wear *me* out."

I threw my sports bra at him.

He caught it deftly, laughing. "So? Who was it?"

I bit my lip, not wanting to lie to the one person who always gave it to me straight, even when it hurt. But I had to. "A guy who works in the Crossfire."

His smile fading, Cary stepped into the room and shut the door behind him. "And you just up and decided to bring him home and fuck his brains out all night? I thought you went to your Krav Maga class."

"I did. He lives near here and I ran into him after class. One thing led to another . . ."

"Should I be worried?" he asked quietly, studying my face as he handed my sports bra back to me. "You haven't had a random screw in a long time."

"It's not like that." I forced myself to hold Cary's gaze, knowing that if I didn't, he'd never believe me. "I'm . . . seeing him. We're having dinner tonight."

"Am I going to meet him?"

"Sure. Not today, though. I'm going to his place."

His lips pursed. "You're not telling me something. Spit it out."

I sidestepped the question. "I saw you kissing Trey in the kitchen this morning."

"Okay."

"Things going good with you two?"

"Can't complain."

Yikes. When Cary was on to something, he wouldn't let it go. I sidestepped again.

"I talked to Brett today," I said as casually as possible, trying not to make a big deal out of it. "He called me at work. And no, he wasn't the guy from last night."

His brows rose. "What'd he want?"

Kicking off my shoes, I headed to the bathroom to wash off what was left of my makeup. "He's coming back to New York for the debut of a music video for 'Golden.' He asked me to go with him."

"Eva—" he began, in that low warning tone parents save for bratty children.

"I want you to come with."

That set him back a bit. "As a chaperone? Don't you trust yourself?"

I looked at his reflection in the mirror. "I'm not getting back together with him, Cary. Not that we were ever really together to begin with, so stop worrying about that. I want you there because I think you'll have fun and I don't want to lead Brett on. He agreed we'd go as friends, but I think the concept needs to be drummed into him, just to be safe. And fair."

"You should've said no."

"I tried."

"No is no, baby girl. Not that difficult."

"Shut up!" I scrubbed at one eye with a makeup remover towelette.

"It's bad enough I got guilted into going! You thought it'd be funny for me to attend that concert without knowing who I'd see there. I don't need shit from you."

Because I was sure to get enough of that from Gideon . . .

Cary scowled. "What the hell do you have to feel guilty for?"

"Brett got his ass kicked because of me!"

"Nooo, he got an ass-kicking because he kissed a beautiful girl without thinking about the consequences. He should've expected you to be taken. And what burrowed up your anal cavity and rotted?"

"I don't need a lecture about Brett, okay?" What I needed was Cary's take on my relationship with Gideon and the concerns I had, but I couldn't reach out to my best friend. That made everything going wrong in my life even more unsettling. I felt totally alone and adrift. "I've told you, I'm not taking that road again."

"Glad to hear it."

I told him what I could of the truth, because I knew he wouldn't judge. "I'm still in love with Gideon."

"Of course you are," he agreed simply. "For what it's worth, I'm sure your breakup is eating at him, too."

I hugged him. "Thank you."

"For what?"

"Being you."

He snorted. "I'm not saying you should wait for him. Whatever Cross's deal is doesn't matter—he snoozes, he loses. But I don't think you're ready to jump into some other dude's bed. You can't do casual sex, Eva. It means something to you; that's why you get so fucked up when you just give it away."

"It never works," I agreed, stepping away to finish cleaning my face. "Will you go with me to the video premiere?"

"Yeah, I'll go."

"Want to bring Trey or Tatiana?"

Shaking his head, he turned to the mirror and arranged his hair with practiced sweeps of his hands. "Then it'd be like a double date. Better if I'm the third wheel. More impact."

I watched his reflection, my mouth curving in a soft smile. "I love you."

He blew me a kiss. "Then take care of yourself, baby girl. That's all I need."

MY favorite housewarming gift was Waterford martini glasses. To me, it was just the right blend of luxury, fun, and usefulness. I'd given a set to a college friend who had no idea what Waterford crystal was but loved appletinis, and I'd given a set to my mother, who didn't drink martinis but loved Waterford. It was a gift I'd even feel comfortable giving to Gideon Cross, a man who had more money than was comprehensible.

But stemware wasn't what I clutched in my hands as I knocked on his door.

Nervous, I shifted on my feet and ran a hand down my hip to smooth my dress. I'd dolled myself up after getting back from the gym, taking the time to really work my New Eva hairstyle and smoky eye shadow. My pale pink lipstick was smudgeproof and I wore a little black dress that was a halter with a low draping neckline and an even lower back.

The short dress showed a lot of leg, which I accentuated with peep-toe Jimmy Choos. I wore the diamond hoops I'd chosen for our first date and the ring he'd given me, a striking piece that had interlacing gold ropes hugged by diamond Xs—the Xs representing Gideon holding on to the various threads of me.

The door opened and I swayed a little on my feet, struck by the gorgeous, sexy-as-sin man who greeted me. Gideon must have been feeling sentimental, too. He had on the same black sweater he'd worn to the nightclub where we'd first really hung out together. It looked amazing on him—the perfect blend of casual and elegant sexiness. Paired with graphite gray dress slacks and bare feet, the effect on me was pure, white-hot desire.

"Christ," he growled. "You look amazing. Next time warn me before I open the door."

I smiled. "Hello, Dark and Dangerous."

5

GIDEON'S MOUTH CURVED in a devastating grin as he held his hand out to me. When my fingers touched his palm, he caught me and drew me inside, pulling me close to place his lips softly over mine. The door shut behind me and he reached past me to lock it, shutting the world out.

My hand clenched around a fistful of his sweater. "You're wearing my favorite sweater."

"I know." Abruptly, he sank into a graceful crouch, taking my hand that he held and placing it on his shoulder. "Let's make you comfortable, angel. You won't need these heels until you're ready for me to fuck you."

My core clenched with anticipation. "What if I'm ready now?"

"You're not. You'll know when the time comes."

As Gideon removed my shoes, I shifted my weight from one foot to the other. "Will I? How?"

He glanced up at me with those intensely blue eyes. He was nearly on his knees, taking my shoes off, yet he was undeniably in command of himself and of me. "I'll be pushing my cock inside you."

I shifted on my feet for a different reason. *Yes, please* . . .

Straightening, he once again loomed over me. His fingertips drifted across my cheek. "What's in the bag?"

"Oh." I mentally shook off the sexual spell he had me under. "Housewarming gift."

I looked around. The space was a mirror image of my own. The apartment was lovely and comfortably inviting. I'd partly expected a semi-lived-in space, mostly bare with only the essentials. Instead, it was very much a home. One that was lit only by candlelight, which cast a warm golden glow on furniture I recognized because it was Gideon's *and* mine.

Stunned, I barely noticed when he took the gift bag and my purse from my fingers. Barefoot, I skirted him, seeing my coffee and end tables placed around his sofa and side chairs; my entertainment center holding his knickknacks and framed photos of the two of us together; my drapes with his unlit floor and table lamps.

On the wall, where my flat-screen TV would be hanging, was a massive photo of me blowing him a kiss, a much larger version of the photo I'd given him that he kept on his desk in his Crossfire office.

I turned slowly, trying to take it all in. He'd shocked me like this once before, when he'd re-created my bedroom in his penthouse, giving me a familiar place to run when things got too intense.

"When did you move in here?" I loved it. The mix of my modern traditional with his old-world elegance was oddly perfect. He'd blended just the right pieces to create a space that was . . . *us.*

"The week Cary was in the hospital."

I glanced at him. "Are you serious?"

That was when Gideon had begun pulling away from me, cutting me off. He'd started hanging out with Corinne again and become difficult to reach.

Getting this place set up must have kept him busy, too.

"I needed to be near you," he said absently, looking into the bag. "I had to be sure I could get to you quickly. Before Nathan could."

Shock rippled through me. At a time when I'd felt Gideon drifting further and further away from me, he'd been physically close. Watching over me. "When I called you from the hospital"—I swallowed past a dry lump—"you had someone with you . . ."

"Raúl. He was coordinating the move-in. I had to get it done before you and Cary came home." He looked up at me. "Towels, angel?" he asked, with more than a hint of amusement.

He pulled the white hand towels embroidered with CROSSTRAINER out of the bag. I'd picked them up at the gym. At the time, I'd been envisioning him having a bare bones bachelor pad. Now, they were ridiculous.

"I'm sorry," I said, still reeling from his disclosure about the apartment. "I had a different idea of what this place looked like."

He pulled the towels away when I reached for them. "Your gifts are always thoughtful. Tell me what you were thinking about when you bought these."

"I was thinking about making you think about me."

"Every minute of every day," he murmured.

"Let me clarify: Me—all hot and sweaty and desperate for you."

"Umm . . . a fantasy I indulge in often."

Abruptly, the memory of Gideon pleasuring himself in my shower punched into my mind. There really were no words for how fucking amazing that sight was. "Do you think about me when you get yourself off?"

"I don't masturbate."

"What? Come on. Every guy does."

Gideon caught my hand and laced our fingers, then drew me toward the kitchen from which the most heavenly smell was emanating. "Let's talk over wine."

"Are you trying to ply me with alcohol?"

"No." He released me and set the bag of towels on the counter. "I know the way to your heart is with food."

I slid onto a bar stool just like the ones in my apartment, touched by his unique way of making me feel at home. "The way to my heart? Or into my pants?"

He smiled as he poured a glass of red wine from a bottle he'd previously opened to let breathe. "You're not wearing pants."

"Not wearing any panties, either."

"Careful, Eva." Gideon shot me a stern look. "Or you'll derail my attempt to seduce you properly before I ride you on every flat surface in this apartment."

My mouth went dry. The look in his eyes when he brought my glass over made me feel flushed and light-headed.

"Before you," he murmured, with his lips to the edge of his glass, "I stroked off every time I took a shower. It was as much a part of my ritual as washing my hair."

That I believed. Gideon was a very sexual man. When we were together, he'd fuck me before bed, first thing in the morning, and sometimes fit in a quickie during the course of the day.

"Since you, only once," he continued. "You were there with me."

I paused with my glass halfway to my mouth. "Really?"

"Really."

I took a drink, gathering my thoughts. "Why did you stop? The last few weeks . . . We went a long time without."

A ghost of a smile curved his lips. "I don't have a drop to waste if I'm going to keep up with you."

I set the wineglass down and pushed at his shoulder. "You're always making me sound like a nymphomaniac!"

"You like sex, angel," he purred. "Nothing wrong with that. You're greedy and insatiable, and I love it. I love knowing that once I get inside you, you're going to suck me dry. Then you'll want to do it again."

I felt my face heat. "For your information, I didn't get off even once while we were apart. Never even got the urge because we weren't together."

He leaned into the counter, resting one elbow on the cool black granite. "Hmm."

"I like fucking you because you're *you*, not because I'm a cock-hungry slut. If you don't like it, grow a gut or stop showering or *something*." I slid off the stool. "Or just say no, Gideon."

I marched into the living room, trying to get away from the unsettled feeling I'd had all day.

Gideon's arms came around me from behind, halting me midstep. "Stop," he said, with the familiar authoritative bite that always turned me on.

I tried to squirm free.

"Now, Eva."

I gave up, my hands falling to my sides to clench my dress.

"Explain what the fuck just happened," he said calmly.

My head bowed and I didn't say anything, because I didn't know what to say. A moment of silence later, he moved, swinging me up into the cradle of his arms and carrying me to the couch. He sat and arranged me on his lap. I snuggled into him.

His chin came to rest on the crown of my head. "You want to pick a fight, angel?"

"No," I mumbled.

"Good. Me neither." His hands stroked up and down my back. "So let's talk instead."

I pressed my nose into his throat. "I love you."

"I know." He tilted his head back, giving me room to nestle.

"I'm not a sex addict."

"I don't see why it'd be a problem if you were. God knows making love with you is my favorite thing to do. In fact, if you ever wanted me to take care of you more often, I'd go so far as to schedule sex with you into my day."

"Oh my God!" I nipped him with my teeth, and he laughed softly.

Gideon wrapped my hair around his fist and tugged my head back. His gaze on my face was soft and serious. "You're not upset about our incredible sex life. It's something else."

Sighing, I admitted, "I don't know what it is. I'm just . . . *off*."

Adjusting me in his lap, Gideon snuggled me closer, pulling me into his warmth. We fit so perfectly together, my curves aligning with his sculpted lines. "Do you like the apartment?"

"I love it."

"Good." His voice was laced with satisfaction. "Obviously, it's an example—taken to the extreme."

My heart rate jumped a little. "Of what our place could look like?"

"We'll start fresh, of course. Everything new."

I was moved by his pronouncement. Still, I had to say, "It was so risky doing this. Moving in here, getting in and out of the building. It makes me nervous just thinking about it."

"On paper, someone lives here. So of course, he'd move furniture in, and come and go. He enters through the garage, just like all the other tenants with cars. When I'm being him, I dress a little differently, take the stairs, and check the security feeds so I know if I'm going to run into anyone before it happens."

The amount of planning involved was mindboggling to me, but then he'd had practice getting to Nathan without a trace. "All this trouble and expense. For me. I can't— I don't know what to say."

"Say you'll plan on moving in with me."

I savored the surge of pleasure his words brought me. "Do you have a time frame in mind for this fresh start?"

"As soon as we can get away with it." His hand on my thigh squeezed gently.

I set my hand over his. There was so much standing in the way of us living together: the lingering trauma of our pasts; my dad, who disliked rich guys and thought Gideon was a cheater; and me, because I liked my apartment and believed that striking out in a new city meant doing as much as I could on my own.

I jumped to the biggest issue for me, though. "What about Cary?"

"The penthouse has an attached guest apartment."

Pulling back quickly, I stared at him. "You'd do that for Cary?"

"No, I'd do it for you."

"Gideon, I . . ." My words trailed off because there were no words. I was awed. Something inside me shifted a little.

"So you're not upset about the apartment," he said. "Something else is on your mind."

I decided to save Brett for last. "I've got a girls' night out on Saturday."

He stilled. Maybe someone who didn't know him as well as I did wouldn't catch that subtle, sharp alertness, but I caught it. "Girls' night doing what, exactly?"

"Dancing. Drinking. The usual."

"Is it a manhunt?"

"No." I licked my dry lips, mesmerized by the change in him. He'd gone from intimately playful to intensely focused. "We're all attached. At least I think we all are. I'm not sure about Megumi's roommate, but Megumi's got a man and you know Shawna's got her chef."

He was suddenly all business when he said, "I'll make the arrangements—car, driver, and security. If you stick with a circuit of my clubs, your security will stay in the car. You want to branch out, he's going in with you."

Blinking in surprise, I said, "Okay."

From the kitchen, the oven timer began beeping.

Gideon went from sitting to standing, with me in his arms, in one powerfully graceful surge. My eyes widened. My blood hummed through my veins. I wrapped my arms around his neck and let him carry me to the kitchen. "I love how strong you are."

"You're easy to impress." Settling me on a bar stool, he gave me a lingering kiss before heading to the oven.

"You cooked?" I wasn't sure why the thought surprised me, but it did.

"No. Arnoldo had ready-to-cook lasagna and a salad delivered."

"Sounds awesome." I knew from having eaten in celebrity chef Arnoldo Ricci's restaurant that the food would be killer.

Grabbing my glass, I wasted the wonderful wine by gulping it down for courage, thinking it was time to tell him what he wouldn't want to hear. I took the plunge and said, "Brett called me at work today."

For a minute or two, I didn't think Gideon heard me. He slid on a pot holder, opened the oven, and pulled out the lasagna without looking my way. It wasn't until he set the pan on the stovetop and glanced at me that I knew for certain he hadn't missed a word.

He tossed the glove onto the counter, grabbed the wine bottle, and came directly to me. Calmly, he took my wineglass and refilled it before he spoke. "I expect he wants to see you when he's in New York next week."

It took me the space of a breath to respond. "You knew he was coming back!" I accused.

"Of course I knew."

Whether that was because Brett's band was signed to Vidal Records or because Gideon was keeping an eye on him, I didn't know. Both reasons were entirely plausible.

"Did you agree to meet up?" His voice was smooth and soft. Dangerously so.

Ignoring the fluttering of nerves in my belly, I held his gaze. "Yes, for the reveal of the new Six-Ninths music video. Cary's going with me."

Gideon nodded, leaving me anxious and clueless about his feelings.

I slid off the stool and went to him. Wrapping me up in his arms, he rested his cheek against the top of my head.

"I'll back out," I offered quickly. "I don't really want to go anyway."

"It's okay." Swaying from side to side, rocking me, he whispered, "I broke your heart."

"That's not why I agreed to go!"

His hands came up and pushed through my hair, combing it back from my forehead and cheeks with a gentleness that brought tears to my eyes. "We can't just forget the last few weeks, Eva. I cut you deep and you're still bleeding."

It struck me then that I hadn't been ready to pick up the pieces of our relationship as if nothing had gone wrong. A part of me was holding a grudge, and Gideon had picked up on it.

I struggled out of his hold. "What are you saying?"

"That I have no right to leave you and hurt you—for whatever reason—then expect you to forget how that felt and forgive me overnight."

"You killed a man for me!"

"You don't owe me anything," he snapped. "My love for you is not an obligation."

It still tore through me like a bullet every time he said he loved me, despite how often he proved it with his actions.

My voice was softer when I said, "I don't want to hurt you, Gideon."

"Then don't." He kissed me with heartrending tenderness. "Let's eat, before the food gets cold."

I changed into a Cross Industries T-shirt and a pair of Gideon's pajama bottoms that I rolled up at the ankles. We took candles over to the coffee table and ate cross-legged on the floor. Gideon kept my favorite sweater on but swapped his slacks for a pair of black lounging pants.

Licking a dab of tomato sauce off my lip, I told him about the rest of my day. "Mark's gathering the nerve to ask his partner to marry him."

"If I'm remembering correctly, they've been together awhile."

"Since college."

Gideon's mouth curved. "I suppose it's still a tough question to ask, even if the answer is a sure thing."

I looked down at my plate. "Was Corinne nervous when she asked you?"

"Eva." He waited until the lengthy silence brought my head up. "We're not going to talk about that."

"Why not?"

"Because it doesn't matter."

I searched his face. "How would you feel if you knew there was someone out there I'd said yes to? Theoretically."

He shot me an irritated look. "That would be different because you wouldn't say yes unless the guy really meant something to you. What I felt was . . . panic. The feeling didn't go away until she broke the engagement."

"Did you buy her a ring?" The thought of him shopping for a ring for another woman hurt me. I looked down at my hand, at the ring he'd bought for me.

"Nothing like that one," he said quietly.

My hand fisted, guarding it.

Reaching over, Gideon set his right hand over mine. "I bought Corinne's ring in the first store I went to. I had nothing in mind, so I picked one that looked like her mother's. Very different circumstances, don't you agree?"

"Yes." I hadn't designed the ring Gideon wore, but I'd searched six shops before I found the right one. It was platinum studded with black diamonds, and it reminded me of my lover, with its cool masculine elegance and bold, dominant style.

"I'm sorry," I said, wincing. "I'm an ass."

He lifted my hand to his lips and kissed my knuckles. "So am I, on occasion."

That made me grin. "I think Mark and Steven are perfect for each other, but Mark has this theory that men get the urge to marry, and then it goes away if it isn't acted on quickly enough."

"I would think it'd be more about the right partner than the right time."

"I've got my fingers crossed for it to work out for them." I picked up my wine. "Want to watch TV?"

Gideon leaned his back against the front of the sofa. "I just want to be with you, angel. I don't care what we're doing."

WE cleaned up the mess from dinner together. As I reached for the rinsed dish Gideon held out for me to put in the dishwasher, he faked me out. He grabbed my hand instead and deftly set the plate on the counter. Catching me around the waist, he spun us into a dance. From the living room, I caught the strains of something beautiful laced with a woman's pure, haunting voice.

"Who is this?" I asked, already breathless from the feel of Gideon's powerful body flexing against mine. The desire that always smoldered between us flared, making me feel vibrant and alive. Every nerve ending sensitized, preparing for his touch. Hunger coiled tight with heated anticipation.

"No clue." He swept me around the island and into the living room.

I surrendered to his masterful lead, loving that dancing was a passion we shared and awed by the obvious joy he felt in just being with me. That same pleasure effervesced within me, lightening my steps until it felt like we were gliding. As we approached the sound system, the music rose in volume. I heard the words *dark and dangerous* in the lyrics and stumbled in surprise.

"Too much wine, angel?" Gideon teased, pulling me closer.

But my attention was riveted to the music. The singer's pain. A tormented relationship she likened to loving a ghost. The words reminded me of the days when I believed I'd lost Gideon forever, and my heart ached.

I looked up into his face. He was watching me with dark, glittering eyes.

"You looked so happy when you were dancing with your dad," he said, and I knew he wanted treasured memories like that between us.

"I'm happy now," I assured him, even as my eyes stung at the sight of his yearning, a longing I knew intimately. If souls could be mated with wishes, ours would be inextricably entwined.

Cupping his nape, I pulled his mouth down to mine. As our lips touched, his rhythm faltered. He stopped, hugging me so tightly my feet left the floor.

Unlike the heartbroken singer, I wasn't in love with a ghost. I was in love with a flesh-and-blood man, one who made mistakes but learned from them, a man who was trying hard to better himself for me, a man who wanted *us* to work as desperately as I did.

"I'm never happier than when I'm with you," I told him.

"Ah, Eva."

He took my breath away with his kiss.

"IT was the kid," I said.

Gideon's fingertips drew circles around my navel. "That's twisted."

We were sprawled lengthwise on the couch, watching my favorite police procedural television show. He was spooned behind me, his chin on my shoulder and his legs tangled with mine.

"That's the way these things work," I told him. "Shock value and all that."

"I think it was the grandmother."

"Oh my God." I tilted my head to look back at him. "And you don't think *that's* twisted?"

He grinned and smacked a kiss on my cheek. "Wanna bet on who's right?"

"I don't gamble."

"Aw, come on." His hand splayed against my belly, anchoring me as he rose up on his elbow to look down at me.

"Nope." I felt him against the curve of my buttocks, a solid, weighty length. He wasn't erect, but that didn't stop him from gaining my attention. Curious, I reached between us and cupped him in my hand.

He hardened instantly. One black brow arched. "You copping a feel, angel?"

I squeezed him gently. "Now I'm hot and bothered, and wondering why my new neighbor isn't putting the moves on me."

"Maybe he doesn't want to push you too far, too fast and scare you off." Gideon's eyes glittered in the light of the television.

"Is that so?"

He nuzzled his nose against my temple. "If he has half a brain, he'd know not to let you get away."

Oh . . . "Maybe I should make the first move," I whispered, wrapping my fingers around his wrist. "But what if he thinks I'm too easy?"

"He'll be too busy thinking he's damned lucky."

"Well, then . . ." I wriggled around to face him. "Howdy, neighbor."

He traced my eyebrow with the tip of his finger. "Hi. I really like the view around here."

"The hospitality isn't bad, either."

"Oh? Plenty of towels?"

I pushed at his shoulder. "Do you want to suck face or not?"

"Suck face?" His head fell back and he laughed, his chest vibrating against me. It was a lusty, full-bodied sound and my toes curled at hearing it. Gideon laughed so rarely.

My hands slid under his sweater and glided over warm skin. My lips moved over his jaw. "Is that a no?"

"Angel, I'll suck on any part of your body I can get my mouth on."

"Start here." I offered him my lips and he took them, sealing his mouth softly over mine. His tongue traced the seam, then dipped inside me, licking and teasing.

I burrowed into his body, moaning when he shifted to lie half over me. My hands slid up and down his back, my leg lifting to hook over his hip. I caught his lower lip between my teeth and stroked the curve with the tip of my tongue.

His groan was so erotic it made me wet.

My back arched as his hand crept beneath the hem of my T-shirt and captured my bare breast, rolling my nipple between his thumb and forefinger.

"You're so soft," he murmured. He kissed his way to my temple, and then buried his face in my hair. "I love touching you."

"You're perfect." I pushed beneath his waistband to grip his bare buttocks. The scent and heat of his skin intoxicated me, made me feel drunk with lust and longing. "A dream."

"You're *my* dream. Christ, you're so beautiful." His mouth covered mine and I fisted a hand in his hair, clutching him to me with my arms and legs wrapped around him.

My world narrowed to just him. The feel of him. The sounds he made.

"I love how much you want me," he said hoarsely. "I couldn't stand being in this alone."

"I'm with you, baby," I promised, my mouth moving feverishly beneath his. "I am *so* with you."

Gideon possessed me with one hand at my nape and the other at my waist. Settling over me, he aligned his hardness to my softness, his cock to my sex, and rolled his hips. I gasped, my nails digging into the rock-hard cheeks of his ass.

"Yes," I moaned shamelessly. "You feel so good."

"It'd feel better inside you," he purred.

I bit his earlobe. "Are you trying to talk me into going all the way?"

"We don't have to go anywhere, angel." He sucked gently on my throat, making my sex clench hungrily. "I can put it in right here. I promise I'll make you feel good."

"I don't know. I've changed my ways. I'm not that kind of girl anymore."

His hand at my waist pushed my pants down. I gave a token wiggle and make a soft sound of protest. My skin tingled where he'd touched me, my body awakening to his demands.

"Shh." Brushing his mouth over mine, he whispered, "If you don't like it once it's in you, I promise I'll pull out."

"Has that line ever worked for anyone?"

"I'm not feeding you lines. I mean every word."

I gripped the steely curves of his butt and rocked up against him, knowing damn well he didn't need any lines. A crook of his finger was all it would take for him to get laid by anyone he wanted.

Thankfully, he only wanted me.

Reveling in his playfulness, I teased, "I bet you say that to all the girls."

"What other girls?"

"You've got a rep, you know."

"But you're the one wearing my ring." As he lifted his head, his fingertips brushed the hair from my temple. "Day One of my life was the day I met you."

The words hit me like a blow. I swallowed hard and whispered, "Okay, that's a winner. You can put it in."

The shadows left his face, chased away by his smile. "God, I'm crazy about you."

I smiled back. "I know."

6

I WOKE IN a cold sweat, my heart pounding violently. I lay in the master bed, panting, my mind clawing up from the depths of sleep.

"Get off me!"

Gideon. My God.

"Don't fucking touch me!"

Throwing off the covers, I scrambled out of bed and ran down the hallway to the guest room. I searched frantically for the switch on the wall, hitting it with the flat of my palm. Light exploded in the room, exposing Gideon writhing on the bed, his legs twisted in the bedding.

"Don't. Ah, Christ . . ." His back arched up from the bed, his hands fisting in the fitted sheet. "It *hurts*!"

"Gideon!"

He jerked violently. I raced to the bedside, my heart twisting to see him flushed and drenched with sweat. I placed my hand on his chest.

"Don't fucking touch me!" he hissed, seizing my wrist and

squeezing it so hard I cried out in pain. His eyes were open, but unfocused, still trapped in his nightmare.

"Gideon!" I struggled to get away.

He jackknifed upward, his lungs heaving and his eyes wild. "Eva."

Releasing me as if I had burned him, he shoved his damp hair out of his face and lunged out of bed. "Jesus. Eva . . . did I hurt you?"

I held my wrist with my other hand and shook my head.

"I want to see," he said hoarsely, reaching for me with trembling hands.

I dropped my arms and stepped into him, hugging him as tightly as I could, my cheek pressed to his sweat-slick chest.

"Angel." He clung to me, shaking. "I'm sorry."

"Shh, baby. It's okay."

"Let me hold you," he whispered, sinking to the floor with me. "Don't let go."

"Never," I promised, my lips whispering over his skin. "Never."

I ran a bath and climbed into the triangular corner tub with him. Sitting behind him on the highest step, I washed his hair and ran soapy hands over his chest and back, washing the icy sweat of the nightmare away. The heat of the water stopped his quivering, but nothing so simple could remove the dark desolation in his eyes.

"Have you ever talked to anyone about your nightmares?" I asked, squeezing warm water out of the sponge onto his shoulder.

He shook his head.

"It's time," I said softly. "And I'm your girl."

He took a long time to speak. "Eva, when you have nightmares . . . are they more like re-creations of actual events? Or does your mind switch them around? Change them?"

"They're mostly memories. True to life. Are yours not?"

"Sometimes. Sometimes they're different. Make-believe."

I absorbed that a minute, wishing I had the training and knowledge to be truly helpful. Instead, I could only love him and listen. I hoped that was enough, because his nightmares were ripping me apart as surely as they were him. "Are they changed in a good way? Or bad?"

"I fight back," he said softly.

"And he still hurts you?"

"Yes, he still wins, but at least I hold him off as long as I can."

I dipped the sponge again, squeezing water over him, trying to maintain a soothing rhythm. "You shouldn't judge yourself. You were only a child."

"So were you."

My eyes closed tightly against the knowledge that Gideon had seen the photos and videos Nathan had taken of me. "Nathan was a sadist. It's natural to struggle against physical pain, so I did. That's not bravery."

"I wish it had hurt me more," he bit out. "I hate that he made me enjoy it."

"You didn't enjoy it. You felt pleasure and that's not the same thing. Gideon, our bodies react to things by instinct, even when we don't consciously want them to." I hugged him from behind, resting my chin on the top of his head. "He was your therapist's assistant, someone you're supposed to be able to trust. He had the training to fuck with your head."

"You don't understand."

"Then make me understand."

"He . . . seduced me. And I let him. He couldn't make me want it, but he made sure I didn't resist."

Moving, I pressed my cheek to his temple. "Are you worried you're bisexual? It won't freak me out if you are."

"No." He turned his head and brushed his mouth across mine, his hands lifting out of the water to link our fingers together. "I've never been attracted to men. But the fact that you'd accept me if I were . . . Right now I love you so much it hurts."

"Baby." I kissed him sweetly, our lips parting and clinging. "I just want you to be happy. Preferably with me. And I really want you to stop hurting yourself over what was done to you. You were raped. You were a victim and now you're a survivor. There's no shame in that."

He turned and pulled me deeper into the water.

I settled beside him, my hand on his thigh. "Can we talk about something? Sexual?"

"Always."

"You told me once that you don't do anal play." I felt him tense. "But you've . . . we've . . ."

"I've had my fingers and tongue inside you," he finished, studying me. He'd altered with the change of subject, his hesitation replaced by calm authority. "You enjoy it."

"Do you?" I asked, before I lost the courage.

He breathed heavily, his cheekbones burnished by the heated water, his face exposed by his slicked-back hair.

After long moments, I feared he wasn't going to answer me. "I'd like to give you that, Gideon, if you want it."

His eyes closed. "Angel."

I reached a hand between his legs, cupping his heavy sac. My middle finger extended beneath him, brushing lightly over the puckered opening. He jerked violently, his legs slamming shut, sending water sloshing to the lip of the tub. His cock hardened like stone against my forearm.

I pulled my trapped hand free and gripped his erection in my fist, stroking, my mouth taking his when he groaned. "I'll do anything for you. There are no limits in our bed. No memories. Just us. You and me. And love. I love you so much."

His tongue thrust into my mouth, a greedy and slightly angry foray. His hand at my waist tightened, his other hand covering mine and urging me to tighten my grip.

Gentle waves lapped against the sides of the bathtub as I pumped his erection. His moan tightened my nipples.

"*I* own your pleasure," I whispered into his mouth. "I'll take it if you won't give it to me."

He growled, his head falling back. "Make me come."

"Any way you want," I vowed.

"WEAR the blue tie. The one that matches your eyes." I had a direct view into the walk-in closet, where Gideon was picking out the suit he'd wear to wrap up the week.

He glanced over to where I sat on the edge of the bed in the master bedroom, a cup of coffee in my hands. His mouth curved in an indulgent smile.

"I love your eyes," I told him with an easy shrug. "They're gorgeous."

He unhooked the tie from the rack and stepped back into the bedroom with a graphite gray suit draped over his forearm. He wore only black boxer briefs, affording me the joy of admiring his leanly ripped body and taut golden skin.

"It's uncanny how often we think alike," he said. "I picked out this suit because the color reminds me of *your* eyes."

That made me smile. I swung my legs, too full of love and happiness to sit still.

Laying his clothes on the bed, Gideon came to me. I tilted my head back to look up at him, my heart beating strong and sure.

He cupped the sides of my head, his thumbs brushing over my eyebrows. "Such a beautiful stormy gray. And so very expressive."

"A totally unfair advantage for you. You read me like a book, while you've got the best poker face I've ever seen."

Bending over, he kissed my forehead. "And yet I can never get away with anything with you."

"So you say." I watched him start to dress. "Listen, I want you to do something for me."

"Anything."

"If you need a date and it can't be me, take Ireland."

He paused in the act of buttoning up his shirt. "She's seventeen, Eva."

"So? Your sister is a beautiful, classy young woman who adores you. She'd do you proud."

Sighing, he grabbed his slacks. "I can't imagine her being anything but bored at the few events appropriate for her to attend."

"You said she'd be bored having dinner at my place and you were wrong about that."

"*You* were there," he argued, yanking up his pants. "She had fun with *you*."

I took a drink of my coffee. "You said anything," I reminded.

"I don't have a problem going dateless, Eva. And I told you I won't be seeing Corinne anymore."

I stared at him over the rim of my mug and didn't say anything.

Gideon shoved his shirttails into his slacks with obvious frustration. "Fine."

"Thank you."

"You could refrain from grinning like the Cheshire cat," he muttered.

"I could."

He stilled, his narrowed eyes sliding down my body to where my robe had fallen away from my bare legs.

"Don't get any ideas, ace. I already put out this morning."

"Do you have a passport?" he asked.

I frowned. "Yes. Why?"

Nodding briskly, he reached for the tie I loved. "You'll need it."

Excitement tingled through me. "For what?"

"For travel."

"Duh." I slid off the bed onto my feet. "Travel to where?"

His eyes held a wicked gleam as he swiftly and expertly knotted his tie. "Somewhere."

"Are you shipping me off to parts unknown?"

"Wouldn't I love to," he murmured. "You and me on a deserted tropical island where you'd be perpetually naked and I could slide into you at any moment."

I set one hand on my hip and shot him a look. "Sunburned *and* bow-legged. Sexy."

He laughed and my toes flexed into the carpet.

"I want to see you tonight," he said, as he shrugged into his vest.

"You just want to put it in me again."

"Well, you did tell me not to stop. Repeatedly."

Snorting, I put my coffee down on the nightstand and shrugged out of my robe. Naked, I crossed the room, skirting him when he made a grab for me. I was opening a drawer to choose one of the lovely Carine Gilson bra and panty sets he kept stocked for me, when he came up behind me, slid his arms beneath mine, and cupped my breasts in both hands.

"I can remind you," he purred.

"Don't you have a job to get to? Because I do."

Gideon pressed against my back. "Come work with me."

"And pour your coffee while waiting for you to fuck me?"

"I'm serious."

"So am I." I spun so quickly to face him that I knocked my purse onto the floor. "I have a job and I like it a lot. You know that."

"And you're good at it." He gripped my shoulders. "Be good at it for me."

"I can't, for the same reason I didn't accept help from my stepfather. I want to make it on my own!"

"I know that. I respect that about you." His hands caressed my arms. "I clawed my way up, too, with the Cross name trying to drag me down. I'd never take the effort away from you. You wouldn't get anything you didn't earn."

I suppressed the twinge of sympathy I felt for Gideon's suffering over his father, a Ponzi scheme swindler who'd taken his own life rather than face jail time. "Do you really think anyone is going to believe I got the job for any reason other than I'm the chick you're sticking it to now?"

"Shut up." He shook me. "You're pissed off and that's fine, but don't talk about us that way."

I pushed at him. "Everyone else will."

Growling, he released me. "You signed up for a CrossTrainer membership even though you've got Equinox and Krav Maga. Explain why."

I pivoted to yank a pair of panties on so I wasn't arguing while buck naked. "That's different."

"It's not."

I faced him again, stepping on stuff that had fallen out of my purse, which only made me madder. "Waters Field and Leaman isn't in competition with Cross Industries! You use the agency's services yourself."

"Do you think you'll never work on a campaign for one of my competitors?"

Standing there in his unbuttoned vest and impeccable tie, he was making it hard for me to think properly. He was beautiful and passionate and everything I'd ever wanted, which made it nearly impossible for me to deny him anything.

"That's not the point. I won't be happy, Gideon," I said with quiet honesty.

"Come here." He held his arms open for me and hugged me when I walked into them. He spoke with his lips against my temple. "One day, the 'Cross' in Cross Industries won't refer to just me."

My anger and frustration simmered. "Can we not talk about this now?"

"One last thing: You can apply for a position just like anyone else, if that's the way you need to do it. I won't interfere. If you get the job, you'd be working on a different floor of the Crossfire and climbing the career ladder all on your own. Whether you advance won't be up to me."

"It's important to you." It wasn't a question.

"Of course it is. We're working hard to build a future together. This is a natural step in that direction."

I nodded reluctantly. "I have to be independent."

His hand cupped my nape, holding me close. "Don't forget what matters most. If you work hard and show skill and talent, that's what people will base their judgments on."

"I have to get ready for work."

Gideon searched my face, then kissed me softly.

He released me and I bent down to pick up my purse. Then I noticed that I'd stepped on my mirrored compact and shattered its case. I wasn't heartbroken over it, because I could always pick up another at Sephora on the way home. What froze my blood was the electrical wire sticking out of the cracked plastic.

Gideon crouched down to help me. I looked at him. "What is this?"

He took the compact from me and broke off more of the shell to expose a microchip with a small antenna. "A bug, maybe. Or a tracking device."

I looked at him with horror. My lips moved silently. *The police?*

"I've got jammers in the apartment," he answered, shocking me further. "And no. There's no way any judge would've authorized a tap on you. There's nothing to justify it."

"Jesus." I fell back on my ass, feeling sick.

"I'll have my guys look at it." He lowered to his knees and brushed the hair back from my face. "Could it be your mother?"

I stared at him helplessly.

"Eva—"

"My God, Gideon." I held him off with an uplifted hand and

grabbed my phone with the other. I dialed Clancy, my stepfather's bodyguard, and the moment he answered, I said, "Is the bug in my compact one of yours?"

There was a pause, then, "Tracking device, not a bug. Yes."

"For fuck's sake, Clancy!"

"It's my job."

"Your job sucks," I shot back, picturing him in my head. Clancy was solid muscle. He wore his dirty-blond hair in a military crew cut and radiated a vibe that was deadly dangerous. But I wasn't afraid of him. "This is bullshit and you know it."

"Keeping you safe became a bigger concern when Nathan Barker showed up again. He was slippery, so I had to cover both of you. The minute his death was confirmed, I turned off the receiver."

I squeezed my eyes shut. "This isn't about the damn tracker! I don't have a problem with that. It's the keeping-me-in-the-dark part that's wrong on so many levels. I feel violated, Clancy."

"I don't blame you, but Mrs. Stanton didn't want you to worry."

"I'm an adult! I get to decide if I worry or not." I shot a look at Gideon when I said that, because what I was saying was totally applicable to him, too.

His arch look told me he got the message.

"You won't hear me arguing," Clancy said gruffly.

"You owe me," I told him, knowing just how I was going to collect. "Big-time."

"You know where to find me."

I killed the call, then sent a text to my mom: We need to talk.

My shoulders sagged with disappointment and frustration.

"Angel."

I shot Gideon a look that warned him not to push me. "Don't you dare make excuses—for yourself or for her."

His eyes were soft and shadowed, but the set of his jaw was resolute.

"I was there when you were told Nathan was in New York. I saw your face. There's no one who loves you who wouldn't do whatever they could to shield you from that."

And that was really hard for me to deal with, because I couldn't deny that I was glad I hadn't known about Nathan until after he was dead. But I also didn't want to be insulated from bad things. They were part of living.

Reaching for his hand, I gripped it tightly. "I feel the same way about you."

"I've taken care of my demons."

"And mine." But we were still sleeping apart from each other. "I want you to go back to Dr. Petersen," I said quietly.

"I went on Tuesday."

"You did?" I couldn't hide my surprise at learning he'd kept his regular schedule.

"Yeah, I did. I only missed the one appointment."

When he'd killed Nathan . . .

His thumb brushed over the back of my hand. "It's just you and me now," he said, as if he'd read my mind.

I wanted to believe that.

I was dragging when I got to work, which wasn't a good omen for the rest of the day. At least it was Friday and I could be a slug over the weekend, which would probably be a necessity Sunday morning if I partied too hard Saturday night. I hadn't had a girls' night out in ages and I felt the need for a good stiff drink or two.

In the previous forty-eight hours, I'd learned that my boyfriend had killed my rapist, one of my exes was hoping to spread me across his sheets, one of my boyfriend's exes was hoping to smear him in the press, and my mother had microchipped me like a damned dog.

Really, how much was a girl supposed to take?

"You ready for tomorrow?" Megumi queried, after she buzzed me through the glass doors.

"Hell, yeah. My friend Shawna texted me this morning and she's in." I mustered a genuine smile. "I arranged for a club limo for us. You know . . . one of those that take you to all the VIP spots, cover included."

"What?" She couldn't hide her excitement, but still had to ask, "How much is that?"

"Nada. It's a favor from a friend."

"Some favor." Her grin made me happy, too. "This is going to be *awesome*! You'll have to tell me the deets over lunch."

"You're on. I expect you to dish about your lunch yesterday, too."

"Talk about mixed signals, right?" she complained. "'We're just having fun,' but he shows his face at my work? I would never pop into a guy's office for an impromptu lunch if we were just messing around."

"Men," I huffed sympathetically, even as I acknowledged that I was grateful for the one who was *mine*.

I went to my desk and got ready to start my workday. When I saw the framed photos of Gideon and me in my drawer, I was struck by the need to reach out to him. Ten minutes later, I'd asked Angus to place an order for black magic roses to be sent to Gideon's office with the note:

You've got me under your spell.
I'm still thinking about you.

Mark came to my cubicle just as I was closing the window on my browser. One look at his face and I could tell he wasn't doing so hot. "Coffee?" I asked.

He nodded and I stood. We headed to the break room together.

"Shawna was over last night," he began. "She said you're going out tomorrow night."

"Yes. Is that still okay with you?"

"Is what still okay?"

"If your sister-in-law and I hang out," I prodded.

"Oh . . . yeah. Sure. Go for it." He ran a restless hand over his short, dark curls. "I think it's cool."

"Great." I knew there was more on his mind, but I didn't want to push. "Should be fun. I'm looking forward to it."

"So is she." He reached for two single-serving coffee pods, while I took mugs from the shelf. "She's also looking forward to Doug getting back. And popping the question."

"Wow. Now *that's* cool! Two weddings in your family in a year. Unless you're planning a long engagement . . . ?"

He handed the first cup of coffee to me and I went to the fridge for half-and-half.

"It's not going to happen, Eva."

Mark's tone was weighted with dejection, and when I turned to face him, his head was down.

I patted his shoulder. "Did you propose?"

"No. There's no point. He was asking Shawna if she and Doug were planning on having kids right away, since she's still in school part-time, and when she said they weren't, he went into this lecture about how marriage is for couples ready for a family. Otherwise, it's better to keep things simple. It's the same crap I once shoveled to him."

I rounded him and lightened my coffee. "Mark, you won't know Steven's answer until you ask him."

"I'm scared," he admitted, looking into his steaming mug. "I want more than we've got, but I don't want to ruin what we have. If his answer is no and he thinks we want different things out of our relationship . . ."

"Cart before the horse, boss."

"What if I can't live with no?"

Ah . . . I could understand that. "Can you live with not knowing for sure either way?"

He shook his head.

"Then you have to tell him everything you've told me," I said sternly.

His mouth quirked. "Sorry to keep dumping this on you. But you're always great at giving me perspective."

"You know what to do. You just want a kick in the ass to do it. I'm always up for ass-kicking."

He smiled full on. "Let's not work on the divorce attorney's campaign today."

"How about the airline instead?" I suggested. "I have some ideas."

"All right, then. Let's hit it."

WE hard-charged through the morning, and I was energized by our progress. I wanted to keep Mark too occupied to worry. Work was a cure-all for me, and it quickly became clear that it was for him as well.

We'd just wrapped up for lunch and I had stopped by my desk to drop off my tablet when I saw the interoffice envelope on my desk. My pulse leaped with excitement and my hands shook slightly as I unwound the thin twine and let the note card inside slide out.

YOU'RE THE MAGIC.
YOU MAKE DREAMS COME TRUE.
X

I held the card to my chest, wishing it were the writer I was holding instead. I was thinking about sprinkling rose petals on our bed when my desk phone rang. I wasn't all that surprised when I heard my mother's breathy bombshell voice on the other end.

"Eva. Clancy talked to me. Please don't be upset! You have to understand—"

"I get it." I opened my drawer and tucked Gideon's precious note into my purse. "Here's the thing: You don't have Nathan as an excuse anymore. If you've got any more bugs or trackers or whatever in my stuff, you better fess up now. Because I promise you, if I find something else moving forward, our relationship will be irrevocably damaged."

She sighed. "Can we talk in person, please? I'm taking Cary out to lunch and I'll just stay over until you get home."

"All right." The irritation that had started prickling at me dissipated just as quickly as it had come up. I loved that my mother treated Cary like the brother he was to me. She gave him the maternal love he'd never had. And they were both so appearance- and fashion-conscious that they always had a blast together.

"I love you, Eva. More than anything."

I sighed. "I know, Mom. I love you, too."

My other line flashed a call from reception, so I said good-bye and answered it.

"Hey." Megumi's voice was low and hushed. "The chick who came by for you once before, the one you wouldn't see, she's here again asking for you."

I frowned, my brain taking a second to latch on to what she was talking about. "Magdalene Perez?"

"Yep. That's the one. What should I do?"

"Nothing." I pushed to my feet. Unlike the last time Gideon's friend-who-wished-she-were-more had come around, I was prepared to deal with her myself. "On my way."

"Can I watch?"

"Ha! I'll be there in a minute. This won't take long, then we'll head out to lunch."

Vanity had me smearing on some lip gloss before I slung my purse over my shoulder and headed out front. Thinking of Gideon's note put the smile on my face that greeted Magdalene when I found her in the waiting area. She stood when I came into view, looking so amazing I couldn't help but admire her.

When I'd first met her, her dark hair had been long and sleek, like Corinne Giroux's. Now, it was cut in a classic bob that showed off the exotic beauty of her face. She wore cream slacks and a black sleeveless shell that had a big bow tied at the hip. Pearls at her ears and throat completed the elegant look.

"Magdalene." I gestured for her to return to her seat and took the armchair on the opposite side of the small conversation table. "What brings you here?"

"I'm sorry to barge in on you at work like this, Eva, but I was visiting Gideon and thought I'd stop here, too. I have something to ask you."

"Oh?" I set my purse down beside me and crossed my legs, smoothing my burgundy skirt. I resented her for being able to spend time with my boyfriend openly when I couldn't. There was no way around it.

"A reporter stopped by my office today, asking personal questions about Gideon."

My fingertips curled into the cushion of the armrest. "Deanna Johnson? You didn't answer her, did you?"

"Of course not." Magdalene leaned forward, setting her elbows on her knees. Her dark eyes were somber. "She's already talked to you."

"She tried."

"She's his type," she pointed out, studying me.

"I noticed," I said.

"The type he doesn't stick with long." Her full red lips twisted ruefully. "He's told Corinne that it's best if they remain long-distance friends, rather than social ones. But I suspect you know that."

I felt a ripple of pleasure over that news. "How would I know?"

"Oh, I'm sure you have ways." Magdalene's eyes sparkled with knowing amusement.

Oddly, I found myself at ease with her. Maybe because she seemed so at ease with herself, which hadn't been the case the previous times we'd crossed paths. "Seems like you're doing good."

"I'm getting there. I had someone in my life who I thought was a friend but was really just toxic. Without him around, I can think again." She straightened. "I've just started seeing someone."

"Good for you." In that respect, I wished her only the best. She'd been horribly used by Gideon's brother, Christopher. She didn't know I knew. "I hope it works out."

"Me, too. Gage is different from Gideon in a lot of ways. He's one of those brooding artist types."

"Deep souls."

"Yes. Very deep, I think. I hope I get to find out for sure." She stood. "Anyway, I don't mean to keep you. I was worried about the reporter and wanted to discuss her with you."

I corrected her as I rose. "You were worried about me discussing Gideon with the reporter."

She didn't deny it. "Bye, Eva."

"Bye." I watched her exit through the glass doors.

"That didn't look too bad," Megumi said, joining me. "No scratching or hissing."

"We'll see how long it lasts."

"Ready for lunch?"

"I'm starved. Let's go."

WHEN I walked in my front door five and a half hours later, Cary, my mom, and a dazzling silver Nina Ricci formal gown laid out on the sofa greeted me.

"Isn't it fantastic?" my mother gushed, looking fantastic herself in a fifties-style fitted dress with cap sleeves and a pattern of tiny cherries. Her blond hair framed her beautiful face in thick, glossy curls. I had to hand it to her; she could make any era look glamorous.

I'd been told my whole life that I looked just like her, but I had my father's gray eyes instead of her cornflower blue, and my abundant curves were from the Reyes side. I had a butt no amount of exercise would rid me of and breasts that prevented me from wearing anything without a lot of support. It still amazed me that Gideon found my body so irresistible when he'd previously been drawn only to tall, slender brunettes.

Dropping my bag and purse on a bar stool, I asked, "What's the occasion?"

"A shelter fund-raiser, a week from Thursday."

I looked at Cary for confirmation that he'd be escorting me. His nod allowed me to shrug and say, "Okay."

My mother beamed, looking radiant. In my honor, she supported charities benefiting abused women and children. When the fund-raisers were formal, she always purchased seats for Cary and me.

"Wine?" Cary asked, clearly picking up on my restless mood.

I shot him a grateful look. "Please."

As he headed off to the kitchen, my mom glided over to me on sexy red-soled slingbacks and pulled me in for a hug. "How was your day?"

"Weird." I hugged her back. "Glad it's over."

"Do you have plans this weekend?" She pulled away, her gaze sliding warily over my face.

That got my back up. "Some."

"Cary tells me you're seeing someone new. Who is he? What does he do?"

"Mom." I got to the point. "Are we good? Clean slate and all that? Or is there something you want to tell me?"

She started to fidget, almost wringing her hands. "Eva. You won't be able to understand what it's like until you have children of your own. It's terrifying. And knowing for certain that they're in danger—"

"Mom."

"And there are additional dangers that come just from being a beautiful woman," she rushed on. "You're connected to powerful men. That doesn't always make you safer—"

"Where are they, Mom?"

She huffed. "You don't have to take that tone with me. I was only trying—"

"Maybe you should go," I cut in coldly, the chill I felt on the inside leaching out through my voice.

"Your Rolex," she snapped, and it was like a slap to my face.

I staggered back a step, my right hand instinctively covering the watch on my left wrist, a treasured graduation gift from Stanton and my mother. I'd had the silly sentimental idea of passing it on to my daughter, should I be lucky enough to have one.

"Are you shitting me?" My fingers clawed at the clasp and the watch fell to the carpet with a muffled thud. It hadn't been a gift at all. It'd been a shackle on my wrist. "You've seriously crossed the line!"

She flushed. "Eva, you're overreacting. It's not—"

"Overreacting? Ha! My God, that's laughable. Really." I shoved two pinched-together fingers in her face. "I'm this close to calling the police. And I've half a mind to sue you for invasion of privacy."

"I'm your mother!" Her voice trailed off, took on a note of pleading. "It's my job to look after you."

"I'm a twenty-four-year-old adult," I said coldly. "By law, I can look after myself."

"Eva Lauren—"

"Don't." I lifted my hands, then dropped them. "Just don't. I'm going to leave now, because I'm so pissed off I can't even look at you. And I don't want to hear from you, unless it's with a sincere apology. Until you admit you're wrong, I can't trust you not to do it again."

I walked to the kitchen and grabbed my purse, my gaze meeting Cary's just as he was coming out with a tray of half-filled wineglasses. "I'll be back later."

"You can't just walk out like this!" my mother cried, clearly on the verge of one of her emotional fits. I couldn't deal with it. Not then.

"Watch me," I muttered under my breath.

My goddamned Rolex. Just thinking of it hurt like hell, because the gift had meant so much to me. Now, it meant nothing at all.

"Let her go, Monica," Cary said, his voice low and soothing. He knew how to deal with hysteria better than anyone. It was crappy sticking him with my mom, but I had to go. If I went to my room, she would just cry and plead at my door until I felt sick. I hated seeing her like that, hated causing her to feel that way.

Exiting my apartment, I went to Gideon's next door, rushing to get inside before the tears overwhelmed me or my mother came after me. There was nowhere else for me to go. I couldn't go out in public shell-shocked and crying. My mother wasn't the only one who had me under surveillance. There was also the possibility of the police, Deanna Johnson, and maybe even some paparazzi.

I got as far as Gideon's couch, sprawling across the cushions and allowing the tears to flow.

7

"ANGEL."

Gideon's voice and the feel of his hands on me pulled me from sleep. I mumbled a protest as he shifted me onto my side, and then the heat of his body was warming my back. One of his muscular arms wrapped around my waist, tucking me close.

Spooned with him, the biceps of his other arm hard beneath my cheek, I slid back into unconsciousness.

WHEN I woke again, it felt like days later. I lay on the couch with my eyes closed for long minutes, soaking in the warmth of Gideon's powerful body and breathing air that smelled of him. After a while, I decided that sleeping longer would only throw off my body clock even more. We'd had a lot of late nights and early mornings since we had gotten back together, and they were taking their toll.

"You've been crying," he murmured, burying his face in my hair. "Tell me what's wrong."

I wrapped my arms over his, snuggling into him. I told him about the watch. "Maybe I overreacted," I finished. "I was tired, which makes me irritable. But God . . . it hurt like hell. It totally ruined a gift that meant a lot to me, you know?"

"I can imagine." His fingers drew gentle circles across my stomach, caressing me through the silk of my shirt. "I'm sorry."

I looked toward the windows and saw that night had fallen. "What time is it?"

"A little after eight."

"What time did you get in?"

"Half past six."

I wriggled around to face him. "Early for you."

"Once I knew you were here, I couldn't stay away. I've wanted to be with you since your flowers arrived."

"You liked them?"

He smiled. "I have to say, reading your words in Angus's handwriting was . . . interesting."

"I'm trying to be safe."

He kissed the tip of my nose. "While still spoiling me."

"I want to. I want to ruin you for other women."

The pad of his thumb brushed over my bottom lip. "You did that the moment I saw you."

"Sweet talker." My depression lifted just from being with Gideon and knowing I was his sole focus at that moment. "You trying to get in my pants again?"

"You're not wearing pants."

"Is that a no?"

"That's a yes, I want under your skirt." His eyes darkened when I nipped his thumb with my teeth. "And inside your hot, wet, tight little cunt. I've wanted that all day. I want it every day. I want it now, but we'll wait until you're feeling better."

"You could kiss it and make it better."

"Kiss what, exactly?"

"Everything. Everywhere."

I knew I could get used to having him all to myself like this. Knew I wanted to. Which was impossible, of course.

Thousands of little pieces of him were committed to thousands of people and projects and commitments. If I'd learned anything from my mother's multiple marriages to successful businessmen, it was that wives were often mistresses, almost invariably taking second place because their husbands were also married to their work. There was a reason why a man became a captain in his chosen field—he gave it his all. The woman in his life got what was left.

Gideon tucked my hair behind my ear. "I want this. Coming home to you."

It always startled me when it seemed like he'd read my thoughts. "Would it have been better if you'd found me barefoot in the kitchen?"

"I wouldn't be opposed, but naked in bed would work best for me."

"I'm a decent cook, but you just want me for my body."

He smiled. "It's the very delicious package holding everything else I want."

"I'll show you mine, if you show me yours."

"Love to." His fingertips slid gently down my cheek. "But first, I want to make sure you're in the right frame of mind after the situation with your mother."

"I'll get over it."

"Eva." His tone warned me that he wouldn't be put off.

I sighed. "I'll forgive her, I always do. I don't have a choice, really, because I love her and I know she means well, even if she is seriously misguided. But this thing with the watch . . ."

"Go on."

I rubbed at the ache in my chest. "It broke something in our relationship. And no matter how we move forward, there's always going to be that crack there that didn't exist before. *That's* what hurts."

Gideon was quiet for a long time. One of his hands slid into my hair, while the other curled possessively over my hip. I waited for him to say what was on his mind.

"I broke something in our relationship, too," he said finally, his voice somber. "I'm afraid it's always going to be between us."

The sadness in his eyes twisted into me, hurting me. "Let me up."

He did, reluctantly, watching me warily as I stood. I hesitated before I unzipped my skirt. "Now I know what it feels like to lose you, Gideon. How badly it hurts. If you shut me out, it's probably going to make me panic a little. You'll just have to be careful of that, and I'll just have to trust that your love is going to stick."

He nodded his understanding and acceptance, but I could see it was eating at him.

"Magdalene came by today," I said, to take his mind off the lingering rift between us.

He tensed. "I told her not to."

"It's okay. She was probably concerned about me nursing a grudge, but I think she realized I love you too much to hurt you."

He sat up as I let my skirt drop. It pooled on the floor, revealing my garters and stockings, which earned me a slow hiss through his clenched teeth. I climbed back onto the couch and straddled his thighs, draping my arms around his neck. His breath was hot through the silk of my shirt, stirring my blood.

"Hey." I ran both hands through his hair, nuzzling my cheek against him. "Stop worrying about us. I think we need to be worrying about Deanna Johnson. What's the worst she could possibly dig up on you?"

His head fell back, his gaze narrowing. "She's my problem. I'll deal with her."

"I think she's after something really juicy. Calling you out as a heartless playboy isn't going to be enough."

"Stop worrying. The only reason I would care is because I don't want my past shoved in your face."

"You're too confident." My fingers went to his vest and began freeing the buttons. I exposed his shirt and removed his tie, draping it carefully over the back of the sofa. "Are you going to talk to her?"

"I'm going to ignore her."

"Is that the right way to handle this?" I went to work on his shirt.

"She wants my attention; she's not going to get it."

"She'll find another way, then."

He settled deeper into the seat back, his neck tilting to look up to me. "The only way for a woman to get my attention is to be you."

"Ace." I kissed him, tugging at his shirttails. He shifted to make it easier for me to pull them out of his pants. "I need you to explain Deanna," I murmured. "What set her off like this?"

He sighed. "She was a mistake in every sense. She made herself available once, and I make it a rule to avoid overly eager women a second time."

"And that doesn't make you sound like an asshole at all."

"I can't change what happened," he said coldly.

I could tell he was embarrassed. He could be as much of a dick as any guy, but he was never proud of it.

"Deanna happened to be covering an event where Anne Lucas was making me uncomfortable," he continued. "I used Deanna to keep Anne from approaching me. I didn't feel good about it afterward and I didn't handle it well."

"I get the picture." I pushed his shirt apart, exposing his warm, firm skin.

Remembering how he reacted after the first time we'd had sex, I could imagine how he'd handled Deanna. With me, he'd immediately shut down and shut me out, leaving me feeling used and worthless.

He'd fought to win me back after that, but the reporter hadn't been so lucky.

"You don't want to lead her on with any contact," I summed up. "She's probably still digging on you."

"I doubt that. I don't think I said more than a dozen words to her altogether."

"You were an ass to me, too. I fell in love with you anyway."

My hands slid lovingly across his hard chest, caressing the light dusting of dark hair before coasting down the thin, silky trail that led below his waistband. His abs quivered beneath my touch, the tempo of his breathing changing.

Sinking to sit on his lap, I adored his body. My thumbs circled the tiny points of his nipples and I watched his reaction, waiting for him to succumb to the subtle pleasure of my touch. I lowered my head and pressed a kiss to his throat, feeling his pulse leap beneath my lips and inhaling the virile scent of his skin. Enjoying him was something I didn't get to do enough of, because he always turned it back around on me.

Gideon groaned, his hand coming up to grip my hair. "Eva."

"I love the way you respond to me," I whispered, seduced by having such an unabashedly sexual male completely at my mercy. "Like you can't help yourself."

"I can't." He let the sleep-tousled strands sift through his fingers. "You touch me like you worship me."

"I do."

"I feel it in your hands . . . your mouth. The way you look at me." His throat worked on a swallow and I followed the movement with my eyes.

"I've never wanted anything more." I caressed his torso, tracing muscled pecs, then the line of every rib. Like a connoisseur admiring the perfection of a priceless work of art. "Let's play a game."

His tongue did a slow sweep along the curve of his lip, making my sex clench with jealousy. He knew it, too. I saw it in the way his eyes glittered dangerously. "Depends on the rules."

"Tonight, you're mine, ace."

"I'm always yours."

I unbuttoned my blouse and shrugged out of it, exposing my white lace demi-bra and matching thong.

"Angel," he breathed, his gaze so hot I felt it slide over my bared flesh. His hands moved to touch and I caught his wrists, staying him.

"Rule number one: I'm going to suck you, stroke you, and tease you all night long. You're going to come until you can't see straight." I cupped him through his slacks, massaging his rigid length with my palm. "Rule number two: You're just going to lie back and enjoy it."

"No returning the favor?"

"No."

"Not happening," he said decisively.

I pouted. "Pretty please."

"Angel, getting you off is ninety-nine percent of the fun for me."

"But then I'm so busy coming I don't get to enjoy you!" I complained. "Just for once—one night—I want you to be selfish. I want you to let go, be an animal, come just because it feels good and you're ready."

His lips thinned. "I can't do that with you. I need you with me."

"I knew you'd say that." Because I'd once told him that feeling used by a man for his pleasure was a trigger for me. I needed to feel loved and wanted, too. Not as an interchangeable female body to ejaculate into, but as Eva, an individual woman who needed genuine affection with sex. "But this is my game and it's played by my rules."

"I haven't agreed to play."

"Hear me out."

Gideon exhaled slowly. "I can't do it, Eva."

"You could do it with other women," I argued.

"I wasn't in love with them!"

I melted. I couldn't help it. "Baby . . . I want this," I whispered. "Real bad."

He made an exasperated noise. "Help me understand."

"I can't hear your heart racing when I'm gasping for breath. I can't feel you shaking when I'm shaking, too. I can't taste you when my mouth is dry from begging you to finish me off."

His beautiful face softened. "I lose my mind every time I come inside you. Let that be enough."

I shook my head. "You've said I'm like your favorite wet dream made real. Those dreams couldn't have all been about getting the girl off. What about the blowjobs? The hand jobs? You love my tits. Don't you want to fuck them until you come all over me?"

"Jesus, Eva." His cock thickened in my grip.

Brushing my parted lips across his, I deftly opened his slacks. "I want to be your dirtiest fantasy," I whispered. "I want to be filthy for you."

"You're already what I want you to be," he said darkly.

"Am I?" I ran my nails lightly down his sides, biting my lower lip when he hissed. "Then do it for me. I love those moments after you've seen to me and you're chasing your own orgasm. When your rhythm and focus changes, and you get ferocious. I know you're just thinking about how good it feels and how hot you are and how hard you're going to come. It makes me feel so good to get you that worked up. I want a whole night of feeling like that."

His hands squeezed my thighs. "With one stipulation."

"What is it?"

"You get tonight. Next weekend, the game's on me."

My mouth fell open. "I get a night, you get a whole weekend?"

"Umm . . . a whole weekend of seeing to you."

"Man," I muttered, "you drive a hard bargain."

His smile was razor sharp. "That's the plan."

"OUR mom says that our dad is a real sex machine."

Gideon glanced at me, grinning, from where he sat beside me on the floor. "You've got a weird catalog of movie lines in that gorgeous head of yours, angel."

I took a swig from my bottled water and swallowed just in time to recite the next line from *Kindergarten Cop*. "My dad's a gynecologist and he looks at vaginas all day long."

His laughter made me so happy I felt as if I could float away. He was bright-eyed and more relaxed than I'd seen him since forever. Some of that had to do with the straight-to-the-point blowjob I'd given him on the couch, followed by a long, slow, slippery hand job in the shower. But a lot of it came from me, I knew.

When I was in a good mood, he was, too. It amazed me that I had a profound influence on such a man. Gideon was a force of nature, his magnetic self-possession so powerful it put everyone around him in his shadow. I saw flashes of it every day and was awed by it, but not nearly as much as I was by the charming, wryly amusing lover I had entirely to myself in our private moments together.

"Hey," I said, "you won't be laughing when your kids tell their teachers the same things about you."

"Since they'd have to hear it from you, I'd know who it was that really needed the spanking."

He turned his head to resume watching the movie, as if he hadn't just knocked the wind out of me. Gideon was a man who'd lived an entirely solitary life, and yet he'd accepted me into it so completely that he could envision a future I was afraid to imagine. I was so scared I'd only be setting myself up for a heartbreak I couldn't survive.

Noting my silence, he set his hand on my bare knee and glanced at me again. "Still hungry?"

My gaze remained trained on the open Chinese take-out boxes on the coffee table in front of us, and the black magic roses, which Gideon had brought home from work so we could enjoy them over the weekend.

Not wanting to make more of his statement than he'd intended, I said, "Only for you."

I put my hand in his lap, feeling the soft heft of his cock within the black boxer briefs I'd allowed him to wear for dinner.

"You are a dangerous woman," he murmured, leaning closer.

Moving quickly, I caught his mouth with my own, sucking on his lower lip. "Have to be," I murmured, "to keep up with you, Dark and Dangerous."

He smiled.

"I need to check in with Cary again," I said with a sigh. "See if Mom's left yet."

"You okay?"

"Yeah." I leaned my head on his shoulder. "There's nothing like a little Gideon therapy to make things look up."

"Did I mention I make house calls? Twenty-four-seven."

I sank my teeth into his biceps. "Let me take care of this, then I'll make you come again."

"I'm good, thanks," he shot back, clearly amused.

"But we haven't played with the girls yet."

He bent down and buried his face in my cleavage. "Hello, girls."

Laughing, I shoved at his shoulders and he pushed me backward until I sprawled on the floor between the sofa and coffee table. He hovered above me, his arms tight and hard from supporting his weight. His gaze roamed, caressing my bra, then my bare tummy, then my thong and garters. The ensemble I wore post-shower was fire-engine red, chosen to keep Gideon revved.

"You're my lucky charm," he said.

I squeezed his biceps. "Really?"

"Yep." He licked the upper swell of my breast. "You're magically delicious."

"Oh my God!" I laughed. "Cheesy."

His eyes smiled at me. "I did warn you about me and romance."

"You lied. You're the most romantic guy I've ever dated. I can't believe you hung those CrossTrainer towels in your bathroom."

"How could I not? And I wasn't kidding about you being lucky." He kissed me. "I've been working on offloading my share of a casino in Milan. Those black magic roses arrived just as a bidder threw in a small winery in Bordeaux that I've had my eye on. Guess what it's called . . . La Rose Noir."

"A winery for a casino, huh? So you remain the god of sex, vice, and recreation."

"Endeavors that help me satisfy you, my goddess of desire, pleasure, and corny one-liners."

I ran my hands down his sides and slid my fingers beneath his waistband. "When do I get to try the wine?"

"When you're helping me brainstorm the advertising campaign for it."

With a sigh, I said, "You don't give up, do you?"

"Not when I want something, no." He rose to his knees and then helped me sit up. "And I want you. Very, very much."

"You have me," I said, using his words.

"I have your heart and your insanely sexy body. Now, I want your brain. I want everything."

"I need to save something for me."

"No. Take me instead." Gideon's hands reached around to cup the bare cheeks of my ass. "Not an even trade in quality, I'm sorry to say."

"You're bargaining like mad today."

"Giroux was happy with his deal. You will be, too, I promise."

"Giroux?" My heart thudded. "No relation to Corinne?"

"Her husband. Although they're estranged and facing divorce, as you know."

"No way. You do business with *her husband*?"

His mouth twisted ruefully. "First time. And likely the last, although I did tell him that I'm involved with a special woman—and she's not his wife."

"The problem is that she's in love with you."

"She doesn't know me." He cupped the back of my head and rubbed our noses together. "Hurry up and call Cary. I'll clean up dinner. Then we'll suck face."

"Fiend."

"Sexpot."

I scrambled up to head to my purse for my phone. Gideon grabbed a garter and snapped it, sending a shock wave of sensation across my skin. Surprisingly aroused by the nip of pain, I slapped his hand away and hurried out of reach.

Cary answered on the second ring. "Hey, baby girl. You still doing okay?"

"Yes. And you're still the best friend ever. Is Mom still hanging around?"

"She bailed a little over an hour ago. You stayin' over at loverman's?"

"Yeah, unless you need me."

"Nah, I'm good. Trey's on his way over now."

That news made me feel a lot better about spending a second night away. "Say hi to him for me."

"Sure. I'll kiss him for you, too."

"Well, if it's from me, don't make it too hot and wet."

"Spoilsport. Hey, remember how you asked me to do some digging on the Good Doctor Lucas? So far, I've come up with a whole lotta nada. He doesn't seem to do much else besides work. No kids. Wife is a doctor, too. A shrink."

I glanced at Gideon, cautiously ensuring that he didn't overhear. "Seriously?"

"Why? Is that important?"

"No, I guess not. I just . . . I guess I expect psychologists to be astute judges of character."

"Do you know her?"

"No."

"What's going on, Eva? You're all cloak-and-dagger lately, and it's starting to piss me off."

Climbing onto a bar stool, I explained as much as I could. "I met Dr. Lucas at a charity dinner one night, then again when you were in the hospital. Both times he said some nasty things about Gideon and I'm just trying to figure out what his deal is."

"Come on, Eva. What else could it be besides Cross banged his wife?"

Unable to reveal a past that wasn't mine to share, I didn't answer. "I'll be home tomorrow afternoon. I've got that girls' night out. You sure you don't want to come?"

"Go ahead, change the subject," Cary bitched. "Yes, I'm sure I don't want to come. I'm not ready to hit the scene. Just thinking about it gives me hives."

Nathan had jumped Cary outside a club, and Cary was still recovering physically from that. Somehow, I'd forgotten that it was the mind that took longer to heal. He played it so cool, but I should've known better. "The weekend after next, you want to fly out to San Diego? See my dad, our friends . . . maybe even Dr. Travis, if we're up for it?"

"Subtle, Eva," he said dryly. "But yeah, sounds good. I may need you to front me some money, since I'm not working right now."

"No problem. I'll make the arrangements and we can square up later."

"Oh, before you hang up. One of your friends called earlier—

Deanna. I forgot to tell you when we talked before. She has news and she wants you to call her back."

I shot a look at Gideon. He caught my eye and something on my face must have given me away, because his eyes took on that familiar hard gleam. He headed toward me with that long, agile stride, the remnants of dinner carted neatly in the original delivery bag.

"Did you tell her anything?" I asked Cary in a low voice.

"*Tell* her anything? Like what?"

"Like something you wouldn't want to tell a reporter, because that's what she is."

Gideon's face took on a stony cast. He passed me to drop the trash in the compactor, then came back to my side.

"You're friends with a reporter?" Cary asked. "Are you nuts?"

"No, I'm not friends with her. I have no idea how she got my home number, unless she called up from the front desk."

"What the hell does she want?"

"An exposé on Gideon. She's starting to get on my bad side. She's all over him like a rash."

"I'll blow her off if she calls back."

"No, don't." I held Gideon's gaze. "Just don't give her any information about anything. Where did you tell her I was?"

"Out."

"Perfect. Thanks, Cary. Call if you need me."

"Have a banging good time."

"Jesus, Cary." Shaking my head, I killed the call.

"Deanna Johnson called you?" Gideon asked, his arms crossing his chest.

"Yep. And I'm about to call her back."

"No, you're not."

"Shut up, caveman. I'm not into that 'me Cross, you Cross little woman' bullshit," I snapped. "In case you've forgotten already, we made a trade. You got me, and I got you. I protect what's mine."

"Eva, don't fight my battles for me. I can take care of myself."

"I know that. You've been doing it your whole life. Now, you've got me. I can handle this one."

Something shifted over his features, so swiftly I couldn't identify whether he was getting pissed. "I don't want you to have to deal with my past."

"You dealt with mine."

"That was different."

"A threat is a threat, ace. We're in this together. She's reaching out to me, which makes me your best shot at figuring out what she's up to."

He threw up one hand in frustration, then raked it through his hair. I had to force myself not to get distracted by the way his entire torso flexed with his agitation—his abs clenching, his biceps hardening. "I don't give a shit what she's up to. You know the truth, and you're the only one who matters."

"If you think I'm going to sit around while she crucifies you in the press, you need to revisit and revise!"

"She can't hurt me unless she hurts you, and it's possible that's what she's really after."

"We won't know unless I talk to her." I pulled Deanna's card out of my purse and dialed, blocking my number from showing on her Caller ID.

"Eva, damn it!"

I put the phone on speaker and set it on the counter.

"Deanna Johnson," she answered briskly.

"Deanna, it's Eva Tramell."

"Eva, hi." The tone of her voice changed, assuming a friendliness we hadn't yet established. "How are you?"

"I'm good. You?" Studying Gideon, I tried to see if hearing her voice had any effect whatsoever. He glared back, looking deliciously pissed off. I'd become resigned to the fact that whatever his mood, I always found him irresistible.

"Things are churning. In my line of work that's always good."

"So is getting your facts straight."

"Which is one of the reasons I called you. I have a source who claims Gideon walked in on a ménage composed of you, your roommate, and another guy, and flew into a rage. The guy ended up in the hospital and is now pressing assault charges. Is that true?"

I froze, my hearing drowned by my roaring blood. The night I'd met Corinne, I'd come home to find Cary in a four-body sexual tangle that included a guy named Ian. When Ian had lewdly—and nakedly—propositioned me to join them, Gideon had refused the offer with his fist.

I looked at Gideon and my stomach cramped. *It was true.* He was being sued. I could see the proof of it in his face, which was devoid of all emotion, his thoughts hidden behind a flawless mask. "No, it's not true," I answered.

"Which part?"

"I have nothing further to say to you."

"I also have a firsthand account of an altercation between Gideon and Brett Kline, allegedly over you being caught in a hot clinch with Kline. Is that true?"

My knuckles whitened as I gripped the edge of the counter.

"Your roommate was recently assaulted," she went on. "Did Gideon have anything to do with that?"

Oh my God . . . "You're out of your mind," I said coldly.

"The footage of you and Gideon arguing in Bryant Park shows him being very aggressive and physically rough with you. Are you in an abusive relationship with Gideon Cross? Is he violent with an uncontrollable temper? Are you afraid of him, Eva?"

Gideon spun on his heel and walked away, striding down the hallway and turning into his home office.

"Fuck you, Deanna," I bit out. "You're going to rip an innocent man's reputation apart because you can't deal with casual sex? Way to represent the sophisticated modern woman."

"He answered the phone," she hissed, "before he was done. He answered the fucking phone and started talking about an inspection at one of his properties. Midconversation he looked at me lying there waiting for him and he said, 'You can go.' Just like that. He treated me like a whore, only I didn't get paid. He didn't even offer me a drink."

I closed my eyes. *Jesus.* "I'm sorry, Deanna. I mean that sincerely. I've met my share of assholes and it sounds like he was one to you. But what you're doing is wrong."

"It's not wrong if it's true."

"But it's not."

She sighed. "I'm sorry you're in the middle of this, Eva."

"No, you're not." I hit the end button and stood with my head bent, holding on to the counter while the room spun around me.

8

I FOUND GIDEON pacing like a caged panther behind his desk. He had an earpiece in his ear and he was either listening or on hold, since he wasn't talking. He caught my eye, his face hard and unyielding. Even dressed in boxer briefs, he seemed invulnerable. No one would be fool enough to take him for anything else. Physically, his power was evident in every slab of muscle. Beyond that, he radiated a ruthless menace that sent a chill down my spine.

The indolent, well-pleasured male I'd eaten dinner with was gone, replaced by an urban predator who dominated his competition.

I left him to it.

Gideon's tablet was what I wanted, and I found it in his briefcase. It was password protected and I stared at the screen for a long while, startled to realize I was shaking. Everything I'd feared was happening.

"Angel."

Looking up, I caught his eye as he appeared from the hallway.

"The password," he explained. "It's *angel.*"

Oh. All the rampant energy inside me vanished, leaving me feeling drained and tired. "You should've told me about the lawsuit, Gideon."

"At this point in time there isn't a lawsuit, only the threat of one," he said without inflection. "Ian Hager wants money, I want nondisclosure. We'll settle privately and be done with it."

I sagged back into the couch, dropping the tablet onto my thighs. I watched as he walked toward me, drinking him in. It was so easy to become dazzled by his looks, enough that one could fail to see how alone he was at heart. But it was past time he learned to include me when he faced difficulties.

"I don't care if it's a nonstarter," I argued. "You should've told me."

His arms crossed his chest. "I meant to."

"You meant to?" I shoved to my feet. "I tell you I'm broken up over my mother not telling me something and you don't say a word about your own secrets?"

For a moment, he remained hard-faced and immovable. Then he cursed under his breath and unfolded. "I came home early, planning to tell you, but then you told me about your mom and I thought that was enough shit for you to deal with in one day."

Deflating, I sank back onto the couch. "That's not the way a relationship works, ace."

"I'm just getting you back, Eva. I don't want all the time we spend together to be about what's wrong and fucked up in our lives!"

I patted the cushion beside me. "Come here."

He took a seat on the coffee table in front of me instead, his spread legs bracketing mine. He caught my hands in both of his, lifting them to his lips to kiss my knuckles. "I'm sorry."

"I don't blame you. But if there's anything else you have to tell me, now would be the time."

He pressed forward, urging me to stretch out on the couch. Coming over me, he whispered, "I'm in love with you."

With everything going wrong, that was the one thing that was totally right.

It was enough.

WE fell asleep on the couch, wrapped up in each other. I drifted in and out of consciousness, plagued by anxiety and thrown off my schedule by our earlier long nap. I was awake enough to sense the change in Gideon, hear his fast breathing, followed by the tightening of his grip on me. His body jerked powerfully, shaking me. His whimper pierced my heart.

"Gideon." I wriggled around to face him, my agitated movements waking him. We'd drifted off with the lights on and I was grateful that he woke to the brightness.

His heart was pounding beneath my palm, a fine mist of sweat blooming on his skin. "What?" he gasped. "What's wrong?"

"You were slipping into a nightmare, I think." I pressed soft kisses over his hot face, wishing my love could be enough to banish the memories.

He tried to sit up and I clung tighter to hold him down.

"Are you okay?" He ran a hand over me, searching. "Did I hurt you?"

"I'm fine."

"God." He fell back and covered his eyes with his forearm. "I can't keep falling asleep with you. And I forgot to take my prescription. Goddamn it, I can't be this careless."

"Hey." I propped myself up on my elbow and ran my other hand down his chest. "No harm done."

"Don't make light of this, Eva." He turned his head and looked at me, his gaze fierce. "Not this."

"I would never." God, he looked so weary, with dark smudges under his eyes and deep grooves framing that wickedly sensual mouth.

"I killed a man," he said grimly. "It's never been safe for you to be with me when I'm sleeping, and that's even truer now."

"Gideon . . ." I suddenly understood why he'd been having his nightmares more frequently. He could rationalize what he'd done, but that didn't alleviate the weight on his conscience.

I brushed the thick strands of hair off his forehead. "If you're struggling, you need to talk to me."

"I just want you safe," he muttered.

"I never feel safer than when I'm with you. I need you to stop beating yourself up for everything."

"It's my fault."

"Wasn't your life perfectly uncomplicated before I came along?" I challenged.

He shot me a wry look. "I seem to have a taste for complicated."

"Then stop bitching about it. And don't move, I'll be right back."

I went to the master bedroom and swapped my garters, stockings, and bra for an oversized Cross Industries T-shirt. Pulling the velour throw off the foot of the bed, I went to Gideon's room and grabbed his medicine.

His gaze followed me as I dropped off the throw and prescription before heading to the kitchen for a bottle of water. In short order, I had him settled in, the both of us huddled together beneath the blanket and the majority of the lights turned off.

I snuggled closer, hooking my leg over his. The medication prescribed for Gideon's parasomnia was no cure, but he was religious about taking it. I loved him all the more for that dedication, because he did it for me. "Do you know what you were dreaming about?" I asked.

"No. Whatever it was, I wish it were you instead."

"Me, too." I laid my head on his chest, listening to his heartbeat slow. "If it had been a dream about me, what would it be like?"

I felt him relax, sinking into the sofa and into me.

"It would be a cloudless day on a Caribbean beach," he murmured.

"A private beach, with a cabana on the white sand, enclosed on three sides with the view in front of us. I'd have you spread out on a chaise longue. Naked."

"Of course."

"You'd be sun-warmed and lazy, your hair blowing in the breeze. You'd be wearing that smile you give me after I've made you come. We would have nowhere to go, no one waiting. Just the two of us, with all the time in the world."

"Sounds like paradise," I murmured, feeling his body growing heavier by the moment. "I hope we swim naked."

"Umm . . ." He yawned. "I need to go to bed."

"I want a bucket of iced beer, too," I said, hoping to detain him long enough that he'd fall asleep in my arms. "With lemons. I'd squeeze the juice over your eight-pack and lick it off."

"God, I love your mouth."

"You should dream about that, then. And all the naughty things it can do to you."

"Give me some examples."

I gave him plenty, talking in a low soothing voice, my hands stroking over his skin. He slipped away from me with a deep exhalation.

I held him close until long after the sun rose.

GIDEON slept until eleven. I'd been strategizing for hours by then and he found me in his office, his desk littered with my notes and drawings.

"Hey," I greeted him, lifting my lips for his kiss as he rounded the desk. He looked sleep-mussed and sexy in his boxer briefs. "Good morning."

He looked over my work. "What are you doing?"

"I want you caffeinated before I explain." I rubbed my hands together, excited. "Want to grab a quick shower while I make you a cup of coffee? Then we'll dig in."

His gaze slid over my face and he gave me a bemused smile. "All right. However, I suggest I grab *you* in the shower. Then we'll have coffee and dig in."

"Save that thought—and your libido—for tonight."

"Oh?"

"I'm going out, remember?" I prodded. "And I'm going to drink too much, which makes me horny. Don't forget to take your vitamins, ace."

His lips twitched. "Well, then."

"Oh, yeah. You'll be lucky if you can crawl out of bed tomorrow," I warned.

"I'll make sure to stay hydrated, then."

"Good idea." I returned my attention to his tablet, but had to look when he walked his very fine ass out of the room.

When I saw him again, he was damp-haired and wearing black sweats that hung low enough on his hips that I knew he was commando underneath. Forcing myself to focus on my plans, I gave him the desk chair and stood next to him.

"Okay," I began, "following the adage that the best defense is a good offense, I've been taking a look at your public image."

He took a sip of his coffee.

"Don't look at me like that," I admonished. "I didn't pay any attention to your personal life, since *I'm* your personal life."

"Good girl." He gave me an approving pat on my behind.

I stuck my tongue out at him. "I'm mostly thinking of how to combat a smear campaign focused on your temper."

"It helps that I haven't previously been known as having one," he said dryly.

Until you met me . . . "I'm a terrible influence on you."

"You're the best thing that ever happened to me."

That earned him a quick, smacking kiss to the temple. "It took me a ridiculous amount of time to find out about the Crossroads Foundation."

"You didn't know where to look."

"Your search optimization really blows," I countered, pulling up the website. "And there's only this splash page, which is pretty, but ridiculously bare. Where are the links and info about the charities that have benefited? Where's the About page on the foundation and what you hope to accomplish?"

"A packet detailing all of that information is sent out to charities, hospitals, and universities twice a year."

"Great. Now, let me introduce you to the Internet. Why isn't the foundation tied to you?"

"Crossroads isn't about me, Eva."

"The hell it isn't." I met his raised brows with my own and shoved a to-do list in front of him. "We're defusing the Deanna bomb before it blows. This website needs to be overhauled by Monday morning, with the addition of these pages and the information I've outlined."

Gideon took a cursory glance at the paper, then picked up his mug and leaned back in his chair. I studiously focused on the mug and not his amazing torso.

"The Cross Industries site should cross-link with the foundation from your Bio page," I continued. "Which also needs an overhaul and updating."

I slid another paper in front of him.

He picked it up and began reading the biography I'd drafted. "This was clearly written by someone in love with me."

"You can't be shy, Gideon. Sometimes you just have to be blunt and say, 'I rock.' There's so much more to you than a gorgeous face, hot body, and insane sex drive. But let's focus on the stuff I don't mind sharing with the world."

Flashing a grin, Gideon asked, "How much coffee have you had this morning?"

"Enough to take you to the mat, so watch out." I bumped my hip into his arm. "I also think you should consider a press release announcing the acquisition of La Rose Noir, so that your name and Giroux's are linked. Remind people that Corinne—who you've been seen around with so much lately—has a husband, so Deanna can't paint you as a total bad guy for cutting Corinne off. *If* she decides to go that route."

He caught me unawares and pulled me into his lap. "Angel, you're killing me. I'll do whatever you want, but you need to understand that Deanna has nothing. Ian Hager isn't going to risk a nice settlement to publicize his story. He'll sign the necessary releases, take the money, and go away."

"But what about—"

"Six-Ninths isn't going to want their 'Golden' girl linked with another guy. Ruins the love story of the song. I'll be speaking to Kline and we'll get on the same page."

"You're talking to Brett?"

"We're in business together," he pointed out, with a twist to his lips, "so yes. And Deanna's using Cary's attack as a bluff. You and I both know there's nothing there."

I considered all that. "You think she's yanking my chain? Why?"

"Because I'm yours, and if she had a press pass to any event we attended together, she knows it." He leaned his forehead against mine. "I can't hide how I feel around you, which is what's made you a target."

"You hid it well enough from me."

"Your insecurity made you blind."

I couldn't argue with that. "So she freaks me out with the threat of the story. What does she achieve?"

He leaned back. "Think about it. The lid is about to blow on a scandal involving you and me. What's the swiftest way to defuse it?"

"Stay away from me. That's what you'd be advised to do. Distancing yourself from the source of a scandal is Crisis Management 101."

"Or do the opposite and marry you," he said softly.

I froze. "Is that—? Are you—?" Swallowing hard, I whispered, "Not now. Not like this."

"No, not like this," Gideon agreed, rubbing his lips back and forth over mine. "When I propose, angel, trust me, you'll know it."

My throat was tight. I could only nod.

"Breathe," he ordered gently. "One more time. Now, reassure me that's not panic."

"Not really. No."

"Talk to me, Eva."

"I just . . ." I blurted it out in a rush. "I want you to ask me when I can say yes."

Tension gripped his body. He leaned back, his eyes wounded beneath his frown. "You couldn't say yes now?"

I shook my head.

His mouth thinned into a determined line. "Lay out what you need from me to make that happen."

I wrapped my arms around his shoulders, so that he'd feel the connection between us. "There's so much I don't know. And it's not that I need to know more in order to make up my mind, because nothing could make me stop loving you. Nothing. I just feel like your hesitance to share things with me means that *you're* not ready."

"I think I followed that," he muttered.

"I can't take the risk that you won't want forever with me. I won't survive you, either, Gideon."

"What do you want to know?"

"Everything."

He made a frustrated noise. "Be specific. Start with something."

The first thing that came to mind was what came out of my mouth, because I'd been buried in his business all morning. "Vidal Records. Why are you in control of your stepfather's company?"

"Because it was going under." His jaw hardened. "My mother had already suffered through one financial meltdown; I wasn't going to let it happen to her again."

"What did you do?"

"I was able to convince her to talk them—Chris and Christopher—into taking the company public, then she sold Ireland's shares to me. In addition to what I acquired, I had the majority."

"Wow." I squeezed his hand. I'd met both Christopher Vidal Sr.—Chris—and Christopher Vidal Jr. As alike as father and son were in appearance, with their dark copper waves and grayish-green eyes, I suspected they were very different men. Certainly I knew Christopher was a douche. I didn't think his father was. At least I hoped he wasn't. "How did that go over?"

Gideon's arch look was all the answer I needed. "Chris would ask for my advice, but Christopher always refused to take it and my stepdad wouldn't choose sides."

"So you did what had to be done." I kissed his jaw. "Thank you for telling me."

"That's it?"

I smiled. "No."

I was about to ask him more when I heard my phone ringing with my mother's ring tone. I was surprised it had taken her so long to call; I'd taken my smartphone off mute around ten o'clock. Groaning, I said, "I have to get that."

He let me up, his hand stroking over my butt as I walked away. When I turned at the doorway to look back, he was poring over my notes and suggestions. I smiled.

By the time I reached my phone on the breakfast bar, it had stopped ringing, but it immediately started up again. "Mom," I answered, jumping in before she started flipping out. "I'm going to come over today, okay? And we'll talk."

"Eva. You have no idea how worried I've been! You can't do this to me!"

"I'll be over in an hour," I interjected. "I just need to get dressed."

"I couldn't sleep last night, I was so upset."

"Yeah, well, I didn't sleep much, either," I retorted. "It's not just about you all the time, Mom. I'm the one who had her privacy violated. You're just the one who got caught doing it."

Silence.

It was rare for me to be assertive with my mother because she always seemed so fragile, but it was time to redefine our relationship or we'd end up not having one. I looked to my wrist for the time, remembered I didn't have a watch anymore, and glanced at the cable box by the television instead. "I'll be over around one."

"I'll send a car for you," she said quietly.

"Thank you. See you soon." I hung up.

I was about to drop my phone back into my purse when it beeped with a text from Shawna: What r u wearing 2nite?

A number of ideas ran through my mind, from casual to outrageous. Even though I was inclined toward outrageous, I was checked by thoughts of Deanna. I had to think about what I'd look like in the tabloids. LBD, I replied, thinking the little black dress was a classic for a reason. Wild heels. Too much jewelry.

☺ Got it! See u at 7, she texted back.

On the way to the bedroom, I paused by Gideon's office and lounged against the doorjamb to watch him. I could watch him for hours; he was such a joy to look at. And I found him very sexy when he was focused.

He glanced up at me with a soft curve to his lips, and I knew he'd been aware of my staring. "This is all very good," he praised, gesturing at his desktop. "Especially considering you pulled this together in a matter of hours."

I preened a little, thrilled to have impressed a businessman whose acumen had made him one of the most successful individuals in the world.

"I want you at Cross Industries, Eva."

My body reacted to the unwavering determination in his voice, which reminded me of when he'd said, *I want to fuck you, Eva*, when he'd first come on to me.

"I want you there, too," I said. "On your desk."

His eyes gleamed. "We can celebrate that way."

"I like my job. I like my co-workers. I like knowing I've earned every milestone I reach."

"I can give you that and more." His fingers tapped against the side of his coffee mug. "I'm guessing you went with advertising because you like the spin. Why not public relations?"

"Too much like propaganda. At least with advertising, you know the bias right away."

"You mentioned crisis management this morning. And clearly"—he gestured at his desk—"you have an aptitude for it. Let me exploit it."

I crossed my arms. "Crisis management is PR and you know it."

"You're a problem solver. I can make you a fixer. Give you real, time-sensitive problems to solve. Keep you challenged and active."

"Seriously." I tapped my foot. "How many crises do you have in a given week?"

"Several," he said cheerfully. "Come on, you're intrigued. I can see it on your face."

Straightening, I pointed out, "You have people to handle that kind of stuff already."

Gideon leaned back in his chair and smiled. "I want more. So do you. Let's have it together."

"You're like the devil himself, you know that? And you're stubborn as hell. I'm telling you, working together would be a bad idea."

"We're working together just fine now."

I shook my head. "Because you agreed with my assessment and suggestions, plus you had me sitting in your lap and you copped a feel of my ass. It's not going to be the same when we're not on the same page and arguing about it in your office in front of other people. Then we'll have to bring that irritation home and deal with it here, too."

"We can agree to leave work at the door." His eyes slid over me, lingering on my legs, which were mostly bared by my silk robe. "I won't have any problem thinking of more enjoyable things."

Rolling my eyes, I backed out of the room. "Sex maniac."

"I love making love with you."

"That's not fair," I complained, having no defense against that. No defense against *him*.

Gideon grinned. "I never said I play fair."

WHEN I entered my apartment fifteen minutes later, it felt weird. The floor plan was identical to Gideon's next door, but reversed. The blending of his furniture and mine had helped to make his space feel like *ours* but had the side effect of making me feel like my home was . . . alien.

"Hey, Eva."

I looked around and saw Trey in the kitchen, pouring milk into two glasses. "Hey," I greeted him back. "How are you?"

"Better."

He looked it. His blond hair, which was usually unruly, had been nicely styled—one of Cary's talents. Trey's hazel eyes were bright, his smile charming beneath his once-broken nose.

"It's good to see you around more," I told him.

"I rearranged my schedule a bit." He held up the milk and I shook my head, so he put it away. "How are you?"

"Dodging reporters, hoping my boss gets engaged, planning on setting one parent straight, fitting in a phone call to the other parent, and looking forward to hitting the town with the girls tonight."

"You're awesome."

"What can I say?" I smiled. "How's school? And work?"

I knew Trey was studying to be a veterinarian and juggling jobs to pay for it. One of those gigs was as a photographer's assistant, which was how he'd met Cary.

He winced. "Both brutal, but it'll pay off someday."

"We should have another movie-and-pizza night when you get a chance." I couldn't help rooting for Trey in the tug-of-war between him and Tatiana. It could just be me, but she'd always seemed very adversarial toward me. And I didn't like the way she'd put herself forward when she met Gideon.

"Sure. I'll see what Cary's schedule is like."

I regretted bringing it up to Trey first instead of Cary, because some of the light left his eyes. I knew he was thinking about Cary having to fit him in between time with Tatiana. "Well, if he's not up for it, we can always go out without him."

His mouth tilted up on one side. "Sounds like a plan."

AT ten minutes to one, I exited the lobby to find Clancy already waiting for me. He waved aside the doorman and opened the town car door for me, but no one looking at him would believe he was just a driver. He carried himself like the weapon he was, and in all the years I'd known him, I couldn't recall ever seeing him smile.

Once he'd resumed his seat behind the wheel, he turned off the police scanner he routinely listened to and pulled his sunglasses down enough to catch my eye in the rearview mirror. "How are you?"

"Better than my mom, I'm guessing."

He was too professional to give anything away in his expression. Instead, he slid his shades back into place and synced my phone to the car's Bluetooth to start my playlist. Then he pulled away from the curb.

Reminded of his thoughtfulness, I said, "Hey. I'm sorry I took it out on you. You were doing a job and you didn't deserve to get bitched at for it."

"You're not just a job, Miss Tramell."

I was silent for a bit, absorbing that. Clancy and I had a distant, polite association. We saw each other quite a bit because he was responsible for getting me to and from my Krav Maga classes in Brooklyn. But I'd never really thought about him having any sort of personal stake in my safety, although it made sense. Clancy was a guy who took pride in his work.

"It wasn't just that one thing, though," I clarified. "A lot of stuff happened before you and Stanton ever came into the picture."

"Apology accepted."

The brusque reply was so like him that it made me smile.

Settling more comfortably into the seat, I looked out the window at the city I'd adopted and loved passionately. On the sidewalk beside me, strangers stood shoulder to shoulder over a tiny counter, eating individual slices of pizza. As close as they were, they were distant, each displaying a New Yorker's ability to be an island in a crashing tide of people. Pedestrians flowed past them in both directions, avoiding a man pushing religious flyers and the tiny dog at his feet.

The vitality of the city had a frenetic pulse that made time seem to move faster here than anywhere else. It was such a contrast to the lazy sensuality of Southern California, where my dad lived and I'd gone to school. New York was a dominatrix on the prowl, cracking a mean whip and tantalizing with every vice.

My purse vibrated against my hip and I reached into it for my phone. A quick glance at the screen told me it was my dad. Saturdays were our weekly catch-up days and I always looked forward to our chats, but I was almost inclined to let the call go to voice mail until I was in a better frame of mind. I was too aggravated with my mom, and my dad had already been overly concerned about me since he'd left New York after his last visit.

He'd been with me when the detectives had come to my apartment to tell me Nathan was in New York. They'd dropped that bomb before they revealed that Nathan had been murdered, and I hadn't been able to hide my fear at the thought of him being so close. My dad had been after me about my violent reaction ever since.

"Hey," I answered, mostly because I didn't want to be at odds with both my parents at the same time. "How are you?"

"Missing you," he replied in the deep, confident voice I loved. My dad was the most perfect man I knew—darkly handsome, self-assured, smart, and rock solid. "How 'bout you?"

"I can't complain too much."

"Okay, complain just a little. I'm all ears."

I laughed softly. "Mom's just driving me a little batty."

"What'd she do now?" he asked, with a note of warm indulgence in his voice.

"She's been sticking her nose in my business."

"Ah. Sometimes we parents do that when we're worried about our babies."

"*You've* never done that," I pointed out.

"I haven't done it *yet*," he qualified. "That doesn't mean I won't, if I'm worried enough. I just hope I could convince you to forgive me."

"Well, I'm on my way to Mom's now. Let's see how convincing she can be. It would help if she'd admit she's wrong."

"Good luck with that."

"Ha! Right?" I sighed. "Can I call you tomorrow?"

"Sure. Is everything all right, sweetheart?"

I closed my eyes. Cop instincts plus daddy instincts meant I rarely got anything by Victor Reyes. "Yep. It's just that I'm almost to Mom's now. I'll let you know how it goes. Oh, and my boss might be getting engaged. Anyway, I have stuff to tell you."

"I may have to stop by the station in the morning, but you can reach me on my cell no matter what. I love you."

I felt a sudden surge of homesickness. As much as I loved New York and my new life, I missed my dad a lot. "I love you, too, Daddy. Talk to you tomorrow."

Killing the call, I looked for my wristwatch, and its absence reminded me of the confrontation ahead. I was upset with my mother about the past, but was most concerned with the future. She'd hovered over me for so long because of Nathan, I wasn't sure she knew any other way to behave.

"Hey." I leaned forward, needing to clarify something that was bothering me. "That day when me, Mom, and Megumi were walking back to the Crossfire and Mom freaked out . . . Did you guys see Nathan?"

"Yes."

"He'd been there before and got his ass beat by Gideon Cross. Why would he go back?"

He glanced at me through the mirror. "My guess? To be seen. Once he made himself known, he kept the pressure up. Likely, he expected to frighten you and managed to scare Mrs. Stanton instead. Effective in either case."

"And no one told me," I said quietly. "I can't get over that."

"He wanted you frightened. No one wanted to give him that satisfaction."

Oh. I hadn't thought of it that way.

"My big regret," he went on, "is not keeping an eye on Cary. I miscalculated, and he paid the price."

Gideon hadn't seen Nathan's attack on Cary coming, either. And God knew I felt guilty about it, too—my friendship was what had put Cary in danger to begin with.

But I was really touched that Clancy cared. I could hear it in his gruff voice. He was right; I wasn't just a job to him. He was a good man who gave his all to everything he did. Which made me wonder: How much did he have left over for the other things in his life?

"Do you have a girlfriend, Clancy?"

"I'm married."

I felt like an ass for not knowing that. What was she like, the woman married to such a hard, somber man? A man who wore a jacket year-round to hide the sidearm he was never without. Did he soften for her and show her tenderness? Was he fierce about protecting her? Would he kill for her?

"How far would you go to keep her safe?" I asked him.

We slowed at a light and he turned his head to look at me. "How far wouldn't I go?"

9

"WHAT WAS WRONG with that one?" Megumi asked, watching the guy in question walk away. "He had dimples."

I rolled my eyes and polished off my vodka and cranberry. Primal, the fourth stop on our club-hopping list, was pumping. The line to get in wrapped around the block and the guitar-heavy tracks suited the club's name, the music pounding through the darkened space with a primitive, seductive beat. The décor was an eclectic mix of brushed metals and dark woods, with the multihued lighting creating animal-print silhouettes.

It should've been too much, but like everything Gideon, it skirted the edge of decadent excess without falling over it. The atmosphere was one of hedonistic abandon and it did crazy things to my alcohol-fueled libido. I couldn't sit still, my feet tapping restlessly on the rungs of my chair.

Megumi's roommate, Lacey, groaned at the ceiling, her dark blond hair arranged in a disheveled updo I admired. "Why don't *you* flirt with him?"

"I might," Megumi said, looking flushed, bright-eyed, and very hot in a slinky gold halter dress. "Maybe *he'll* commit."

"What do you want out of commitment?" Shawna asked, nursing a drink as fiery red as her hair. "Monogamy?"

"Monogamy is overrated." Lacey slid off her bar stool at our tallboy table and wriggled her butt, the rhinestones on her jeans glittering in the semidarkness of the club.

"No, it's not." Megumi pouted. "I happen to like monogamy."

"Is Michael sleeping with other women?" I asked, leaning forward so I didn't have to shout.

I had to lean back right away to make room for the waitress, who brought another round and cleared the previous one away. The club's uniform of black stiletto boots and hot pink strapless minidresses stood out in the crowd, making it easy to know who to flag. It was also really sexy—as was the staff wearing them. Had Gideon had any hand in picking the outfit? And if so, had anyone modeled it for him?

"I don't know." Megumi picked up her new drink and sucked at her straw with a sad face. "I'm afraid to ask."

Grabbing one of the four shot glasses in the center of the table and a lime wedge, I shouted, "Let's do shots and dance!"

"Fuck yeah!" Shawna tossed back her shot of Patrón without waiting for the rest of us, then shoved a lime in her mouth. Dropping the juiceless wedge into her empty glass, she shot us all a look. "Hurry up, laggers."

I went next, shuddering as the tequila washed away the tang of cranberry. Lacey and Megumi went together, toasting each other with a loud *"Kanpai!"* before downing theirs.

We hit the dance floor en masse, Shawna leading the way in her electric blue dress that was damn near as bright under the black lights as the club uniform. We were swallowed into the mass of writhing dancers, quickly finding ourselves pressed between steamy male bodies.

I let go, giving myself over to the grinding beat of the music and the sultry atmosphere of the rocking club. Lifting my hands in the air, I swayed, releasing the lingering tension from the long, pointless afternoon with my mother. At some point, I'd lost my trust in her. As much as she promised that things would be different without Nathan, I found I couldn't believe her. She'd crossed the line too many times.

"You're beautiful," someone yelled by my ear.

I looked over my shoulder at the dark-haired guy curved against my back. "Thanks!"

It was a lie, of course. My hair clung to my sweat-damp temples and neck in a sticky tangle. I didn't care. The music raged on, songs sliding into each other.

I reveled in the utter sensuality of the venue and the shameless drive for casual sex that everyone seemed to exude. I was pressed between a couple—the girlfriend at my back and her boyfriend at my front—when I spotted someone I knew. He must have seen me first, because he was already working his way toward me.

"Martin!" I yelled, breaking out of my bump-and-grind sandwich. In the past, I'd only crossed paths with Stanton's nephew during the holidays. We'd met up once since I moved to New York, but I hoped we would eventually see each other more.

"Eva, hi!" He caught me up in a hug, then pulled back to check me out. "You look fantastic. How are you?"

"Let's get a drink!" I shouted, feeling too parched to hold a conversation at the decibel level required in the crowd.

Grabbing my hand, he led me out of the crush and I pointed to my table. The moment we sat down, the waitress was there with another vodka and cranberry.

It'd been that way all night, although I'd noted that my drinks were getting darker as the hours progressed, a sure sign that the vodka-to-cranberry ratio was slowly becoming more cranberry than not. I knew that was deliberate and was suitably impressed by Gideon's ability to carry his instructions from club to club. Since no one was stopping me from supplementing with shots, I didn't mind too much.

"So," I began, taking a welcome sip before rolling the icy-cold tumbler across my forehead. "How have you been?"

"Great." He grinned, looking quite handsome in a camel-hued V-neck T-shirt and black jeans. His dark hair wasn't nearly the length of Gideon's, but it fell attractively across his forehead, framing eyes that I knew were green although no one would be able to tell in the club's lighting. "How's the ad biz treating you?"

"I love my job!"

He laughed at my enthusiasm. "If only we could all say that."

"I thought you liked working with Stanton."

"I do. Like the money, too. Can't say I love the job, though."

The waitress brought his scotch on the rocks, and we clinked glasses.

"Who are you here with?" I asked him.

"A couple friends"—he looked around—"who are lost in the jungle. You?"

"Same." I caught Lacey's eye on the dance floor and she gave me two thumbs up. "Are you seeing anyone, Martin?"

His smile widened. "No."

"You like blondes?"

"Are you hitting on me?"

"Not quite." I raised my brows at Lacey and jerked my head toward Martin. She looked surprised for a minute, then grinned and rushed over.

I introduced them and felt pretty good about the way they hit it off. Martin was always fun and charming, and Lacey was vivacious and attractive in a unique way—more charismatic than beautiful.

Megumi made her way back over and we did another round of shots before Martin asked Lacey to dance.

"You got any other hot guys in your pocket?" Megumi asked, as the couple melted away.

I was wishing I had my smartphone in my pocket. "You're miserable, girl."

She looked at me for a long minute. Then her lips twisted. "I'm drunk."

"That, too. Want another shot?"

"Why not?"

We did a shot each, polishing them off just as Shawna came back with Lacey, Martin, and his two friends, Kurt and Andre. Kurt was gorgeous, with sandy brown hair, square jaw, and cocky smile. Andre was cute, too, with a mischievous twinkle in his dark eyes and shoulder-length dreadlocks. He focused on Megumi, which cheered her right up.

Our expanded group was roaring with laughter in no time.

"And when Kurt came back from the bathroom," Martin finished his story, "he sacked the whole restaurant."

Andre and Martin started howling. Kurt threw limes at them.

"What does that mean?" I asked, smiling even though I didn't get the punch line.

"It's when you leave your sac hanging out of your fly," Andre explained. "At first people can't figure out what it is they're seeing, then they try to figure out if you just somehow don't know your nads are swinging in the breeze. No one says a word."

"No shit?" Shawna nearly fell off her chair.

We got so rowdy, our waitress asked us to tone it down—with a smile. I caught her by the elbow before she walked away. "Is there a phone I can use?"

"Just ask one of the bartenders," she said. "Tell them Dennis—he's the manager—okayed it and they'll hook you up."

"Thanks." I slid off my seat as she moved on to another table. I had no idea who Dennis was, but I'd just been going with the flow all night, knowing Gideon would've set up everything flawlessly. "Anyone up for water?" I asked the group.

I got booed and pelted with wadded-up napkins. Laughing, I went to the bar and waited for an opening to ask for Pellegrino and the phone. I dialed Gideon's cell number, since it was the one I had memorized. I figured it was safe since I was calling from a public place he owned.

"Cross," he answered briskly.

"Hi, ace." I leaned into the bar and covered my other ear with my hand. "I'm drunk-dialing you."

"I can tell." His voice changed for me, slowed and grew warm. It captivated me even over the music. "Are you having a good time?"

"Yes, but I miss you. Did you take your vitamins?"

He had a smile in his voice when he asked, "Are you horny, angel?"

"It's your fault! This club is like Viagra. I'm hot and sweaty and dripping in pheromones. And I've been a bad girl, you know. Dancing like I'm single."

"Bad girls get punished."

"Maybe I should be really bad, then. Make the punishment worth it."

He growled. "Come home and be bad with me."

The thought of him at home, ready for me, made me even more eager for him. "I'm stuck here 'til the girls are done, which looks to be a while."

"I can come to you. Within twenty minutes, you could have my cock inside you. Do you want that?"

I glanced around the club, my entire body vibrating with the hard-driving music. Imagining him here, fucking me in this no-holds-barred place, made me squirm with anticipation. "Yes. I want that."

"Do you see the skywalk?"

Turning around, I looked up and saw the suspended walkway hugging the walls. Dancers dry-fucked to the music from twenty feet above the dance floor. "Yes."

"There's a section where it wraps around a mirrored corner. I'll meet you there. Be ready, Eva," he ordered. "I want your cunt naked and wet when I find you."

I shivered at the familiar command, knowing it meant he'd be rough and impatient. *Just what I wanted.* "I'm wearing a—"

"Angel, a crowd of millions couldn't hide you from me. I found you once. I'll always find you."

Longing seared my veins. "Hurry."

Reaching over to replace the receiver on the business side of the bar, I grabbed my mineral water and drank until the bottle was empty. Then I headed to the bathroom, where I waited in line forever in order to get ready for Gideon. I was giddy with booze and excitement, so thrilled that my boyfriend—arguably one of the busiest men in the world—would drop everything to . . . service me.

I licked my lips, shifting on my feet.

I hurried through the ladies' room to a stall, ditching my panties before hitting the sink and mirror to freshen up with a damp napkin. Most of my makeup had melted off, leaving me with smudged eyes and cheeks reddened by heat and exertion. My hair was a mess, both wildly mussed and wet around my face.

Oddly, I didn't look half bad. I looked sexual and ready.

Lacey was in line and I stopped by her as I inched my way through the crowded bathroom threshold.

"Having fun?" I asked her.

"Yeah!" She grinned. "Thanks for introducing me to your cousin."

I didn't bother to correct her. "You're welcome. Can I ask you something? About Michael?"

Shrugging, she said, "Go for it."

"You went out with him first. What didn't you like about him?"

"No chemistry. Good-looking guy. Successful. Sadly, I didn't want to fuck him."

"Toss him back," the girl next in line interjected.

"I did."

"Okay." I could totally respect not progressing with a relationship lacking sexual heat, but I was still bothered by the situation. I didn't like seeing Megumi so bummed. "I'm going to go grind against some hot guy."

"Hit it, girl," Lacey said with a nod.

I took off in search of the stairs to the skywalk. I found them guarded by a bouncer policing the number of bodies allowed to venture up. There was a line and I eyed it with dismay.

As I debated how much of a delay I was facing, the bouncer unfolded his powerful arms from across his chest and pressed his earpiece deeper into his ear with one hand, clearly focusing on whatever was being relayed through his receiver. He could have been Samoan or Maori, with dark caramel skin, a shaved head, and massive barrel chest and biceps. He had a baby face and was downright adorable when his fierce scowl was replaced by a wide grin.

His hand dropped away from his ear and he crooked a finger at me. "You Eva?"

I nodded.

He reached behind him and unhooked the velvet rope blocking the stairway. "Head on up."

A roar of protests came from those who were waiting. I offered an apologetic smile, then raced up the metal stairs as fast as my heels would allow. When I reached the top, a female bouncer let me through and pointed to my left. I saw the corner Gideon had mentioned, where two mirrored walls connected and the skywalk wrapped around it in an L shape.

I weaved my way through writhing bodies, my pulse rate increasing with every step. The music was less loud up here and the air more humid. Sweat glistened on exposed skin and the elevation lent a sense of danger, even though the glass railing surrounding the skywalk was shoulder-high. I was almost to the mirrored section when I was caught around the waist and pulled back into a man's rolling hips.

Looking over my shoulder, I saw the guy I'd danced with before, the one who'd called me beautiful. I smiled and started dancing, closing my eyes to lose myself in the music. When his hands started to slide over my waist, I caught them, pinning them to my hips with my own. He laughed and dipped his knees, aligning his body with mine.

We were three songs out before I felt the ripple of awareness that told me Gideon was nearby. The electrical charge swept over my skin, heightening every sensation. Abruptly the music was louder, the temperature hotter, the sensuality of the club more arousing.

I smiled and opened my eyes, spotting him arrowing toward me. I was instantly hot for him, my mouth watering as I ate up the sight of him in a dark T-shirt and jeans, his hair pulled back from that breathtaking face. No one seeing him would put him together with Gideon Cross, the international mogul. This guy appeared younger and rougher, distinctive only for his incredible smokin' hotness. I licked my lips with anticipation, leaning into the guy behind me and rubbing my ass voluptuously into the next roll of his hips.

Gideon's hands fisted at his sides, his posture aggressive and predatory. He didn't slow as he neared me, his body on a collision course with mine. Turning, I met him the last step, surging into him. Our bodies crashed together, my arms encircling his shoulders and my hands pulling his head down so I could take his mouth in a wet, hungry kiss.

With a growl, Gideon cupped my ass and yanked me up hard against him, my feet leaving the floor. He bruised my lips with the ferocity of his passion, his tongue filling my mouth with hard, deep plunges that warned me of the violent shades of his lust.

The guy I'd been dancing with came up behind me, his hands in my hair and his lips at my shoulder blade.

Gideon pulled back, his face a gorgeous mask of fury. "Get lost."

I looked at the guy and gave a shrug. "Thanks for the dance."

"Anytime, beautiful." He caught the hips of a girl walking by and moved away.

"Angel." With a growl, Gideon pressed me into the mirror, his hard thigh thrust between my legs. "You're a bad girl."

Shameless and eager, I rode him, gasping at the feel of denim against my tender sex. "Only for you."

He gripped my bare buttocks beneath my dress, spurring me on. His teeth caught the shell of my ear, my silver chandelier earrings brushing my neck. He was breathing hard, low rumbles vibrating in his chest. He smelled so good and my body responded, trained to associate his scent with the wildest, hottest of pleasures.

We danced, straining together, our bodies moving as if there were no clothes between us. The music pounded around us, through us, and he moved his amazing body to it, captivating me. We'd danced before, ballroom style, but never like this. This sweaty, dirty grinding. I was surprised, turned on, fell even deeper in love.

Gideon watched me with a hooded gaze, seducing me with his need and his uninhibited moves. I was lost in him, wrapped around him, clawing to get closer.

He kneaded my breast through the thin black jersey of my spaghetti-strapped dress. The built-in shelf bra was no barrier. His fingers stroked, then tugged the hardened point of my nipple.

As I moaned, my head fell back against the mirror. Dozens of people surrounded us and I didn't care. I just needed his hands on me, his body against mine, his breath on my skin.

"You want me," he said harshly, "right here."

I quivered at the thought. "Would you?"

"You want them to watch. You want them to see me fuck my cock into your greedy little cunt until you're dripping in cum. You want me to prove you're mine." His teeth sank into the top of my shoulder. "Make you feel it."

"I want to prove that *you're* mine," I shot back, shoving my hands into the pockets of his jeans to feel his hard ass flex. "I want everyone to know it."

Gideon hitched one arm beneath my rear and lifted me, his other hand slapping flat against a pad on the wall by the mirror. I heard a faint beeping, and then a door opened in the mirror at my back and we stepped into almost total darkness. The concealed entrance closed behind us, muting the music. We were in an office, with a desk, a seating area, and a 180-degree view of the club through two-way mirrors.

He put me down and spun me, pinning my front to the transparent side of the glass. The club was spread out before me, the dancers on the skywalk only inches away. His hands were up my skirt and in the bodice of my dress, fingers sliding into my cleft and rolling my nipple.

I was snared. His big body covered mine, his arms around me, torso to hips, his teeth in my shoulder holding me in place. He owned me.

"Tell me if it's too much," he murmured, his lips drifting up my throat. "Safeword before I scare you."

Emotion flooded me, gratitude for this man who always—*always*—thought of me first. "I provoked you. I want to be taken. I want you wild."

"You're so hot for it," he purred, pumping two fingers quick and hard into me. "You were made for fucking."

"Made for you," I gasped, my breath fogging the glass. I was on fire for him, my desire pouring out from the inside, from the well of love I couldn't contain.

"Did you forget that tonight?" His hand left my sex to reach between us and yank open his fly. "When other men were touching you, rubbing against you? Did you forget you're mine?"

"Never. I never forget." My eyes closed as his erection, so stiff and warm, rested heavily against the bare cheek of my ass. He was hot for it, too. Hot for me. "I called you. Wanted you."

His lips moved over my skin, forging a scorching trail to my mouth. "Take me, then, angel," he coaxed, his tongue touching mine with teasing licks. "Put me inside you."

Arching my back, I reached between my legs, my hand circling his thickness. He bent his knees, lining himself up for me.

I paused, turning my head to press my cheek to his. I loved that I could have this with him . . . be this way with him. Circling my hips, I stroked my clit with the wide crest of his cock, making him slick with my arousal.

Gideon squeezed my swollen breasts, plumping them. "Lean into me, Eva. Push away from the glass."

With my palm to the two-way mirror, I pushed back, my head pillowed on his shoulder. He wrapped my throat with his hand, gripped my hip, and thrust so hard into me that my feet left the floor. He held me there, suspended in his arms, filled with his cock, his groan cascading over my senses.

On the other side of the glass, the club raged on. I abandoned myself to the wickedly intense pleasure of seemingly exhibitionist sex, an illicit fantasy that always drove us wild.

I writhed, unable to bear the decadent pressure. My hand between my legs reached lower, cradled his sac. He was tight and full, so ready. And inside me . . . "Oh God. You're so hard."

"I was made to fuck you," he whispered, sending shivers of delight through me.

"Do it." I set both hands on the glass, beyond needy. "Do it now."

Gideon lowered me to my feet, his hands steadying me as I bent at the waist, opening myself to him so he could slide deep. A low, keening cry escaped as he seized my hips and angled me, knowing just how to position me to make me fit him. He was too big for me, too long and thick. The stretching was intense. Delicious.

My core trembled, clenching desperately around him. He made a rough sound of pleasure, pulling out just a little before sliding back slowly. Again, then again. The wide crest of his cock massaging the bundle of nerves deep inside me that only he'd ever reached.

Fingers clawing restlessly, leaving steamy trails on the glass, I moaned. I was achingly aware of the distant throb of the music and the mass of people I saw as clearly as if they were in the room with us.

"That's it, angel," he said urgently. "Let me hear how much you like it."

"Gideon." My legs shook violently on a particularly skillful stroke, my weight supported only by the glass and his secure hold.

I was unbearably excited, greedy, feeling both the submission of my pose and the dominance of being serviced. I could do nothing but take what Gideon gave me, the rhythmic slide and retreat, the sounds of his hunger. The scrape of his jeans against my thighs told me he'd pushed them down only far enough to free his cock, a sign of impatience that thrilled me.

One of his hands left my hip, then returned to rest atop my ass. I felt the pad of his thumb, wet from his mouth, rubbing over the tight pucker of my rear.

"No," I begged, afraid I'd lose my mind. But it wasn't my safeword—*Crossfire*—and I flowered open for him, giving way under the questing pressure.

He growled as he claimed that dark place. He came over me, his other hand moving to finger my sex, to spread me and rub my pulsing clit. "Mine," he said gruffly. "You're mine."

It was too much. I came with a scream, shaking violently, my hands squeaking on the glass as my sweaty palms slipped. He began pounding the ecstasy into me, his thumb in my rear an irresistible torment, his clever fingers on my clit driving me insane. One orgasm rolled into another, my sex rippling along his plunging cock.

He made a rough sound of desire and swelled inside me, chasing his climax. I gasped, "Don't come! Not yet."

Gideon's tempo slowed, his breathing harsh in the darkness. "How do you want me?"

"I want to watch you." I moaned as my core tightened again. "Want to see your face."

He withdrew and pulled me upright. Turned and lifted me. Pressed me to the glass and thrust hard into me. In that moment of possession, he gave me what I needed. The glazed look of helpless pleasure, the instant of vulnerability before the lust seized his control.

"You want to watch me lose it," he said hoarsely.

"Yes." I pulled the straps from my shoulders and exposed my breasts, lifting and squeezing them, toying with my nipples. The glass was vibrating with the beat against my back; Gideon was vibrating against my front, his body barely reined.

I pressed my lips to his, absorbing his panting breaths. "Let go," I whispered.

Holding me effortlessly, he withdrew, dragging the thick, heavy crown across the hypersensitive tissues inside me. Then he powered into me, taking me to my limits.

"Ah, God." I writhed in his grip. "You're so deep."

"Eva."

He fucked me hard, thrusting like a man possessed. I held on, trembling, spread wide for the relentless drives of his rigid penis. He was lost to instinct, the insistent desire to mate. Raw moans spilled from him, making me so hot and slick that my body offered no resistance, welcoming his desperate need.

It was rough and messy and sexy as hell. His neck arched and he gasped my name.

"Come for me," I demanded, tightening around him, squeezing.

His whole body jerked hard, then shuddered. His mouth twisted in a grimace of agonized bliss, his eyes losing their focus as the climax built.

Gideon came with an animal roar, spurting so hard I felt it. Over and over, heating me from the inside with thick washes of semen.

My lips were all over him, my arms and legs holding tight.

He collapsed against me, his lungs heaving for breath.

Still coming.

10

THE FIRST THING I saw when I woke up Sunday morning was an amber bottle labeled HANGOVER CURE in an old-fashioned font. A raffia bow adorned the neck and a cork stopper kept the stomach-turning contents safe. The "cure" worked, as I'd learned the last time Gideon had given me the stuff, but the sight of it reminded me of how much alcohol I'd consumed the night before.

Squeezing my eyes shut, I groaned and buried my head in the pillow, willing myself back to sleep.

The bed shifted. Warm, firm lips drifted down my bare spine. "Good morning, angel mine."

"You sound ridiculously pleased with yourself," I muttered.

"Pleased with you, actually."

"Fiend."

"I was referring to your crisis management suggestions, but of course the sex was phenomenal, as always." His hand slid beneath the sheet that was pooled around my waist and he squeezed my ass.

I lifted my head and found him propped against the headboard beside me with his laptop on his thighs. He looked mouthwatering, as usual, completely relaxed in drawstring lounging pants. I was certain I was looking far less attractive. I'd taken the limo home with the girls, then met up with Gideon at his apartment. It was nearly dawn before I'd finished with him and I'd been so tired, I crashed with hair still wet from a hasty shower.

A tingle of pleasure moved through me at finding him next to me. He'd slept in the guest room, and he had an office to work in. The fact that he chose to work in the bed I slept in meant he'd just wanted to be near me, even while I was unconscious.

I turned my head to look at the bedside clock, but my gaze snagged on my wrist instead.

"Gideon . . ." The watch that had been placed on my arm while I slept enchanted me. The Art Deco–inspired timepiece sparkled with hundreds of tiny diamonds. The band was a creamy satin and the mother-of-pearl face was branded with both Patek Philippe and Tiffany & Co. "It's *gorgeous*."

"There are only twenty-five of those in the world, which isn't nearly as unique as you are, but then, what is?" He smiled down at me.

"I love it." I pushed up onto my knees. "I love you."

He shoved his laptop aside in time for me to straddle him and hug him tightly.

"Thank you," I murmured, touched by his thoughtfulness. He would've gone out for it while I was at my mother's or maybe just after I left with the girls.

"Umm. Tell me how to earn one of these naked hugs every day."

"Just be you, ace." I rubbed my cheek against his. "You're all I need."

I slid out of bed and padded over to the bathroom with the small amber bottle in my hand. I guzzled the contents down with a shudder, brushed my teeth and hair, and then washed my face. I pulled on a robe and returned to the bedroom, finding Gideon gone and his laptop lying open in the middle of the bed.

I passed him in his office, seeing him standing with his feet planted wide and his arms crossed, facing the window. The city stretched out in front of him. Not the skyline view he had in his Crossfire office or his penthouse, but a closer vantage. More grounded and immediate. The connection with the city more intimate.

"I don't share your concern," he said briskly into his earpiece mic. "I'm aware of the risk . . . Stop talking. The subject isn't open to debate. Draw up the agreement as specified."

Recognizing that all-business note of steel in his voice, I kept walking. I still wasn't sure exactly what was in the bottle, but I suspected it was vitamins and liquor of some sort. Hair of the dog. It was warming my belly and making me feel lethargic, so I went to the kitchen and made a cup of coffee.

Supplied with caffeine, I plopped down on the couch and checked my smartphone for messages. I frowned when I saw that I'd missed three calls from my dad, all before eight in the morning in California. I also noted a dozen missed calls from my mom, but I figured Monday was soon enough to deal with her again. And there was a text from Cary that shouted, CALL ME!

I called my dad back first, trying to swallow a quick drink of coffee before he answered.

"Eva."

The anxious way my dad said my name told me something was wrong. I sat up straighter. "Dad . . . Is everything all right?"

"Why didn't you tell me about Nathan Barker?" His voice was hoarse and filled with pain. Goose bumps swept across my skin.

Oh, fuck. He *knew*. My hand shook so badly, I spilled hot coffee on my hand and thigh. I didn't even feel it; I was so panicked by my father's anguish. "Dad, I—"

"I can't believe you didn't tell me. Or Monica. My God . . . She should've said something. Should've told me." He sucked in a shaky breath. "I had the right to know!"

Sorrow spread through my chest like acid. My dad—a man whose self-control rivaled Gideon's—sounded like he was crying.

I set my mug on the coffee table, my breathing fast and shallow. Nathan's sealed juvenile records had broken open upon his death, exposing the horror of my past to anyone who had the knowledge and means to find it. As a cop, my dad had those means.

"There's nothing you could've done," I told him, stunned, but trying to hold it together for his sake. My smartphone beeped with an incoming call, but I ignored it. "Before or after."

"I could've been there for you. I could've taken care of you."

"Daddy, you did. Putting me together with Dr. Travis changed my life. I didn't really start dealing with anything until then. I can't tell you how much that helped."

He groaned, and it was a low sound of torment. "I should've fought your mother for you. You should've been with me."

"Oh, God." My stomach cramped. "You can't blame Mom. She didn't know what was happening for a long time. And when she did find out, she did everything—"

"She didn't *tell me*!" he shouted, making me jump. "She should've fucking told me. And how could she not know? There must've been signs . . . How could she not see them? Jesus. *I* saw them when you came to California."

I sobbed, unable to contain my anguish. "I begged her not to tell you. I made her promise."

"That wasn't your decision to make, Eva. You were a child. She knew better."

"I'm sorry!" I cried. The insistent, relentless beeping of an incoming call pushed me over the edge. "I'm so sorry. I just didn't want Nathan to hurt anyone else I loved."

"I'm coming to see you," he said, with a sudden burst of calm. "I'm getting the next flight out. I'll call you when I land."

"Dad—"

"I love you, sweetheart. You're everything."

He hung up. Shattered, I sat there in a daze. I knew the knowledge of what had been done to me would eat my father alive, but I didn't know how to combat that darkness.

My phone started vibrating in my hand and I just stared down at the screen, seeing my mother's name and unable to think of what to do.

Standing on unsteady feet, I dropped my cell on the low table as if it had burned me. I couldn't talk to her then. I didn't want to talk to anyone. I just wanted Gideon.

I stumbled down the hallway, my shoulder sliding along the wall. I heard Gideon's voice as I neared his office and my tears came faster, my steps quickening.

"I appreciate that you thought of me, but no," he said in a low, firm voice that was different from the one I'd heard him using before. It was gentler, more intimate. "Of course we're friends. You know why . . . I can't give you what you want from me."

I rounded the corner into his office and saw him at his desk, his head down as he listened.

"Stop," he said icily. "This isn't the tack you want to take with me, Corinne."

"Gideon," I whispered, my hand gripping the doorjamb with white-knuckled force.

He glanced up, then straightened abruptly, surging to his feet. The scowl on his face fled.

"I have to go," he said, pulling the earpiece from his ear and dropping it on the desk as he rounded it. "What's wrong? Are you sick?"

He caught me as I rushed into him, needing him. Relief flooded me as he pulled me close and held me tight.

"My dad found out." I pressed my face to his chest, my mind filled with echoes of my father's pain. "He knows."

Gideon swung me up in his arms, cradling me. His phone started ringing. Cursing under his breath, he walked out of the room.

In the hallway, I could hear my phone rattling on the coffee table. The irritating sound of two phones going off simultaneously ratcheted up my anxiety.

"Let me know if you need to get that," he said.

"It's my mom. I'm sure my dad's called her already, and he's so angry. God . . . Gideon. He's devastated."

"I understand how he feels."

He carried me into the guest bedroom and kicked the door closed behind him. Laying me on the bed, he grabbed the remote off the nightstand and turned on the television, lowering the volume to a level that drowned out all other sound but my hiccupping sobs. Then he lay down beside me and hugged me, his hands rubbing up and down my back. I cried until my eyes felt raw and I had nothing left.

"Tell me what to do," he said when I quieted.

"He's coming here. To New York." My stomach knotted at the thought. "He's trying to fly out today, I think."

"When you find out, I'll go with you to pick him up."

"You can't."

"The hell I can't," he said without heat.

I offered my mouth and sighed when he kissed me. "I should really go alone. He's hurt. He won't want anyone else to see him that way."

Gideon nodded. "Take my car."

"Which one?"

"Your new neighbor's DB9."

"Huh?"

He shrugged. "You'll know it when you see it."

I didn't doubt that. Whatever it was, the car would be sleek, fast, and dangerous—just like its owner.

"I'm scared," I murmured, my legs tangling even tighter with his. He was so strong and solid. I wanted to hang on to him and never let go.

His fingers sifted through my hair. "Of what?"

"Things are already fucked up between my mom and me. If my parents have a falling-out, I don't want to get stuck in the middle. I know they wouldn't handle it well—especially my mom. They're crazy in love with each other."

"I hadn't realized that."

"You didn't see them together. Major sizzle," I explained, remembering that Gideon and I had been separated when I learned the sexual chemistry between my parents was still white-hot. "And my dad confessed to still being in love with her. Makes me sad to think about it."

"Because they're not together?"

"Yes, but not because I want one big happy family," I qualified. "I just hate the thought of going through life without the person you're in love with. When I lost you—"

"You've *never* lost me."

"It was like part of me died. Going through a whole lifetime like that . . ."

"Would be hell." Gideon ran his fingertips across my cheek and I saw the bleakness in his eyes, the lingering specter of Nathan haunting him. "Let me handle Monica."

I blinked at him. "How?"

His lips curled on one side. "I'll call her and ask how you're dealing with everything and how you're doing. Start the process of publicly working my way back to you."

"She knows I told you everything. She might break down on you."

"Better me than you."

That was almost enough to make me smile. "Thank you."

"I'll distract her and get her thinking about something else." He reached for my hand and touched my ring.

Wedding bells. He didn't say it, but I got the message. And of course that was what my mother would think. A man in Gideon's position didn't come back to a woman through her mother—especially one like Monica Stanton—unless his "intentions" were serious.

That was an issue we'd tackle another day.

FOR the next hour, Gideon pretended like he wasn't hovering. He stayed close, following me from room to room on some pretext or another. When my stomach growled, he tugged me immediately into the kitchen, pulling together a plate of sandwiches, potato chips, and prepared macaroni salad.

We ate at the island, and I let the comfort of his attentiveness soothe my nerves. As rough as things were, he was there for me to lean on. It made a lot of the troubles we were facing seem surmountable.

What *couldn't* we accomplish, as long as we stayed together?

"What did Corinne want?" I asked. "Besides you."

His features hardened. "I don't want to talk about Corinne."

There was an edge to his voice that niggled at me. "Is everything all right?"

"What did I just say?"

"Something lame that I'm choosing to ignore."

He made an exasperated noise, but relented. "She's upset."

"Screaming upset? Or crying upset?"

"Does it matter?"

"Yes. There's a difference between being mad at a guy and being a teary mess over him. For example: Deanna is mad and can plot your destruction; I was a teary mess and could barely crawl out of bed every day."

"God. Eva." He reached over and set his hand over mine. "I'm sorry."

"Cut it out with the apologies, already! You'll make it up to me having to deal with my mother. So is Corinne mad or teary?"

"She was crying." Gideon winced. "Christ. She lost it."

"I'm sorry you're dealing with that. Don't let her guilt-trip you, though."

"I used her," he said quietly, "to protect you."

I set my sandwich down and narrowed my gaze at him. "Did you or did you not tell her that all you could offer was friendship?"

"You know I did. But I also deliberately fostered the impression that we might be more, for the sake of the press and the police. I sent her mixed signals. *That's* what I feel guilty about."

"Well, stop. That bitch tried to make me think you'd banged her"—I wiggled two fingers—"*twice*. And the first time she did, it hurt so bad I'm still getting over it. Plus she's married, for fuck's sake. She's got no business making moves on my man when she's got her own."

"Back up to the part about banging her. What are you talking about?"

I explained the incidents—the lipstick-on-the-cuff disaster at the Crossfire and my impromptu visit to Corinne's apartment, when she'd tried to play it like she'd just got done screwing him.

"Well, that changes things considerably," he said. "There's nothing more she and I need to say to each other."

"Thank you."

He reached over to tuck my hair behind my ear. "We'll eventually be on the other side of all this."

"Whatever will we do with ourselves then?" I muttered.

"Oh, I'm sure I can think of something."

"Sex, right?" I shook my head. "I've created a monster."

"Don't forget work—together."

"Oh my God. You don't quit."

He crunched on a chip and swallowed. "I want you to see the revamped Crossroads and Cross Industries websites when we're done with lunch."

I wiped my mouth with a napkin. "Really? That was fast. I'm impressed."

"Let's have you look at them first before you decide that."

GIDEON knew me well. Work was my escape and he put me to it. He set me up with his laptop in the living room, made my phone stop ringing, then went into his office to call my mother.

For the first few minutes after he'd left me alone, I listened to the low murmur of his voice and tried to focus on the websites he'd pulled up for me, but it was no use. I was too scattered to pay attention. I ended up calling Cary instead.

"Where the fuck are you?" he barked by way of greeting.

"I know it's been crazy," I said quickly, having no doubt my mother and father would've been calling the apartment Cary and I shared when I didn't answer my smartphone. "I'm sorry."

The background noise on Cary's end told me he was somewhere out on the streets.

"Mind telling me what's going on? Everyone's calling me—your parents, Stanton, Clancy. They're all looking for you and you're not answering your cell. I've been freaking out wondering what happened to you!"

Crap. I closed my eyes. "My dad found out about Nathan."

He was silent, the sounds of distant traffic and honking the only indication he was still on the line. Then, "Holy shit. Oh, baby girl. That's bad."

The compassion in his voice made my throat too tight to speak. I didn't want to cry any more.

The background noise suddenly muted, as if he'd stepped into someplace quiet. "How is he?" Cary asked.

"He's torn up. God, Cary, it was *awful.* I think he was crying. And he's furious with Mom. That's probably why she's calling so much."

"What's he going to do?"

"He's flying out to New York. I don't know when, but he said he'd be calling when he landed."

"He's flying out *now*? Like today?"

"I think so," I said miserably. "I'm not sure how he's managing to get time off work again so soon."

"I'll fix up the guest room when I get home, if you haven't done it already."

"I'll take care of it. Where are you?"

"Catching lunch and a matinee with Tatiana. I had to get out for a while."

"I'm so sorry you've been fielding my calls."

"Not a big deal," he dismissed, in his usual Cary way. "I was more worried than anything. You haven't been around much lately. I don't know what you're doing or *who* you're doing. You're not acting like yourself."

The note of accusation in his tone deepened my remorse, but there was nothing I could share. "I'm sorry."

He waited, as if for an explanation, then said something under his breath. "I'll be home in a couple hours."

"All right. See you then."

I hung up, then called my stepfather.

"Eva."

"Hi, Richard." I dug right in. "Did my dad call Mom?"

"Just a moment." There was silence on the phone for a minute or two, then I heard a door shut. "He did call, yes. It was . . . unpleasant for your mother. This weekend has been very hard on her. She's not well, and I'm concerned."

"This is hard on all of us," I said. "I wanted to let you know that my dad is coming back to New York and I'll need to spend some quiet time with him."

"You need to talk to Victor about being a little more understanding of what your mother went through. She was on her own, with a traumatized child."

"You need to understand that we've got to give him time to come to grips with this," I shot back. My tone was harsher than I intended, but reflective of my feelings. I was not going to be forced to take sides between my parents. "And I need you to deal with Mom and get her to stop calling me and Cary nonstop. Talk to Dr. Petersen if you have to," I suggested, referring to my mother's therapist.

"Monica's on the phone now. I'll discuss it with her when she's free."

"Don't just discuss it. Do something about it. Hide the phones somewhere if that's what it takes."

"That's extreme. And unnecessary."

"Not if she doesn't quit!" My fingers drummed on the coffee table. "You and me, we're both guilty of tiptoeing around Mom—*Oh no, don't upset Monica!*—because we'd rather just give in than deal with her meltdowns. But that's emotional extortion, Richard, and I'm done paying out."

He was silent, then, "You're under a lot of strain right now. And—"

"You think?" In my head I was screaming. "Tell Mom I love her and I'll call when I can. Which won't be today."

"Clancy and I are available if you need anything," he said stiffly.

"Thank you, Richard. I appreciate that."

I hung up and fought the urge to throw the phone at the wall.

I'D managed to calm down enough to go over the Crossroads website before Gideon reappeared from his office. He looked wiped and a bit dazed, which was to be expected, considering. Dealing with my mom when she was upset was a challenge for anyone, and Gideon didn't have much experience to fall back on.

"I warned you," I said.

He lifted his arms over his head and stretched. "She'll be all right. I think she's tougher than she lets on."

"She was stoked to hear from you, wasn't she?"

He smirked.

I rolled my eyes. "She thinks I need a rich man to take care of me and keep me safe."

"You've got one."

"I'm going to assume you meant that in a noncaveman way." I stood. "I have to head out and get ready for my dad's visit. I'll need to be home at night for however long he's here, and it's probably not wise for you to sneak into my apartment. If he mistakes you for a burglar, it won't be pretty."

"It's also disrespectful. I'll use the time to be seen at the penthouse."

"So we've got a plan." I stood and scrubbed at my face before admiring my new watch. "At least I've got a lovely way to count the minutes until we're together again."

He came to me, catching me by the nape. His thumb drew tantalizing circles on the back of my neck. "I need to know you're okay."

I nodded. "I'm tired of Nathan running my life. I'm working toward that fresh start."

I imagined a future in which my mom wasn't a stalker, my dad was back on solid footing, Cary was happy, Corinne was in another country far away, and Gideon and I weren't ruled by our pasts.

And I was finally ready to fight for it.

11

MONDAY MORNING. TIME to go to work. I hadn't heard from my dad, so I got ready to head in. I was digging in my closet when a knock came on my bedroom door.

"Come in," I yelled.

A minute later, I heard Cary shout back, "Where the hell are you?"

"In here."

His shadow darkened the doorway. "Any word from your dad?"

I glanced at him. "Not yet. I sent him a text and didn't get a reply."

"So he's still on the plane."

"Or he missed a connection. Who knows?" I scowled at my clothes.

"Here." He came in and stepped around me, pulling a pair of gray linen palazzo pants off the bottom rack and a black lace cap-sleeved shirt.

"Thank you." And because he was close, I hugged him.

His returning hug was so tight it squeezed the air out of me. Startled by his exuberance, I held him for a long while, my cheek over his heart. For the first time in a few days, he was dressed in jeans and a T-shirt, and as usual, he managed to look striking and expensive.

"Everything okay?" I asked him.

"I miss you, baby girl," he murmured into my hair.

"Just trying to make sure you don't get sick of me." I tried to sound like I was teasing, but his tone niggled at me. It lacked all the vivacity I was so used to hearing in it. "I'm taking a cab to work, so I've got some time. Why don't we have a cup of coffee?"

"Yeah." He pulled back and smiled at me, looking boyishly beautiful.

Taking my hand, he led me out of the closet. I tossed my clothes on an armchair before we headed out to the kitchen.

"Are you going out?" I asked.

"I've got a shoot today."

"Well, that's good news!" I headed to the coffeemaker while he went to pull half-and-half out of the fridge. "Sounds like another occasion to dig into the case of Cristal."

"No way," he scoffed. "Not with everything that's going on with your dad."

"What else are we going to do? Sit around staring at each other? There's nothing more that can be done. Nathan is dead and even if he weren't, what he did to me is long over." I pushed a steaming mug over to him and filled another. "I'm ready to shove his memory in a cold, dark hole and forget about him."

"Over for you." He lightened my coffee and slid it back. "It's still news to your dad. He'll want to talk about it."

"I am *not* talking about it with my dad. I'm not talking about it *ever*."

"He might not go along with that."

I turned and faced him, leaning back into the counter with my mug cradled between my hands. "All he needs is to see me doing okay. This isn't about him. It's about me, and I'm surviving. Pretty well, I think."

He stirred his coffee, a thoughtful look on his face.

"Yeah, you are," he said after a few seconds. "Are you going to tell him about your mystery man?"

"He's not a mystery. I just can't talk about him, and that has nothing to do with our friendship. I trust you and love you and rely on you like always."

His green eyes challenged me over the rim of his mug. "Doesn't seem like it."

"You're my best friend. When I'm old and gray, you'll still be my best friend. Not talking about the guy I'm seeing isn't going to change that."

"How am I not supposed to feel like you don't trust me? What's the big deal with this guy that you can't even give me a name or anything?"

I sighed and told him a partial truth. "I don't know his name."

Cary stilled, staring. "You're shitting me."

"I never asked him what it is." As evasive answers went, it begged to be challenged. Cary gave me a long look.

"And I'm not supposed to be worried?"

"Nope. I'm comfortable with the whole thing. We're both getting what we need and he cares about me."

He studied me. "What do you call him when you're coming? You've got to be shouting something if he's any good at it. Which I assume he is, since you obviously aren't getting to know each other by talking."

"Uh . . ." That tripped me up. "I think I just say, 'Oh, God!' "

Throwing his head back, he laughed.

"How are you holding up with juggling two relationships?" I asked.

"I'm good." He shoved one hand in his pocket and rocked back on his heels. "I think Tat and Trey are as close to monogamy as I've ever been. It's working out for me so far."

I found the whole arrangement fascinating. "Ever worry about shouting out the wrong name when you're coming?"

His green eyes sparkled. "Nope. I just call 'em all *baby*."

"Cary." I shook my head. He was incorrigible. "Are you going to introduce Tatiana to Trey?"

He shrugged. "I don't think that's the best idea."

"No?"

"Tatiana's a bitch on a good day, and Trey's just a nice guy. Not a great combo, in my book."

"You once told me you didn't like Tatiana very much. Has that changed?"

"She is who she is," he said dismissively. "I can live with it."

I stared at him.

"She needs me, Eva," he said quietly. "Trey wants me, and I think he loves me, but he doesn't need me."

That I understood. It was nice to be needed sometimes. "Gotcha."

"Who says there's only one person in the world who can give us everything?" He snorted. "I'm not sure I'm buying that. Look at you and your no-name guy."

"Maybe a mix-and-match situation can work for people who don't get jealous. It wouldn't work for me."

"Yeah." He held out his mug and I tapped it with my own.

"So Cristal and . . . ?"

"Hmm . . ." His lips pursed. "Tapas?"

I blinked. "You want to take my dad out?"

"Bad idea?"

"It's a great idea, if we can get him to go along with it." I smiled. "You rock, Cary."

He winked at me and I felt a little more settled.

Everything in my life seemed to be shaken up, most especially my relationships with the people I loved most. That was hard for me to deal with, because I relied on them to keep me on an even keel. But maybe when everything settled down, I'd be a bit stronger. Able to stand a bit straighter on my own.

It would be worth all the turmoil and pain if so.

"Want me to fix your hair?" Cary asked.

I nodded. "Please."

When I got to work, I was disappointed to find a very unhappy Megumi. She gave me a lethargic wave as she buzzed me in, then dropped back into her chair.

"Girl, you need to kick Michael to the curb," I said. "This is *not* working out for you."

"I know." She brushed back the long bangs of her asymmetrical bob. "I'm going to break it off the next time I see him. I haven't heard from him since Friday, and I'm driving myself crazy wondering if he picked up anyone while doing his bachelor barhopping thing."

"Eww."

"I know, right? It's just not cool worrying about if the guy you're sleeping with is shagging someone else."

I couldn't help but be reminded of my earlier conversation with Cary. "Me and Ben and Jerry's are only a phone call away. Holler if you need us."

"Is that your secret?" She gave a short laugh. "What flavor got you over Gideon Cross?"

"I'm not over him," I admitted.

She nodded sagely. "I knew that. But you had fun on Saturday, right? And he's an idiot, by the way. One day, he's going to figure that out and coming crawling back."

"He called my mom over the weekend," I said, leaning over the desk and lowering my voice. "Asking about me."

"Whoa." Megumi leaned forward, too. "What did he say?"

"I don't know the details."

"Would you get back together with him?"

I shrugged. "I can't say. Depends on how well he grovels."

"Totally." She high-fived me. "Your hair looks great, by the way."

I thanked her and headed to my cubicle, mentally preparing my request to take off from work if my dad called. I'd barely turned the corner at the end of the hall when Mark bounded out of his office with a huge grin.

"Oh my God." I stopped midstep. "You look insanely happy. Let me guess. You're engaged!"

"I am!"

"Yay!" I dropped my purse and bag on the floor and clapped. "I'm so excited for you! Congratulations."

Bending down, he picked up my stuff. "Come into my office."

He gestured me in ahead of him, then closed the glass door behind us.

"Was it tough?" I asked him, taking a seat in front of his desk.

"Toughest thing I've ever done." Mark handed me my bags. Sinking into his chair, he rocked back and forth. "And Steven let me stew over it. Can you believe that? He knew all along I was going to propose. Said he could tell by how I freaked out I was."

I grinned. "He knows you well."

"And he waited a minute or two before he answered me. And let me tell you, it seemed like hours."

"I bet. So was all of his anti-marriage talk a front?"

He nodded, still grinning. "His pride took a hit when I put him off before, so he wanted a little payback. Said he'd always known I'd come around eventually. Wanted to make me work for it when I finally did."

It sounded like Steven, who was playful and gregarious. "So where did you pop the question?"

He laughed. "I couldn't do it somewhere with atmosphere, right? Like the candlelit restaurant or the nice dark bar after the show. No, I had to wait until the limo dropped us off at home at the end of the night and we were standing outside our brownstone and I knew I was going to lose my chance. So I just blurted it out right there on the street."

"I think that's really romantic."

"I think *you're* a romantic," he shot back.

"Who cares about wine and roses? Anyone can do that. Showing somebody you can't live without them? *That's* romance."

"As usual, you make a good point."

I blew on my nails and buffed them on my shirt. "What can I say?"

"I'll let Steven give you all the details at lunch on Wednesday. He's told the story so many times already, he's got the delivery down pat."

"I can't wait to see him." As excited as Mark was, I was sure Steven was bouncing off the walls. The big, muscled contractor had a personality as vibrant as his bright red hair. "I'm so thrilled for you both."

"He's going to rope you into helping Shawna with the planning, you know that, right?" He sat up and set his elbows on the table. "Besides his sister, he's recruiting every woman we know. I'm sure the whole thing will be over-the-top craziness all the way."

"Sounds fun!"

"You say that now," he warned, his dark eyes laughing. "Let's grab some coffee and get this week started, shall we?"

I stood. "Um, I hate to ask this, but my dad is making an emergency trip into the city this week. I'm not sure when he'll be coming in. It could be today. I'll need to pick him up and get him settled when he arrives."

"Do you need to take some time off?"

"Just to get him situated in my apartment. A few hours at most."

Mark nodded. "You said 'emergency trip.' Is everything all right?"

"It will be."

"Okay. I don't have a problem with you taking time when you need it."

"Thank you."

As I dropped my stuff off at my desk, I thought—for the millionth time—how much I loved my job and my boss. I understood how much Gideon wanted to keep me close and I appreciated the vision of us building something together, but my work nurtured me as an individual. I didn't want to give that up, and I didn't want to end up resenting him if he kept pushing me to do so. I'd have to come up with an argument Gideon would accept.

I started working on it as Mark and I headed to the break room.

ALTHOUGH Megumi hadn't yet kissed Michael good-bye, I took her out to lunch at a nearby deli with delicious wraps and a decent selection of Ben & Jerry cups. I chose Chunky Monkey, she went with Cherry Garcia, and we both enjoyed the cool treat in the middle of the hot day.

We sat at a small metal table in the back, the remnants of our lunch on a tray between us. The deli wasn't as crazed during the noon hour as some of the other restaurants and full-service eateries in the area were, which suited us both fine. We could hold a conversation without raising our voices.

"Mark's floating," she said, licking her spoon. She wore a lime green dress that went really well with her dark hair and pale skin. Megumi always dressed in bold colors and styles. I envied her ability to pull them off so well.

"I know." I smiled. "It's so cool to see someone that happy."

"Guilt-free happiness. Unlike this ice cream."

"What's a little guilt every now and then?"

"A fat ass?"

I groaned. "Thanks for the reminder that I have to hit the gym today. I haven't worked out in days."

Unless one counted mattress gymnastics . . .

"How do you stay motivated?" she asked me. "I know I should go, but I can always find an excuse not to."

"And you keep that amazing figure anyway?" I shook my head. "You make me sick."

Her lips quirked. "Where do you work out?"

"I alternate between a regular gym and a Krav Maga studio in Brooklyn."

"Do you go after work or before?"

"After. I am *not* a morning person," I said. "Sleep is my friend."

"Would you mind if I tag along sometime? I don't know about that Krav what-a, but the gym. Where do you go?"

I swallowed a bit of chocolate and was about to reply when I heard a phone ringing.

"Are you going to get that?" Megumi asked, which alerted me to the fact that the phone was mine.

The burner phone, which was why I didn't recognize it.

I dug it out quickly and answered with a breathless "Hello?"

"Angel."

For a second, I savored the rasp of Gideon's voice. "Hey. What's up?"

"My attorneys just notified me that the police might have a suspect."

"What?" My heart stopped. My stomach began to revolt against lunch. "Oh my God."

"It's not me."

I don't remember getting back to the office. When Megumi asked me for the name of my gym, she had to ask twice. The fear I felt was like nothing I'd ever suffered before. It was so much worse when you felt it on behalf of someone you loved.

How could the police possibly suspect someone else?

I had the horrible feeling they were just trying to shake Gideon up. Shake me up.

If that was the goal, it was working. At least on me. Gideon had sounded calm and collected during our brief conversation. He'd told me not to get upset, that he just wanted to warn me that the police might come by with more questions. Or they might not.

Jesus. I walked slowly back to my desk, my nerves shot. I felt like I'd gulped down an entire pot of coffee. My hands were trembling and my heart was beating too fast.

I sat down at my desk and tried to get back to work, but I couldn't concentrate. I stared at my monitor and didn't see anything.

What if the police did have a suspect who wasn't Gideon? What would we do? We couldn't let an innocent person go to prison.

And yet there was a tiny voice in my head whispering that Gideon would be safe from prosecution if someone else were convicted of the crime.

The moment the thought entered my mind, I felt sick over it. My gaze went to the photo of my dad. He was in his uniform, looking dashingly handsome standing next to his patrol car.

I was so confused, so frightened.

When my smartphone started vibrating on my desk, I jumped. Dad's name and number flashed on the screen. I answered quickly. "Hey! Where are you?"

"Cincinnati. I'm switching planes."

"Hang on, let me write down your flight info." I snagged a pen and jotted down the details he gave me. "I'll be waiting for you when you land. I can't wait to see you."

"Yeah . . . Eva. Sweetheart." He sighed heavily. "I'll see you soon."

He hung up, and the subsequent silence was deafening. I knew then that the strongest emotion he was feeling was guilt. It colored his voice and made my chest ache.

Standing, I made my way over to Mark's office. "I just heard from my dad. His flight lands at LaGuardia in a couple hours."

He looked at me, then frowned, his gaze searching. "So go home, get ready, and pick him up."

"Thanks." That one word would have to do. Mark seemed to understand that I didn't want to stick around and talk.

I used the burner phone to send a text while I took a cab ride home: Heading to the apt. Leaving in 1 hour to get dad. Can u talk?

I needed to know what Gideon was thinking . . . how he was feeling. I was a wreck and I didn't know what to do about it.

When I got home, I changed into a simple, lightweight summer dress and sandals. I answered a text from Martin, agreeing that it was great we'd hung out Saturday night and that we should do it again. I double-checked the kitchen, making sure all of my dad's favorite foods that I'd stocked up on were exactly where I'd put them. I checked the guest room again, even though I'd gone over it the day before. I got online and checked my dad's flight.

Done. I had enough time left over to drive myself crazy.

I did a search for "Corinne Giroux and husband" on Google, looking specifically at images.

What I discovered was that Jean-François Giroux was a really good-looking guy. Hot, actually. Not as hot as Gideon, but then who was? Gideon was in a league by himself, but Jean-François was a head-turner in his own right, with dark wavy hair and eyes the color of pale jade. He was tan and had a goatee, which *really* worked for him. He and Corinne made a stunning couple.

My burner phone rang and I lunged to my feet in a rush, stumbling around the coffee table to get to it. I snatched it out of my purse and answered, "Hello?"

"I'm next door," Gideon said. "I don't have a lot of time."

"I'm coming."

I grabbed my purse and left my place. One of my neighbors was just unlocking her door, so I offered a polite, distant smile and pretended to wait for the elevator. The moment I heard her go inside her apartment, I darted over to Gideon's door. It opened before I could use my key.

The Gideon who greeted me was in jeans and T-shirt, with a ball cap on his head. He caught my hand and pulled me inside, tugging the hat off before lowering his mouth to mine. His kiss was surprisingly sweet, his firm lips soft and warm.

I dropped my purse and wrapped my arms around him, snuggling into him. The feel of his strength eased my anxiety enough to allow me to take a deep breath.

"Hi," he murmured.

"You didn't have to come home." I could only imagine how doing so had disrupted his day. Changing clothes, making the trip back and forth . . .

"Yes, I did. You need me." His hands slid up my back, and then he pulled away just enough to look down into my face. "Don't worry about this, Eva. I'll take care of it."

"How?"

His blue eyes were cool, his expression one of confidence. "Right now, I'm waiting on more information. Who are they looking at? Why are they looking at him? Chances are very good that it won't pan out. You know that."

I search his face. "What if they do?"

"Will I let someone else pay for my crime?" His jaw tightened. "Is that what you're asking?"

"No." I smoothed his brow with my fingertips. "I know you won't let that happen. I'm just wondering how you'll prevent it."

His scowl deepened. "You're asking me to predict the future, Eva. I can't do that. You just have to trust me."

"I do," I promised fervently. "But I'm still scared. I can't help being freaked out."

"I know. I'm worried, too." His thumb brushed over my bottom lip. "Detective Graves is a very intelligent woman."

His observation clicked with me. "You're right. That makes me feel better."

I didn't know Shelley Graves, not really. But in the few interactions I'd had with her, she'd struck me as being intelligent *and* street-smart. I hadn't factored her into the equation, and I should have. It was odd to be in a position where I both feared who she was and appreciated it.

"You set up for your dad?"

The reminder brought some of the jitters back. "Everything's ready. Except me."

His eyes softened. "Any idea how you're going to handle him?"

"Cary went back to work today, so we'll celebrate with champagne and then head out to dinner."

"You think he's going to be up for that?"

"I don't know if *I'm* up for it," I admitted. "It's screwy to be making plans to drink Cristal and kick up my heels in the middle of everything going on. But what else can I do? If my dad doesn't see I'm okay, he's not going to get over finding out about Nathan. I have to show him all of that ugliness is in the past."

"And you need to let me handle the rest," he admonished. "I *will* take care of you, of *us*. Focus on your family for a while."

Stepping back, I grabbed his hand and led him toward the couch. It was weird being home so early after going in to work. Seeing the brightness of the afternoon sun beating down on the city outside the windows had me feeling out of step, reinforcing the notion that we'd stolen time to be together.

I sat, curled my legs, and faced him, watching as he settled beside me. We were so alike in many ways, including our pasts. Did Gideon need to get everything out in the open with his family, too? Is that what he'd need to fully heal?

"I know you have to get back to work," I said, "but I'm glad you came home for me. You're right—I needed to see you."

He lifted my hand to his lips. "Do you know when your father's heading back to California?"

"No."

"My appointment with Dr. Petersen would've made tomorrow a late night for us anyway." Gideon looked at me with a slight smile. "We'll find a way to be together."

Having him near . . . touching him . . . seeing him smile . . . hearing those words. I could get through anything as long as I had him next to me after a long day.

"Can I have five minutes?" I asked.

"You can have whatever you want, angel," he said softly.

"Just this." I slid closer and curved into his side.

Gideon's arm came around my shoulders. Our hands linked together in our laps. We formed a perfect circle. Not as glittering as the rings we wore on our fingers, but priceless all the same.

After a moment, I felt him lean into me. He sighed. "I needed this, too."

I hugged him tighter. "It's okay to need me, ace."

"I wish I needed you a little less. Just enough to make it bearable."

"What would be the fun in that?"

His soft laugh made me fall even harder for him.

GIDEON had been right about the DB9. As I watched the parking attendant pull the sleek metallic gray Aston Martin to a stop in front of me, I thought it was pretty much Gideon on wheels. It was sex with a gas pedal; so much brute elegance it damn near made my toes curl.

I was scared as hell to get behind the wheel.

Driving in New York was *nothing* like driving in Southern California. I hesitated before accepting the keys from the bow-tied attendant, debating the wisdom of just calling for a town car.

The burner phone started ringing and I fumbled for it quickly. "Hello?"

"Just do it," Gideon purred. "Stop worrying and drive it."

I spun around, my gaze searching for security cameras. Awareness shivered down my spine. I could *feel* Gideon's gaze on me. "What are you doing?"

"Wishing I were with you. I'd love to spread you across the hood and fuck you real slow. Push my cock deep inside you. Give those shocks a workout. Umm. God, I'm hard."

And he was making me wet. I could listen to him endlessly; I loved his voice so much. "I'm scared I'm going to screw up your pretty car."

"I don't give a shit about the car, only about your safety. So scratch it up all you want, just don't get hurt."

"If that was supposed to calm me down, it didn't work."

"We could have phone sex until you come, that should do it."

I narrowed my gaze at the parking attendants, who were pretending not to watch me. "Should I be worried about what got you so horny in the short time since I was with you?"

"Thinking about you driving the DB9 turns me on."

"Does it now?" I fought to hold back a smile. "Remind me, which one of us has the transportation fetish?"

"Slide behind the wheel," he coaxed. "Imagine I'm in the passenger seat. My hand between your legs. My fingers fucking your soft, slick cunt."

Stepping closer to the car on shaky legs, I muttered, "You must have a death wish."

"I'd take my cock out and stroke it with my fist while I fingered you, get us both good and hot."

"Your lack of respect for this vehicle's upholstery is appalling." I settled into the driver's seat and spent a minute figuring out how to move it forward.

His voice rasped through the car's sound system. "How does it feel?"

It totally figured that he'd synced my burner phone to the car's Bluetooth. Gideon always thought of everything.

"Expensive," I answered. "You're crazy for letting me drive this."

"I'm crazy about *you*," he replied, sending delight skipping through me. "LaGuardia is programmed in the GPS."

It made me feel good to know that coming home to see me had lightened his mood so much. I knew just how he felt. It meant a lot to know he felt the same way.

I pulled up the GPS, then hit the button to put the transmission into drive. "You know what, ace? I want to blow you while you're driving this thing. Throw a pillow across this center console here and suck your cock for *miles*."

"I'm going to take you up on that. Tell me how she feels."

"Smooth. Powerful." I waved at the attendants as I eased out of the subterranean parking garage. "Very responsive."

"Just like you," he murmured. "Of course, you're my favorite ride."

"Aw, that's sweet, baby. And you're my favorite joystick." I merged carefully into traffic.

He laughed. "I better be your only joystick."

"But I'm not your only ride," I pointed out, loving him so much in that moment because I knew he was looking out for me, making sure I was comfortable. Back in California, driving had been like breathing to me, but I hadn't been behind the wheel of a car since I moved to New York.

"You're the only one I enjoy naked," he said.

"That's real lucky for you, because I'm very possessive."

"I know." His voice was filled with masculine satisfaction.

"Where are you?"

"At work."

"Multitasking, I'm sure." I stepped on the gas and prayed as I cut across lanes. "What's a little calming distraction for your girlfriend in the midst of world entertainment domination?"

"I'd stop the world from spinning for you."

That silly line oddly touched me. "I love you."

"Liked that one, did you?"

I grinned, startled and pleased by his ridiculous sense of humor.

I was hyperaware of my surroundings. There were signs in every direction prohibiting everything. Driving in Manhattan was a fast trip to nowhere. "Hey, I can't turn left or right. I think I'm heading for the Midtown Tunnel. I could lose you."

"You'll never lose me, angel," he vowed. "Wherever you go, however far, I'll be right here with you."

WHEN I spotted my dad outside the baggage claim area, I lost all the confidence Gideon had instilled in me since I'd left work. Dad looked drawn and haggard, his eyes reddened and his jaw shadowed by stubble.

I felt the sting of tears as I walked toward him, but I blinked them back, determined to reassure him. Holding my arms open, I watched him drop his carry-on and then all the air left my lungs as he hugged me tightly.

"Hi, Daddy," I said, with a tremor in my voice I hoped he missed.

"Eva." His lips pressed hard to my temple.

"You look tired. When's the last time you slept?"

"On the leg out of San Diego." He pulled back and looked at me with gray eyes that were the same as mine. He searched my face.

"Do you have more luggage?"

He shook his head, still studying me.

"Are you hungry?" I asked.

"I grabbed something in Cincinnati." Finally, he backed up and retrieved his bag. "But if you're hungry . . . ?"

"Nope. I'm good. But I was thinking we could take Cary out for dinner later, if you're up for it. He went back to work today."

"Sure." He paused with his bag in his hand, looking a bit lost and unsure.

"Dad, I'm okay."

"*I'm* not. I want to hurt something and there's nothing for me to hit."

That gave me an idea.

Grabbing his hand, I started leading him out of the airport. "Hold that thought."

12

"He's really making Derek work for it," Parker noted, wiping the light sheen of sweat off his shaved head with a hand towel.

I turned to watch, seeing my father wrestling with the instructor who was twice his size, and my dad wasn't a small guy. Standing over six feet tall and weighing in at two hundred pounds of solid, rippling muscle, Victor Reyes was a formidable opponent. Plus, he'd told me he was going to check out Krav Maga himself after I'd shared my interest in it, and it seemed he had—he had some of the moves down pat. "Thanks for letting him jump in."

Parker looked at me, his dark eyes steady and calm in that way he had. He'd been teaching me more than just how to defend myself. He had also taught me to focus on the steps to be taken, not the fear.

"Usually I'd say class isn't the place to bring your anger," he said, "but Derek needed the challenge."

Although he didn't ask it, I could feel the unspoken question in the air. I decided it was best to answer it, since Parker was doing me a favor by letting my dad monopolize his co-instructor. "He just found out that someone hurt me a long time ago. Now it's too late to do anything about it and he's having a hard time with that."

He reached down and grabbed the bottle of water sitting just off the side of the training mat. After a minute, he said, "I have a daughter. I can imagine how that feels."

When he looked at me before taking a drink, I saw the understanding in his thickly lashed dark eyes and I was reassured that I'd brought my dad to the right place.

Parker was easygoing and had a great smile, and was genuine in a way that I'd rarely come across. But he had an air about him that warned people to tread carefully. One knew right away that it would be stupid to try to pull anything over on him. His street smarts were as obvious as his tribal tattoos.

"So you bring him here," he said, "let him work it out and let him see you taking care of your own protection. Good idea."

"I don't know what else to do," I confessed. Parker's studio was located in a revitalizing area of Brooklyn. It was a converted warehouse, and the exposed brick and giant sliding loading-bay doors added to the atmosphere of tough chic. It was a place where I felt confident and take-charge.

"I've got some ideas." He grinned and jerked his chin toward the mat. "Let's show him what you can do."

I dropped my towel over my water bottle and nodded. "Let's."

I didn't see any of the uniformed parking attendants as we pulled into the underground garage of my apartment building. Since I wanted to do the honors myself anyway, that worked for me. I slid the DB9 into an empty slot and cut the engine. "Fabulous. Right by the elevator."

"So I see," my dad said. "Is this your car?"

I'd been waiting for that question. "No. A neighbor's."

"Friendly neighbor," he said dryly.

"A cup of sugar. An Aston Martin. It's all the same, right?" I glanced at him with a smile.

He looked so tired and worn, and not from the workout. The weariness came from the inside, and it was killing me.

Turning the car off, I released my seat belt and turned to look at him. "Dad. I . . . It's shredding me to see you torn up over this. I can't stand it."

Heaving out his breath, he said, "I just need some time."

"I never wanted you to find out." I reached out and gripped his hand. "But I'll be glad you did, if we can put Nathan behind us for good."

"I read the reports—"

"God. Daddy . . ." I swallowed back a rush of bile. "I don't want that stuff in your head."

"I knew there was something wrong." He stared at me with such sorrow and pain in his eyes it hurt to look into them. "The way Cary went to sit beside you when Detective Graves said Nathan Barker's name . . . I knew you weren't telling me something. I kept hoping you would."

"I've tried very hard to put Nathan in my past. You were one of the few things in my life he hadn't infected. I wanted to keep it that way."

His grip on my hand tightened. "Tell me the truth. Are you okay?"

"Dad. I'm the same daughter you came to see a couple weeks ago. The same daughter who hung out with you in San Diego. I'm *okay.*"

"You were pregnant—" His voice broke and a tear slid down his cheek.

I brushed it away, ignoring my own. "And I will be again someday. Maybe more than once. Maybe you'll be crawling with grandkids."

"Come here."

Leaning across the console, he hugged me. We sat in the car for a long time, crying. Getting it out.

Was Gideon watching the security feeds, sending me silent support? It gave me comfort to think he might be.

DINNER out that night wasn't quite as boisterous a meal as usual for Cary, my dad, and me, but it wasn't as grim as I'd feared it might be. The food was great, the wine better, and Cary was snarking out.

"She was worse than Tatiana," he said, talking about the model he'd shared the shoot with that day. "She kept going on about her 'good side,' which I personally thought was her ass as it walked out the door."

"You've done shoots with Tatiana?" I asked, then explained to my dad, "She's a girl Cary's seeing."

"Oh, yeah." Cary licked red wine off his lower lip. "We work together a lot, actually. I'm the Tatiana Tamer. She starts one of her fits and I calm her down."

"How do— Never mind," I said quickly. "I don't want to know how."

"You already know." He winked.

I looked at my dad and rolled my eyes.

"How about you, Victor?" Cary asked around a bite of sautéed mushroom. "You seeing anyone?"

My dad shrugged. "Nothing serious."

That was by his choice. I'd seen how women acted around him—they fell all over themselves trying to get his attention. My dad was hot, with an amazing body, gorgeous face, and Latin sensuality. He had his pick of women and I knew he wasn't a saint, but he never seemed to meet anyone who really got to him. I'd recently realized that was because my mother had gotten there first.

"You think you'll ever have more kids?" Cary asked him, surprising me with the question.

I'd long ago become resigned to being an only child.

My dad shook his head. "Not that I'm opposed to the idea, but Eva is more than I ever thought I'd have in my life." He looked at me with so much love it made my throat tight. "And she's perfect. Everything I could ever hope for. I'm not sure there's room in my heart for anyone else."

"Aw, Daddy." I leaned my head into his shoulder, so glad he was with me, even if it was for the worst possible reason.

When we got back to the apartment, we decided to watch a movie before calling it a night. I went to my room to change and was stoked to find a gorgeous bouquet of white roses on my dresser. The card, written in Gideon's distinctive bold penmanship, made me almost giddy.

I'M THINKING OF YOU, AS ALWAYS.
AND I'M HERE.
YOURS, G.

I sat on the bed, hugging the card, certain he was thinking of me that very moment. It was also starting to sink in that he'd been thinking of me every moment of the weeks we'd been apart, too.

That night, I fell asleep on the couch after watching *Dredd*. I woke briefly to the feeling of being lifted and carried to my room, smiling sleepily as my dad tucked me into bed like a child and kissed my forehead.

"Love you, Daddy," I murmured.

"Love you, too, sweetheart."

I woke up before my alarm the next morning and felt better than I had in a long while. I left a note on the breakfast bar telling my dad to call me if he wanted to get together for lunch. I wasn't sure if he had anything planned for the day. I knew Cary had a shoot in the afternoon.

During the cab ride to work, I answered a text from Shawna squeeing over her brother's engagement to Mark. So happy for all of u, I texted back.

I'm drafting u! she shot back.

I smiled down at my phone. What's that? Signal's breaking up . . . Can't read u . . .

As the cab stopped in front of the Crossfire, the sight of the Bentley at the curb gave me the usual thrill. When I hopped out, I peeked into the front seat and waved when I saw Angus sitting inside.

He stepped out, setting his chauffeur hat on his head. Like Clancy, you couldn't tell he was carrying a sidearm by looking at him; he wore it so comfortably.

"Good morning, Miss Tramell," he greeted me. Although he wasn't a young man and his red hair was liberally threaded with silver, I'd never had any doubts about Angus's ability to protect Gideon.

"Hi, Angus. It's good to see you."

"You're looking lovely today."

I glanced down at my pale yellow dress. I'd chosen it because it was bright and cheery, which was the impression I wanted my dad to have of me. "Thank you. I hope your day rocks." I backed up toward the revolving door. "See you later!"

His pale blue eyes were kind as he tipped his hat to me.

When I got upstairs, I found Megumi looking more like her usual self. Her smile was wide and real, and her eyes had the sparkle I enjoyed seeing every morning.

I stopped by her desk. "How are you?"

"Good. Michael's meeting me for lunch and I'm ending it. Nice and civilized."

"That's a killer outfit you've got on," I told her, admiring the emerald green dress she wore. It was fitted and had leather piping that gave it just the right amount of edge.

She stood and showed off her knee-high boots.

"Very Kalinda Sharma," I said. "He's going to be scrambling to hold on to you."

"As if," she scoffed. "These boots were made for walking. He didn't call me back until last night, which made it nearly four days without contact. Not totally unreasonable, but I'm ready to find a guy who's crazy about me. A guy who thinks about me as much as I'm thinking about him and hates it when we can't be together."

I nodded, thinking about Gideon. "It's worth it to hold out for one. Do you want me to give you a bailout phone call during your lunch?"

She grinned. "Nah. But thank you."

"All right. Let me know if you change your mind."

I headed back to my desk and dug right in to work, determined to get ahead to make up for leaving early the day before. Mark was fired up, too, segueing from work only long enough to tell me that Steven had a binder full of wedding ideas he'd been collecting for years.

"Why am I not surprised?" I said.

"I shouldn't be." Mark's mouth curved with affection. "He's kept it in his office all this time so I wouldn't know about it."

"Did you get a look at it?"

"He went through the whole thing with me. It took *hours*."

"You're going to have the wedding of the century," I teased.

"Yeah." The word held more than a little exasperation, but his expression remained so happy I couldn't stop smiling.

My dad called just before eleven.

"Hey, sweetheart," he said, in reply to my usual work greeting. "How's your day going?"

"Great." I leaned back in my chair and looked at the picture of him. "How'd you sleep?"

"Hard. I'm still trying to wake up."

"Why? Go back to bed and be lazy."

"I wanted to let you know that I'm going to take a rain check on lunch. We'll get together tomorrow. Today, I need to talk to your mom."

"Oh." I knew that tone. It was the same one he used when he pulled people over, that perfect mixture of authority and disapproval. "Listen. I'm not going to step in the middle of this with you two. You're both adults and I'm not picking sides. But I have to say that Mom wanted to tell you."

"She should have."

"She was alone," I pressed on, my feet tapping restlessly on the carpet, "going through a divorce and the trial against Nathan, and dealing with my recovery. I'm sure she desperately wanted a shoulder to lean on—you know how she is. But she was drowning in guilt. I could've gotten her to agree to anything then, and I did."

He was quiet on the other end of the line.

"I just want you to keep that in mind when you talk to her," I finished.

"All right. When will you be home?"

"A little after five. Want to go to the gym? Or back to Parker's studio?"

"Let me see how I'm feeling when you get in," he said.

"Okay." I forced myself to ignore how anxious I was over the upcoming conversation between my parents. "Call me if you need anything."

We hung up and I got back to work, grateful for the distraction.

When lunch rolled around, I decided to grab something quick and bring it back to my desk to work through the hour. I braved the midday sauna outside to hit the local Duane Reade for a bag of beef jerky and a bottled health drink. I'd skipped my workouts pretty frequently since Gideon and I had gotten back together, and I figured it was time to pay a penalty for that.

I was debating the wisdom of sending Gideon an "I'm thinking of you" note when I twirled through the revolving front door of the Crossfire. Just a little something to say thanks for the flowers, which had made a tough day more bearable.

Then I saw the woman I'd prefer never to see again—Corinne Giroux. And she was talking to my man, with her palm resting intimately against his chest.

They stood off to the side, sheltered by a column outside the stream of traffic heading in and out of the security turnstiles. Corinne's long black hair fell nearly to her waist, a glossy curtain that stood out even against her classic black dress. Both she and Gideon were in profile so I couldn't see her eyes, but I knew they were a gorgeous aquamarine hue. She was a beautiful woman and together, they made a stunning couple. Especially right then, with both of them dressed in black, the only spot of color being Gideon's blue tie. My favorite one.

Abruptly, Gideon's head turned and found me, as if he'd felt me watching him. The instant our gazes met, I felt that soul-deep recognition pierce through me, that primitive awareness I'd only ever felt with him. Elementally, something inside me knew he was *mine*. Had known it from the moment I first laid eyes on him.

And some other woman had her hands on him.

My brows rose in a silent *WTF?* At that moment, Corinne followed his gaze. She didn't look happy to see me paused in the middle of the massive lobby, staring at them.

She was lucky I didn't go up to her and yank her away from him by her hair.

Then she cupped his jaw, urged his attention back to her, and lifted onto her tiptoes to press a kiss against his hard mouth, and I really considered doing it. Even took a step toward them.

Gideon's head jerked back just before she accomplished her goal, his hands catching her by the arms and thrusting her away.

Reining in my temper, I exhaled my irritation and left him to it. I can't say I didn't feel jealous, because of course I did—Corinne could be with him publicly and I couldn't. But I didn't have the sick fear in my gut I'd felt before, the horrible insecurity that told me I was going to lose the man I loved more than anything.

It was weird not to feel that panic. There was still a little voice in my head cautioning me against being too confident, telling me it'd be better to be afraid, to guard myself from getting hurt. But for once, I was able to ignore it. After all Gideon and I had been through, all that we were still going through, all he'd done for me . . . it was harder to disbelieve than to believe.

Despite everything, we were stronger than we'd ever been.

I hopped on an elevator and headed up to work, my thoughts drifting to my parents. I was choosing to take it as a good sign that neither my mother nor Stanton had called to bitch about my dad. I crossed my fingers and hoped that when I got home we could all put Nathan behind us for good. I was so ready for that. Beyond ready to move on to the next phase of my life, whatever that might be.

The elevator car slowed to a stop on the tenth floor and the doors opened to the high-pitched whirring sound of power tools and the rhythmic banging of hammers. Directly ahead of the elevator, plastic sheeting hung from the ceiling. I hadn't realized any part of the Crossfire was under construction, and I peered around the people in front of me, trying to get a look.

"Anyone getting out?" the guy nearest the door asked, looking over his shoulder.

I straightened and shook my head, even though he hadn't been talking to me personally. No one else moved. We waited for the doors to close and shut out the construction noise.

But they didn't move, either.

When the guy began hitting the elevator buttons to no avail, I realized what was going on.

Gideon.

Smiling to myself, I said, "Excuse me, please."

The occupants of the car shifted to let me out and another guy stepped out with me. The doors closed behind us and the car continued on.

"What the hell?" the guy said, scowling as he turned and surveyed the other three elevators. He was a little taller than me, but not much, and wore dress slacks with a short-sleeved shirt and tie.

The ding announcing the arrival of another car was nearly drowned out by the construction noise. When the doors to that elevator opened, Gideon stepped out, looking suave and dashing and irritated.

I wanted to jump him, he looked so hot. Plus, I'll admit it totally turned me on when he went all alpha male on me.

I'd stop the world from spinning for you. Sometimes, it felt like he did.

Grumbling under his breath, the short-sleeved guy walked into Gideon's vacated elevator and left us.

Gideon's hand went to his hips, his jacket parting to reveal the sleekness of his suit. All three pieces were black with a subtle sheen that was unmistakably costly. His dress shirt was black and his cuff links were a familiar gold and onyx.

He was dressed as he'd been that very first day I'd met him. At the time, I'd wanted to climb up his scrumptious body and screw him senseless.

All these weeks later, that hadn't changed.

"Eva," he began in that toe-curlingly sexy voice of his. "It's not what you think. Corinne came by because I'm not taking her calls—"

I held up my hand to cut him off and glanced at his gift, my beautiful watch, on my other wrist. "I've got thirty minutes. I'd rather fuck you than talk about your ex, if you don't mind."

He stood silent and unmoving for a long minute, staring at me, trying to gauge my mood. I watched his brain and body switch gears, adjusting from aggravation to awareness. His gaze narrowed, his eyes darkened. A flush came to his cheekbones and his lips parted on a sharp breath. His weight shifted as his blood heated and his cock thickened, his sexuality stirring like a panther stretching after a lazy nap.

I could almost feel the sexual current crackle between us, sparking to life. I responded to it as I'd been trained to do, softening and quickening, my core clenching gently. Begging for him. The commotion around us only made me hornier, adding urgency to the beat of my heart.

Gideon reached into an inner pocket of his jacket and withdrew his phone. He speed-dialed, then lifted the phone to his ear, his eyes locked with mine. "I'm running thirty minutes late. If that won't work for Anderson, reschedule."

He hung up, casually dropping his phone back in his pocket.

"I'm so hot for you right now," I told him, my voice husky with want.

Reaching down, he adjusted himself, then approached me, his eyes smoldering. "Come on."

He set his hand at the small of my back in that way I loved so much, the pressure and warmth hitting a spot that sent tingles of anticipation through me. I looked up at him over my shoulder and saw the slight smile on his mouth, proof that he knew what that innocent touch was doing to me.

We pushed through plastic sheeting, leaving the bank of elevators behind us. In front of us was sunlight and cement and hanging sheeting everywhere I looked. Through the plastic I could see the watery, foggy shadows of workers. I heard music that was nearly drowned out by the din, and men shouting to each other.

Gideon led me through the plastic, knowing his way. His silence was spurring me on, the weight of expectation growing with every step we took. We reached a door and he opened it, urging me into a room that would be someone's corner office.

The city was spread out before me, the view of the modern urban jungle dotted with buildings that wore their history proudly. Steam billowed into the cloudless blue sky at irregular intervals, and the cars seemed to flow along the streets like tributaries.

I heard the door lock behind me and I turned to face Gideon, catching him shrugging out of his jacket. There was furniture in the room. A desk and chairs, and a seating area positioned in the corner. All of it was draped in tarps, the space still unfinished.

With methodical deliberation, he removed his vest, tie, and shirt. I watched him, obsessed with the masculine perfection of him. "We could be interrupted," he said. "Or overheard."

"Would that bother you?"

"Only if it bothers you." He approached me with his fly open and the waistband of his boxer briefs clearly visible in the gap.

"You're provoking me. You'd never risk us being interrupted."

"Not that I'd stop. I can't think of anything capable of stopping me once I'm inside you." He took my purse from my hand and dropped it into one of the chairs. "You've got too many clothes on."

Wrapping his arms around me, Gideon lowered the zipper at my back with practiced ease, his lips whispering across mine. "I'll try not to get you too messy."

"I like messy." I stepped out of my dress and was about to unhook my bra when he tossed me over his shoulder.

I squealed in surprise, smacking his taut ass with both of my hands. He spanked me hard enough to sting, then threw my dress aside so perfectly it landed directly across his jacket. He was walking across the room when his hand reached up and tugged my panties down below the curve of my butt.

He caught the edge of the tarp draped over the couch and threw it back, then sat me down, crouching in front of me. As he pulled my underwear past my strappy heels, he asked, "Everything okay, angel?"

"Yeah." I smiled and touched his cheek, knowing that question encompassed everything from my parents to my job. He always checked to see where my head was at before he took over my body. "Everything's good."

Gideon pulled my hips to the very edge of the sofa with my legs on either side of him, exposing my cleft to his gaze. "So tell me what's got this pretty cunt so greedy today."

"You."

"Excellent answer."

I pushed at his shoulder. "You're wearing the suit you wore when I met you. I wanted to fuck you so bad then, but I couldn't do anything about it. Now I can."

He pressed my thighs wide with gentle hands, his thumb stroking over my clit. My sex quivered as pleasure pulsed through me.

"And now *I* can," he murmured, his dark head lowering.

I grasped desperately at the cushion beneath me, my stomach tightening as his tongue licked leisurely through my slit. He rimmed the trembling opening to my sex, teasing me before his tongue sank into me. I arched violently, my back bowing while he tormented the tender flesh.

"Let me tell you how I imagined you that day," he purred, circling my clit with the tip of his tongue, his hands holding me down when I would've bucked into the caress. "Spread beneath me on black satin sheets, your hair fanned all around you, your eyes wild and hot from the feel of my cock pounding into your tight, silky cunt."

"God. Gideon," I moaned, seduced by the sight of him savoring me so intimately. It was a fantasy come true—the dark and dangerous sex god in the breathtaking suit, servicing me with that sculpted mouth made for driving women wild.

"I imagined your wrists pinned down by my hands," he went on roughly, "me forcing you to take it over and over. Your hard little nipples swollen from my mouth. Your lips red and wet from sucking my cock. The room filled with those sexy sounds you make . . . those helpless whimpers when you can't stop coming."

I whimpered then, biting my lip as he fluttered over my clit with the wicked lash of his tongue. I hooked one leg over his bare shoulder, the heat of his skin scorching the sensitive flesh at the back of my knee. "I want what you want."

His grin flashed. "I know."

He sucked me, drawing on the tight bundle of nerves. I climaxed with a breathless cry, my legs shaking with the rush of release.

I was still quivering with pleasure when he urged me back lengthwise on the couch, his big body looming over me, his cock thrusting upward from where he'd shoved his briefs down just enough to free it. I reached for him, wanting to feel him in my hands, but he caught my wrists and pinned my arms.

"I like you like this," he said darkly. "Held prisoner for my lust."

Gideon's eyes were intent on my face, his lips glistening from my climax, his chest heaving. I was mesmerized by the difference between the virile male about to take me like an animal and the civilized businessman who'd inspired my searing lust to begin with.

"I love you," I told him, panting as the broad head of his cock slid heavily through my swollen cleft. He pushed against me, parting the slick opening.

"Angel." With a groan, he buried his face in my throat and surged inside me, the thick length of his rigid penis tunneling deep. Gasping my name, he ground his hips against me, trying to get deeper, shoving and circling, screwing. "Christ, I need you."

The desperation in his voice took me by surprise. I wanted to touch him, but he held me down, his hips working restlessly. The feel of him inside me, so hot, the wide crest rubbing and massaging, was driving me out of my mind. I screwed him back, unable to stop, the two of us straining together.

His lips brushed against my temple. "When I saw you standing in the lobby just now, in your pretty yellow dress, you looked so bright and beautiful. So perfect."

My throat tightened. "Gideon."

"The sun was shining behind you, and I thought you couldn't possibly be real."

I struggled to get my hands free. "Let me touch you."

"I came after you because I couldn't stay away and when I found you, you wanted me." He held both my wrists in one hand and cupped my butt in the other, lifting me as he pulled out, then thrust deep.

I moaned, rippling around him, my sex sucking ravenously at his thickness. "Oh God, it's so good. You feel so good . . ."

"I want to come all over you, come inside you. I want you on your knees and on your back. And *you want me this way*."

"I need you this way."

"I push inside you and I can't take it." His mouth lowered to mine, sucking erotically. "I need you so much."

"Gideon. Let me touch you."

"I've captured an angel." His kiss was wild and wet, passionate. His lips slanted over mine, his tongue fucking deep and fast. "And I put my greedy hands all over you. I defile you. And you love it."

"I love *you*."

He stroked into me and I writhed, my thighs grasping his pumping hips. "Fuck me. Oh, Gideon. Fuck me hard."

Digging his knees in, he gave me what I begged for, powering into me. His cock plunged into me over and over, his groans and fevered words of lust gusting against my ear.

My core tightened, my clit throbbing with every impact of his pelvis against mine. His heavy sac smacked against the curve of my buttocks and the couch thumped against the bare concrete, inching forward as Gideon pounded into me, every muscle in his body flexing on his downstrokes.

The obscene sounds of furious sex drowned out the awareness of the workers only yards away. The race to climax drove us both, our bodies the outlet for the violence of our emotions.

"I'm going to come in your mouth," he growled, sweat sliding down his temple.

Just the thought of him finishing that way set me off. My sex spasmed in climax, clutching and grabbing at his driving cock, the endless pulses of orgasm radiating outward to my fingers and toes. And still he didn't stop, his hips circling and lunging, expertly pleasuring me until I sagged limp beneath him.

"Eva. *Now.*" He reared back and I followed, scrambling to my knees and sliding my mouth down his glistening erection.

At the first hint of suction, he was coming, spilling over my tongue in powerful bursts. I swallowed repeatedly, drinking him down, relishing the gruff sounds of satisfaction that rumbled from his chest.

His hands were in my hair, his head bowed over me, sweat glistening on his abs. My mouth slid up and down his cock, my cheeks hollowing on drawing pulls.

"Stop," he gasped, pulling me off. "You'll make me hard again."

He was still hard, but I didn't point that out.

Gideon cupped my face in his hands and kissed me, our flavors mingling. "Thank you."

"What are you thanking me for? You did all the work."

"There's no work involved in fucking you, angel." His slow smile was pure satiated male. "I'm grateful for the privilege."

I sank back onto my heels. "You're killing me. You can't be that gorgeous and sexy and say stuff like that. It's overload. It fries my brain. Sends me into a meltdown."

His smile widened and he kissed me again. "I know the feeling."

13

MAYBE IT WAS because I'd just gotten laid myself that I saw the signs on Megumi. Or maybe my sex radar, as Cary called it, wasn't on the fritz anymore. Whatever the reason, I knew my friend had slept with the guy she'd been planning on breaking up with and I could tell she wasn't happy about it.

"Is it on or off?" I asked leaning on the reception counter.

"Oh, I broke it off," she said glumly. "After I hit it with him again first. I figured it'd be liberating. Plus who knows how long my next dry spell will last."

"Are you second-guessing your decision to end it?"

"Not really. He just acted all hurt about it, like I'd used him for sex. Which I guess I did, but he's a no-strings-attached guy. I figured he wouldn't have a problem with a no-strings-attached nooner."

"So now your head's all fucked up." I gave her a sympathetic smile.

"Remember, this is the guy who hadn't called you since Friday. He got lunch with a beautiful girl and an orgasm, not a bad deal."

Her head canted to the side. "Yeah."

"Yeah."

Her mood visibly lifted. "Are you working out tonight, Eva?"

"I should, but my dad's in town and I'm playing it on his schedule. If we go, you're welcome to tag along, but I won't know until after work."

"I don't want to intrude."

"Is that an excuse I hear?"

Her grin was sheepish. "Maybe a little one."

"If you want, you can come home with me after work and meet him. If he wants to work out, you can borrow something of mine to wear. If not, we can come up with something else to do."

"I'd like that."

"Okay, then we're set." It would be good for both of us. It would give my dad another look at the normalcy in my life and it would keep Megumi from torturing herself over Michael. "We'll head out at five."

"You live here?" Megumi tipped her head back to look at my apartment building. "Nice."

Like the others on the tree-lined street, it had history and showed it off with the kinds of architectural detailing contemporary builders didn't use anymore. The building had been updated and now sheltered residents with a modern glass overhang above the entrance. The addition meshed surprisingly well with the façade.

"Come on," I said to her, smiling at Paul as he opened the door for us.

When we exited the elevator on my floor, I forced myself not to glance at Gideon's door. What would it be like to take a friend home to a place I shared with Gideon?

I wanted that. Wanted to build that with him.

I unlocked my apartment and took Megumi's purse when we stepped inside. "Make yourself at home. I'm just going to let my dad know we're here."

She stared wide-eyed at the open floor plan of the living room and kitchen. "This place is huge."

"We don't need all this room, really."

She grinned. "But who's going to complain?"

"Right."

I was turning toward the hallway leading to the guest room when my mom emerged from the hall leading to my bedroom and Cary's, which was on the opposite side of the living area. I came to a halt, startled to see her wearing my skirt and blouse. "Mom? What are you doing here?"

Her reddened eyes locked on a point somewhere around my waist, her skin pale enough to make her makeup look overdone. That was when I realized she was wearing my cosmetics, too. Although we'd been mistaken for sisters on occasion, my gray eyes and soft olive skin tone came from my dad and necessitated a different color palette than the pastels my mom used.

Queasiness spread through my stomach. "Mom?"

"I have to go." She wouldn't meet my gaze. "I hadn't realized it was so late."

"Why are you wearing my clothes?" I asked, even though I *knew*.

"I spilled something on my dress. I'll get these back to you." She rushed past me, coming to another abrupt stop when she saw Megumi.

I couldn't move; my feet felt rooted to the carpet. My hands fisted at my sides. I knew the walk of shame when I saw it. My chest tightened with anger and disappointment.

"Hi, Monica." Megumi came forward to give her a hug. "How are you?"

"Megumi. Hi." My mom clearly scrambled for more to say. "It's great to see you. I wish I could stay and hang out with you girls, but I really have to run."

"Is Clancy here?" I asked, not having paid attention to the other vehicles on the street when I'd arrived.

"No, I'll grab a cab." She still didn't look directly at me, even when she turned her head in my direction.

"Megumi, would you mind sharing a cab with my mom? I'm sorry to flake on you, but I'm suddenly not feeling well."

"Oh, sure." She searched my face and I could see her picking up on my change of mood. "No problem."

My mom looked at me then and I couldn't think of a thing to say to her. I was almost as disgusted by the look of guilt on her face as I was by the thought of her cheating on Stanton. If she was going to do it, she could at least own it.

My dad chose that moment to join us. He walked into the room dressed in jeans and a T-shirt, with bare feet and hair still damp from a shower.

As always, my luck was impeccably bad.

"Dad, this is my friend Megumi. Megumi, this is my dad, Victor Reyes."

As my dad walked to Megumi and shook her hand, my parents gave each other a wide berth. The precaution did nothing to stop the electricity arcing between them.

"I'd thought maybe we could hang out," I told him to fill the sudden awkward silence, "but now I'm not feeling up to it."

"I have to go," my mom said again, grabbing her purse. "Megumi, did you want to ride with me?"

"Yes, please." My friend hugged me good-bye. "I'll call you later and see how you're feeling."

"Thanks." I caught her hand and squeezed it before she pulled away.

The moment the door shut behind them, I headed to my room.

My dad came after me. "Eva, wait."

"I don't want to talk to you right now."

"Don't be childish about this."

"Excuse me?" I rounded on him. "My stepdad pays for this apartment. He wanted me to have a place with great security so I'd be safe from Nathan. Were you thinking about that when you were fucking his wife?"

"Watch your mouth. You're still my daughter."

"You're right. And you know what?" I backed up toward the hallway. "I've never been ashamed about that until now."

I lay on my bed and stared up the ceiling, wishing I could be with Gideon, but knowing he was in therapy with Dr. Petersen.

I texted Cary instead: I need u. Come home ASAP.

It was close to seven when the knock came on my bedroom door. "Baby girl? It's me. Let me in."

I rushed to open it and surged into him, hugging him tight. He picked me up so that my feet left the floor and carried me into the room, kicking the door shut behind him.

He dropped me on the bed and took a seat beside me, his arm around my shoulders. He smelled good, his cologne familiar. I leaned into him, grateful for his unconditional friendship.

After a few minutes, I told him. "My parents slept with each other."

"Yeah, I know."

I tilted my head back to look up at him.

He grimaced. "I heard 'em when I was heading out to the shoot this afternoon."

"Eww." My stomach churned.

"Yeah, doesn't work for me, either," he muttered. His fingers sifted through my hair. "Your dad's on the couch looking beat. Did you say something to him?"

"Unfortunately. I was mean, and now I'm feeling awful about it. I need to talk to him but it's weird, because the person I'm feeling most loyal to is Stanton. I don't even like the guy half the time."

"He's been good to you, and to your mom. And getting cheated on is never cool."

I groaned. "I'd be less freaked about it if they'd gone somewhere else. I mean, it'd still be wrong, but these are Stanton's digs. That makes it worse."

"It does," he agreed.

"How would you feel about moving?"

His brows rose. "Because your parents shagged here?"

"No." I stood and started pacing. "Security was the reason we got this place. It made sense to let Stanton help out when Nathan was a threat and safety was a priority, but now . . ." I looked at him. "It's all different now. It doesn't seem right anymore."

"Move where? Someplace else in New York we can afford on our own? Or out of New York altogether?"

"I don't want to leave New York," I assured him. "Your work is here. Mine, too."

And Gideon.

Cary shrugged. "Sure. Whatever. I'm game."

Walking over to where he still sat on my bed, I hugged him. "Would you mind ordering something in for dinner while I talk to my dad?"

"Got anything particular in mind?"

"Nope. Surprise me."

I joined my dad on the couch. He'd been surfing through my tablet but put it aside when I sat.

"I'm sorry about what I said earlier," I began. "I didn't mean it."

"Yeah, you did." He scrubbed wearily at the back of his neck. "And I don't blame you. I'm not proud of myself right now. And I have no excuse. I knew better. She knew better."

Pulling my legs up, I sat facing him with my shoulder resting against the back of the sofa. "You guys have a lot of chemistry. I know what that's like."

He shot me an examining glance, his gray eyes stormy and serious. "You have that with Cross. I saw it when he came over for dinner. Are you going to try to work things out with him?"

"I'd like to. Would you have a problem with that?"

"Does he love you?"

"Yes." My mouth curved. "But more than that, I'm . . . necessary to him. There's nothing he wouldn't do for me."

"So why aren't you together?"

"Well . . . it's complicated."

"Isn't it always?" he said ruefully. "Listen. You should know . . . I've loved your mother since the moment I saw her. What happened today shouldn't have happened, but it meant something to me."

"I get it." I reached for his hand. "So what happens now?"

"I head home tomorrow. Try to get my head on straight."

"Cary and I were talking about coming out to San Diego the weekend after next. We thought we'd drop in and just hang out. See you and Dr. Travis."

"Did you talk to Travis about what happened to you?"

"Yes. You saved my life hooking me up with him," I said honestly. "I can't thank you enough for that. Mom had been sending me to all these stuffy shrinks and I just couldn't connect with any of them. I felt like a case study. Dr. Travis made me feel like I was normal. Plus I met Cary."

"Are you two done talking about me?" As if on cue, Cary walked into the room waving a take-out menu. "I know I'm fascinating, but you might want to save your jaws for the Thai food we've got coming. I ordered a ton of it."

My dad caught an eleven o'clock flight out of New York, so I had to leave it to Cary to see him off. We said our good-byes before I left for work, promising to make plans for the trip to San Diego the next time we talked.

I was in the back of a cab on the way to work when Brett called. For just a moment, I debated letting the call go to voice mail, and then I got over it and answered. "Hi, you."

"Hello, gorgeous." His voice rolled over my senses like warm chocolate. "Ready for tomorrow?"

"I will be. What time is the video launch? When do we need to be in Times Square?"

"We're supposed to arrive at six."

"Okay. I don't know what to wear."

"You'll look amazing no matter what you've got on."

"Let's hope. How's the tour going?"

"I'm having the time of my life." He laughed, and the husky, sexy sound brought back memories. "It's a helluva long way from Pete's."

"Ah, Pete's." I'd never forget that bar, although some of the nights I'd spent there were a bit hazy. "Are you excited about tomorrow?"

"Yeah, I get to see you. I can't wait."

"That's not what I meant, and you know it."

"I'm excited about the video launch, too." He laughed again. "I wish I could see you tonight, but I'm taking a red-eye into JFK. Plan on dinner tomorrow, though."

"Can Cary come? I invited him to the video launch already. You two know each other, so I figured you wouldn't mind. Too much, anyway."

He snorted. "You don't need a cockblocker, Eva. I can restrain myself."

The cab pulled over in front of the Crossfire and the driver stopped the meter. I pushed cash through the Plexiglas slot and slid out, leaving the door open for the guy rushing over to hop in. "I thought you liked Cary."

"I do, but not as much as I like having you to myself. How about we compromise and agree that Cary comes to the launch and you come to dinner alone?"

"All right." I figured it wouldn't hurt to make the situation easier for Gideon to deal with by picking a restaurant he owned. "How about I make the reservation?"

"Awesome."

"I've got to run. I'm just getting to work."

"Text me your address, so I know where to pick you up."

"Will do." I spun through the revolving door and headed toward the turnstiles. "We'll talk tomorrow."

"I'm looking forward to it. See you around five."

Tucking my phone away, I entered the nearest open elevator. When I got upstairs and was buzzed through the glass security doors, I was greeted by Megumi's phone thrust in my face.

"Can you believe this?" she asked.

I pulled back enough to bring the screen into focus. "Three missed calls from Michael."

"I *hate* guys like him," she complained. "Hot and cold and all over the place. They want you until they have you, then they want something else."

"So tell him that."

"Really?"

"Straight up. You could just avoid his calls, but that'll drive you crazy. Don't agree to meet with him, though. Having sex with him again would be bad."

"Right." Megumi nodded. "Sex is bad, even when it's really good."

Laughing, I headed back to my cubicle. I had other things to do besides referee someone else's love life. Mark was juggling several accounts at once, with three campaigns rolling into the final stages. Creatives were at work and mock-ups were slowly making their way across his desk. That was my favorite part—seeing all the strategizing come together.

By ten o'clock, Mark and I were deep into debating the various approaches to a divorce attorney's ad campaign. We were trying to find the right mix of sympathy for a difficult time in a person's life and the most prized qualities of a lawyer—the ability to be cunning and ruthless.

"I'm never going to need one of these," he said, somewhat out of the blue.

"No," I replied, once my brain caught up to the fact that he was talking about divorce attorneys. "You never will. I'm dying to congratulate Steven at lunch. I'm really so thrilled for you two."

Mark's grin exposed his slightly crooked teeth, which I thought were cute. "I've never been happier."

It was nearing eleven and we'd switched to a guitar manufacturer's campaign when my desk phone rang. I ran out to my cubicle to grab it and had my usual greeting cut off by a squeal.

"Oh my God, Eva! I just found out we're both going to be at that Six-Ninths thing tomorrow!"

"Ireland?"

"Who else?" Gideon's sister was so excited, she sounded younger than her seventeen years. "I *love* Six-Ninths. Brett Kline is so freakin' hot. So is Darrin Rumsfeld. He's the drummer. He's fine as hell."

I laughed. "Do you happen to like their music, too?"

"Pfft. That's a given. Listen"—her voice turned serious—"I think you should try talking to Gideon tomorrow. You know, just kinda walk by and say hi. If you open the door, he'll totally barge through it, I swear. He misses you like crazy."

Leaning back in my chair, I played along. "You think so?"

"It's so obvious."

"Really? How?"

"I don't know. Like how his voice changes when he talks about you. I can't explain it, but I'm telling you, he's dying to get you back. You're the one who told him to bring me along tomorrow, didn't you?"

"Not precisely—"

"Ha! I knew it. He always does what you tell him." She laughed. "Thanks, by the way."

"Thank him. I'm just looking forward to seeing you again."

Ireland was the one person in Gideon's family for whom he felt untarnished affection, although he tried hard not to show it. I thought maybe he was afraid to be disappointed or afraid he might ruin it somehow. I wasn't sure what the deal was, but Ireland hero-worshipped her brother and he'd kept his distance, even though he needed love terribly.

"Promise me you'll try to talk to him," she pressed. "You still love him, right?"

"More than ever," I said fervently.

She was quiet for a minute, then said, "He's changed since he met you."

"I think so. I've changed, too." I straightened when Mark stepped out of his office. "I have to get back to work, but we'll catch up tomorrow. And make plans for that girls' day we talked about."

"Sweet. Catch you later!"

I hung up, pleased that Gideon had followed through and made plans with Ireland. We were making progress, both together and on our own.

"Baby steps," I whispered. Then I got back to work.

AT noon, Mark and I headed out to meet Steven at a French bistro. Once we entered the restaurant, it was easy to spot Mark's partner, even with the size of the place and the number of diners.

Steven Ellison was a big guy—tall, broad shouldered, and heavily muscled. He owned his own construction business and preferred to be working the job sites with his crew. But it was his gloriously red hair that really drew the eye. His sister Shawna had the same hair—and the same fun-loving nature.

"Hey, you!" I greeted him with a kiss on the cheek, able to be more familiar with him than I was with my boss. "Congratulations."

"Thank you, darlin'. Mark is finally going to make an honest man out of me."

"It'd take more than marriage to do that," Mark shot back, pulling out my chair for me.

"When haven't I been honest with you?" Steven protested.

"Um, let's see." Mark got me settled in my seat, then took the one beside me. "How about when you swore marriage wasn't for you."

"Ah, I never said it wasn't for *me*." Steven winked at me, his blue eyes full of mischief. "Just that it wasn't for most people."

"He was really twisted up over asking you," I told him. "I felt bad for the guy."

"Yeah." Mark flipped through the menu. "She's my witness to your cruel and unusual punishment."

"Feel bad for me," Steven retorted. "I wooed him with wine, roses, and violin players. I spent days practicing my proposal. I still got shot down."

He rolled his eyes, but I could tell there was a wound there that hadn't quite healed. When Mark placed his hand over his partner's and squeezed, I knew I was right.

"So how'd he do it?" I asked, even though Mark had told me.

The waitress, asking if we wanted water, interrupted us. We held her back a minute and ordered our food, too, and then Steven started relaying their anniversary night out.

"He was sweating like mad," he went on. "Wiping at his face every other minute."

"It's summer," Mark muttered.

"And restaurants and theaters are climate controlled," Steven shot back. "We went through the whole night with him like that and finally headed home. I got to thinking he wasn't going to do it. That the night was gonna end and he still wasn't going to get the damn words out. And there I am wondering if I'll have to ask him again, just to get it over with. And if he says no again—"

"I didn't say no the first time," Mark interjected.

"—I'm going to deck him. Just knock his ass out, toss him on a plane, and head to Vegas, because I'm not getting any younger here."

"Definitely not mellowing with age, either," Mark grumbled.

Steven gave him a look. "So we're climbing out of the limo, and I'm trying to remember that fan-fucking-tastic proposal I came up with before, and he grabs my elbow and blurts out, 'Steve, damn it. You *have* to marry me.' "

I laughed, leaning back as the waitress put my side salad in front of me. "Just like that."

"Just like that," Steven said, with an emphatic nod.

"Very heartfelt." I gave Mark a thumbs-up. "You rocked it."

"See?" Mark said. "I got it done."

"Are you writing your own vows?" I asked. "Because that'll be really interesting."

Steven guffawed, snagging the attention of everyone nearby.

I swallowed the cherry tomato I was munching on and said, "You know I'm dying to see your wedding binder, right?"

"Well, it just so happens . . ."

"You didn't." Mark shook his head as Steven reached down and pulled a bulging binder out of a messenger bag on the floor by his chair.

It was so packed that papers were sticking out of the top, bottom, and side.

"Wait 'til you see this cake I found." Steven pushed the breadbasket aside to make room to open the binder.

I bit back a grin when I saw the dividers and table of contents.

"We are *not* having a wedding cake in the shape of a skyscraper with cranes and billboards," Mark said firmly.

"Really?" I asked, intrigued. "Let me see."

When I got home that night, I dropped my purse and bag off in their usual place, kicked off my shoes, and went straight to the couch. I sprawled across it, staring up the ceiling. Megumi was going to meet me at CrossTrainer at six thirty, so I didn't have a lot of time, but I felt like I just needed a breather. Starting my period the afternoon before had me riding the edge of irritation and grumpiness, with a dash of exhaustion tossed in for shits and giggles.

I sighed, knowing I was going to have to deal with my mom at some point. We had a ton of crap to work through, and putting it off was starting to bug me. I wished it were as easy to work things out with her as it was with my dad, but that wasn't an excuse to avoid addressing our issues. She was my mother and I loved her. It was hard on me when we weren't getting along.

Then my thoughts drifted to Corinne. I guess I should have figured that a woman who would leave her husband and move from Paris to New York for a man wasn't going to give up on him easily, but still. She had to know Gideon well enough to realize hounding him wasn't going to work.

And Brett . . . what was I going to do about him?

The intercom buzzed. Frowning, I pushed to my feet and headed over to it. Had Megumi misunderstood and thought we were meeting here? Not that I minded, but . . .

"Yes?"

"Hi, Eva," the guy at the front desk said cheerfully. "NYPD detectives Michna and Graves are here."

Crap. Everything else lost significance in that moment. Fear spread through me with crawling fingers of ice.

I wanted a lawyer with me. Too much was on the line.

But I didn't want to seem like I had anything to hide.

I had to swallow twice before I could answer. "Thanks. Can you send them up, please?"

14

MY HEART WAS pounding as I hurried to my purse and silenced the burner phone, tucking it into a zippered pocket. I turned around, looking for anything that might be out of place, anything I should hide. There were the flowers in my bedroom and the card.

Unless the detectives had a warrant, though, they could only take note of what was in plain sight.

I ran to shut my door, then went ahead and shut Cary's, too. I was breathing hard when the doorbell rang. I had to force myself to slow down and walk calmly to the living room. When I reached the front door, I took a deep, calming breath before opening it.

"Hello, detectives."

Graves, a rail-thin woman with a severe face and foxlike blue eyes, was in the lead. Her partner, Michna, was the quieter of the two, an older man with receding gray hair and a paunch. They had a rhythm between the two of them—Graves was the heavy who kept the subjects occupied and off-balance. Michna was obviously good at fading into the background while his cop's eyes cataloged everything and missed nothing. Their success rate had to be pretty high.

"Can we come in, Miss Tramell?" Graves asked in a tone that made the question a demand. She'd tied her curly brown hair back and wore a jacket to cover her holstered gun. There was a satchel in her hand.

"Sure." I pulled the door open wider. "Can I get you anything? Coffee? Water?"

"Water would be great," Michna said.

I led them to the kitchen and pulled bottled water out of the fridge. The detectives waited at the breakfast bar—Graves with her eyes pinned to me while Michna scoped out his surroundings.

"You just get home from work?" he asked.

I figured they knew the answer, but replied anyway. "A few minutes ago. Would you like to sit in the living room?"

"Here's good," Graves said in her no-nonsense way, putting the worn leather satchel on the counter. "We'd just like to ask you a few questions, if you don't mind. And show you some photos."

I stilled. Could I bear to see any of the photos Nathan had taken of me? For a wild moment, I thought they might be pictures taken at the death scene or even autopsy shots. But I knew that was highly unlikely. "What's this about?"

"Some new information has come to light that could be related to Nathan Barker's death," Michna said. "We're pursuing all leads, and you may be able to help."

I took a deep, shaky breath. "I'm happy to try, of course. But I don't see how I can."

"Are you familiar with Andrei Yedemsky?" Graves asked.

I frowned at her. "No. Who's that?"

She dug in her bag and pulled out a sheaf of eight-by-ten photos, setting them down in front of me. "This man. Have you seen him before?"

Reaching out with shaking fingers, I pulled the top photo toward me. It was of a man in a trench coat, talking to another man about to climb into the back of a waiting town car. He was attractive, with extremely blond hair and tanned skin. "No. He's not someone you'd forget meeting, either." I looked up at her. "Should I know him?"

"He had pictures of you in his home. Candid shots of you on the street, coming and going. Barker had the same photos."

"I don't understand. How did he get them?"

"Presumably from Barker," Michna said.

"Is that what this Yedemsky guy said? Why would Nathan give him pictures of me?"

"Yedemsky didn't say anything," Graves said. "He's dead. Murdered."

I felt a headache coming on. "I don't understand. I don't know anything about this man, and I have no idea why he'd know anything about me."

"Andrei Yedemsky is a known member of the Russian mob," Michna explained. "In addition to smuggling alcohol and assault weapons, they've also been suspected of trafficking women. It's possible Barker was making arrangements to sell or trade you for that purpose."

I backed away from the counter, shaking my head, unable to process what they were saying. Nathan stalking me was something I could believe. He'd hated me on sight, hated that his father had remarried instead of mourning his mother forever. He'd hated me for getting him locked up in psychiatric treatment, and my being awarded the five-million-dollar settlement he thought of as his inheritance. But the Russian mob? Sex trafficking? I couldn't comprehend that at all.

Graves flipped through the photos until she came to one of a platinum sapphire bracelet. An L-square ruler framed it—unmistakably a forensics shot. "Do you recognize this?"

"Yes. That belonged to Nathan's mother. He had it altered to fit him. He never went anywhere without it."

"Yedemsky was wearing it when he died," she said without inflection. "Possibly as a souvenir."

"Of what?"

"Of Barker's murder."

I stared at Graves, who knew better. "You're suggesting Yedemsky could be responsible for Nathan's death? Then who killed Yedemsky?"

She held my gaze, understanding the motivation behind my question. "He was taken out by his own people."

"You're sure about that?" I needed to know that *they* knew Gideon wasn't involved. Yes, he'd killed for me—to protect me—but he'd never kill just to avoid going to jail.

Michna frowned at my query. It was Graves who replied. "There's no doubt. We have the hit on surveillance footage. One of his associates didn't take too kindly to Yedemsky sleeping with his underage daughter."

Hope surged, followed by chilling fear. "So what happens now? What does this mean?"

"Do you know anyone who has connections to the Russian mob?" Michna asked.

"God, no," I said vehemently. "That's . . . another world. I'm having trouble believing Nathan had any connections. But then it's been years since I knew him . . ."

I rubbed at the tightness in my chest and looked at Graves. "I want to put this behind me. I want him to stop ruining my life. Is that ever going to happen? Is he going to haunt me even after he's dead?"

She quickly and efficiently collected the photos, her face impassive. "We've done all we can. Where you go from here is up to you."

I showed up at CrossTrainer at quarter after six. I went because I'd told Megumi I would and I'd already flaked on her once. I also felt a tremendous restlessness, an urge to move that I had to exhaust before it drove me insane. I'd sent a text to Gideon as soon as the detectives left, telling him I needed to see him later, but I hadn't heard back by the time I'd put my purse in a locker.

Like all things Gideon, CrossTrainer was impressive in both size and amenities. The three-story club—one of hundreds around the country—had everything a fitness enthusiast could want, as well as spa services and a smoothie bar.

Megumi was slightly overwhelmed and needed help with some of the high-tech machinery, so she was taking advantage of the trainer-supervised workout for new members and guests. I got on a treadmill. I started out at a brisk walk, warming up, and then eventually progressed to a run. Once I hit my stride, I let my thoughts run, too.

Was it possible that Gideon and I were free to pick up the pieces of our lives and move on? How? Why? My mind raced with questions that I needed to ask Gideon—with the hope that he was as clueless as I was. He couldn't be involved in Yedemsky's death. I wouldn't believe he was.

I ran until my thighs and calves burned, until sweat ran down my body in steady streams and my lungs ached with the effort of breathing.

It was Megumi who finally got me to stop, waving her hand in my line of sight as she moved in front of my treadmill. "I am so totally impressed right now. You're a machine."

I slowed my pace to a jog, then a walk, before stopping altogether. Grabbing my towel and water bottle, I stepped off, feeling the effects of pushing myself too long and hard.

"I hate running," I confessed, still panting. "How'd your workout go?"

Megumi looked chic even in gym clothes. Her chartreuse racerback tank had bright blue threading that matched her spandex leggings. The ensemble was summer-bright and stylish.

She bumped shoulders with me. "You make me feel like an underachiever. I just did a circuit and checked out the hot guys. The trainer I worked with was good, but I wish I'd gotten *that* guy instead."

I followed the point of her finger. "That's Daniel. Want to meet him?"

"Yes!"

I walked with her toward the mats in the center of the open space, waving at Daniel when he lifted his gaze and caught sight of us. Megumi quickly yanked out the rubber band holding her hair back, but I thought she'd looked great with it on, too. She had beautiful skin and I envied her mouth.

"Eva, great seeing you." Daniel extended his hand to me for a shake. "Who's this you have with you?"

"My friend Megumi. She just joined today."

"I saw you working with Tara." He flashed Megumi his megawatt smile. "I'm Daniel. If you ever need help with anything, just let me know."

"I'm going to take you up on that," she warned, as she shook his hand.

"Please do. Do you have any particular fitness goals?"

As they started talking more in-depth, my gaze wandered. I checked out the equipment, looking for something easy I could do while I waited for them to wrap it up. Instead I found a familiar sight.

Tossing my towel over my shoulder, I noticed my not-so-favorite reporter on the floor. I took a deep breath and walked over, watching her do curls with a ten-pound hand weight. Her dark brown hair was in a fishtail braid, her long legs on display in skintight shorts, and her stomach tight and flat. She looked great. "Hi, Deanna."

"I'd ask if you come here often," she replied, setting the weight back on the rack and standing, "but that's too clichéd. How are you, Eva?"

"I'm good. You?"

Her smile had the edge that never failed to get my back up. "Doesn't it bother you that Gideon Cross buries his sins under all his money?"

So Gideon had been right about Ian Hager disappearing once he'd gotten paid. "If I really thought you were after the truth, I'd give it to you."

"It's all true, Eva. I've talked to Corinne Giroux."

"Oh? How's her husband?"

Deanna laughed. "Gideon should hire you to manage his public image."

That struck uncomfortably close to home. "Why don't you just go to his office and chew him out? Let him have it. Throw a drink in his face or slap him."

"He wouldn't care. It wouldn't make a damn bit of difference to him."

I wiped at the sweat still sliding down my temples and admitted that might be true. I knew damn well Gideon could be a coldhearted ass. "Either way, you'd probably feel a whole lot better."

Deanna snatched her towel off the bench. "I know exactly what'll make me feel better. Enjoy the rest of your workout, Eva. I'm sure we'll be talking again soon."

She sauntered off and I couldn't shake the feeling that she was on to something. It made me twitchy not knowing what it was.

"Okay, I'm done," Megumi said, joining me. "Who was that?"

"No one important." My stomach chose that moment to growl, loudly announcing that I'd burned off the boeuf bourguignon I'd had for lunch.

"Working out always makes me hungry, too. You want to grab dinner?"

"Sure." We set off toward the showers, skirting equipment and other members. "I'll call Cary and see if he wants to join us."

"Oh, yes." She licked her lips. "Have I told you I think he's delicious?"

"More than once." I waved bye to Daniel before we left the floor.

We reached the locker room and Megumi tossed her towel in the discard bin just inside the entrance. I paused before dropping mine, my thumb rubbing over the embroidered CrossTrainer logo. I thought of the towels hanging in Gideon's bathroom.

Maybe next time I'd be calling him, too, asking him to join friends and me for dinner.

Maybe the worst was over.

WE found an Indian restaurant near the gym and Cary showed up for dinner with Trey, the two of them walking in with their hands linked together. Our table was right in front of the street-level window by the entrance, which lent the pulse of the city to our dining experience.

We sat on cushions on the floor, drank a little too much wine, and let Cary run commentary on the people passing by. I could almost see little hearts in Trey's eyes when he looked at my best friend, and I was happy to see Cary being openly affectionate in return. When Cary was really into someone, he held himself back from touching him or her. I deliberately chose to see his frequent, casual touching with Trey as a sign of the two men growing closer, rather than Cary losing interest.

Megumi got another call from Michael while we were eating, which she ignored. When Cary asked if she was playing hard to get, she told him the story.

"If he calls again, let me answer it," he said.

"Oh, God, no," I groaned.

"What?" Cary blinked innocently. "I can say she's too tied up to get to the phone and Trey can bark out sex commands in the background."

"Diabolical!" Megumi rubbed her hands together. "Michael's not the right guy for that, but I'm sure I'll take you up on that offer someday, knowing my luck with men."

Shaking my head, I dug stealthily into my purse for the burner phone and was bummed to see there was still no reply from Gideon.

Cary made a show of peering over the table. "You hoping for a booty call from loverman?"

"What?" Megumi's mouth fell open. "You're seeing someone and didn't tell me?"

I shot a narrow-eyed look at Cary. "It's complicated."

"It's the total opposite of complicated," Cary drawled, rocking back on his pillow. "It's straight-up lust."

"What about Cross?" she asked.

"Who?" Cary shot back.

Megumi persisted. "He wants her back."

It was Cary's turn to glare at me. "When did you talk to him?"

I shook my head. "He called Mom. And he didn't say he wanted me back."

Cary's smile was sly. "Would you ditch your new loverman for a repeat with Cross, the marathon man?"

Megumi poked me in the leg. "Gideon Cross is a marathon man in bed? Holy shit . . . And he looks like that. Jesus." She fanned herself with her hand.

"Can we *please* stop talking about my sex life?" I muttered, looking to Trey for a little support.

He jumped in. "Cary tells me you two are going to a video premiere tomorrow. I didn't realize music videos were a big thing anymore."

I grasped at the lifeline gratefully. "I know, right? Surprises me, too."

"And then there's good ol' Brett," Cary said, leaning across the table toward Megumi like he was about to impart a secret. "We'll call him backstage man. Or backseat man."

I stuck my fingers in my glass and flicked water at him.

"Why, Eva. You're making me wet."

"Keep it up," I warned," and you'll be soaked."

I still hadn't heard from Gideon by the time we got home at quarter to ten. Megumi had taken the subway back to her place, while Cary, Trey, and I shared a cab back to the apartment. The guys headed straight to

Cary's room, but I lingered in the kitchen, debating whether I should run next door and see if Gideon was there.

I was about to pull my keys out of my purse when Cary came into the kitchen, shirtless and barefoot.

He grabbed whipped cream out of the fridge but paused before he headed back out. "You okay?"

"Yep, I'm good."

"You talk to your mom yet?"

"No, but I'm planning on it."

He leaned his hip against the counter. "Anything else on your mind?"

I shooed him off. "Go have fun. I'm all right. We can talk tomorrow."

"About that. What time should I be ready?"

"Brett wants to pick us up at five, so can you meet me at the Crossfire?"

"No problem." He leaned over and pressed a kiss to the top of my head. "Sweet dreams, baby girl."

I waited until I heard Cary's door shut, then grabbed my keys and went next door. The moment I entered the dark and quiet apartment, I knew Gideon wasn't there, but I searched the rooms anyway. I couldn't shake the feeling that something was . . . off.

Where was he?

Deciding to call Angus, I walked back to my apartment, grabbed the burner phone, and took it into my bedroom.

And found Gideon gripped in a nightmare.

Startled, I shoved my door shut and locked it. He thrashed on my bed, his back arching with a hiss of pain. He was still dressed in jeans and a T-shirt, his big body stretched atop the comforter as if he'd fallen asleep waiting for me. His laptop had been knocked to the floor, still open, and papers were crackling under the violence of his movements.

I rushed to him, trying to figure out a way to wake him that wouldn't put me in danger, knowing he'd hate himself if he hurt me by accident.

He growled, a low feral sound of aggression. "Never," he bit out. "You'll *never* touch her again."

I froze.

His body jerked violently, and then he moaned and curled to his side, shuddering.

The sound of his pain galvanized me. I climbed onto the bed, my hand touching his shoulder. The next moment I was on my back, pinned as he loomed over me, his eyes fixed and sightless. Fear paralyzed me.

"You're going to know what it feels like," he whispered darkly, his hips ramming against mine in a sick imitation of the love we shared.

I turned my head and bit his biceps, my teeth barely denting the rigid muscle.

"Fuck!" He yanked away from me and I dislodged him as Parker had taught me to do, throwing him to the side and freeing myself to leap from the bed and run.

"Eva!"

Spinning, I faced him, my body poised to fight.

He slid from the bed, nearly landing on his knees before he found his balance and straightened. "I'm sorry. I fell asleep . . . Christ, I'm sorry."

"I'm fine," I said, with forced calm. "Relax."

He raked a hand through his hair, his chest heaving. His face was sheened with sweat, his eyes reddened. "God."

I stepped closer, fighting the lingering fear. This was part of our lives. We both had to face it. "Do you remember the dream?"

Gideon swallowed hard and shook his head.

"I don't believe you."

"Damn it. You have to—"

"You were dreaming about Nathan. How often do you do that?" I reached him and took his hand.

"I don't know."

"Don't lie to me."

"I'm not!" he snapped, bristling. "I rarely remember my dreams."

I pulled him toward the bathroom, deliberately keeping him moving forward both physically and mentally. "The detectives came to see me today."

"I know."

The hoarseness of his voice concerned me. How long had he been asleep and dreaming? The thought of him tormented by his own mind, alone and in pain, wounded me. "Did they visit you, too?"

"No. But they've been making inquiries."

I flicked the lights on and he stopped, his grip tightening to make me stop, too. "Eva."

"Hop in the shower, ace. We'll talk when you're done."

He cupped my face in his hands, his thumbs brushing over my cheekbone. "You're moving too fast. Slow down."

"I don't want to get hung up every time you have a nightmare."

"Take a minute," he murmured, lowering his forehead to rest against mine. "I frightened you. *I'm* frightened. Let's just take a minute and deal with that."

I softened, my hand coming up to rest over his racing heart.

He buried his nose in my hair. "Let me smell you, angel. Feel you. Say I'm sorry."

"I'm okay."

"It's not okay," he argued, his voice still low and coaxing. "I should've waited for you at our place."

I rested my cheek against his chest, loving the idea of "our" place. "I've been checking my phone all night, waiting for a text or message."

"I worked late." His hands slid under my shirt, brushing over the bare skin of my back. "Then I came here. I wanted to surprise you . . . make love to you . . ."

"I think we might be free," I whispered, clutching at his shirt. "The detectives . . . I think we're going to be okay."

"Explain."

"Nathan had this bracelet he always wore—"

"Sapphires. Very feminine."

I looked up at him. "Yes."

"Go on."

"They found it on the arm of a dead mob guy. Russian Mafia. They're running with the theory that it was a criminal association gone bad."

Gideon stood very still, his gaze narrowed. "That's interesting."

"It's *weird*. They were talking about photos of me and sex trafficking, which just doesn't mesh with—"

His fingers pressed against my lips, quieting me. "It's interesting because Nathan was wearing that bracelet when I left him."

I watched Gideon take a shower while I brushed my teeth. His soapy hands slid over his body with economical indifference, his movements brisk and rough. There was none of the intimate worship I caressed him with, none of the awe or love. He was done in minutes, stepping out of the shower in all his nude glory before grabbing a towel and scrubbing away the water on his skin.

He came up behind me when he was done, gripping my hips and pressing a kiss to my nape. "I don't have any underworld ties," he murmured.

I finished rinsing my mouth and looked at him through the mirror. "Does it bother you to have to say that to me?"

"I'd rather say it than have you ask."

"Someone went to a lot of trouble to protect you." Turning, I faced him. "Could it be Angus?"

"No. Tell me how the mob guy died."

My fingertips drifted over the ridges of his abdomen, loving the way the muscles flexed and clenched in response to my touch. "One of his own took him out. Retaliation. He was under surveillance, so Graves said they've got proof of that."

"So it's someone connected, then. To either the mob or the authorities, or both. Whoever's responsible, they chose a fall guy who could take the blame and not pay for it."

"I don't care who arranged it, just so long as you're safe."

He kissed my forehead. "We need to care," he said softly. "To protect me, they have to know what I did."

15

SHORTLY AFTER FIVE in the morning, I went from unconscious to wide awake in a heartbeat. The remnants of a dream clung to me, one in which I'd still believed Gideon and I had broken up. Loneliness and grief weighed me down, pinning me to the bed for several minutes. I wished Gideon were beside me. I wished I could just roll over and press my body to his.

Partly due to my period, we hadn't had sex the night before. Instead, we had enjoyed the simple comfort of just being together. We'd curled up on my bed and watched television until the exhaustion of my overkill run on the treadmill pulled me under.

I loved those quiet moments when we just held each other. When the sexual attraction simmered just beneath the surface. I loved the feel of his breath on my skin and the way my curves fit into his hard planes as if we'd been designed for each other.

Sighing, I knew what had me on edge. It was Thursday and Brett was coming to New York, if he wasn't in the city already.

Gideon and I were just starting to find a new rhythm again, which made it the worst possible time for Brett to come back into my life. I was anxious about something going wrong, some gesture or look that would be misconstrued and cause fresh problems for Gideon and me to work through.

It'd be the first time Gideon and I would be out together in public since our "breakup." That was going to be torture. Standing next to Brett while my heart was with Gideon.

Sliding from bed, I went to the bathroom and cleaned up, and then pulled on a pair of shorts and a tank top. I needed to be with Gideon. We needed to spend some time together before the day started with a vengeance.

I moved quietly from my apartment to his, feeling slightly naughty as I ran down the corridor to his—*our*—front door.

Once I'd gone inside, I tossed my keys on the breakfast bar and headed down the hallway to the guest room. He wasn't there and my heart sank, but I kept searching, because I could *feel* him. There was a tingling awareness I experienced only when he was nearby.

I found him in the master bedroom, his arms wrapped around my pillow as he slept partially on his stomach. The sheet clung to his hips, leaving his powerful back and sculpted arms bare, and revealing just a hint of the topmost curve of his amazing ass.

He looked like an erotic fantasy come to life. And he was *mine.*

I loved him so much.

And I wanted him to wake up to me, at least once, with pleasure instead of fear, sadness, and regret.

I undressed quietly in the early light of dawn, my thoughts spinning with ways I could pleasure my man. I wanted to run my hands and mouth all over him, make him breathless and hot, feel his body quiver. I wanted to reaffirm our connection to each other, my whole and irrevocable commitment to him, before the harsh realities we faced came between us.

As my knee sank into the mattress, he stirred. I crawled to him, pressing my lips to the small of his back and working my way up slowly.

"Umm. Eva," he said in a husky voice, lightly stretching beneath me.

"You better hope it's me, ace." I nipped his shoulder blade. "This would turn out bad for you, if not."

I lowered onto him, laying my body over his. His warmth was divine and I took a moment to savor it.

"It's early for you," he murmured, resting easily, just as content as I was to be touching each other.

"Way," I agreed. "You're hugging my pillow."

"Smells like you. Helps me sleep."

I brushed his hair aside and pressed my lips to his throat. "That's a beautiful thing to say. I wish I could lie around like this with you for the entire day."

"You remember I want to take you away this weekend."

"Yes." I ran my hand over his biceps, my fingers gliding over the hard muscle. "I can't wait."

"We'll leave as soon as you get off work on Friday and fly back just in time for work Monday. You won't need anything but your passport."

"And you." I kissed his shoulder, then spoke in a nervous rush. "I want you and came prepared to have you, but it could be messy. I mean, it's the tail end, so maybe not, but if period sex isn't your thing—which I'd totally get, because it has *never* been my thing—"

"*You're* my thing, angel. I'll take you any way I can get you."

He flexed, warning me he was going to turn around. I slid to the side, watching his body roll with a fluid rippling of muscle.

"Sit up for me," I told him, thinking he was even more amazing than I'd given him credit for. Or more horny, which I would never hold against him. "With your back against the headboard."

He arranged himself to my liking, looking sleepy-eyed and sexy, his jaw shadowed with stubble. I climbed into his lap, straddling him. I took a long moment to savor the attraction between us, the delicious and provocative edge of danger he exuded even while at rest. Because Gideon wasn't tamed and never would be. Just like a panther still had its claws, even when they were sheathed.

That was one of my joys. He gentled for me but remained true to himself. He was still the man I'd fallen in love with—hard with rough edges—yet he'd changed, too. He was all things to me, everything I wanted and needed in one imperfect man.

Smoothing his hair back from his face, I traced the curve of his lower lip with the tip of my tongue. His hands, so warm and strong, gripped my hips. His mouth opened, his tongue touching mine.

"I love you," I whispered.

"Eva." Tilting his head, he took over the kiss, deepening it. His lips, so firm yet soft, pressed against mine. His tongue stroked deep, licking and tasting. The soft rasp of it against the tender flesh inside my mouth caused goose bumps to spread in a wave over my skin. His cock began to thicken and lengthen between us, the silky flesh hot against my lower belly.

My nipples tightened, aching, and I shimmied, rubbing them against his chest.

One of his hands cupped my nape, capturing me, holding me steady as he kissed me passionately. His mouth slanted across mine, seeking and ravenous, sucking on my lips and tongue. Moaning, I arched into him, my fingers clutching at his black hair.

"Christ, you turn me on," he growled, pulling his knees up. He urged me back, his body forming a cradle that supported me. His hands cupped my breasts, his thumbs circling the hard points of my nipples. "Look at you. You're so fucking gorgeous."

Warmth spread through me. "Gideon . . ."

"Sometimes you're this icy, hands-off blonde." His jaw tightened and he slipped one hand between my legs, his fingers gliding gently through my cleft. "And then you're like this. So hot and needy. Wanting my hands all over you, my cock inside you."

"I'm like this *for you*. This is what you do to me. What you've been doing to me from the moment I met you."

Gideon's gaze slid over me, followed by his hand. As his fingertips caressed the outside curve of my breast and stroked over my clit at the same time, I shivered.

"I want you," he said gruffly.

"And here I am—naked."

His mouth curved in a slow, sexy smile. "I couldn't miss that."

The tip of his finger circled my opening. I lifted a little to give him better access, my hands sliding over his shoulders.

"But I wasn't talking about sex," he murmured. "Although I want that, too."

"With me."

"Only you," he agreed. His thumb brushed feather light over my nipple. "Forever and always."

I moaned and reached for his cock, gripping him in my hands, stroking him from root to tip.

"I look at you, angel, and I want you so badly. I want to be with you, listen to you, talk to you. I want to hear you laugh and hold you when you cry. I want to sit next to you, breathe the same air, share the same life. I want to wake up to you like this every day forever. I *want* you."

"Gideon." I leaned forward and kissed him softly. "I want you, too."

He teased the tip of my breast, tugging and rolling the hardened peak between his fingers. He rubbed my clit and a soft sound escaped me. Gideon hardened in my hands, his body responding to my growing desire.

The room was lightening as the sun rose higher, but the world outside seemed a lifetime away. The intimacy of the moment was both searing and sweet, filling me with joy.

My hands caressed his erection with tender reverence, my only goal to please him and show him how much I loved him. He touched me the same way, his eyes windows to a wounded soul that needed me as much as I needed him.

"I'm happy with you, Eva. You make me happy."

"I'll make you happy the rest of your life," I promised him. My hips churned, desire sliding hot and thick through my veins. "There's nothing I want more."

Leaning forward, Gideon flicked the tip of his tongue over my nipple, a quick swipe that sent a sharp ache through my breast. "I love your tits. Did you know that?"

"Ah, so that's what did you in—the rack."

"Keep teasing me, angel. Give me an excuse to spank you. I love your ass, too."

He pressed a hand to my back, arching me toward his mouth. Hot wetness surrounded the sensitive peak of my breast. His cheeks hollowed on a deep suck and my sex echoed his mouth, hungry for his cock.

I felt him everywhere, all around me and inside me. His heat and warmth. His passion. In my hands, his cock was hard and throbbing, the plush head slick with pre-cum.

"Tell me you love me," I pleaded.

Gideon's eyes met mine. "You know I do."

"Imagine if I never said the words to you. If you never heard them from me."

His chest expanded on a deep breath. "Crossfire."

My hands stilled on him.

He swallowed, his throat working. "It's your word for when things get to be too much, when it's too intense. It's my word, too, because that's how you make me feel. All the time."

"Gideon, I . . ." He'd made me speechless.

"When you say it, it means stop." His fingertips left my breast and slid down my cheek. "When I say it, it means never stop. Whatever you're doing to me, I need you to keep doing it."

Lifting, I hovered above him. "Let me."

"Yes." His fingers left my cleft, and a heartbeat later his cock was filling me, the flared crown stretching sensitive tissues.

"Slow," he ordered softly, his gaze hooded as he licked his fingers with long, sensuous laps of his tongue. He looked so wicked, so shamelessly decadent.

"Help me." It was always more difficult for me to take him this way, using only gravity and the weight of my body. As desperate as he'd made me, he was still a tight fit.

He caught my hips, sliding me up and down leisurely, working me onto his thick erection. "Feel every inch, angel," he crooned. "Feel how hard you make me."

My thighs trembled as he rubbed over a tender spot inside me. I gripped his wrists, my sex rippling.

"Don't come," he warned, with that authoritative bite that practically ensured I would. "Not until you've taken all of me."

"Gideon." The slow, steady friction of his careful penetration was driving me insane.

"Think of how good it feels when I'm in you, angel. When your greedy little cunt has something to tighten down on when you're coming."

I tightened down on him then, seduced by the coaxing rasp in his voice. "Hurry."

"You're the one who has to let me in." His eyes gleamed with humor. He urged me to lean back, changing the angle of my descent.

I slid onto him, taking him to the root in one smooth, slick glide. "Oh!"

"Fuck." His head fell back, his breathing quick and rough. "You feel amazing. You're squeezing me like a fist."

"Baby." I couldn't hide the plea in my voice. He was so hard and thick inside me, so deep I could barely catch my breath . . .

He shot me a look that scorched. "I want *this*. You and me, nothing between us."

"Nothing," I said fervently, panting. Wriggling. Losing my mind. I needed to come so badly.

"Shh. I've got you." Lifting his thumb to his mouth, Gideon licked the pad, then reached between us, rubbing my clit with expertly applied pressure. Heat bloomed across my skin in a mist of sweat, the flush spreading until I felt feverish.

I climaxed in a searing rush of pleasure, my sex spasming in hard, desperate clutches. His growl was a sound of pure animal sexuality, his cock swelling in response to the covetous milking of my body.

But he didn't come, which made my orgasm all the more intimate. I was open, vulnerable, wrenched by desire. And he watched me fall apart with those haunting blue eyes, his control absolute. The fact that he didn't move, just held himself deep, enhanced the feeling of connection between us.

A tear slid down my cheek, the orgasm pushing my emotions over the edge.

"Come here," he said hoarsely, his hands sliding up my back and pulling me into him. He licked the tear away, then nudged me sweetly with the tip of his nose. My breasts pressed against his chest, my arms went around his waist, slipping into the space between him and the headboard. I held him close, my body quivering with aftershocks.

"You're so beautiful," he murmured. "So soft and sweet. Kiss me, angel."

Tilting my head, I offered him my mouth. The melding was hot and wet, an erotic mixture of his unsated lust and my overwhelming love.

I pushed my fingers into his hair, cupping the back of his head to hold him still. He did the same to me, the two of us communicating without words. His lips sealed over mine, his tongue fucking my mouth even as his cock remained unmoving inside me.

I felt the undercurrent of strain in his kiss and his touch, and I knew he worried about the day's events, too. I arched my back, curving into him, wishing I could make us inseparable. His teeth caught my lower lip, sinking gently into the swollen curve. I whimpered and he murmured, soothing me with rhythmic strokes of his tongue.

"Don't move," he said hoarsely, restraining me with his grip at my nape. "I want to come just feeling you around me."

"Please," I breathed. "Come in me. Let me feel you."

We were completely entwined, grasping and pulling at each other, his cock rigid inside me, our hands in each other's hair, our lips and tongues mating frantically.

Gideon was mine, completely. Yet still some part of my mind was stunned that I had him like this, that he was naked in a bed we shared, in an apartment we shared, that he was inside me, a part of me, taking every bit of my love and passion and giving me back so much more.

"I love you," I moaned, tightening my core and squeezing him. "I love you so much."

"Eva. God." He shuddered, coming. He groaned into my mouth, his hands flexing against my scalp, his breath gusting hard across my lips.

I felt him spurting inside me, filling me, and I trembled with another orgasm, the pleasure pulsing gently through me.

His hands roamed restlessly, rubbing up and down my back, his kiss that perfect blend of love and desire. I felt his gratitude and need, recognized it because I felt the same way.

It was a miracle that I'd found him, that he could make me feel this way, that I could love a man so deeply and completely and sexually with all the baggage I carried. And that I could offer the same refuge to him in return.

Laying my cheek against his chest, I listened to his heart pounding, his perspiration mingling with mine.

"Eva." He exhaled harshly. "Those answers you want from me . . . I need you to ask the questions."

I held him for a long minute, waiting for our bodies to recover and my own panic to subside. He was still inside me. We were as close as we could be, but it wasn't enough for him. He had to have more, on every front. He wasn't going to quit until he possessed every part of me and infiltrated every aspect of my life.

Pulling back, I looked at him. "I'm not going anywhere, Gideon. You don't have to push yourself if you're not ready."

"I am ready." His gaze held mine, blazing with power and determination. "I need *you* to be ready. Because it won't be long before I'm going to ask you a question, Eva. And I'm going to need you to give me the right answer."

"It's too soon," I whispered, my throat tight. I lifted slightly, trying to gain some distance, but he pulled me back and held me down. "I don't know if I can."

"But you're not going anywhere," he reminded, his jaw set. "And neither am I. Why put off the inevitable?"

"That's not the way you need to look at it. We've got too many triggers. If we're not careful, one or both of us will shut down, cut the other one—"

"Ask me, Eva," he commanded.

"Gideon—"

"Now."

Frustrated by his obstinacy, I stewed for a minute, then decided that whatever the reason, there *were* questions that needed answers no matter what. "Dr. Lucas. Do you know why he lied to your mother?"

His jaw worked as he clenched his teeth, his eyes turning hard and cold. "He was protecting his brother-in-law."

"What?" I sat back, my thoughts spinning. "Anne's brother? The woman you were sleeping with?"

"Fucking," he corrected harshly. "Everyone in Anne's family is in the mental health field. The whole fucked-up lot of them. She's a shrink. Did any of your Google searches dig *that* up?"

I nodded absently, more concerned with the vehemence with which he said the word *shrink*, practically spitting it out. Was that why he hadn't gotten help before? And how much did he love me to make the effort to see Dr. Petersen despite his loathing?

"I didn't know it right away," he went on. "I couldn't figure out why Lucas lied. He's a pediatrician, for chrissakes. He's supposed to care about kids."

"Screw that. He's supposed to be human!" Rage filled me, a white-hot desire to find Lucas and hurt him. "I can't believe he could look me in the eye like he did and say all that shit he said."

Blaming Gideon for everything . . . trying to drive a wedge between us . . .

"It wasn't until I met you that I finally started to get it," he said, his hands tightening around my waist. "He loves Anne. Maybe as much as I love you. Enough to overlook her cheating and cover up for her brother to spare her the truth. Or embarrassment."

"He shouldn't be practicing medicine."

"I don't disagree."

"So why is his office in one of your buildings?"

"I bought the building because his practice is in it. Helps me keep an eye on him and how well he's doing . . . or not."

Something about the way he said "or not" led me to wonder: Did he have anything to do with Lucas's less profitable times? I remembered when Cary had been taken to the hospital and how special arrangements had been made for him and for me, because Gideon was such a generous benefactor. How much could he influence?

If there were ways to put Lucas at a disadvantage, I was certain Gideon knew them all.

"And the brother-in-law?" I asked. "What happened to him?"

Gideon's chin lifted and his gaze narrowed. "The statute of limitations ran out for me, but I confronted him, told him if he ever went into practice or laid a hand on another child I'd set up an unlimited fund dedicated to prosecuting him civilly and criminally on behalf of his victims. Shortly after that, he killed himself."

The last was said without inflection, which made the hairs on my nape stand on end. I shivered with a sudden chill that came from inside me.

He rubbed his hands up and down my arms, trying to warm me, but he didn't pull me into him. "Hugh was married. Had a child. A boy. Just a few years old."

"Gideon." I hugged him, understanding. He'd lost a father to suicide, too. "What Hugh chose to do isn't your fault. You're not responsible for the decisions he made."

"Aren't I?" he asked, with that ice in his voice.

"No, you're not." I held him as tight as I could, willing my love into his tense, rigid body. "And the boy . . . His father's death might have prevented him from experiencing what you did. Have you thought of that?"

His chest lifted and fell roughly. "Yes, I've thought of it. But he doesn't know what his father was. He only knows that his dad is gone, by choice, and he's left behind. He'll believe his father didn't care enough about him to stay."

"Baby." I pulled his head toward me, urging him to rest against me. I didn't know what to say. I couldn't make excuses for Geoffrey Cross and I knew Gideon was thinking of him, as well as the boy he himself had once been. "You didn't do anything wrong."

"I need you to stay, Eva," he whispered, his arms finally coming around me. "And you're holding back. It's driving me crazy."

I rocked gently, cradling him. "I'm being cautious because you're so important to me."

"I know it's not fair to ask you to be with me"—his head tilted back—"when we can't even sleep in the same bed, but I'll love you better than anyone else could. I'll take care of you and make you happy. I know I can."

"You do." I brushed his hair back from his temples and wanted to cry when I saw the longing on his face. "I want you to believe I'll stay with you."

"You're afraid."

"Not of you." I sighed, trying to pull the words together in a way that made sense. "I can't . . . I can't just be an extension of you."

"Eva." His features softened. "I can't change who I am, and I don't want to change who you are. I just want us to be who we are—together."

I kissed him. I didn't know what to say. I wanted us to live the same life, too, to be together in every way we could be. But I also believed that neither of us was ready.

"Gideon." I kissed him again, my lips clinging to his. "You and me, we're barely strong enough on our own. We're getting better all the time, but we're not there yet. It's not just about the nightmares."

"Tell me what it's about, then."

"Everything. I don't know . . . It's not right for me to live in a place Stanton pays for anymore now that Nathan isn't a threat. And especially not now that my parents hooked up."

His brows shot up. "Excuse me?"

"Yeah," I confirmed. "Total mess."

"Move in with me," he said, rubbing my back to comfort me.

"So . . . I skip right over making it on my own? Am I always going to live off someone else?"

"For fuck's sake." He made a frustrated noise. "Would you feel better if we shared the rent?"

"Ha! Like I could afford your penthouse, even paying just a third of it. And there's no way Cary could."

"So we'll move in here or next door, if you want, and take over the lease. I don't care where, Eva."

I stared at him, wanting what he was offering but afraid I'd miss a big pitfall that would hurt us.

"You came to me as soon as you got up this morning," he pointed out. "You don't like being away from me, either. Why torture ourselves? Sharing the same space should be the least of our problems."

"I don't want to screw this up," I told him, my fingers brushing over his chest. "I *need* us to work, Gideon."

He caught my hand and pressed it over his heart. "I need us to work, too, angel. And I want mornings like this and nights like last night while we do it."

"No one even knows we're seeing each other. How do we go from being broken up to living together?"

"We start today. You're taking Cary with you to the video launch. I'll come up to the both of you with Ireland, say hi—"

"She called me," I interrupted, "and told me to go up to you. She wants us to get back together."

"She's a smart girl." He smiled and I felt a little thrill at the thought that he might be opening up to her. "So one of us will approach the other, make small talk, and I'll say hi to Cary. You and I won't have to fake the attraction between us. Tomorrow, I'll take you out to lunch. Bryant Park Grill would be ideal. We'll make a show of it."

It all sounded wonderful and easy, but . . . "Is it safe?"

"Finding Nathan's bracelet on a criminal's corpse opens the door to reasonable doubt. That's all we need."

We looked at each other, sharing the feeling of hope, the sense of excitement and expectation in a future that had seemed so much more uncertain just yesterday.

He touched my cheek. "You made a reservation at Tableau One for tonight."

I nodded. "Yeah, I had to use your name to get on the list, but Brett asked me out to dinner and I wanted us to go to a place connected with you."

"Ireland and I have a reservation at the same time. We'll join you."

I shifted awkwardly, nervous at the thought, and Gideon thickened inside me. "Uh . . ."

"Don't worry," he murmured, his focus clearly shifting to more heated thoughts. "It'll be fun."

"Yeah, right."

Banding his arms around my hips and shoulder blades, Gideon scooped me up and moved, rolling and putting me beneath him. "Trust me."

I was going to reply, but he kissed me quiet and fucked me senseless.

I showered and dressed at Gideon's, then hurried back down the hallway to my apartment for my purse and bag, trying not to look like I was sneaking around. It was easy to get ready at Gideon's apartment, since he'd stocked the bathroom with all my usual toiletries and cosmetics, and had purchased enough clothes and underwear for me to never have to wear anything from my own closet.

It was too much, but that was the way he was.

I was rinsing off the mug I'd used for a quick cup of coffee when Trey came into the kitchen.

He smiled sheepishly. Dressed in a pair of Cary's sweats and his own shirt from last night, he looked right at home. "Good morning."

"Back atcha." I put the mug in the dishwasher and faced him. "I'm glad you came to dinner."

"Me, too. I had fun."

"Coffee?" I asked him.

"Please. I have to get ready for work, but I'm dragging."

"I've had those days." I fixed him a cup and slid it over.

He took the mug and lifted it in a salute of thanks. "Can I ask you something?"

"Shoot."

"Do you like Tatiana, too? Is it weird for you, having us both around?"

I shrugged. "I don't really know Tatiana, to be honest. She doesn't hang with Cary and me the way you do."

"Oh."

I started heading out and squeezed his shoulder before I passed him. "Have a good one."

"You, too."

I checked my phone while taking a cab to work. I almost wished I'd walked, since the cabbie kept the front windows down and was apparently averse to wearing deodorant. The only saving grace was that it was faster than walking.

There was a text from Brett sent around six in the morning: On the ground. Can't wait to c u 2nite!

I sent him back a smiley face.

Megumi looked good when I met up with her at work, which made me happy, but Will was looking glum. As I was putting my purse in a drawer, he stopped by my cubicle and rested his crossed arms along the low wall.

"What's the matter?" I asked him, looking up at him from my chair.

"Help. Need carbs."

Laughing, I shook my head. "I think it's sweet that you're suffering through this diet for your girl."

"I shouldn't complain," he said. "She's lost like five pounds—that I didn't think she had to lose, mind you—and she looks amazing and has all this energy. But God . . . I feel like a slug. My body's not built for this."

"Are you asking me out to lunch?"

"Please." He clasped his hands together like he was praying. "You're one of the few women I know who actually enjoys eating."

"I've got the butt to show for it, too," I said ruefully. "But sure. I'm game."

"You're the best, Eva." He backed up and bumped into Mark. "Oops. Sorry."

Mark grinned. "No problem."

Will headed back to his cubicle and Mark turned his smile to me.

"We've got the Drysdel team coming in at nine thirty," I reminded him.

"Right. And I've got an idea I'd like to run past strategy before they get here."

I grabbed my tablet and stood, thinking we'd be running down to the wire. "You're living on the edge, boss."

"Only way to do it. Come on."

The day flew by and I rushed full-bore all through it, filled with restless energy. Getting up so early, then eating a plate of pierogi for lunch, didn't slow me down.

I wrapped up exactly at five and did a quick change in the bathroom, switching from my skirt and blouse into a more casual jersey dress in pale blue. I slipped on a pair of wedge sandals, swapped out my diamond studs for silver hoops, and turned my ponytail into a messy bun. Then I headed down to the lobby.

As I moved toward the revolving entrance door, I saw Cary standing outside on the sidewalk talking to Brett. I slowed, giving myself a minute to absorb the sight of my old flame.

Brett's short-cropped hair was naturally dark blond, but he'd had the tips dyed platinum and the look was a good one for him, with his tanned skin and irises of a beautiful emerald green. On stage he was usually shirtless, but today he was dressed in black cargo pants and bloodred T-shirt, his arms covered in sleeves of tattoos that writhed over his muscles.

He turned his head then, looking inside the lobby, and I started walking again, my stomach fluttering a little when he caught sight of me, and his ruggedly handsome face was softened by a smile that revealed a killer dimple.

Jesus, he was sexy as hell.

Feeling a little too exposed, I pulled out my sunglasses and slipped them on. Then I took a deep breath as I spun through the revolving doors, my gaze shifting to the Bentley parked just behind Brett's limo.

Brett whistled. "Damn, Eva. You're more gorgeous every time I see you."

I shot a strained smile at Cary, my pulse racing madly. "Hey."

"You look great, baby girl," he said, reaching for my hand.

Out of the corner of my eye, I saw Angus step out of the Bentley. In that moment of distraction, I totally missed Brett reaching for me. A split second after I registered his hands at my waist, I realized he was going to kiss me and barely turned my head in time. His lips touched the corner of my mouth, feeling warm and familiar. I stumbled back, tripping over Cary, who caught me by the shoulders.

Flushed with embarrassment and disoriented, I looked anywhere but at Brett.

And found myself looking into the icy blue eyes of Gideon.

16

STANDING FROZEN JUST outside the revolving doors of the Crossfire, Gideon stared at me with such intensity I squirmed.

Sorry, I mouthed, feeling awful, knowing how I would've felt if Corinne had gotten her lips on him the other day.

"Hi," Brett greeted me, too focused on me to pay attention to the dark figure standing with his fists and jaw clenched just a few feet away.

"Hey." I could feel Gideon watching me, and it was painful not to go to him. "Ready?"

Without waiting for the guys, I yanked the limo door open and crawled in. I'd barely gotten my ass on the seat when I pulled the burner phone out of my purse and sent a quick text to Gideon: I love you.

Brett settled on the bench seat beside me, and then Cary slid in.

"I've been seeing your pretty mug everywhere, man," Brett said, talking to Cary.

"Yeah." Cary shot me a crooked smile. He looked great in distressed jeans and designer T-shirt, with leather cuffs on his wrists that matched his boots.

"Did the rest of the band fly in with you?" I asked.

"Yep, they're all here." Brett flashed that dimple at me again. "Darrin crashed the minute we got to the hotel."

"I don't know how he drums for hours. It's exhausting just watching."

"When you're high off the rush of being on stage, energy isn't a problem."

"How's Erik?" Cary asked with more than casual interest, making me wonder—not for the first time—if he and the band's bassist had ever hooked up. As far as I knew, Erik was straight, but there had been little signs here and there that made me think he might have experimented a little with my best friend.

"Erik's dealing with some issues that have come up on the tour," Brett replied. "And Lance hooked up with a girl he met when we were in New York the last time. You'll be seeing them all in a few minutes."

"The life of a rock star," I teased.

Brett shrugged and smiled.

I looked away, regretting my decision to bring Cary along. Because having him there meant I couldn't say what I needed to say to Brett—that I was in love with someone else and there was no hope for us.

A relationship with Brett would be entirely different from what I had with Gideon. I'd have had a lot of time on my own while he was on tour. I could do all the things I thought I should do before settling down—living by my own means and spending time unattached with friends and by myself. Kind of the best of both worlds: having a boyfriend but enjoying plenty of individuality.

But although I was worried about jumping from college into a lifetime commitment, I had no doubts that Gideon was the man I wanted. We were just out of sync with our timing—I thought there was no reason to rush, while he thought there was no reason to wait.

"We're here," Brett said, looking out the window at the crowd.

Despite the muggy heat of the day, Times Square was packed as usual. The ruby-red glass stairs in Duffy Square were full of people taking pictures of each other, and pedestrian traffic clogged the overflowing sidewalks. Police officers dotted the corners, keeping a sharp eye out for trouble. Street performers outshouted each other, and the smells emanating from food carts competed with the much less savory smell of the street itself.

Massive electronic billboards plastered on the sides of buildings fought for attention, including one of Cary with a female model wrapped around him from behind. Cameramen and boom operators loitered around a mobile video screen, which was attached to a traveling platform and positioned in front of the bleacherlike stair seating.

Brett climbed out of the limo first and was immediately bombarded by the excited screams of avid fans—most were female. He flashed that killer smile and waved, then reached in a hand to help me out. My reception was much less warm, especially after Brett put his arm around my waist. Cary's appearance, however, started a hum of murmurs. When he slipped on a pair of shades, he elicited his own swell of excited yells and catcalls.

I was overwhelmed by the sensory input but quickly focused when I spotted Christopher Vidal Jr. talking with the host of an entertainment gossip show. Gideon's brother was dressed for business in shirt, tie, and navy slacks. His dark auburn hair caught the eye even in the early evening shade cast by the towering buildings surrounding us. He waved when he caught sight of me, which turned the host's gaze to me as well. I waved back.

The rest of Six-Ninths stood in front of the bleachers signing autographs, clearly enjoying the attention. I looked at Brett. "Go do your thing."

"Yeah?" He studied me, trying to make sure I was okay with him abandoning me.

"Yeah." I waved him off. "This is for you. Enjoy it. I'll be here when it's time for the show."

"Okay." He smiled. "Don't go anywhere."

He bounded off. Cary and I walked over to the tent bearing the Vidal Records logo. Protected from the crowds by private security, it was a tiny oasis in the madness of Times Square.

"Well, baby girl, you've got your hands full with him. I forgot how it was with you two."

"*Was* being the operative word," I pointed out.

"He's different from before," he went on. "More . . . settled."

"That's great for him. Especially with all that's going on in his life right now."

He scoped me out. "Aren't you even the slightest bit interested in seeing if he can still bang you brainless?"

I shot him a look. "Chemistry is chemistry. And I'm sure he's had plenty of chances to bone up on his already fabulous skills."

"Bone up, ha! That's punny." He waggled his brows at me. "You seem solid."

"Ah, now that would be an illusion."

"Well, look who's here," he murmured, turning my attention to Gideon, who was approaching with Ireland at his side. "And heading straight toward us. If there's a brawl over you, I'm watching from the bleachers."

I shoved at him. "Thanks."

It amazed me that Gideon could look so cool in his suit when it was still so hot. Ireland looked fantastic in a low-rise flared skirt and tummy-baring fitted tank top.

"Eva!" she shouted, running over and leaving her brother behind. She met me with a hug, then pulled back to check me out. "Awesome! He's got to be kicking himself."

I looked around her at Gideon, searching his face for any signs that he was pissed about Brett. Ireland turned and hugged Cary, too, surprising him. In the meantime, Gideon walked straight up to me, grabbed me gently by the upper arms, and kissed both of my cheeks French style.

"Hello, Eva." His voice was flavored with a soft rasp that had my toes curling. "It's good to see you."

I blinked up at him, not having to fake my astonishment at all. "Uh, hi. Gideon."

"Doesn't she look delish?" Ireland asked, making no attempt at subtlety.

Gideon's eyes never left my face. "She always does. I need a minute of your time, Eva."

"Sure." I shot a what-the-fuck look at Cary and let Gideon lead me to a corner of the tent. We'd taken a few steps when I said, "Are you mad? Please don't be."

"Of course I am," he said evenly. "But not at you or him."

"O-kay." I had no idea what that meant.

He stopped and faced me, raking a hand through his gorgeous hair. "This situation is intolerable. I could stand it when there was no other choice, but now . . ." His gaze was fierce on my face. "You're mine. I need the world to know that."

"I've told Brett that I'm in love with you. Cary, too. My dad. Megumi. I've never lied about how I feel about you."

"Eva!" Christopher came up to me and pulled me into him for a kiss on the cheek. "I'm so glad Brett brought you. You know, I had no idea you two used to be an item."

I managed a smile, hyperaware of Gideon's gaze. "It was a long time ago."

"Not that long." He grinned. "You're here, aren't you?"

"Christopher," Gideon said, by way of greeting.

"Gideon." Christopher's smile didn't waver, but he noticeably cooled. "You didn't have to come. I've got this covered."

They were half brothers but had so little in common physically.

Gideon was taller, bigger, and undeniably dark in both coloring and demeanor. Christopher was a handsome man with a sexy smile, but he had none of Gideon's sizzling magnetism.

"I'm here for Eva," Gideon said smoothly, "not the show."

"Really?" Christopher looked at me. "I thought you and Brett were working things out."

"Brett's a friend," I replied.

"Eva's personal life is none of your business," Gideon said.

"It shouldn't be yours, either." Christopher looked at him with such hostility it made me uncomfortable. "The fact that 'Golden' is a true story, and that Brett and Eva are here together, is a great marketing angle for Vidal and the band."

"The song is the end of that story."

Christopher frowned and reached into his pocket, pulling out his smartphone. He read the screen, then scowled at his brother. "Call Corinne, will you? She's going nuts trying to reach you."

"I talked to her an hour ago," Gideon said.

"Stop giving her mixed signals," Christopher snapped. "If you didn't want to talk to her, you shouldn't have gone over to her place last night."

I tensed, my pulse leaping. I looked at Gideon, saw his jaw tighten, and remembered how I'd waited for a reply text from him. He'd been at my place when I got home, but he'd never explained why he hadn't texted me back. He certainly hadn't said anything about going to Corinne's apartment.

And hadn't he said he wasn't taking her calls?

I backed away with my stomach in knots. I'd felt off all day, and facing the simmering dislike between Gideon and Christopher was too much on top of it. "Excuse me."

"Eva," Gideon said sharply.

"It was good seeing you both," I murmured, playing my scripted part before turning away and heading the few feet over to Cary.

Gideon caught up with me after only two steps, gripping me by the elbow and whispering in my ear. "She's calling my phone and work all the time. I had to talk with her."

"You should've told me."

"We had more important things to talk about."

Brett glanced over at us. He was too far away for me to see his expression, but his posture looked tight. People, all of them pushing to get closer, surrounded him and he was focused on me instead.

Damn it. He'd seen me with Gideon and it was spoiling what should be a wonderful experience for him. As I'd feared, the whole outing was a mess.

"Gideon," Christopher said tightly from behind us. "I wasn't finished talking to you."

Gideon glanced at him. "I'll get to you in a minute."

"You'll talk to me now."

"Walk away, Christopher." Gideon stared at his brother so coldly I shivered despite the heat. "Before you make a scene that takes all the attention away from Six-Ninths."

Christopher seethed for a long minute, then seemed to realize his brother wasn't kidding. He cursed under his breath and turned, only to be confronted by Ireland.

"Leave them alone," she said, with her hands on her hips. "I want them to get back together."

"You stay out of this."

"Whatever." She wrinkled her nose at him. "Come show me around."

He paused, his gaze narrowed. Then he sighed and took her by the elbow, leading her away. I realized they were close.

It made me sad that Gideon didn't have that kind of bond with them.

Gideon brought my attention back to him with a brush of fingertips to my cheek, a soft caress that conveyed so much love . . . and possession. No one looking at us could mistake the claim. "Tell me you know nothing happened with Corinne."

I sighed. "I know you didn't do anything with her."

"Good. She's not acting like herself. I've never seen her so . . . Damn it. I don't know. Needy. Irrational."

"Devastated?"

"Maybe. Yes." His face softened. "She wasn't like this when she broke our engagement."

I felt bad for both of them. Ugly good-byes weren't fun for anyone. "She walked away that time. This time, it's you. It's always harder being the one left behind."

"I'm trying to settle her down, but I need you to promise me that she's not going to get in between us."

"I won't let her. And you're not going to worry about Brett."

It took him a few seconds, but he finally said, "I'll worry, but I'll handle it."

I could tell it wasn't an easy concession for him to make.

His lips thinned. "I have to go deal with Christopher. Are we okay?"

Nodding, I said, "I'm good. You?"

"As long as Kline doesn't kiss you." The warning was clear in his voice.

"Same goes."

"If he kisses me, he's getting decked."

I laughed. "You know what I meant."

He caught my hand and rubbed his thumb over my ring. "Crossfire."

My heart hurt in the best way. "Love you, too, ace."

BRETT disengaged from his fans and headed over to the tent, looking grim.

"Having fun yet?" I asked him, hoping to keep him feeling positive.

"He wants you back," he said bluntly.

I didn't hesitate. "Yes."

"If you're going to give him a second chance, I should get one, too."

"Brett—"

"I know it's tough with me being on the road—"

"And based in San Diego," I pointed out.

"—but I can make it out here often enough and you can always meet up with me, see some new places. Plus, the tour ends in November. I can come stay out here for the holidays." He looked at me with those green eyes of his, and the attraction hummed between us. "Your dad's still in SoCal, so you've got more than one reason to come out."

"You'd be reason enough. But, Brett . . . I don't know what to say. I'm in love with him."

He crossed his arms and looked exactly like the wickedly delicious bad boy he was. "I don't care. It's not going to work out for you with him, and I'll be around, Eva."

Staring at him, I realized nothing would convince him but time.

Brett stepped closer, then reached out to run his hand down my arm. He stood over me, his body curved into mine. I remembered other times we'd stood like this, the moments right before he pressed me back against something and fucked me hard.

"It's only going to take once," he murmured in my ear, his voice sinful as always. "One time inside you and you'll remember how it is between us."

I swallowed past a dry throat. "That's not going to happen, Brett."

His mouth curved in a slow smile, revealing that decadent dimple. "We'll see about that."

"I can't believe they're so much hotter in person," Ireland said, looking over at where the guys were doing their prelaunch interview with the TV show host. "You, too, Cary."

He smiled, his teeth dazzlingly white. "Well, thank you, darlin'."

"So . . ." She looked at me with those blue eyes that were so like Gideon's. "You used to date Brett Kline?"

"Not really. Honestly, we just used to mess around."

"Did you love him?"

I thought about that for a minute. "I think I was close, maybe. I could have fallen in love with him under different circumstances. He's a great guy."

Her lips pursed.

"What about you?" I asked. "Are you seeing anyone?"

"Yes." Her lips twisted ruefully. "I really like him—a lot—but it's weird, because he can't let his parents know he's dating me."

"Why not?"

"His grandparents lost most of their money to that scheme Gideon's dad ran."

My gaze went to Cary, whose brows were lifted above the line of his shades.

"That's not your fault," I said, angry on her behalf.

"Rick says his parents think it's 'convenient' that Gideon is so rich now," she muttered.

"Convenient? They think it's *convenient*?"

"Angel."

I turned around at the sound of Gideon's voice, not having realized he'd come up behind me. "What?"

He just stared at me. I was irritated enough that it took me a minute to note the hint of a smile on his face.

"Don't start," I told him, narrowing my gaze in warning. I turned back to Ireland. "Tell Rick's parents to look up the Crossroads Foundation."

"If you're done being offended for my sake," Gideon said, coming up so close behind me that he brushed up against me, "they're about five minutes from starting the video."

My gaze searched out Brett, who'd rejoined the crowd, and found him waving me over.

I looked at Cary.

"Go on," he said with a jerk of his chin. "I'll hang here with Ireland and Cross."

I headed over to the band, smiling when I saw how excited they were. "Big moment, guys," I said to them.

"Ah, well." Darrin grinned. "This whole event was set up just to get us on this TV show and Internet simulcast. It was the only way Vidal could get them to give us any coverage. Let's hope it pays off, because fuckin' A, it's hot as hell out here."

The host announced the exclusive premiere of the video, and then the screen switched from showing the logo of the show to the start of the video and the first chords of the song began.

The black screen suddenly lit up, revealing Brett sitting on a stool in front of a mic in a puddle of light, just as he'd been at the concert. He began to sing, his voice deep and rough. Crazy sexy. The effect his voice had on me was powerful and immediate, just as it'd always been.

The camera slowly backed away from Brett, revealing a dance floor in front of the stage where he sang. There was a crowd dancing, but they were cast in black and white while a lone blonde was strikingly colored.

I stilled as shock spread through me. The camera was careful to film only her backside and profile, but the girl was undeniably meant to be me. She was my height, with the same hair color and style as mine before I'd recently cut it. She had my curvy butt and hips, and her profile was similar enough to mine to understand immediately who she was meant to be.

The next three minutes of my life passed in a horrified daze. "Golden" was a sexually charged song and the actress did all the things Brett sang about—dropping to her knees for a Brett lookalike, making out with him in a bar restroom, and straddling his lap in the back of a classic '67 Mustang just like the one Brett owned. Those intimate memories were intercut with shots of the real Brett still singing onstage with the rest of the guys in the band.

The fact that actors were playing us helped me deal with it a little better, but one glance at Gideon's stony face told me it didn't matter to him. He was seeing one of the wildest times in my life relived before his eyes and it was very real to him.

The video ended with a shot of Brett looking soulful and tormented, a single tear sliding down his cheek.

I pulled away and faced him.

His smile slowly faded when he got a good look at my expression.

I couldn't believe how personal the video was. I was freaking out that millions of people were going to see it.

"Wow," the host said, leaning into the band with mic in hand. "Brett, you really put yourself out there with this. Was it the song that brought you and Eva back together?"

"In a roundabout way, yeah."

"And Eva, did you play yourself in the video?"

I blinked, realizing he was outing me as *the* Eva on national television. "No, that's not me."

"How do you feel about 'Golden'?"

I licked my dry lips. "It's an amazing song by an amazing band."

"About an amazing love story." The host smiled into the camera and rambled on, but I tuned him out, my gaze searching for Gideon. I couldn't spot him anywhere.

The host talked to the band a bit more and I wandered away, searching. Cary came up to me with Ireland in tow.

"Some video," he drawled.

I looked at him miserably before my gaze slid over to Ireland. "Do you know where your brother is?"

"Christopher's schmoozing. Gideon left." She winced apologetically. "He asked Christopher to take me home with him."

"Damn it." I dug in my purse for the burner phone and typed out a quick text: I love you. Tell me you'll c me 2nite.

I waited for a reply. When it didn't come after a few minutes, I just held the phone in my hand, willing it to vibrate.

Brett ambled up to me. "We're done here. Wanna bail?"

"Sure." I turned to Ireland. "I'm out of town the next two weekends, but let's get together after that."

"I'll keep my schedule open," she said, hugging me hard.

Turning to Cary, I caught his hand and squeezed it. "Thanks for coming."

"Are you kidding? I haven't been this entertained in a long time." He and Brett did some complicated handshake. "Good job, man. I'm stoked for you."

"Thanks for coming. We'll catch you later."

Brett set his hand at the small of my back and we took off.

17

GIDEON DIDN'T SHOW up at Tableau One.

In a way, I was grateful, because I didn't want Brett thinking I'd planned the interruption. Outside his long-term hopes for our relationship, Brett was someone who'd been important to me in the past and I wanted to be friends with him, if possible.

But I was preoccupied with imagining what Gideon was thinking and feeling.

I picked at my dinner, too unsettled to eat. When Arnoldo Ricci stopped by to say hello, looking very dashing and handsome in his white chef coat, I felt bad that so much of his fine food was still on my plate.

The celebrity chef was a friend of Gideon's. Gideon was a silent partner in Tableau One, which was the reason I'd chosen the restaurant. If he had any doubts about how the dinner with Brett would go, he'd have people to ask that he trusted.

Of course, I hoped Gideon would trust me enough to believe *me*, but I knew our relationship had its issues and our mutual possessiveness was just one of them.

"It's good to see you, Eva," Arnoldo said with his lovely Italian accent. He pressed a kiss to my cheek, then pulled out one of the empty chairs at our table and sat.

Arnoldo extended his hand to Brett. "Welcome to Tableau One."

"Arnoldo's a Six-Ninths fan," I explained. "He came to the concert with Gideon and me."

Brett's lips twisted ruefully as the two men shook hands. "Nice to meet you. Did you see both shows?"

He was referring to the brawl he'd had with Gideon. Arnoldo understood. "I did. Eva is very important to Gideon."

"She's important to me, too," Brett said, grabbing his frosty mug of Nastro Azzurro beer.

"Well, then." Arnoldo smiled. "*Che vinca il migliore.* May the best man win."

"Ugh." I sat back in my chair. "I'm not a prize. Or I should say: I'm no prize."

Arnoldo shot me a look. Obviously he didn't wholly disagree with me. I didn't blame him; he knew I'd kissed Brett and had seen the effect it'd had on Gideon.

"Is there a problem with your meal, Eva?" Arnoldo asked. "If you liked it, your plate would be empty."

"You serve big helpings," Brett pointed out.

"And Eva is a big eater."

Brett looked at me. "You are?"

I shrugged. Was he catching on to how little we really knew about each other? "One of my many flaws."

"Not to me," Arnoldo said. "How did the video show go?"

"I think it went well." Brett searched my face as he answered.

I nodded, not wanting to spoil what was supposed to be a celebratory time for the band. What was done, was done. I couldn't fault Brett's intentions, only his execution. "They are well on the road to megastardom."

"And I can say I knew you when." Arnoldo smiled at Brett. "I bought your first single on iTunes when it was still your only single."

"Appreciate the support, man," Brett said. "We wouldn't have made it without our fans."

"You wouldn't have made it if you weren't so good." Arnoldo looked at me. "You will have dessert, won't you? And more wine."

As Arnoldo settled back in his chair, I realized he intended to fill the role of chaperone. When I glanced at Brett, I could tell from his wry smile that he caught that, too.

"So," Arnoldo began, "tell me how Shawna is doing, Eva."

I sighed inwardly. At least Arnoldo was a babysitter who was fun to look at.

BRETT's hired driver dropped me off at my apartment a little after ten. I invited Brett up, because I couldn't see any way to avoid it that wasn't rude. He took in the exterior of the building with some surprise, as well as the night doorman and the front desk.

"You must have a smokin' job," he said as we walked toward the elevators.

The clicking of heels on marble chased after me. "Eva!"

I cringed at the sound of Deanna's voice. "Reporter alert," I whispered, before turning around.

"That's a bad thing?" he asked, turning with me.

"Hi, Deanna." I greeted her with a strained smile.

"Hello." Her dark eyes raked Brett from head to toe, and then she thrust her hand at him. "Brett Kline, right? Deanna Johnson."

"A pleasure, Deanna," he said, turning on the charm.

"What can I do for you?" I asked her as they shook hands.

"Sorry for interrupting you on your date. I didn't realize you two were back together until I saw you at the Vidal event earlier." She smiled at Brett. "I take it there's no harm done from your altercation with Gideon Cross?"

Brett's brows rose. "You lost me."

"I'd heard you and Cross exchanged a few blows in an argument."

"Someone's got a big imagination."

Had Gideon talked to him? Or had media training taught Brett the pitfalls to avoid?

I hated that Deanna had been nearby earlier, watching me. Or, more accurately, watching Gideon. He was the one she was fixated on. I was just easier to access.

Her answering smile was brittle. "Bad source, I guess."

"It happens," he said easily.

She turned her attention back to me. "I saw Gideon with you today, Eva. My photographer got some great shots of you two. I stopped by to ask you for a statement, but now that I see who you're with, would you comment on the status of your relationship with Brett?"

She directed the question at me, but Brett stepped in, grinning and flashing that dazzling dimple. "I think 'Golden' says it all. We've got history and friendship."

"That's a great quote, thanks." Deanna eyed me. I eyed her right back. "Okay. I don't want to hold you up. I appreciate your time."

"Sure." I caught Brett's hand and tugged it. "Good night."

I hurried him to the elevators and didn't relax until the doors closed.

"Can I ask why a reporter's so interested in who you're dating?"

I glanced at him. He was lounging against the handrail, his hands gripping the brass on either side of his hips. The pose was hot and he was undeniably sexy, but my thoughts were with Gideon. I was anxious to be with him and talk to him.

"She's an ex of Gideon's with a grudge."

"And that doesn't send up any flags for you?"

I shook my head. "Not like you're probably thinking."

The elevator arrived on my floor and I led the way to my apartment, hating that I had to walk by Gideon's to get there. Had he felt like this when he'd spent time with Corinne? Weighted with guilt and worry?

I opened the door and was sorry that Cary wasn't hanging out on the couch. It didn't even seem like my roommate was home. The lights were off, which was a strong indicator that he was out. He always left lights on in his wake when he was around.

Hitting the switch, I turned in time to see Brett's face when the recessed ceiling fixtures lit up the place. I always felt weird when people first realized I had money.

He looked at me with a frown. "I'm rethinking my career choice."

"My job doesn't pay for this. My stepdad does. For now, anyway." I went to the kitchen and dropped my purse and bag off on a bar stool.

"You and Cross hang in the same circles?"

"Sometimes."

"Am I too different for you?"

The question unsettled me, even though it was perfectly valid. "I don't judge people by their money, Brett. Do you want something to drink?"

"Nah, I'm good."

I gestured toward the couch and we settled there.

"So, you didn't like the video," he said, laying his arm over the back of the sofa.

"I didn't say that!"

"Didn't have to. I saw your face."

"It's just really . . . personal."

His green eyes were hot enough to make me flush. "I haven't forgotten one thing about you, Eva. The video proves that."

"That's because there wasn't a whole lot for you to remember," I pointed out.

"You think I don't know you, but I bet I've seen sides of you Cross never has and never will."

"That's true in reverse."

"Maybe," he conceded, his fingers tapping silently into the cushion. "I'm supposed to fly out at the butt-crack of dawn tomorrow, but I'll catch a later flight. Come with me. We've got shows in Seattle and San Francisco over the weekend. You can head back Sunday night."

"I can't. I have plans."

"The weekend after that we're in San Diego. Come there." His fingers slid down my arm. "It'll be like old times, with twenty thousand extra people."

I blinked. What were the chances that we'd be home at the same time? "I've got plans to be in SoCal then. Just me and Cary."

"So we'll hook up next weekend."

"Meet up," I corrected, standing when he did. "Are you leaving?"

He stepped closer. "Are you asking me to stay?"

"Brett . . ."

"Right." He gave me a rueful smile and my heart raced a little. "We'll see each other next weekend."

We walked together to the door.

"Thank you for inviting me along today," I told him, feeling oddly sorry that he was going so soon.

"I'm sorry you didn't like the video."

"I do like it." I caught his hand. "I do. You did a great job with it. It's just weird seeing myself from the outside, you know?"

"Yeah, I get it." He cupped my cheek with his other hand and bent in for a kiss.

I turned my head and he nuzzled me instead, the tip of his nose rubbing up and down my cheek. The light scent of his cologne, mingled with the scent of his skin, teased my senses and brought back heated memories. The feel of his body standing so close to mine was achingly familiar.

I'd once had a mad crush on him. I had wanted him to feel the same way about me in return and now that he did, it was bittersweet.

Brett gripped my upper arms and groaned softly, the sound vibrating through me. "I remember how you feel," he whispered, his voice deep and husky. "On the inside. I can't wait to feel it again."

I was breathing too fast. "Thank you for dinner."

His lips curved against my cheek. "Call me. I'll call you no matter what, but it'd be nice for you to call me sometime. Okay?"

I nodded and had to swallow before speaking. "Okay."

He was gone a moment later and I was running to my purse for the burner phone. There was no message from Gideon. No missed call or text.

Grabbing my keys, I left my apartment and hurried to his, but it was dark and lifeless. I knew the moment I entered that he wasn't there without having to check the artfully colored glass bowl he emptied his pockets into.

Feeling like something was very off, I headed back to my place. I dropped my keys on the counter and went to my room, heading straight for the bathroom and a shower.

The unsettled feeling in my stomach wouldn't go away, even as I washed the stickiness and grime of the hot afternoon down the drain. I scrubbed shampoo into my scalp and thought over the day, growing angrier by the moment because Gideon was off somewhere doing whatever, instead of being home with me working things out.

And then I sensed him.

Rinsing soap out of my eyes, I turned and found him yanking off his tie as he stepped into the room. He looked tired and worn, which troubled me more than anger would have.

"Hey," I greeted him.

He watched me as he stripped with quick, methodical movements. Magnificently naked, he joined me in the shower, walking right into me and pulling me into a tight embrace.

"Hey," I said again, hugging him back. "What's the matter? Are you upset about the video?"

"I hate the video," he said bluntly. "I should've screened the damn thing when I realized the song was about you."

"I'm sorry."

He pulled back and looked down at me. The mist from the shower was slowly dampening his hair. He was infinitely sexier than Brett. And the way he felt about me—and I felt about him in return—was infinitely deeper. "Corinne called right before the video finished. She was . . . hysterical. Out of control. It concerned me and I went to see her."

I took a deep breath, fighting off a flare of jealousy. I had no right to feel that way, especially after the time I'd spent with Brett. "How did that go?"

He urged my head back with gentle fingers. "Close your eyes."

"Talk to me, Gideon."

"I will." As he rinsed the suds from my hair, he said, "I think I figured out what the problem is. She's been taking antidepressants and they're not the right prescription for her."

"Oh, wow."

"She was supposed to let the doctor know how they were working out, but she didn't even realize she's been acting so bizarre. It took hours of talking to her to get her to see it, and then pinpoint why."

I straightened and wiped my eyes, trying to stem my growing irritation over another woman monopolizing my man's attention. I couldn't discount her making up a problem just to keep Gideon spending time with her.

He swapped places with me, sidestepping under the shower spray. Water coursed down his amazing body, running lovingly over the hard ridges and slabs of muscle.

"So what now?" I asked.

He shrugged grimly. "She'll see her doctor tomorrow to discuss getting off the pills or switching to something else."

"Are you supposed to walk her through that?" I complained.

"She's not my responsibility." His gaze held mine, telling me without words that he understood my fear and worry and anger. Just as he'd always understood me. "I told her as much. Then I called Giroux and told him, too. He needs to come take care of his wife."

He reached for his shampoo, which rested on a glass shelf with the rest of his personal shower items. He'd moved his stuff into my place pretty much the minute I agreed to date him, just as he had stocked his place with duplicates of my everyday items.

"She was provoked, though, Eva. Deanna visited her earlier tonight with pictures she took of you and me at the video launch."

"Fabulous," I muttered. "That explains why Deanna was here waiting to ambush me."

"Was she really?" he purred dangerously, making me pity Deanna—for about half a second. She was digging herself a nice grave.

"She probably got shots of you showing up at Corinne's place and wanted to rile me." I crossed my arms. "She's stalking you."

Gideon tipped his head back into the water to rinse, his biceps flexing as he ran his fingers through his hair.

He was so flagrantly, sexually, beautifully male.

I licked my lips, aroused by the sight of him despite my irritation with his exes. I closed the distance between us and squeezed some of his body wash into my palm. Then I ran my hands over his chest.

Groaning, he looked down at me. "I love your hands on me."

"That's good, since I can't keep my hands off you."

He touched my cheek, his eyes soft. He searched my face, maybe gauging whether I was wearing the fuck-me look or not. I didn't think I was. I wanted him, that never stopped, but I also wanted to enjoy just being with him. That was hard when he was blowing my mind.

"I needed this," he said. "Being with you."

"It seems like so much is coming at us, doesn't it? We can't catch a break. If it's not one thing, it's another." My fingertips traced the hard ridges of his abdomen. Desire hummed between us, and that wonderful sense of being near someone who was precious and necessary. "But we're doing okay, aren't we?"

His lips touched my forehead. "We're hanging in pretty good, I'd say. But I can't wait to take you away tomorrow. Get out of here for a while, away from everyone, and just have you all to myself."

I smiled, delighted by the thought. "I can't wait, either."

I woke when Gideon slipped out of my bed.

Blinking, I noted that the television was still on, though muted. I'd fallen asleep curled up with him, enjoying our time alone together after all the hours and days we'd been forced to spend apart.

"Where are you going?" I whispered.

"To bed." He touched my cheek. "I'm crashing hard."

"Don't go."

"Don't ask me to stay."

I sighed, understanding his fear. "I love you."

Bending over me, Gideon pressed his lips to mine. "Don't forget to put your passport in your purse."

"I won't forget. Are you sure I shouldn't pack something?"

"Nothing." He kissed me again, his lips clinging to mine.

Then he was gone.

I wore a light jersey wrap dress to work on Friday, something that could go from work to a long flight easily. I had no idea how far Gideon was taking me, but knew I'd be comfortable no matter what.

When I got to work, I found Megumi on the phone, so we waved at each other and I headed straight to my cubicle. Ms. Field stopped by just as I settled into my chair.

The executive chairman of Waters Field & Leaman looked powerful and confident in a soft gray pantsuit.

"Good morning, Eva," she said. "Have Mark stop by my office when he gets in."

I nodded, admiring her triple-strand black pearl necklace. "Will do."

When I passed along the request to Mark five minutes later, he shook his head. "Betcha we didn't get the Adrianna Vineyards account."

"You think?"

"I hate those damned cattle-call RFPs. They're not looking for quality and experience. They just want someone who's hungry enough to give their services away."

We'd dropped everything to meet the deadline for the request for proposal, which had been given to Mark to spearhead because he'd done such an amazing job with the Kingsman Vodka account.

"Their loss," I told him.

"I know, but still . . . I want to win 'em all. Wish me luck that I'm wrong."

I gave him a thumbs-up and he headed to Christine Field's office. My desk phone rang as I was pushing to my feet to grab a cup of coffee from the break room.

"Mark Garrity's office," I answered, "Eva Tramell speaking."

"Eva, honey."

I exhaled at the sound of my mother's watery voice. "Hi, Mom. How are you?"

"Will you see me? Maybe we could have lunch?"

"Sure. Today?"

"If you could." She took a breath that sounded like a sob. "I really need to see you."

"Okay." My stomach knotted with concern. I hated hearing my mother so upset. "Do you want me to meet you somewhere?"

"Clancy and I will come get you. You take lunch at noon, right?"

"Yes. I'll meet you at the curb."

"Good." She paused. "I love you."

"I know, Mom. I love you, too."

We hung up and I stared down at the phone.

How was our family going to move forward from here?

I sent a quick text to Gideon, letting him know I'd have to take a rain check on lunch. I needed to get my relationship with my mom back on track.

Knowing I needed more coffee to tackle the day ahead, I set off to fill up.

I left my desk exactly at noon and headed down to the lobby. As the hours passed, I grew more and more excited about getting away with Gideon. Away from Corinne, and Deanna, and Brett.

I'd just passed through the security turnstiles when I saw him.

Jean-François Giroux stood at the security desk, looking distinctly European and very attractive. His wavy dark hair was longer than it had been in the pictures I'd seen of him, his face less tan and his mouth harder, framed by a goatee. The pale green of his eyes was even more striking in person, even though they were red with weariness. From the small carry-on at his feet, I suspected he'd come straight to the Crossfire from the airport.

"*Mon Dieu.* How slow are the elevators in this building?" he asked the security guard in a clipped French accent. "It's impossible that it should take twenty minutes to come down from the top."

"Mr. Cross is on his way," the guard replied staunchly, remaining in his chair.

As if he sensed my gaze, Giroux's head swiveled toward me and his gaze narrowed. He pushed away from the counter, striding toward me.

The cut of his suit was tighter than Gideon's, narrower at the waist and calves. The impression I got of him was too neat and rigid, a man who assumed power by enforcing rules.

"Eva Tramell?" he asked, startling me with his recognition.

"Mr. Giroux." I offered my hand.

He took it, then surprised me by leaning in and kissing both of my cheeks. Perfunctory, absentminded kisses, but that wasn't the point. Even for a Frenchman, it was a familiar gesture from someone who was a total stranger to me.

When he stepped back, I looked at him with raised brows.

"Would you have time to speak with me?" he asked, still holding my hand.

"I'm afraid not today." I tugged away gently. Anonymity was created just by being in a massive space crowded with people rushing to and fro, but with Deanna lurking around, I couldn't be too careful about who I was seen with. "I have a lunch date and then I'm leaving directly after work."

"Tomorrow, perhaps?"

"I'll be out of town this weekend. Monday would be the earliest."

"Out of town. With Cross?"

My head canted to the side as I examined him, trying to read him. "That's really none of your business, but yes."

I told the truth so he'd know that Gideon had a woman in his life who wasn't Corinne.

"Does it not bother you," he said, his tone noticeably cooling, "that he used my wife to make you jealous and bring you back to him?"

"Gideon wants to be friends with Corinne. Friends spend time together."

"You're blond, but surely you can't be so naïve as to believe that."

"You're stressed," I countered, "but surely you know you're being an ass."

I registered Gideon's presence before I felt his hand on my arm.

"You'll apologize, Giroux," he interjected with dangerous softness. "And do so sincerely."

Giroux shot him a look so filled with anger and loathing, it made me shift restlessly on my feet. "Making me wait is classless, Cross, even for you."

"If the insult were intentional, you'd know it." Gideon's mouth thinned into a line as sharp as a blade. "The apology, Giroux. I've never been anything but polite and respectful to Corinne. You will show Eva the same courtesy."

To the casual observer, his pose was loose and relaxed, but I felt the fury in him. I sensed it in both men—one hot and one icy cool, the tension building by the moment. The space around us felt like it was closing in, which was insane considering how wide and deep the lobby was, and how high the ceiling soared.

Afraid they'd come to blows right there, regardless of being in such a populated space, I reached over and caught Gideon's hand in mine, giving it a light squeeze.

Giroux's gaze dropped to our linked hands, then rose to meet my eyes. *"Pardonnez-moi,"* he said, inclining his head slightly to me. "You are not at fault here."

"Don't let us hold you up," Gideon murmured to me, his thumb brushing over my knuckles.

But I lingered, hating to walk away. "You should be with your wife," I said to Giroux.

"She should be with me," he corrected.

I reminded myself that he hadn't come after her when she'd left him. He'd been too busy blaming Gideon instead of fixing his marriage.

"Eva," my mom called, having come inside to find me. She approached on nude Louboutins, her slender body draped in a soft silk halter dress in a matching hue. In the dark marble-lined lobby, she was a bright spot.

"Let's get you on your way, angel," Gideon said. "Give me a minute, Giroux."

I hesitated before walking away. "Good-bye, Monsieur Giroux."

"Miss Tramell," he said, tearing his gaze away from Gideon. "Until next time."

I left because I didn't have a choice, but I didn't like it. Gideon walked me over to intercept my mom, and I looked at him, letting him see the worry on my face.

His eyes reassured me. I saw the same latent power and uncompromising control that I'd recognized when we first met. He could handle Giroux. He could handle anything.

"Enjoy your lunch," Gideon said, kissing my mom's cheek before facing me and giving me a quick, hard kiss on the mouth.

I watched him walk away and was unnerved by the intensity with which Giroux's eyes followed his return.

My mom's arm linking with mine brought my attention to her.

"Hi," I said, trying to push my unease away. I waited for her to ask if the guys were going to join us, since she loved nothing more than spending time with rich handsome men, but she didn't.

"Are you and Gideon trying to work things out?" she asked instead.

"Yes."

I glanced at her before I preceded her through the revolving door. She looked more fragile than ever, her skin pale and her eyes lacking their usual sparkle. I waited until she joined me outside, my senses struggling to adjust to the change wrought by stepping out of the cool, cavernous lobby into the sweltering heat and explosion of noise and activity on the street.

I smiled at Clancy as he opened the back door to the town car. "Hey, Clancy."

As my mom slid gracefully into the back of the car, he smiled back. At least I think it was a smile. His mouth twitched a little.

"How are you?" I asked him.

He gave me a brisk nod in reply. "And you?"

"Hanging in there."

"You'll be all right," he said, just as I slid into the car beside my mom. He sounded a lot more confident about that than I felt.

THE first few minutes of lunch were filled with an awkward silence. Sunlight flooded the New American bistro my mom had selected, which only made the unease between us more obvious.

I waited for my mom to start things off, since she was the one who wanted to talk. I had plenty to say, but first I needed to know what the priority was for her. Was it the trust she'd broken by putting a tracking device in my Rolex? Was it her cheating on Stanton with my dad?

"That's a beautiful watch," she said, looking at my new one.

"Thank you." My hand covered it, protecting it. The timepiece was priceless to me, and deeply personal. "Gideon bought it for me."

She looked horrified. "You didn't tell him about the tracker, did you?"

"I tell him everything, Mom. We don't have any secrets."

"Maybe *you* don't. What about him?"

"We're solid," I said confidently. "And getting stronger every day."

"Oh." She nodded, her short curls swaying gently. "That's . . . wonderful, Eva. He can take good care of you."

"He already does, in the way I need him to, which has nothing to do with his money."

My mother's lips tightened at my bitter tone. She didn't actually frown, something she studiously avoided to protect the flawlessness of her skin. "Don't be so quick to dismiss money, Eva. You never know when or why you'll need it."

Irritation simmered through me. She'd put money first my whole life, no matter who she hurt—like my father—in the process.

"I don't," I argued. "I just won't let it rule my life. And before you blurt out something like, oh it's easy for me to say that, I can guarantee if Gideon lost every cent he had, I'd still be with him."

"He's too smart to lose it all," she said tightly. "And if you're lucky, you'll never have anything happen that will drain you financially."

I sighed, exasperated with the topic. "We're never going to see eye to eye on this, you know."

Her beautifully manicured fingers stroked over the handle of her silverware. "You're so angry at me."

"Do you realize Dad's in love with you? He's so in love with you, he can't move on. I don't think he'll ever get married. He'll never have a steady woman in his life who'll take care of him."

She swallowed hard and a tear slid down her cheek.

"Don't you dare cry," I ordered, leaning forward. "This isn't about you. You're not the victim here."

"I'm not allowed to feel pain?" she retorted, her voice harder than I'd ever heard it. "I'm not allowed to cry over a broken heart? I love your father, too. I would give anything for him to be happy."

"You don't love him enough."

"Everything I've done is for love. *Everything.*" She laughed humorlessly. "My God . . . I wonder how you can stand to be with me when you hold such a low opinion."

"You're my mother and you've always been on my side. You're always trying to protect me, even if you go about it the wrong way. I love you and Dad both. He's a good man who deserves to be happy."

She took a shaky sip of water. "If it weren't for you, I'd wish we had never met. We both would've been happier that way. There's nothing I can do about it now."

"You could be with him. Make him happy. You seem to be the only woman who can."

"That's impossible," she whispered.

"Why? Because he's not rich?"

"Yes." Her hand went to her throat. "Because he's not rich."

Brutal honesty. My heart sank. There was a bleak look in her blue eyes I'd never seen before. What drove her to need money so desperately? Would I ever know or understand? "But *you're* rich. Isn't that enough?"

Over the course of three divorces, she'd amassed millions in personal wealth.

"No."

I stared at her, incredulous.

She looked away, her three-carat diamond studs catching the light and glittering with a rainbow of colors. "You don't understand."

"So explain it to me, Mom. Please."

Her gaze returned to me. "Maybe someday. When you're not so upset with me."

Sitting back in my chair, I felt a headache building. "Fine. I'm upset because I don't understand, and you won't explain because I'm upset. We're getting nowhere fast."

"I'm sorry, honey." Her expression was pleading. "What happened between your father and me—"

"Victor. Why don't you ever say his name?"

She flinched. "How long will you punish me?" she asked quietly.

"I'm not trying to punish you. I just don't get it."

It was crazy that we were sitting in a bright, busy space filled with people and dealing with painful personal crap. I wished she'd had me over to her place instead, the home she shared with Stanton. But I guessed she had wanted the buffer of an audience to keep me from totally losing it.

"Listen," I said, feeling tired. "Cary and I are going to move out of the apartment, get something on our own."

My mom's shoulders straightened. "What? Why? Don't be reckless, Eva! There's no need—"

"There is, though. Nathan's gone. And Gideon and I want to spend more time together—"

"What does that have to do with you moving away?" Her eyes flooded with tears. "I'm *sorry*, Eva. What more can I say?"

"This isn't about you, Mom." I tucked my hair behind my ear, fidgeting because her crying always got to me. "Okay, honestly, it does feel weird living in a place Stanton pays for after what happened between you and Dad, but more than that, Gideon and I want to live together. It just makes sense to start fresh someplace."

"Live together?" My mother's tears dried up. "Before marriage? Eva, no. That would be a horrible mistake. What about Cary? You brought him out to New York with you."

"And he'll stay with me." I didn't feel like telling her I hadn't brought up the Gideon-as-a-roommate idea to Cary yet, but I was confident he'd be okay with it. I would be around more and the rent would be easier to bear when split in thirds. "It'll be the three of us."

"You don't live with a man like Gideon Cross if you're not married to him." She leaned forward. "You have to trust me on this. Wait for the ring."

"I'm not in a rush to get married," I said, even as my thumb rubbed over the back of my ring.

"Oh my God." My mother shook her head. "What are you saying? You love him."

"It's too soon. I'm too young."

"You're twenty-four. That's the perfect age." Determination straightened my mother's spine. For once, that didn't bother me, because it restored some of her spirit. "I'm not going to let you ruin this, Eva."

"Mom—"

"No." Her eyes took on a calculating gleam. "Trust me and slow down. I'll handle this."

Crap. That wasn't at all reassuring when she was on Gideon's side of the marriage argument and not mine.

18

I WAS STILL thinking about my mom when I left the Crossfire at five o'clock. The Bentley waited at the curb and as I walked up to it, Angus climbed out and smiled at me.

"Good evening, Eva."

"Hi." I smiled back. "How are you, Angus?"

"Excellent." He rounded the rear of the car and opened the back door for me.

I searched his face. How much did he know about Nathan and Gideon? Did he know as much as Clancy? Or even more than that?

Slipping into the cool backseat, I pulled out my smartphone and called Cary. It went to voice mail, so I left a message. "Hey, just reminding you that I'll be gone this weekend. Would you do me a favor and think about moving into a place we share with Gideon, and we can talk about it when I get back? Someplace new, that we can all afford. Not that he has to worry about that," I added, imagining Cary's expression. "Okay. If you need me and you can't reach me on my cell, send me an e-mail. Love you."

I'd just hit the end button when the door opened and Gideon joined me. "Hi, ace."

He caught me by the back of the neck and kissed me, his mouth sealing over mine. His tongue licked into my mouth, tasting me, making my thoughts grind to a halt. I was breathless when he let me go.

"Hi, angel," he said roughly.

"Wow."

His mouth curved. "How was lunch with your mom?"

I groaned.

"That good, huh?" He caught my hand. "Tell me about it."

"I don't know. It was weird."

Angus got in the driver's seat and pulled into traffic.

"Weird?" Gideon prompted. "Or uncomfortable?"

"Both." I looked out the tinted window as we slowed due to traffic. The sidewalks were clogged with people, but they were moving briskly. It was the cars that were stuck. "She's so focused on money. That's nothing new, but I'm used to her acting like it's just common sense to want financial security. Today, she seemed . . . sad. Resigned."

His thumb stroked soothingly over my knuckles. "Maybe she's feeling guilty for cheating."

"She should! But I don't think that's it. I think it's something else, but I don't have a clue."

"Do you want me to look into it?"

I turned my head to meet his gaze. I didn't answer right away, thinking it over. "I do, yes. But I feel icky about it, too. I researched you, Dr. Lucas, Corinne . . . I keep digging for people's secrets instead of just asking about them outright."

"So ask her," he said, in that matter-of-fact male way.

"I did. She said she'd talk about it when I wasn't upset."

"Women," he scoffed, with warm amusement in his eyes.

"What did Giroux want? Did you know he was coming by?"

He shook his head. "He wants someone to blame for his marriage troubles. I'm convenient."

"Why doesn't he stop blaming and start fixing? They need to go into counseling."

"Or get a divorce."

I stiffened. "Is that what you want?"

"What I want is you," he purred, releasing my hand to grab me instead and pull me onto his lap.

"Fiend."

"You have no idea. I have diabolical plans for you this weekend."

The heated look he raked me with had my thoughts shifting in a much naughtier direction. I was pulling his head down for a kiss when the Bentley turned, and it was suddenly dark. Looking around, I realized we'd pulled into a parking garage. We drove around two levels, pulled into a spot, then immediately pulled out again.

Along with four other black Bentley SUVs.

"What's going on?" I asked, as we headed back toward the exit with two Bentleys in front of us and two behind us.

"Shell game," he said, nuzzling my throat.

We pulled back out into traffic, heading in different directions.

"Are we being followed?" I asked.

"Just being cautious." His teeth sank gently into my flesh, making my nipples hard. Supporting my back with one arm, he brushed the side of my breast with his thumb. "This weekend is ours."

He'd taken my mouth in a lush, deep kiss when we pulled into another parking garage. We slid into a spot and the door was yanked open. I was trying to figure out what was going on, when Gideon swung his legs to the side and slipped out of the Bentley with me held firmly in his arms, only to immediately step into the back of another car.

We were on the road again in less than a minute, with the Bentley pulling out into traffic in front of us and heading in the opposite direction.

"This is insane," I said. "I thought we were leaving the country."

"We are. Trust me."

"I do."

His eyes were soft on my face. "I know you do."

We didn't have any more stops on the way to the airport. We pulled right onto the tarmac after a brief security check, and I preceded Gideon up the short flight of steps into one of his private jets. The cabin was luxurious yet understated in its elegance, with sofa seating on the right and table and chairs on the left. The flight attendant was a handsome young guy with black dress slacks and vest embroidered with the Cross Industries logo and his name, Eric.

"Good evening, Mr. Cross. Miss Tramell," Eric greeted us with a smile. "Would you like something to drink as we prepare for takeoff?"

"Cranberry and Kingsman for me," I said.

"The same," Gideon replied, shrugging out of his jacket and handing it over to Eric, who waited while Gideon stripped off his vest and tie, too.

I watched appreciatively, throwing in a whistle for good measure. "I'm liking this trip already."

"Angel." He shook his head, his eyes laughing.

A gentleman in a navy suit entered the plane. He greeted Gideon warmly, shook my hand when introduced, then requested our passports. He was gone as quickly as he'd come, and the cabin door was closed. Gideon and I were buckled in at the table with our drinks when the plane started taxiing down the runway.

"Are you going to tell me where we're headed?" I asked, lifting my drink in a toast.

He clinked his crystal tumbler against mine. "Don't you want it to be a surprise?"

"Depends on how long it takes to get there. I might go crazy with curiosity before we land."

"I expect you'll be too busy to think about it." His mouth curved. "This is a mode of transportation, after all."

"Oh." I glanced back, seeing the little hallway of doors at the back of the plane. One would be a lavatory, one an office, and the other a bedroom. Expectation coursed through me. "How much time have we got to kill?"

"Hours," he purred.

My toes curled. "Oh, ace. The things I'm going to do to you."

He shook his head. "You're forgetting this is my weekend to have you any way I want. That was the deal."

"On our trip? That doesn't seem fair."

"You said that before."

"It was true then, too."

His smile widened and he took a drink. "As soon as the captain gives the go-ahead to get up, I want you to head into the bedroom and get naked. Then lie on the bed and wait for me."

One of my brows arched. "You love the idea of having me rolling around naked waiting for you to fuck me."

"I do, yes. I recall the reverse being a fantasy of yours."

"Hmm." I took a drink, relishing the way the vodka went down icy and smooth, then heated in my stomach.

The plane leveled out and the captain made a brief announcement freeing us to move about the cabin.

Gideon shot me a look that said, *Well? Run along now.*

Narrowing my gaze at him, I got up, taking my drink with me. I took my time, provoking him. And making myself more excited. I loved being at his mercy. As much as I loved making him lose his mind over me, I couldn't deny that his control was a major turn-on. I knew how absolute that control could be, which made it possible for me to trust him completely. I didn't think there was anything I wouldn't allow him to do to me.

Which was a conviction that would be tested sooner rather than later, I realized when I entered the sleeping cabin and saw the red silk-and-suede restraints lying so prettily on the white comforter.

Turning my head, I looked at Gideon only to find him gone. His empty glass sat on the table, the square cubes of ice glittering like diamonds.

My heart thudded. I stepped into the room, tossing back the rest of my drink. I couldn't bear to be restrained during sex, unless it was by Gideon. By his hands or the weight of his muscled body. We'd never gone beyond that. I wasn't sure I could.

I set my empty tumbler on the nightstand, my hand shaking slightly. I didn't know if that was due to fear or excitement.

I knew Gideon would never hurt me. He worked so hard to make sure I was never afraid. But what if I disappointed him? What if I couldn't give him what he needed? He'd mentioned bondage before and I knew one of his fantasies was to have me completely restrained and open to him, my body spread and helpless for him to use. I understood that desire, the need to feel total and utter possession. I felt that way toward him.

I undressed. My movements were slow and careful, because my pulse was already thrumming too quickly. I was practically panting, the anticipation painfully acute. I hung my clothes on a hanger in the small closet, then climbed gingerly onto the raised bed. I was holding the restraints in my hands, doubting and second-guessing myself, when Gideon walked in.

"You're not lying down," he said gently, closing and locking the door behind him.

I held up the restraints.

"Custom made, just for you." He approached, his nimble fingers already freeing the buttons of his shirt. "Crimson is your color."

Gideon undressed as slowly as I had, affording me the opportunity to appreciate every inch of skin he exposed. He knew the rippling of his muscles beneath the rough silk of his tanned flesh would be an aphrodisiac to me.

"Am I ready for this?" I asked softly.

His gaze stayed on my face as he removed his pants. When he stood in just his black boxer briefs, his cock a thick bulge in the front, he answered, "Never more than you can take, angel. I promise you that."

Taking a deep breath, I lay back, setting the cuffs on my belly. He came to me, his face tight with lust. He settled on the bed beside me and lifted my hand to his mouth, kissing my wrist. "Your pulse is racing."

I nodded, not knowing what to say.

He picked up the cuffs, deftly unhooking the strip of crimson silk that held the two suede wrist pieces together. "Being bound helps you surrender, but it doesn't have to be literal. It just has to be enough to get you in the right headspace."

My stomach quivered as he laid the strap across it. He set one cuff on his thigh and held up the other.

"Give me your wrist, angel."

I extended my hand to him, my breathing quickening as he fastened the suede snugly. The feel of the primitive material against my fluttering pulse was surprisingly arousing.

"That's not too tight, is it?" he asked.

"No."

"You should feel the constriction enough to be constantly aware of it, but it shouldn't hurt you."

I swallowed. "It doesn't hurt."

"Good." He bound my other wrist similarly, then straightened to admire his handwork. "Beautiful," he murmured. "Reminds me of the red dress you wore the first time I had you. That was it for me, you know. You devastated me. There was no coming back from that."

"Gideon." My apprehension left me, chased away by the warmth of his love and desire. I was precious to him. He would never push me further than I could go.

"Reach up and grip the sides of the pillow," he ordered.

I did, and the tightening of my wrists made me even more aware of the cuffs. I felt bound. Captured.

"Feel it?" he asked, and I understood.

I loved him so much in that moment it hurt. "Yes."

"I'm going to tell you to close your eyes," he went on, standing and taking off the final bit of clothing he wore. He was heavily aroused, his thick cock bobbing under its own weight, the wide crown shiny with pre-cum. My mouth flooded, hunger pulsing through me. He was so hot for me, so hungry, and yet you'd never know it from his voice or the calm he radiated.

His perfect restraint made me wet. Gideon was the best of everything for me, a man who wanted me ferociously—which I so urgently needed to feel secure—but with enough self-possession to keep from overwhelming me.

"I want you to keep your eyes closed if you can," he continued, his voice low and soothing, "but if it gets to be too much, open them. But say your safeword first."

"Okay."

He picked up the satin strap and ran it lightly over my skin. The cool metal of the fastener at one end caught on my nipple, making it pucker. "Let's be very clear about this, Eva. Your safeword isn't for me. It's for *you*. All you have to say to me is *no* or *stop*, but just like wearing the cuffs makes you feel bound, saying your safeword will put your mind in the right place. Do you understand?"

I nodded, growing more comfortable and eager by the moment.

"Close your eyes."

I followed the command. Almost instantly, I became sharply aware of the pressure at my wrists. The vibration and dull hum of the plane's engines became more pronounced. My lips parted. My breathing sped up.

The strap glided over my cleavage to my other breast. "You're so beautiful, angel. Perfect. You have no idea what it does to me seeing you like this."

"Gideon," I whispered, desperately in love with him. "Tell me."

His splayed fingertips touched my throat, and then began a slow slide down my torso. "My heart's beating as fast as yours."

I arched and shivered beneath his slightly ticklish touch. "Good."

"I'm so hard it hurts."

"I'm wet."

"Show me," he said roughly. "Spread your legs." His fingers slid through my cleft. "Yes. You're slick and hot, angel."

My sex clenched hungrily, my entire body responding to his touch.

"Ah, Eva. You've got the greediest cunt. I'm going to spend the rest of my life keeping it satisfied."

"You should start now."

He laughed softly. "Actually, we're starting with your mouth. I need you to suck me off so I can fuck you straight through until we land."

"Oh my God," I moaned. "Please tell me it's not a ten-hour flight."

"I might have to spank you for that," he purred.

"But I'm a good girl!"

The mattress dipped as he climbed onto it. I felt him work his way toward me until he knelt beside my shoulder. "Be a good girl now, Eva. Turn toward me and open your mouth."

Eager, I obeyed. The silky soft crest of his cock brushed over my lips and I opened wider, absorbing the shock of pleasure I felt at the sound of his tormented groan. His fingers pushed into my hair, his palm cupping the back of my neck. Holding me where he wanted me.

"God," he gasped. "Your mouth is just as greedy."

The position I was in, on my back with my hands gripping the pillow, prevented me from taking more than the thick head. I mouthed him, my tongue flickering over the sensitive hole at the tip, thrilled by the joy of focusing on Gideon. Going down on him wasn't selfless for me. In fact, it was mostly for me that I loved it so much.

"That's it," he encouraged, rocking his hips to fuck my mouth. "Suck my cock just like that . . . so good, angel. You make me come so hard."

I breathed him in, feeling my body respond to his scent, instinctively reacting to its mate. With all of my senses saturated with Gideon, I gave myself over to our mutual pleasure.

I dreamed I was falling, and it jerked me awake.

My heart raced from the surprise, and then I realized the plane had dropped suddenly. Turbulence. I was fine. And so was Gideon, who'd fallen asleep beside me. That made me smile. I'd almost passed out when he'd finally given me an orgasm after fucking me so thoroughly I was nearly incoherent with the need to come. It was only fair that he'd be a little wiped out, too.

A quick glance at my watch told me we'd been in the air almost three hours. I guessed we'd napped about twenty minutes, maybe even less than that. I was pretty sure he'd been at me for close to two hours. I could still feel the echo of his thick cock sliding in and out of me, stroking and rubbing all of my sensitive spots.

I slid carefully out of bed, not wanting to wake him, and was super quiet when closing the pocket door that concealed the en suite lavatory.

Outfitted with dark wood and chrome fixtures, the lavatory was both masculine and elegant. The toilet had armrests, which made it look like a throne, and a frosted window allowed sunlight into the space. A walk-in shower had a hand wand showerhead that looked very tempting, but I was still wearing the crimson cuffs. So I took care of business, washed my hands, then spotted hand lotion in one of the drawers.

The fragrance was subtle but wonderful. As I rubbed it on, a wicked idea entered my mind. Grabbing the tube, I took it back to the bedroom with me.

The sight that greeted me when I reentered made my breath catch.

Gideon sprawled across the queen-size bed, dwarfing it with his beautiful golden body. One arm was tossed over his head, the other draped across his pecs. He had one leg bent and fallen off to the side, while the other stretched out until his foot hung off the end of the mattress. His cock lay heavily across his lower abs, the crown nearly reaching his navel.

God, he was so virile. Stunningly so. And powerful, his entire body a study in physical strength and grace.

And yet I could bring him to his knees. That humbled me.

He woke when I climbed onto the bed, blinking up at me.

"Hey," he said gruffly. "Come here."

"I love you," I told him, lowering into his outstretched arms. His skin felt like warm silk and I snuggled into him.

"Eva." He took my mouth in a sweet, hungry kiss. "I'm not nearly done with you."

Taking a deep breath of courage, I set the tube of lotion on his stomach. "I want to be inside you, ace."

He glanced down, frowning, then stilled. I was close enough to feel his breathing change. "That isn't our deal," he said carefully.

"I think we need to revisit and revise. Besides, it's still Friday, so it's not quite the weekend yet."

"Eva—"

"It turns me on just thinking about it," I whispered, wrapping my legs around his thigh and rubbing against him, letting him feel that I was wet. The coarse hair sliding against my sensitive sex made me moan, as did the sense of being shameless and naughty. "You say stop and I will. Just let me try."

His teeth ground audibly.

I kissed him. Pressed my body against him. When Gideon was

walking me through something new, he talked me through it. But with him, sometimes talking wasn't the answer. Sometimes it was best to help him turn his mind off.

"Angel—"

I slid over him, straddling him, setting the lotion aside so he wasn't thinking about it so much. If I took him someplace new, I didn't want either of us to overthink it. And if it didn't feel natural, I wouldn't do it. What we had together was too precious to spoil.

Running my hands down his chest, I gentled him, let him feel my love for him. How I worshipped him. There was nothing I wouldn't do for him, except give up.

His arms came around me, one hand pushing into my hair, the other settling at the small of my back, urging me closer. His mouth was open to me, his tongue licking and tasting. I sank into the kiss, angling my head to get at him.

His cock hardened between us, thickening against my belly. He arched his hips upward, increasing the pressure between us, and moaned into my mouth.

I moved across his cheek to his throat, licking the salt from his skin before latching on. I sucked rhythmically, scoring him with my teeth, marking him. With his hand at my nape, he held me close, rough sounds of pleasure vibrating against my lips.

Pulling back, I looked at the bright red hickey I'd left him with. "Mine," I whispered.

"Yours," he vowed roughly, his eyes hooded and hot.

"Every inch of you." I moved lower, finding and teasing the flat disks of his nipples. I licked over the tiny points, then around them, my touch feather light until I suckled him.

Gideon hissed as my cheeks hollowed on a drawing pull, his hands falling away to grip the comforter on either side of his hips.

"Inside and out," I said softly, as I turned to his other nipple and lavished similar attention on it.

As I made my way down his straining body, I felt his tension grow. When my tongue rimmed his navel, he jerked violently.

"Shh," I soothed him, rubbing my cheek against his throbbing cock.

He'd washed up after our earlier round, leaving him smelling clean and delectable. His sac hung heavily between his legs, the satiny flesh bared by his meticulous grooming. I loved that he was as smooth as I was. When he was inside me, the connection was complete in every way, the sensations emphasized by touching skin to skin.

With my hands on his inner thighs, I urged him to spread open wider, giving me room to settle comfortably. Then I licked along the seam of his taut sac.

Gideon growled. The untamed, animalistic sound sent a ripple of apprehension through me. Still, I didn't stop. I couldn't. I wanted him too much.

Using only my mouth, I worshipped him, sucking softly and caressing him with my tongue. Then I suspended his testicles on the pads of my thumbs, lifting them to access the sensitive skin beneath. His balls drew up, the skin tightening and pulling close to his body. My tongue reached a little lower, an exploratory foray toward my ultimate goal.

"Eva. Stop." He panted. "I can't. Don't."

My mind raced as I continued to touch him, my hand gripping his cock and stroking it. He was still too much inside his own head, too focused on what was to come instead of what was happening now.

But I knew how to get him to focus on something else.

"Why don't we do this together, ace?" Shifting, I turned around, straddling him backward.

His hands grabbed my hips before I was fully balanced, yanking my sex down to his waiting mouth. I cried out in surprise as he latched onto my clit, sucking hungrily. Swollen and sensitive from earlier, I could hardly bear the sudden rush of pleasure. He was wild and ravenous, his passion driven by his frustration and fear.

Wrapping my lips around his cock, I gave him back what he was giving to me.

As I sucked hard on the head of his erection, his groan vibrated against my clit and nearly made me come. He held me to him, his fingers digging into my hips with bruising force.

I loved it. He was unraveling, and while he was afraid of what that meant, it thrilled me. He didn't trust himself with me, but I trusted him. It was a level of trust we'd worked hard for, shed tears and blood for, and I valued it more than anything else in my life.

Fisting his cock, I pumped him, lapping up the surges of pre-cum that spilled from him. I'd just realized he was trembling when he wrenched us to our sides, placing us side by side instead of one on top of the other.

He ate me hard and fast, his tongue pushing into my sex and driving me mad with furious thrusts. I touched the pucker of his anus with the tip of my finger, my mouth sliding feverishly up and down his thickness. He shuddered and the low sound that escaped him sent goose bumps racing across my sweat-misted skin.

My hips were working without volition, grinding my slick sex against his working mouth. I was moaning uncontrollably, my core trembling with tiny shivers of delight. He was fucking me so good with his tongue . . . driving me insane.

And then his fingertip was mimicking mine, rubbing against my rear entrance. My free hand searched blindly for the lotion.

Gideon pushed the tube into my grip, a much-needed sign of consent.

I'd barely flipped the cap open when his finger pushed inside me. As I arched my back, his cock slipped out of my mouth and I gasped his name, my body absorbing the shock of his unexpected entry. He'd lubed his fingers before passing the tube.

For a moment, I was overwhelmed by him. He was everywhere—around me, inside me, plastered against me. And he wasn't gentle. His finger in my rear plunged and retreated, fucking me, his forcefulness still tinged with that hint of anger. I was pushing him where he didn't want to go and he was punishing me with pleasure that came too quick to manage.

I was gentler with him. Opening my mouth, I sucked his cock. I let the lotion warm on my fingers before I rubbed it against him. And I waited for him to push out for me, to flower open, before I pushed inside with a single finger.

The sound that rattled from him then was like nothing I'd ever heard. It was the cry of a wounded animal, but filled with soul-deep pain. He froze against me, breathing hard against my sex, his finger buried deep, his hard body quivering.

I pulled my mouth off him and crooned, "I'm in you now, baby. You're doing so good. I'm going to make you feel so good."

He gasped when I slid a little deeper, my fingertip gliding over his prostate. *"Eva!"*

His cock swelled even further, turning red, the thick veins standing out along its length, pre-ejaculate spurting onto his lower belly. He was hard as stone, curving up to a point just past his navel. I'd never seen him so aroused and it made me so hot.

"I've got you." I stroked gently inside him, my tongue licking along his raging hard-on. "I love you so much, Gideon. I love touching you like this . . . seeing you this way."

"Ah, Christ." He shook violently. "Fuck me, angel. Now," he bit out, as I rubbed him again. *"Hard."*

I swallowed his erection and gave him what he demanded, massaging the spot inside him that made him curse and writhe, his body fighting the bombardment of sensation. His hands left me, his big frame arching away, but I held on with my lips and hands, driving him onward.

"Ah, God," he sobbed, ripping the comforter in his fists, the tearing sound reverberating through the enclosed space. "Stop. Eva. No more. Damn it!"

I pressed inside the same moment I sucked hard outside and he came with such force, I choked on the heated flood. He spurted across my lips as I pulled away, over his stomach and my breasts, releasing in a gushing torrent that made it hard to believe he'd already come twice in as many hours. I could feel the contractions against my fingertip, the wrenching pulses that propelled the semen from his cock.

It wasn't until his body stilled that I pulled away, turning around shakily to pull him into my arms. We were a sweaty, sticky mess and I loved that it didn't matter.

Gideon buried his damp face between my breasts and cried.

19

GIDEON'S CHOSEN LOCATION was paradise. His pilot took us over the Windward Islands, flying low over the impossibly beautiful blue waters of the tranquil Caribbean into a private airport not far from our ultimate destination, the Crosswinds resort.

We were both still pretty shell-shocked when the plane landed. Gideon had had the orgasm of his life, after all. We had our passports stamped with our hair still wet, our hands linked tightly together. We hardly spoke, either to each other or to anyone else. I think we were both too raw.

We slid into a waiting limousine and Gideon poured himself a stiff drink. His face gave nothing away, his guard up and impenetrable. I shook my head when he held up the crystal decanter in silent query.

He settled on the seat beside me and put his arm around my shoulders.

I snuggled into him, draping my legs over his lap. "Are we okay?"

He pressed a hard kiss to my forehead. "Yes."

"I love you."

"I know." He tossed back his drink and set the empty tumbler in a cup holder.

We didn't say anything else on the long drive from the airport to the resort. It was dark by the time we arrived, but the open-air lobby was brightly lit. Framed by lush potted plants and decorated in dark woods and colorful ceramic tiles, the front desk welcomed guests with a care-free yet elegant style.

The hotel manager was waiting on the circular front drive as we rolled to a stop. His appearance was immaculate, his smile wide. He was clearly excited to have Gideon in residence and doubly so that Gideon knew his name—Claude.

Claude spoke animatedly, as we followed along behind him with our hands linked firmly together. No one could tell from looking at Gideon how intimate and exposed to each other we'd been only an hour or so before. While my hair had dried in a messy mop, his looked as gorgeous and sexy as ever. His suit was perfectly pressed and beautifully worn, while my dress looked a little limp after the long day. My makeup had washed off in the shower, leaving me pale with the remnants of raccoon eyes.

Yet Gideon's possessiveness toward me was clear in the way he gripped me, and how he steered me into our suite in front of him with his hand at the small of my back. He made me feel safe and accepted, even though he was in his work persona and I wasn't at my best, which reflected on him.

I loved him for that.

I just wished he weren't so quiet. It made me worry. And it totally made me doubt my decision to push him after he'd told me to stop more than once. What the hell did I know about what he needed to get better?

As the manager continued to talk to Gideon, I moved slowly through the massive living area, with its wide-open terrace and white couches spread across bamboo floors. The master bedroom was equally impressive, with a large bed framed by mosquito netting and another open terrace that led directly to a private swimming pool with an infinity edge that made it look like part of the shimmering ocean just beyond it.

A warm breeze blew in, kissing my face and sifting through my hair. The rising moon cast a trail over the ocean, and the distant sounds of laughter and reggae made me feel isolated in a way that wasn't quite pleasant.

Nothing was right when Gideon was off.

"Do you like it?" he asked quietly.

I turned to face him and heard the front door shut in the other room. "It's fantastic."

He gave a curt nod. "I ordered dinner in. Tilapia and rice, some fresh fruit and cheese."

"Awesome. I'm starving."

"There are clothes for you in the closet and drawers. You'll find bikinis, too, but the pool and beach are private, so you don't need them unless you want them. If there's anything missing, just let me know and we'll get it brought in."

I stared at him, noting the several feet between us. His eyes glittered in the soft light cast by the dimmed cam lighting and bedside table lamps. He was edgy and distant, and I felt tears building in the back of my throat.

"Gideon . . ." I held my hand out to him. "Did I make a mistake? Did I break something between us?"

"Angel." He sighed. He came close enough to catch my hand and lift it to his lips. Up close I could see how his gaze darted away, as if he had a hard time looking at me. A sick feeling settled in my gut. "Crossfire."

The one word came out so low, I almost thought I'd imagined it. Then he pulled me into his arms and kissed me sweetly.

"Ace." Pushing onto my tiptoes, I cupped the back of his neck and kissed him back with everything I had.

He pulled away too quickly. "Let's change for dinner before it gets here. I could stand being in less clothes."

I stepped back reluctantly, acknowledging that he had to be hot in his suit, but still sensing that something wasn't right. That feeling worsened when Gideon left the room to change and I realized we wouldn't be sharing the same bedroom.

I kicked off my shoes in the walk-in closet that was filled with way too many clothes for a weekend trip. Most were white. Gideon liked me in white. I suspected it was because he thought of me as his angel.

Did he still think of me that way now? Or was I the devil? A selfish bitch who made him face demons he'd rather forget?

I changed into a simple cotton slip dress in black, which matched my funereal mood. I felt like something had died between us.

Gideon and I had stumbled many times before, but I'd never felt this level of withdrawal from him. This discomfort and unease.

I'd felt it with other guys, when they were getting ready to tell me they didn't want to see me anymore.

Dinner arrived and was neatly laid out on the terrace table overlooking the secluded beach. I saw a white tent cabana on the sand and remembered Gideon's dream of us rolling around on a chaise for two by the water, making love.

My heart hurt.

I gulped two glasses of crisp, fruity white wine and went through the motions of eating, even though I'd lost my appetite. Gideon sat across from me in loose white linen drawstring pants and nothing else, which just made everything worse. He was so handsome, so goddamned sexy it was impossible not to stare at him. But he was miles away from me. A silent, forceful presence that made me *want* with every fiber of my soul.

The emotional gulf between us was growing. I couldn't reach across it.

I pushed my plate away once I'd cleared it and realized Gideon had hardly eaten at all. He'd just forked his food around and helped me drain the bottle of wine.

Taking a deep breath, I told him, "I'm sorry. I should've . . . I didn't . . ." I swallowed hard. "I'm sorry, baby," I whispered.

Shoving back from the table with a loud screech of the chair legs across the tile, I hurried away from the patio.

"Eva! Wait."

My feet hit the warm sand and I ran toward the ocean, pulling my dress off and colliding with water that felt as hot as a bath. It was shallow for several feet, then dropped off suddenly, plunging me in below my head. I bent my knees and sank, grateful to be submerged and hidden as I cried.

The weightlessness soothed my heavy heart. My hair billowed around me and I felt the soft brush of fish as they darted past the invader in their silent, peaceful world.

Being yanked back into reality had me sputtering and flailing.

"Angel." Gideon growled and took my mouth, kissing me hard and furious as he stalked out of the water and up the beach. He took me to the cabana and dropped me onto the chaise, covering me with his body before I fully caught my breath.

I was still dizzy when he groaned and said, "Marry me."

But that wasn't why I said, "Yes."

GIDEON had gone into the water after me with his pants on. The soaked linen clung to my bare legs as he sprawled over me and kissed me as if he were dying of a thirst only I could quench. His hands were in my hair, holding me still. His mouth was frantic, his lips swollen like mine, his tongue greedy and possessive.

I lay beneath him unmoving. Shocked. My startled brain quickly caught up.

He'd been agonizing over popping the question, not because he was leaving me.

"Tomorrow," he bit out, rubbing his cheek against mine. The first tingle of stubble roughened his jaw, the sensation jolting me into a deeper awareness of where we were and what he wanted.

"I—" My mind stuttered to a halt again.

"The word is *yes*, Eva." He pushed up and stared down at me fiercely. "Real simple—yes."

I swallowed hard. "We can't get married tomorrow."

"We can," he said emphatically, "and we will. I need it, Eva. I need the vows, the legality . . . I'm going crazy without them."

I felt the world spinning, like I was on one of those fun-house barrel rides that revolve so fast you're stuck to the wall with centrifugal force when the floor drops away from your feet. "It's too soon," I protested.

"You can say that to me after the flight over?" he snapped. "You fucking *own* me, Eva. I'll be damned if I don't own you back."

"I can't breathe," I gasped, inexplicably panicked.

Gideon rolled, pulling me on top of him, his arms banding around me. Possessing me. "You want this," he insisted. "You love me."

"I do, yes." I dropped my forehead to his chest. "But you're rushing into—"

"You think I'd ask you this on the fly? For God's sake, Eva, you know me better than that. I've been planning this for weeks. It's all I've thought about."

"Gideon . . . we can't just run off and elope."

"The hell we can't."

"What about our families? Or friends?"

"We'll get married again for them. I want that, too." He brushed the wet hair off my cheek. "I want pictures of us in the newspapers, magazines . . . everywhere. But that will take months. I can't wait that long. This is for us. We don't have to tell anyone, if you don't want. We can call it an engagement. It can be our secret."

I stared at him, not knowing what to say. His urgency was both romantic and terrifying.

"I asked your dad," he went on, shocking me all over again. "He didn't have any—"

"What? When?"

"When he was in town. I had an opportunity and I took it."

For some reason, that hurt. "He didn't tell me."

"I told him not to. Told him it wasn't going to happen right away. That I was still working on getting you back. I recorded it, so you can listen to the conversation if you don't believe me."

I blinked down at him. "You recorded it?" I repeated.

"I wasn't leaving anything to chance," he said unapologetically.

"You told him it wouldn't be right away. You lied to him."

His smile was razor sharp. "I didn't lie. It's been a few days."

"Oh my God. You're crazy."

"Possibly. If so, you've made me this way." He pressed a hard kiss to my cheek. "I can't live without you, Eva. I can't even imagine trying. Just the thought makes me insane."

"*This* is insane."

"Why?" He frowned. "You know there's no one else for either of us. What are you waiting for?"

Arguments rushed through my mind. Every reason we should wait, every possible pitfall seemed crystal clear. But nothing came out of my mouth.

"I'm not giving you any options here," he said decisively, twisting up and standing with me cradled in his arms. "We're doing this, Eva. Enjoy your last remaining hours as a single woman."

"Gideon," I gasped, my head thrashing as the orgasm poured through me.

His sweat dripped onto my chest, his hips tireless as he stroked his magnificent penis into me over and over, rolling and thrusting, shallow then deep.

"That's it," he praised hoarsely, "squeeze my dick just like that. You feel so good, angel. You're going to make me come again."

I panted for breath, boneless and tired from his unrelenting demands. He'd woken me twice before, taking me with skilled precision, imprinting onto my brain and my body that I belonged to him. That I was his and he could do whatever he wanted to me.

It made me so hot.

"Umm . . ." He purred, sliding his cock deep. "You're so creamy with my cum. I love the way you feel when I've been at you all night. A lifetime of this, Eva. I'll never stop."

I draped my leg over his hip, holding him in me. "Kiss me."

His wickedly curved mouth brushed over mine.

"Love me," I demanded, my nails digging into his hips as he flexed inside me.

"I do, angel," he whispered, his smile widening. "I do."

When I woke, he was gone.

I stretched in a tangle of sheets that smelled of sex and Gideon and breathed in the salt-tinged breeze drifting through the open patio doors.

I lay there for a while, thinking over the night and the day before. Then the weeks before, and the few months since I'd met Gideon. Then beyond that. Back to Brett and others I had dated. Back to a time when

I'd been so certain I would never find a man who loved me for who I was, with all my emotional scars and baggage and neediness.

What else could I say besides yes, now that by some miracle I'd found him?

Rolling out of bed, I felt a flutter of excitement at the thought of finding Gideon and agreeing to marry him without reservation. I loved the idea of eloping with him, of our first vows spoken in private, with no one watching who harbored doubts or dislike or bad wishes. After all we'd both been through, it made perfect sense for our new beginning to be filled with nothing but love and hope and happiness.

I should've known he'd plan it all perfectly, from the privacy to the exclusive locale. Of course we'd get married on a beach. Beaches held fond memories for both of us, not the least of which was our last time away at the Outer Banks.

When I saw the breakfast tray on the coffee table in the bedroom's seating area, I smiled. There was a white silk robe draped over the back of the chair, too.

Gideon never missed a trick.

I pulled the robe on and reached to pour myself a cup of coffee, wanting a caffeine boost before I searched for him in the suite and gave him my answer. That was when I saw the prenuptial agreement tucked beneath the covered breakfast plate.

My hand froze halfway to the carafe. The agreement was tastefully arranged beneath the single red rose in a slender white vase, with the silverware gleaming from an artfully folded cloth napkin.

I don't know why I was so surprised and . . . crushed. Of course, Gideon would've planned everything down to the last detail—starting with the prenup. After all, hadn't he tried to start our relationship with an agreement?

All of my giddy happiness left me in a rush. Deflated, I turned away from the tray and headed into the shower instead. I took my time washing up, moving in slow motion. I decided I'd rather say no than read a legal document that put a price on my love. A love that was precious and priceless to me.

Still, I feared it was too late, that the damage was already done. Just knowing he'd had a prenup drafted changed everything and I couldn't blame him for that. For God's sake, he was Gideon Cross. One of the twenty-five richest men in the world. It was inconceivable that he *wouldn't* demand a prenuptial agreement. And I wasn't naïve. I knew better than to dream of Prince Charming and castles in the sky.

Showered and clothed in a light sundress, I pulled my hair back in a wet ponytail and went for the coffee. I poured a cup, added cream and sweetener, then slid the prenup free and stepped out to the patio.

Down on the beach, preparations were under way for the wedding. A flower-covered arch had been placed by the shoreline and braided white ribbon had been draped across the sand to mark an impromptu aisle.

I chose to sit with my back to the view, because it hurt to look at it.

I took a sip of coffee, let it soak into me, then took another. I was halfway done with my cup when I gathered enough courage to read the damn legalese. The opening few pages detailed the assets we owned separately prior to marriage. Gideon's holdings were staggering. *When did he find time to sleep?* I thought the dollar amount attributed to me was wrong, until I considered how long the principal had been sitting in investments.

Stanton had taken my five million and doubled it.

It struck me then how stupid I was for just sitting on it, instead of investing it where it could help those who needed it. I'd been acting like that blood money didn't exist when I should've been putting it to work. I made a mental note to tackle that project as soon as I got back to New York.

After that, the reading got interesting.

Gideon's first stipulation was that I take the Cross name as my own.

I could keep Tramell as an additional middle name, but with no hyphenation as a surname. *Eva Cross*—it was nonnegotiable. And so very like him. My domineering lover made no apologies for his caveman tendencies.

His second stipulation was that I accept ten million from him upon the wedding, doubling my personal estate just for saying *I do*. Every year thereafter, he gave me more. I would receive bonuses for each child we had together, be paid for going to couples therapy with him. I agreed to counseling and mediation in the event of a divorce. I agreed to share a residence with him, bimonthly vacations, date nights . . .

The more I read, the more I understood. The prenup didn't protect Gideon's assets at all. He gave them freely, going so far as to stipulate up front that fifty percent of everything he acquired from our marriage onward was irrefutably mine. Unless he cheated. If that happened, it cost him severely.

The prenup was designed to protect his heart, to bind me and bribe me to stay with him no matter what. He was giving everything he had.

He joined me on the terrace when I flipped to the last page, strolling out in a pair of partially buttoned jeans and nothing else. I knew his perfectly timed arrival wasn't coincidental. He'd been watching me from somewhere, gauging my reaction.

I brushed the tears from my cheeks with studied nonchalance. "Good morning, ace."

"Morning, angel." He bent and pressed a kiss to my cheek before taking the chair at the end of the table to my left.

A member of the staff came out with breakfast and coffee, arranging the place settings quickly and efficiently before disappearing as swiftly as he'd appeared.

I looked at Gideon, at the way the tropical breeze adored him and played with that sexy mane of hair. Sitting there as he was, so virile and casual, he wasn't at all the cut-and-dried presentation of dollar signs I'd seen in the prenup.

Allowing the pages to flip back to the first page, I set my hand on top of it and said, "Nothing in this document can keep me married to you."

He took a quick, deep breath. "Then we'll revisit and revise. Name your terms."

"I don't want your money. I want this," I gestured at him. "Especially this." I leaned forward and placed my hand over his heart. "You're the only thing that can hold me, Gideon."

"I don't know how to do this, Eva." He caught my hand and held it pressed flat to his chest. "I'm going to fuck up. And you'll want to run."

"Not anymore," I argued. "Haven't you noticed?"

"I noticed you running into the ocean last night and sinking like a damn stone!" Leaning forward, he held my gaze. "Don't argue the prenup on principle. If there are no deal breakers for you in it, live with it. For me."

I sat back. "You and I have a long way to go," I said softly. "A document can't force us to believe in each other. I'm talking about trust, Gideon."

"Yeah, well—" He hesitated. "I don't trust myself not to fuck this up, and you don't trust that you've got what I need. We trust each other just fine. We can work on the rest together."

"Okay." I watched his eyes light up and knew I was making the right decision, even if I was still partially convinced that it was a decision we were making too soon. "I do have one revision."

"Name it."

"You just did. The name issue."

"Nonnegotiable," he said flatly, with an empathic swipe of his hand for good measure.

I arched a brow. "Don't be a fucking Neanderthal. I want to take my dad's name, too. He's wanted that and it's bothered him my whole life. This is my chance to fix it."

"So, Eva Lauren Reyes Cross?"

"Eva Lauren Tramell Reyes Cross."

"That's a mouthful, angel," he drawled, "but do what makes you happy. That's all I want."

"All I want is you," I told him, leaning forward to offer him my mouth for a kiss.

His lips touched mine. "Let's make it official."

I married Gideon Geoffrey Cross barefoot on a Caribbean beach with the hotel manager and Angus McLeod as witnesses. I hadn't realized Angus was there, but I was pleased that he was.

It was a quick, beautifully simple ceremony. I could tell from the beaming smiles of the reverend and Claude that they were honored to officiate over Gideon's nuptials.

I wore the prettiest dress I'd found in the closet. Strapless and ruched from breasts to hips, with petals of organza floating down to my feet, it was a sweet yet sexy romantic gown. My hair was up in an elegantly messy knot with a red rose tucked into it. The hotel provided a bouquet of white-ribboned jasmine.

Gideon wore graphite gray slacks and an untucked white dress shirt. He went barefoot, too. I cried when he repeated his vows, his voice strong and sure, even while his eyes betrayed a heated yearning.

He loved me so much.

The entire ceremony was intimate and deeply personal. Perfect.

I missed my mom and dad and Cary. I missed Ireland and Stanton and Clancy. But when Gideon bent to seal our marriage with a kiss, he whispered, "We'll do this again. As many times as you want."

I loved him so much.

Angus stepped up to kiss me on both cheeks. "It does me good to see you both so happy."

"Thank you, Angus. You've taken good care of him for a long time."

He smiled, his eyes glistening as he turned to Gideon. He said something so heavily accented by his Scottish heritage, I couldn't be sure it was any form of English at all. Whatever it was, it made Gideon's eyes shine, too. How much of a surrogate father had Angus been to Gideon over the years? I would always be grateful to him for giving Gideon support and affection when he desperately needed it.

We cut a small cake and toasted with champagne on the terrace of our suite. We signed the register the reverend offered and were given our certificate of marriage to sign as well. Gideon's fingers brushed over it reverently.

"Is this what you needed?" I teased him. "This piece of paper?"

"I need you, Mrs. Cross." He pulled me close. "I wanted this."

Angus took both the certificate and prenup with him when he made himself scarce. Both had been duly notarized by the hotel manager and would end up wherever Gideon kept such things.

As for Gideon and me, we ended up in the cabana, tangled naked with each other. We sipped chilled champagne, touched each other playfully and greedily, and kissed lazily as the day crawled by.

That was perfect, too.

"So, how are we handling this when we get back?" I asked him, as we ate a candlelit dinner in the dining room of our suite. "The whole we-ran-off-and-got-hitched explanation."

Gideon shrugged and licked melted butter off his thumb. "However you want."

I pulled the meat out of a crab leg and considered the options. "I want to tell Cary for sure. And I think my dad will be okay with it. I kind of talked around it when I called him earlier and he told me you'd asked him, so he's prepared. I don't think Stanton will care much either way, no offense."

"None taken."

"I'm worried about my mom, though. Things are already rough

between us. She'll be totally stoked that we're married"—I paused a minute, absorbing that for the millionth time—"but I don't want her to think that I left her out because I'm mad at her."

"Let's just tell her and everyone else we're engaged."

I dunked the crabmeat into drawn butter, thinking I wanted to get *very* used to seeing Gideon shirtless and sated and relaxed. "She'll have a conniption if we live together before the wedding."

"Well, then she'll have to plan fast," he said dryly. "You're my wife, Eva. I don't care if anyone else knows it or not, *I* know it. And I want to come home to you, have coffee in the morning with you, zip up the back of your dresses, and unzip them at night."

Watching him snap a crab leg with his hands, I asked, "Will you wear a wedding band?"

"I'm looking forward to it."

That made me smile. He paused and stared at me.

"What?" I prompted, when he didn't say anything. "Do I have butter splashed on my face?"

He sat back with a deep exhalation. "You're beautiful. I love looking at you."

I felt my face heat. "You're not so bad yourself."

"It's starting to go away," he murmured.

My smile faded. "What? What's going away?"

"The . . . worry. It feels safe, doesn't it?" He sipped his wine. "Settled. It's a good feeling. I like it. A lot."

I hadn't had as much time to get used to the idea of being married, but as I sat back and really thought about it, I had to agree. He was mine. No one could doubt it now. "I like it, too."

He lifted my hand to his lips. The ring he'd given me caught the candlelight and glimmered with multihued fire. It was a tastefully large Asscher-cut diamond in a vintage setting. I loved the timeless sophistication of it, but more so because it was the ring his father had married his mother with.

Even though Gideon was deeply wounded by his parents' betrayals, their time together as a family of three was the last true happiness he remembered before meeting me.

And he swore he wasn't romantic.

He caught me admiring the ring. "You like it."

"I do." I looked at him. "It's one of a kind. I was thinking we could do something unusual with our home, too."

"Oh?" He squeezed my hand and resumed eating.

"I understand the need to sleep apart, but I don't like having doors and walls between us."

"I don't, either, but your safety comes first."

"How about a master suite with two bedrooms connected by a bathroom with no doors. Just archways or passageways. So technically, we're still in the same open space."

He considered that a minute, then nodded. "Draw it up and we'll bring in a designer to make it happen. We'll continue staying on the Upper West Side for now while we have the penthouse refinished. Cary can take a look at the adjoining one-bedroom apartment and make any changes he wants at the same time."

I rubbed my bare foot along the back of his calf as a thank-you. The sounds of music drifted in on the evening wind, reminding me that we weren't alone on a deserted island.

Was Angus having a good time somewhere? Or was he stuck standing outside the door to our suite?

"Where's Angus?" I asked.

"Around."

"Is Raúl here, too?"

"No. He's in New York working out how Nathan's bracelet ended up where it did."

"Oh." I suddenly lost my appetite. Picking up my napkin, I wiped my fingers. "Should I be worried?"

It was a rhetorical question, since I'd never stopped worrying. The mystery of who was responsible for sending the police in another direction was always there, niggling at the back of my mind.

"Someone handed me a get-out-of-jail-free card," he said evenly, licking his lower lip. "I expected that was going to cost me something, but no one's approached me yet. So, I'll approach them."

"Once you find them."

"Oh, I'll find them," he murmured darkly. "Then we'll know why."

Beneath the table, I wrapped my legs around his and held on.

WE danced on the beach by the light of the moon. The lush humidity was sensuous at night, and we reveled in it. Gideon shared my bed that night, even though I could tell how difficult it was for him to take the risk. I couldn't imagine sleeping alone on my wedding night and trusted that his prescription combined with the previous night's lack of sleep would help him sleep deeply. It did.

Sunday, he gave me the choice of going to a fabulous waterfall or taking the resort's catamaran out to sea or rafting down a jungle river. I smiled and told him next time, and then I had my wicked way with him.

We lazed around all day, skinny-dipping in the private pool and napping when the mood struck us. It was after midnight when we left, and I was sorry to go. The weekend had been far too short.

"We've got a lifetime of weekends," he murmured as we drove back to the airport, reading my mind.

"I'm selfish with you. I want you all to myself."

When we boarded the jet, the clothes we'd had at our disposal at the resort came with us. It made me smile, thinking of how little we'd worn over the two days.

I took the cosmetic case into the bedroom so I could brush my teeth before sleeping the duration of the flight home. That was when I saw the patent leather and brass luggage tag attached to it, engraved with *Eva Cross*.

Gideon slipped into the lavatory behind me and kissed my shoulder. "Let's crash, angel. We need some sleep before work."

Pointing at the luggage tag, I said, "Was my saying yes really that much of a foregone conclusion?"

"I was prepared to hold you hostage until you did."

I didn't doubt him. "I'm flattered."

"You're married." He smacked me on the ass. "Now hurry up, Mrs. Cross."

I hurried and slipped into the bed beside him. He immediately spooned behind me, tucking me close.

"Sweet dreams, baby," I whispered, wrapping my arms over his around my middle.

His mouth curved against my neck. "My dreams already came true."

20

IT WAS WEIRD going to work on Monday morning and having no one realize my life was profoundly different. Who knew how much saying a few words and slipping on a ring of metal could change a person's perception of themselves?

I wasn't just Eva, the New York newbie trying to make it on her own in the big city with her best friend. I was a mogul's wife. I had a whole new set of responsibilities and expectations. Just thinking about it intimidated me.

Megumi stood as she buzzed me through the security doors at Waters Field & Leaman. She was dressed with unusual sedateness in a black sleeveless dress with an asymmetrical hemline and bright fuchsia heels. "Wow. You've got an amazing tan! I'm so jealous."

"Thanks. How'd your weekend go?"

"Same old, same old. Michael stopped calling." Her nose wrinkled. "I miss the harassment. Made me feel wanted."

I shook my head at her. "You're nuts."

"I know. So tell me where you went. And did you go with the rock star or Cross?"

"My lips are sealed." Although I was tempted to reveal everything. The only thing that held me back was that I hadn't told Cary yet and he needed to come first.

"No way!" Her dark eyes narrowed. "Are you seriously not going to tell me?"

"Of course I will." I winked. "Just not right now."

"I know where you work, you know," she called after me as I headed down the hallway to my cubicle.

When I reached my desk, I got ready to type a quick text to Cary and discovered that he'd sent me a few over the weekend that hadn't come through until later. They certainly hadn't been there when I'd placed my usual Saturday call to my dad.

Wanna have lunch? I texted.

When I didn't get a reply right away, I silenced my phone and set it in my top drawer.

"Where did you spend the weekend?" Mark asked me as he came in to work. "You've got a great tan."

"Thanks. I lazed it up in the Caribbean."

"Really? I've been scoping out the islands for possible honeymoon spots. Would you recommend it for that, wherever you stayed?"

I laughed, happier than I'd been in long time. Maybe in forever. "Absolutely."

"Get me the deets. I'll add the spot to the list of possibilities."

"You have honeymoon scouting duty?" I stood so we could grab coffee together before we started the day.

"Yep." Mark's mouth quirked on one side. "I'll leave the wedding stuff to Steven, since he's been planning for so long. But the honeymoon is mine."

He sounded so happy, and I knew just how he felt. His good mood made the start of my day even better.

THE smooth sailing ended when Cary called my desk phone shortly after ten o'clock.

"Mark Garrity's office," I answered. "Eva Tramell—"

"—needs an ass-kicking," Cary finished. "I can't remember the last time I was this mad at you."

I frowned, my stomach tightening. "Cary, what's wrong?"

"I'm not going to talk about important shit on the phone, Eva, unlike some people I know. I'll meet you for lunch. And just so you're aware, I turned down a go-see this afternoon to set you straight, because that's what friends do," he said angrily. "They make time in their schedule to talk about things that matter. They don't leave cutesy voicemail messages and think that handles it!"

The line went dead. I sat there, shocked and a bit scared.

Everything in my life ground to a screeching halt. Cary was my anchor. When things weren't right with us, I scattered real quick. And I knew it was the same for him. When we were out of touch, he started fucking up.

I dug out my cell phone and called him back.

"What?" he snapped. But it was a good sign that he'd answered.

"If I screwed up," I said quickly, "I'm sorry and I'll fix it. Okay?"

He made a rough sound. "You fucking piss me off, Eva."

"Yeah, well, I'm good at pissing people off, if you haven't noticed, but I hate when I do it to you." I sighed. "It's going to drive me nuts, Cary, until we can work it out. I need us solid, you know that."

"You haven't acted like it matters lately," he said gruffly. "I'm an afterthought and that fucking hurts."

"I'm always thinking about you. If I haven't shown it, that's my bad."

He didn't say anything.

"I love you, Cary. Even when I'm messing up."

He exhaled into the receiver. "Get back to work and don't stress about this. We'll deal with it at lunch."

"I'm sorry. Really."

"See you at noon."

I hung up and tried to concentrate, but it was hard. It was one thing having Cary angry with me; it was totally another to know I'd hurt him. I was one of the very few people in his life he trusted not to let him down.

AT eleven thirty, I received a small pile of interoffice envelopes. I was thrilled when one of them revealed a note from Gideon.

MY GORGEOUS, SEXY WIFE,
I NEVER STOP THINKING ABOUT YOU.
YOURS,
X

My feet tapped out a little happy dance beneath my desk. My skewed day righted itself a little.

I wrote him back.

Dark and Dangerous,
I'm madly in love with you.
Your ball and chain,
Mrs. X

I tucked it in an envelope and dropped it in my out-box.

I was drafting a reply to the artist working on a gift card campaign when my desk phone rang. I answered with my usual greeting and heard a reply in a familiar French accent.

"Eva, it's Jean-François Giroux."

Sitting back in my chair, I said, "*Bonjour,* Monsieur Giroux."

"What time is best for us to meet today?"

What the hell did he want from me? I supposed if I wanted to know, I'd have to follow through. "Five o'clock? There's a wine bar not too far from the Crossfire."

"That would be fine."

I gave him directions and he hung up, leaving me feeling somewhat whiplashed by the call. I swiveled in my chair, thinking. Gideon and I were trying to move forward with our lives, but people and issues from our pasts were still trying to hold us back. Would the announcement of our marriage, or even an engagement, change that?

God, I hoped so. But was anything ever that easy?

Glancing at the clock, I refocused on work and returned to writing my e-mail.

I was down in the lobby by five after noon, but Cary hadn't arrived yet. As I waited for him, my nerves started getting to me. I'd gone over my brief conversation with Cary again and again and knew he was right. I had convinced myself he'd be okay with having Gideon join our living arrangements because I couldn't imagine facing the alternative—having to choose between my best friend and my boyfriend.

And now there was no choice. I was married. Ecstatically so.

Still, I found myself grateful that I'd tucked my wedding ring into the zippered pocket of my purse. If Cary felt a growing distance between us, finding out I'd gotten hitched over the weekend wouldn't help.

My stomach twisted. The secrets between us were mounting. I couldn't stand it.

"Eva."

I jerked out of my thoughts at the sound of my best friend's voice. He was striding toward me wearing loose-fitting cargo shorts and a V-neck T-shirt. He kept his shades on, and with his hands shoved in his pockets, he seemed distant and cool. Heads turned as he walked by and he didn't notice, his attention on me.

My feet moved. I was hurrying toward him before I thought of it, then ran straight into him so hard, his breath left him with a grunt. I hugged him, my cheek pressed to his chest.

"I missed you," I said, meaning it with all my heart, even though he wouldn't know exactly why.

He muttered something under his breath and hugged me. "Pain in the ass sometimes, baby girl."

Pulling back, I looked up at him. "I'm sorry."

He linked his fingers with mine and led me out of the Crossfire. We went to the place with the great tacos that we'd gone to the last time he had met me for lunch. They also had great slushy virgin margaritas, which were perfect on a steamy summer day.

After waiting in line about ten minutes, I ordered only two tacos, since I hadn't hit the gym in way too long. Cary ordered six. We snagged a table just as its former occupants cleared away, and Cary inhaled a taco before I'd barely taken the wrapper off my straw.

"I'm sorry about the voice mail," I said.

"You don't get it." He swiped a napkin across lips that turned sane women into giggling girls when he smiled. "It's the whole situation, Eva. You leave me a message telling me to think about sharing a place with Cross, *after* you tell your mom that it's a done deal and *before* you fall off the face of the earth for the weekend. I guess however I feel about it means jack shit to you."

"That's not true!"

"Why would you want a roommate when you're living with a boyfriend anyway?" he asked, clearly getting warmed up. "And why would you think I'd want to be a third wheel?"

"Cary—"

"I don't need any fucking handouts, Eva." His emerald eyes narrowed. "I've got places I can crash, other people I can room with. Don't do me any favors."

My chest tightened. I wasn't ready to let Cary go yet. Someday in the future, we'd be heading our separate ways, maybe only seeing each other on special occasions. But that time wasn't now. It couldn't be. Just thinking about it screwed with my head.

"Who says I'm doing it for you?" I shot back. "Maybe I just can't bear the thought of not having you nearby."

He snorted and ripped a bite out of his taco. Chewing angrily, he swallowed his food down with a long draw on his straw. "What am I, your three-year chip marking your recovery? Your celebratory token for Eva Anonymous?"

"Excuse me." I leaned forward. "You're mad, I get it. I've said I'm sorry. I love you and I love having you in my life, but I'm not going to sit here and get kicked because I fucked up."

I pushed away from the table and stood. "I'll catch you later."

"You and Cross getting married?"

Pausing, I looked down at him. "He asked. I said yes."

Cary nodded, as if that were no surprise, and took another bite. I grabbed my purse from where it hung on the back of my chair.

"Are you afraid of living alone with him?" he asked around his chewing.

Of course he'd think that. "No. He'll be sleeping in his own bedroom."

"Has he been sleeping in a separate room the last few weekends you've been shacking up with him?"

I stared. Did he know for a fact that Gideon was the "loverman" I'd been spending time with? Or was he just fishing? I decided I didn't care. I was tired of lying to him. "Mostly, yes."

He set his taco down. "Finally, some truth out of you. I was beginning to think you'd forgotten how to be honest."

"Fuck you."

Grinning, he gestured at my vacant chair. "Sit your ass back down, baby girl. We're not done talking."

"You're being a jerk."

His smile faded and his gaze hardened. "Being lied to for weeks makes me cranky. Sit down."

I sat and glared at him. "There? Happy?"

"Eat. I've got shit to say."

Exhaling my frustration, I slung my purse over the chair again and faced him with my brows raised.

"If you think," he began, "that being sober and working steadily broke my bullshit meter, now you know better. I knew you were nailing Cross again from the moment you started back up."

Biting into my taco, I shot him a skeptical look.

"Eva honey, don't you think that if there were another man in New York who could bang it out all night like Cross, I would've found him by now?"

I coughed and nearly spit out my food.

"No one's lucky enough to find two guys like that in a row," he drawled. "Not even you. You should've had a dry spell or at least a couple of really bad lays first."

I threw my wadded-up straw wrapper at him, which he dodged with a laugh.

Then he sobered. "Did you think I would judge you for getting back together with him after he jacked up?"

"It's more complicated than that, Cary. Things were . . . a mess. There was a lot of pressure. Still is, with that reporter stalking Gideon—"

"Stalking him?"

"Totally. I just didn't want . . ." *You exposed. Vulnerable. Open to accusation as an accomplice after the fact.* "I just had to let it play out," I finished lamely.

He let that sink in, then nodded. "And now you're going to marry him."

"Yes." I took a drink, needing to loosen the lump in my throat. "But you're the only one who knows that besides us."

"Finally, a secret you let me in on." His lips pursed for a few seconds. "And you still want me to live with you."

I leaned forward again, holding out my hand for his. "I know you can do something else, go somewhere else. But I'd rather you didn't. I'm not ready to be without you yet, married or not."

He gripped my hand so tightly, my bones pressed together. "Eva—"

"Wait," I said quickly. He was far too serious all of a sudden. I didn't want him to cut me off before I put everything out there. "Gideon's penthouse has an adjacent one-bedroom apartment he doesn't use."

"A one-bedroom apartment. On Fifth Avenue."

"Yeah. Great, right? All yours. Your own space and entrance and view of Central Park. But still connected to me. The best of both worlds." I rushed on, hoping to say something he'd latch on to. "We'll stay on the Upper West Side for a bit, while I make changes to the penthouse. Gideon says we can have whatever changes you want made to your apartment done at the same time."

"My apartment." He stared at me, which made me even more nervous. A man and a woman tried to squeeze between our table and the back of an occupied chair that was pushed too far out into the walkway, but I ignored them.

"I'm not talking about a handout," I assured him. "I've been thinking that I'd like to put that money I've been sitting on to work. Create a foundation or something to decide how to use it in support of causes and charities we believe in. I need your help. And I'll pay you for it. Not just for your input, but for your face. I want you to be the foundation's first spokesperson."

Cary's grip on my hand slackened.

Alarmed, I tightened mine. "Cary?"

His shoulders sagged. "Tatiana's pregnant."

"What?" I felt the blood drain from my face. The little restaurant was hopping, and the shouting of orders behind the counter and the clatter of trays and utensils made it hard to hear, but I'd caught the two words that fell out of Cary's mouth as if he'd shouted them at me. "Are you kidding?"

"I wish." He pulled his hand away and scooped back the bangs that draped over one eye. "Not that I don't want a kid. That part's cool. But . . . fuck. Not now, you know? And not with her."

"How the hell did she get pregnant?" Cary was religious about protecting himself, knowing damn well he lived a high-risk lifestyle.

"Well, I shoved my dick in her and pushed it around—"

"Shut up," I bit out. "You're *careful*."

"Yeah, well, putting a sock on it isn't guaranteed protection," he said wearily, "and Tat doesn't take the pill because she says it makes her break out and eat too much."

"Jesus." My eyes stung. "Are you sure it's yours?"

He snorted. "No, but that doesn't mean it's not. She's six weeks along, so it's possible."

I had to ask. "Is she going to keep it?"

"I don't know. She's thinking it over."

"Cary . . ." I couldn't hold back the tear that slid down my cheek. My heart was aching for him. "What are you going to do?"

"What can I do?" He slumped back in his chair. "It's her decision."

His powerlessness had to be killing him. After his mother had given birth to him, unwanted, she'd used abortion as birth control. I knew that haunted him. He'd told me so. "And if she decides to go through with the pregnancy? You'll have a paternity test done, right?"

"God, Eva." He looked at me with reddened eyes. "I haven't thought that far ahead yet. What the hell am I supposed to say to Trey? Things are just starting to smooth out between us and I've got to hit him with this? He's going to dump me. It's over."

Sucking in a deep breath, I straightened in my chair. I couldn't let Cary and Trey fall apart. Now that Gideon and I were good, it was time to fix all the other areas of my life I'd been neglecting. "We'll take it a step at a time. Figure things out as we go. We'll get through this."

He swallowed hard. "I need you."

"I need you, too. We'll stick together and work it out." I managed a smile. "I'm not going anywhere and neither are you. Except to San Diego this weekend," I amended hastily, reminding myself to talk to Gideon about that.

"Thank God." Cary sat forward again. "What I wouldn't give to shoot hoops at Dr. Travis's right now."

"Yeah." I didn't play basketball, but I knew I could use a one-on-one with Dr. Travis myself.

What would he say when he learned how far off the rails we'd slid in the few months we'd been in New York? We had spun some big dreams the last time we'd all sat down together. Cary had wanted to star in a Super Bowl ad and I'd wanted to be the one behind the scenes of that ad. Now he was facing the possibility of a baby and I was married to the most complicated man I had ever met.

"Dr. Trav's gonna flip," Cary muttered, reading my mind.

For some reason, that made us both laugh 'til we cried.

WHEN I got back to my desk, I found another small pile of interoffice envelopes. Catching my lower lip between my teeth, I searched each one until I found the one I was hoping for.

I CAN THINK OF MANY USES FOR THAT CHAIN,
MRS. X.
YOU WILL ENJOY THEM ALL IMMENSELY.
YOURS,
X

Some of the dark clouds from lunch floated away.

AFTER Cary's mind-blowing revelation, meeting Giroux after work barely registered on my what-else-could-possibly-go-wrong-next scale.

He was already at the wine bar when I arrived. Dressed in perfectly pressed khakis and white dress shirt rolled up at the sleeves and open at the throat, he looked good. Casual. But that didn't make him seem more relaxed. The man was strung tight as a bow, vibrating with tension and whatever else was eating at him.

"Eva," he greeted me. With that overt friendliness I hadn't liked the first time, he kissed me on both cheeks again. *"Enchanté."*

"Not too blond for you today, I take it?"

"Ah." He gave me a smile that didn't reach his eyes. "I deserved that."

I joined him at his table by the window and we were served shortly after.

The place had the look of an establishment that had been around a long time. Tin tiles covered the ceiling, while the aged hardwood floors and intricately carved bar suggested the place had been a pub at some point in its history. It had been modernized with chrome fixtures and a wine rack behind the bar that could have been an abstract sculpture.

Giroux openly studied me as the server poured our wine. I had no idea what he was looking for, but he was definitely searching for something.

As I took a sip of a lovely shiraz, he settled comfortably in his chair and swirled his wine around in his glass. "You've met my wife."

"I have, yes. She's very beautiful."

"Yes, she is." His gaze dropped to his wine. "What else did you think of her?"

"Why does it matter what I think?"

He looked at me again. "Do you see her as a rival? Or a threat?"

"Neither." I took another drink and noticed a black Bentley SUV easing into a tight spot at the curb just outside the window I sat beside. Angus was behind the wheel and apparently uncaring of the No Parking sign he was camping out in front of.

"You are that certain of Cross?"

My attention returned to Giroux. "Yes. But that doesn't mean I don't wish you would pack up your wife and take her back to France with you."

His mouth quirked on one side in a grim smile. "You are in love with Cross, yes?"

"Yes."

"Why?"

That made me smile. "If you think you can figure out what Corinne sees in him by what *I* see in him, forget it. He and I, we're . . . different with each other than we are with other people."

"I saw that. With him." Giroux took a drink, savoring it before swallowing.

"Forgive me, but I don't know why we're sitting here. What do you want from me?"

"Are you always so direct?"

"Yes." I shrugged. "I get impatient with being confused."

"Then I will be direct as well." He reached out and caught my left hand. "You have a tan line from a ring. A sizable one, it appears. An engagement ring, perhaps?"

I looked at my hand and saw he was right. There was a square-sized spot on my ring finger that was a few shades lighter than the rest of my skin. Unlike my mother, who was pale, I'd inherited my father's warm skin tone and I tanned easily.

"You're very perceptive. But I would appreciate you keeping your speculations to yourself."

He smiled and for the first time, it was genuine. "Perhaps I will get my wife back after all."

"I think you could, if you tried." I sat up, deciding it was time to leave. "You know what your wife told me once? She said you're indifferent. Instead of waiting for her to come back, you should just take her back. I think that's what she wants."

He stood when I did, standing over me. "She has chased Cross. I do not think a woman who chases will find a man chasing her attractive."

"I don't know about that." I pulled a twenty out of my pocket and set it on the table, despite his scowl at the sight of it. "She said yes when you asked her to marry you, didn't she? Whatever you did before, do it again. Good-bye, Jean-François."

He opened his mouth to speak, but I was already halfway out the door.

ANGUS was waiting beside the Bentley when I exited the wine bar.

"Would you like to go home, Mrs. Cross?" he asked, as I slipped into the back.

His greeting made me grin. Combined with my recent conversation with Giroux, it sparked an idea. "Actually, I'd like to make a stop, if you don't mind."

"Not at all."

I gave him directions, then sat back and relished the building anticipation.

It was half past six when I was ready to call it a day, but when I asked Angus where Gideon was, I learned he was still in his office.

"Will you take me to him?" I asked.

"Of course."

Returning to the Crossfire after hours was weird. Although there were still people moving through the lobby, it had a different feel from the daytime. When I reached the top floor, I found the glass security doors to Cross Industries propped open and a cleaning crew at work emptying trash cans, wiping down the glass, and vacuuming.

I headed directly to Gideon's office, noting the number of empty desks, which included that of Scott, his assistant. Gideon stood behind his, an earpiece in his ear, and his jacket hung on the coat rack in the corner. His hands were on his hips and he was talking, his lips moving rapidly and his face a mask of concentration.

The wall across from him was covered in flat screens streaming news from around the world. To the right of that was a bar with jeweled decanters on lighted glass shelves that were the only spot of color in the office's cool palette of black, white, and gray. Three distinct seating areas offered comfortable spaces for less formal meetings, while Gideon's black desk was a miracle of modern technology, serving as the conduit for all the electronics in the room.

Surrounded by his expensive toys, my husband looked nothing short of edible. The beautifully tailored lines of his vest and pants showed off the perfection of his body, and the sight of him at his command center, wielding the power that had built his empire, did crazy things to my heart. The floor-to-ceiling windows that surrounded him on two sides allowed the view of the city to make an imposing backdrop, yet the vista didn't diminish him in any way.

Gideon was master of all he surveyed, and it showed.

Reaching into my purse, I unzipped the small pocket and drew out the rings inside it, slipping mine on. Then I stepped closer to the glass wall and double doors that separated him from everyone else.

His head swiveled toward me and his gaze heated at the sight of me. He hit a button on his desk, and the double doors swung open automatically. A moment later, the glass turned opaque, ensuring that no one lingering in the office would be able to see us.

I went in.

"I agree," he said, to whomever he was talking to. "Get it done and report back to me."

As he pulled off his earpiece and dropped it on his desk, his gaze never left me. "You're a welcome surprise, angel. Tell me about your meeting with Giroux."

I shrugged. "How did you know?"

His mouth tilted up on one side and he shot me a look that said, *Really? You're going to ask?*

"Are you here for a while?" I queried.

"I have a conference call with the Japanese division in half an hour, then I'm done. We'll go to dinner afterward."

"Let's get something to take home and eat with Cary. He's having a baby."

Gideon's brows shot up. "Come again?"

"Well, he might be having a baby." I sighed. "He's messed up over it and I want to be there for him. Plus, he should get used to having you around again."

He raked me with an assessing glance. "You're messed up over it, too. Come here." He rounded the desk and opened his arms. "Let me hold you."

I dropped my purse on the floor, kicked off my heels, and walked right into him. His arms came around me, and his lips, so firm and warm, pressed against my forehead.

"We'll figure it out," he murmured. "Don't worry."

"I love you, Gideon."

His embrace tightened.

Leaning back, I looked up into his gorgeous face. His eyes were so blue, seemingly even more so with the touch of sun he'd gotten during our trip away. "I have something for you."

"Oh?"

I backed up, catching his left hand before it dropped away from me. Holding it, I slid the ring I'd just bought him onto his finger, twisting it to fit over his last knuckle. He was still the entire time. When I released his hand so he could get a better look, it didn't move at all from where it'd been when I was holding it, as if he'd frozen in place.

Canting my head, I admired the ring on him, thinking it had just the effect I was looking for. But when a moment passed without a word from him, I looked up and saw him staring at his hand as if he'd never seen it before.

My heart sank. "You don't like it."

His nostrils flared on a deep breath and he turned over his hand to look at the backside, which was the same. The design I'd chosen wrapped continuously around.

The platinum wedding band was very much like the ring he wore on his right hand. It had the same beveled grooves cut into the precious metal, which gave it a similar industrial, masculine look. But the wedding band was garnished with rubies, making it impossible to miss. The bloodred hue stood out against his tanned skin and dark suits, a conspicuous sign of my possession.

"It's too much," I said quietly.

"It's always too much," he said hoarsely. And then he was on me, his hands cupping my head and his lips on mine, kissing me fiercely.

I grabbed his wrists, but he moved too quickly, lifting me up by the waist so my feet left the floor, and then carrying me to the same couch where he'd first laid his body over mine so many weeks ago.

"You don't have time for this," I gasped.

He sat me down with my butt on the edge of the sofa. "This won't take long."

He wasn't kidding. Reaching beneath my skirt, he slid my panties down my legs, then spread them wide and lowered his head.

There in his office, where I'd just admired his power and commanding presence, Gideon Cross knelt between my thighs and ate me with ruthless skill. His tongue fluttered over my clit until I writhed with the need to come, but it was the sight of him—in his suit, in his office, servicing me so thoroughly—that brought me to climax with a cry of his name.

I was shivering with pleasure while he licked inside me, the sensitive tissues trembling around the shallow plunges of his wickedly knowledgeable tongue. When he opened his fly and freed his erection, I was desperate for him, my body arching toward him in a shameless silent plea.

Gideon took the heavy length of his cock in hand and stroked the thick crest through my cleft, coating himself in the slickness of my orgasm. The fact that we were both still dressed except for what we needed to get out of the way made it all the hotter.

"I want you to submit," he said darkly. "Bend over and spread wide. I'm going to fuck you deep."

A whimper escaped me at the thought and I scrambled to obey. Aware of how tall he was, I moved to the side of the couch and folded over the armrest, reaching behind me to pull up my skirt.

He didn't hesitate. With a powerful thrust of his hips, he was inside me, stretching me. *"Eva."*

Gasping, I clawed at the sofa cushions. He was thick and hard and so, so deep. With my stomach pressed over the curve of the couch arm, I swore I could feel him pressing outward from the inside.

Folding over me, he wrapped his arms around me and sank his teeth into the side of my neck. The primitive claiming made my sex clench around him, caressing him.

He growled and ran his lips over me, lightly abrading me with the hint of evening stubble on his jaw. "You feel so good," he said hoarsely. "I love fucking you."

"Gideon."

"Give me your hands."

Unsure of what he wanted, I slid my arms closer to my body and he circled my wrists with his fingers, pulling my hands gently around to the small of my back.

Then he was fucking me. Pounding into my sex with relentless drives, using my arms to pull me back to meet the thrusts of his hips. His heavy sac smacked against my clitoris, the rhythmic slaps spurring me toward another orgasm. He grunted on every plunge, mirroring my cries.

His race to orgasm was wildly exciting, as was his complete control of my body. I could only lie there and take it, take his lust and hunger, servicing him as he had me. The friction of his thrusts was delicious, a steady rubbing and pulling that made me crazed with desire.

I wished I could see him; see his eyes when they lost their focus and pleasure took him, his face a grimace of agonized ecstasy. I loved that I could affect him so fiercely, that my body felt so good to him, that sex with me shattered his defenses.

He shuddered and cursed. His cock lengthened, thickening as his balls tightened and drew up. "Eva . . . Christ. I love you."

I felt the lash of his semen inside me, pumping hot and thick. I bit my lip to stem my cry. I was so hot for him, so close.

Releasing my wrists, he wrapped me up, the fingers of one hand sliding into my cleft and rubbing my swollen clit. I came while he was still pumping, my sex milking his spurting cock as he emptied himself inside me. His lips were on my cheek, his breath gusting hot and moist across my skin, low rumbles spilling from his chest as he came hard and long.

We were both panting as our orgasms eased, leaning heavily on each other.

Swallowing hard, I spoke breathlessly. "I guess you like the ring."

His rough laugh filled me with joy.

FIVE minutes later, I lay wilted and sated on the couch, unable to move. Gideon sat at his desk looking pristine and perfect, radiating the health and vitality of a well-fucked male.

He went through the teleconference without a hitch in his stride, speaking mostly English, but opening and closing with conversational Japanese, his voice deep and smooth. His gaze slid over me now and again, his mouth curving in a ghost of a smile laced with undeniable masculine triumph.

I supposed he was entitled to it, considering I had so many post-orgasmic endorphins floating through my system I felt almost drunk.

Gideon finished his call and stood, shrugging out of his jacket again. The gleam in his eyes told me why.

Mustering the energy to raise my brows, I asked, "We're not leaving?"

"Of course we are. But not yet."

"Maybe you should cut back on those vitamins, ace."

His lips twitched as he freed the buttons of his vest. "I've spent too many days fantasizing about fucking you on that couch. We haven't covered even half of those fantasies yet."

I stretched, deliberately enticing him. "Can we still be naughty now that we're married?"

From the spark that lit his amazing eyes, I could guess his views on that.

By the time we left the Crossfire at nearly nine o'clock, Gideon had answered the question definitively.

21

Gideon and I were sitting on the floor of my living room eating pizza in our sweats when Cary came in a little after ten o'clock. Tatiana was with him. I reached across Gideon for a packet of Parmesan cheese and whispered, "Baby mama."

He winced. "She's trouble. Poor guy."

That was my thought exactly as the tall blonde walked in and wrinkled her nose rudely at our pizza. Then she caught sight of Gideon and flashed a come-hither smile.

I took a deep breath and told myself to let it go.

"Hey, Cary," Gideon greeted my best friend before tossing his arm over my shoulder and burying his face in my neck.

"Hey," Cary said. "What are you guys watching?"

"*End of Watch*," I answered. "It's really good. You two want to join us?"

"Sure." Cary caught Tatiana's hand and led her toward the couch.

She didn't have the grace to hide her disapproval of the idea.

They sat on the couch and settled into a comfortable tangle that was obviously familiar for them. Gideon pushed the pizza box their way. "Help yourselves, if you're hungry."

Cary snagged a slice, while Tatiana complained about him jostling her. I was bummed that she couldn't be more comfortable hanging out. If she was going to have Cary's baby, she was going to be in my life, and I hated the thought of that relationship being awkward.

In the end, they didn't stay in the living room long. She insisted that the handheld camera shots in the movie made her queasy, and Cary took her back to his room. A short while later, I thought I heard her laughing, making me think her biggest problem was the need to keep Cary all to herself. I could understand that insecurity. I was intimately familiar with it myself.

"Relax," Gideon murmured, urging me to lean into his chest. "We'll work it out with them. Give it some time."

I caught his left hand hanging over my shoulder and toyed with his ring.

He pressed his lips to my temple and we finished watching the movie.

ALTHOUGH Gideon slept in his apartment next door, he came over early enough to zip me into a sheath dress and fix me some coffee. I'd just finished putting on some pearl earrings and was stepping into the hallway when Tatiana appeared heading from the direction of the kitchen with two water bottles in her hands.

She was buck naked.

My temper almost boiled over, but I kept my tone calm. The pregnancy certainly didn't show, but knowing about it was reason enough to skip the shouting match. "Excuse me. You need to have clothes on if you're going to walk around my apartment."

"It's not just your apartment," she shot back, tossing her tawny mane over her shoulder as she moved to pass me.

I thrust my arm across the hallway, blocking her way. "You don't want to play games with me, Tatiana."

"Or what?"

"You'll lose."

She stared at me for a long minute. "He'll pick me."

"If it came to that, he'd resent you and you'd lose anyway." I dropped my arm. "Think about that."

Cary's door opened behind me. "What the fuck are you doing, Tat?"

Turning my head, I saw my best friend filling his doorway wearing only his boxers. "Giving you a good excuse to buy her a nice robe, Cary."

His jaw tightened and he waved me off, opening his door wider in a silent order for Tatiana to get her bare ass back in there.

I resumed my trek to the kitchen, my teeth grinding together. My mood worsened when I found Gideon in the kitchen, leaning back into the counter and leisurely drinking his coffee. He wore a black suit and pale gray tie and looked unbearably handsome.

"Enjoy the show?" I asked tightly. I hated that he'd seen another woman naked. And not just any woman, but a model with the lean, willowy body type he'd been known to prefer.

He lifted one shoulder in a careless shrug. "Not especially."

"You like 'em tall and skinny." I reached for the cup of coffee waiting for me on the counter beside him.

Gideon set his left hand over mine. The rubies on his wedding band sparkled in the bright kitchen lights. "Last I checked, the wife I can't resist was petite and voluptuous. Spectacularly so."

I closed my eyes, trying to push past my jealousy. "Do you know why I chose your ring?"

"Red is our color," he said quietly. "Red dresses in limos. Red fuck-me heels at garden parties. A red rose in your hair when you married me."

That he understood soothed me. I turned into him, pressing my body to his.

"Umm," he purred, hugging me close. "You're a soft, delicious little handful, angel."

I shook my head, my anger melting into exasperation.

He nuzzled his nose against my cheek. "I love you."

"Gideon." Tilting my head back, I offered my mouth and let him kiss my bad mood away.

The feel of his lips on mine never stopped making my toes curl. I was slightly dazed when he pulled back and murmured, "I have my appointment with Dr. Petersen tonight. I'll call you when I'm finished and we'll see what we want to do about dinner."

"Okay."

He smiled at my blissfully nonchalant reply. "I can set up an appointment for us to see him Thursday."

"Make it for next Thursday, please," I said, sobering. "I hate to miss any more therapy, but Mom wants me and Cary to go to a charity gala this Thursday. She bought me a dress and everything. I'm afraid if I don't go, she'll take it the wrong way."

"We'll go together."

"Yeah?" Gideon in a tuxedo was an aphrodisiac to me. Of course, Gideon in anything or nothing turned me on, too. But in a tux . . . Dear God, he was sizzling.

"Yes. It's as good a time as any to be seen out together again. And to announce our engagement."

I licked my lips. "Can I take advantage of you in the limo?"

His eyes laughed at me. "By all means, angel mine."

WHEN I got to work, Megumi wasn't at her desk so I didn't get to see how she was faring. It kind of gave me an excuse to call Martin, though, and see if things with him and Lacey had panned out after our wild night at Primal.

I pulled out my smartphone to program a reminder and saw that my mom had left a voice mail the night before. I listened to it on the way to my desk. She wanted to see if I wanted hair and makeup done before the dinner on Thursday, suggesting that she come over with a beauty crew and we could get dolled up together.

When I reached my desk, I texted her back, letting her know I loved the idea, but time would be tight, since I wouldn't be getting off work until five.

I was settling in for the day when Will stopped by.

"Got plans for lunch?" he asked, looking cute in a plaid shirt only he could pull off so well and a solid navy tie.

"Not another carb feast, please. My butt can't take it."

"No." He grinned. "Natalie's past the brutal phase of her diet, so it's getting better. I was thinking a soup and salad bar."

I smiled. "I'm game for that. Want to see if Megumi wants to come?"

"She's not here today."

"Oh? Is she sick?"

"Don't know. I only heard about it because I was the one who had to call the temp agency for someone to cover for her."

I sat back with a frown. "I'll give her a call on my break and see how she's feeling."

"Tell her I said hi." He drummed a beat on the top of my cubicle wall and headed off.

THE rest of the day passed in a blur. I left a message for Megumi on my break, then tried to reach her again after work as Clancy drove me to

Brooklyn for my Krav Maga class. "Have Lacey call me back if you're feeling too sick," I said in my voice mail message. "I just want to know you're okay."

I killed the call, then sat back and appreciated the grandeur of the Brooklyn Bridge. Going through the massive stone arches soaring over the East River always felt like traveling to a different world. Below, the waterway was dotted with commuter ferries and a lone sailboat heading out into the busy New York harbor.

We reached the long off-ramp in less than a minute and I turned my attention back to my phone.

I called Martin.

"Eva," he answered cheerfully, clearly recognizing my number from his contact list. "I'm glad to hear from you."

"How are you?"

"I'm good. You?"

"Hanging in there. We should get together sometime." I smiled at a cop who was artfully directing traffic at the hugely complicated intersection on the Brooklyn side. She kept things moving with a whistle between her teeth and fluid hand gestures that had serious sass to them. "We could grab a drink after work or double-date for dinner."

"I'd like that. Are you seeing someone in particular?"

"Gideon and I are working things out."

"Gideon Cross? Well, if anyone can hook him, it'd be you."

I laughed and wished I had my ring on. I didn't wear it around during the day the way Gideon wore his. He didn't care who knew he was taken or by whom, but I still had everyone in my life to tell. "Thanks for the vote of confidence. What about you? You seeing anyone?"

"Lacey and I are dabbling. I like her. She's a lot of fun."

"That's great. I'm glad to hear it. Listen, if you talk to her today, can you ask her to let me know how Megumi's doing? She's out sick and I just want to make sure she's all right and doesn't need anything."

"Sure thing." The receiver filled with a sudden rush of noise, the unmistakable sound of him stepping outside. "Lacey's out of town, but she's supposed to give me a call tonight."

"Thank you. I appreciate it. You're on the move, so I'll let you go. Let's plan on getting together next week and we'll work out the details in the next couple of days."

"Sounds good. I'm glad you called."

I smiled. "Me, too."

We hung up and because I felt like reaching out, I sent a text to Shawna and another to Brett. Just quick hellos with smiley faces.

When I looked up, I caught Clancy looking at me in the rearview mirror.

"How's Mom?" I asked.

"She'll be fine," he said, in his usual no-nonsense way.

I nodded and looked out the window, catching sight of a gleaming steel bus stop shelter displaying Cary's billboard. "Family is so hard sometimes, you know."

"I know."

"You have any brothers or sisters, Clancy?"

"One of each."

What were they like? Were they tough as nails and deadly like Clancy? Or was he the black sheep? "Are you close, if you don't mind my asking?"

"We're tight. My sister lives out of state, so I don't see her much, but we talk on the phone once a week at least. My brother's in New York, so we catch up more often."

"Cool." I tried to picture a relaxed Clancy tossing back beers with someone who resembled him, but couldn't pull it off. "Does he work security, too?"

"Not yet." His mouth did that little lip twitch, almost-smile thing. "He's with the FBI for now."

"Is your sister in law enforcement?"

"She's in the Marines."

"Whoa. Awesome."

"Yes, she is."

I studied him and his military crew cut. "You were in the service, too, weren't you?"

"I was." He didn't volunteer any more than that.

When I opened my mouth to pry further, we turned a corner and I realized we'd reached the former warehouse where Parker had his studio.

I grabbed my gym bag and got out before Clancy could open the door for me. "See you in an hour!"

"Knock 'em out, Eva," he said, watching me until I got inside.

The door had barely closed behind me when I saw a familiar brunette I would've rather not seen again. Ever. She stood to the side, just off the training mats, with her arms crossed. She was dressed in black workout pants with a bright blue stripe down the sides that matched her fitted long-sleeve shirt. Her brown curly hair was scraped back into an unforgiving ponytail.

She turned. Cool blue eyes raked me from head to toe.

Facing the inevitable, I took a deep breath and approached her. "Detective Graves."

"Eva." She gave me a curt nod. "Great tan."

"Thanks."

"Cross take you away for the weekend?"

Not exactly a casual question. My back went up. "I had some time off."

Her thin mouth quirked on one side. "Still cautious. Good. What does your dad think of Cross?"

"I believe my dad trusts my judgment."

Graves nodded. "I'd keep thinking about Nathan Barker's bracelet if I were you. But then, loose ends make me twitchy."

A shiver of unease ran down my back. The whole thing made me twitchy, but who could I talk to about it? No one but Gideon, and I knew him too well to doubt that he was doing everything in his considerable power to solve that mystery.

"I need a sparring partner," the detective said suddenly. "You're up."

"Uh, what?" I blinked at her. "Is that . . . ? Can we . . . ?"

"The case has gone cold, Eva." She stalked onto the mat and began to stretch. "Hurry up. I don't have all night."

GRAVES kicked my ass. For such a rail-thin, wiry woman, she packed some strength. She was focused, precise, and ruthless. I actually learned a lot from her over the hour and a half we sparred, most especially never to let down my guard. She was lightning quick and swift to exploit any advantage.

When I stumbled into my apartment a little after eight, I headed straight to the bathtub. I soaked in vanilla-scented water, surrounded by candles, and hoped Gideon would show up before I pruned.

He ended up coming in just as I was wrapping a towel around me, his damp hair and jeans telling me he'd showered after a visit with his trainer.

"Hi, ace."

"Hi, wife." He came up to me, tugged open my towel, and lowered his head to my breast.

My breath left me when he sucked a nipple into his mouth, drawing rhythmically until it hardened.

Straightening, he admired his handiwork. "God, you're sexy."

I lifted onto my tiptoes and kissed his chin. "How'd things go tonight?"

He looked at me with a wry curve to his lips. "Dr. Petersen congratulated us, then went on about how important couples therapy would be."

"He thinks we got married too soon."

Gideon laughed. "He didn't even want us having sex, Eva."

Wrinkling my nose, I resecured my towel and grabbed a comb for my wet hair.

"Let me," he said, taking the comb and leading me to the wide lip of the tub. He urged me to sit.

As he combed my hair, I told him about seeing Detective Graves at my Krav Maga class.

"My lawyers tell me the case has been shelved," Gideon said.

"How do you feel about that?"

"You're safe. That's all that matters."

There was no inflection in his voice, which told me it mattered to him more than he'd tell me. I knew that somewhere, deep down inside him, Nathan's murder was haunting him. Because *I* was haunted by what Gideon had done for me and we were two halves of the same soul.

That was why Gideon had wanted us to get married so badly. I was his safe place. I was the one person who knew every dark, tormented secret he had, and I loved him desperately anyway. And he needed love more than anyone I'd ever met.

There was a vibration against my shoulder and I teased, "Is that a new toy in your pocket, ace?"

"Should've turned the damn thing off," he muttered, digging his phone out. He looked at the screen, then answered with a clipped, "Cross."

I heard a woman's agitated voice coming through the receiver, but I couldn't make out the words.

"When?" After hearing the answer, he asked, "Where? Yes. I'm on my way."

He hung up and raked a hand through his hair.

I stood. "What's wrong?"

"Corinne's in the hospital. My mother says it's bad."

"I'll get dressed. What happened?"

Gideon looked at me. Goose bumps swept across my skin. I'd never seen him look so . . . shattered.

"Pills," he said hoarsely. "She swallowed a bottle of pills."

WE took the DB9. While we waited for the attendant to bring the car to us, Gideon called Raúl, telling him to meet us at the hospital to take over the Aston Martin when we arrived.

When Gideon slid behind the wheel, he drove with tight focus; every turn of the wheel and press of the accelerator was skilled and precise. Enclosed in the small space with him, I knew he'd shut down. Emotionally, he was unreachable. When I placed my hand on his knee to offer comfort and support, he didn't even twitch. I wasn't sure he even felt it.

Raúl was waiting for us when we pulled up to the emergency room. He opened the door for me, then rounded the hood and took the driver's seat after Gideon got out. The gleaming car was moved out of the drop-off driveway before we walked through the automatic doors.

I took Gideon's hand, but I wasn't sure he felt that, either. His attention was riveted on his mother, who stood when we entered the private waiting area we'd been directed to. Elizabeth Vidal barely glanced at me, going straight to her son and hugging him.

He didn't hug her back. But he also didn't pull away. His grip on my hand tightened.

Mrs. Vidal didn't even acknowledge me. Instead, she turned her back to me and gestured at the couple seated together nearby. They were clearly Corinne's parents. They'd been talking to Elizabeth when Gideon and I came in, which seemed odd to me since Jean-François Giroux was standing alone by the window, looking as much like an outsider as Elizabeth was making me feel.

Gideon's hold on my hand slackened as his mother pulled him toward Corinne's family. Feeling awkward standing in the doorway alone, I went to Jean-François.

I greeted him softly. "I'm very sorry."

He looked at me with dead eyes, his face seeming to have aged a decade since we'd met at the wine bar the day before. "What are you doing here?"

"Mrs. Vidal called Gideon."

"Of course she did." He looked over to the seating area. "One would think he was her husband and not I."

I followed his gaze. Gideon was crouched in front of Corinne's parents, holding her mother's hand. A sick feeling of dread spread through me, making me cold.

"She would rather be dead than live without him," he said tonelessly.

I looked back at him. Suddenly, I understood. "You told her, didn't you? About our engagement."

"And look how well she took the news."

Jesus. I took a shaky step toward the wall, needing the support. How could she not know what a suicide attempt would do to Gideon? She couldn't be that blind. Or had his reaction, his guilt, been her aim all along? It made me sick to think of anyone being that manipulative, but there was no denying the result. Gideon was back at her side. At least for now.

A doctor entered the room, a kind-looking woman with cropped silvery blond hair and faded blue eyes. "Mr. Giroux?"

"Oui." Jean-François stepped forward.

"I'm Dr. Steinberg. I'm treating your wife. Could we speak privately for a moment?"

Corinne's father stood. "We're her family."

Dr. Steinberg smiled gently. "I understand. However, it's Corinne's husband I need to speak with. I can tell you that Corinne will be fine after a few days' rest."

She and Giroux stepped out of the room, which effectively cut off the sound of their voices, but they were still visible through a glass wall. Giroux towered over the much shorter doctor, but whatever she said to him had him crumbling visibly. The tension in the waiting room ratcheted up to an unbearable degree. Gideon stood beside his mother, his attention snared by the heartrending scene unfolding before us.

Dr. Steinberg reached out and placed a hand on Jean-François's arm, still speaking. After a moment, she stopped and left him. He just stood there, staring at the floor, his shoulders slumped as if a great weight pressed down on them.

I was about to go to him, when Gideon moved first. The moment he stepped outside the waiting room, Giroux lunged at him.

The thud as the two men collided was teeth-rattling in its violence. The room shook as Gideon slammed into the thick glass wall.

Someone shouted in surprise, then yelled for security.

Gideon threw Giroux off and blocked a punch. Then he ducked, avoiding a blow to the face. Jean-François bellowed something, his face contorted with fury and pain.

Corinne's father rushed out at the same moment security arrived with stun guns drawn and aimed. Gideon shoved Jean-François off again, defending himself without once throwing a punch of his own. His face was stony, his eyes cold and nearly as lifeless as Giroux's.

Giroux shouted at Gideon. With the door left open by Corinne's father, I caught part of what was said. The word *enfant* needed no translation. Everything inside me went deathly still, all sound lost to the buzzing in my ears.

Everyone rushed out of the room as both Gideon and Giroux were flex-cuffed and hustled toward a service elevator by the guards. I blinked when Angus appeared in the doorway, certain I was imagining him.

"Mrs. Cross," he said softly, approaching me carefully with his cap in his hands.

I could only imagine how I looked. I was stuck on the word *baby* and what that could possibly mean. After all, Corinne had been in New York as long as I'd known Gideon . . . but her husband hadn't been.

"I've come to take you home."

I frowned. "Where's Gideon?"

"He texted me and asked me to come get you."

My confusion turned into a sharp pain. "But he needs me."

Angus took a deep breath, his eyes filled with something that looked like pity. "Come with me, Eva. It's late."

"He doesn't want me here," I said flatly, latching on to the one thing I was beginning to comprehend.

"He wants you home and comfortable."

My feet felt rooted to the floor. "Is that what the text said?"

"That's what he's thinking."

"You're being kind." I started to walk, running on autopilot.

I passed one of the orderlies picking up the mess made when Giroux had been shoved into a cart of supplies. The way he avoided looking at me seemed to confirm the harsh reality.

I'd been set aside.

22

GIDEON DIDN'T COME home that night. When I checked his apartment on my way out to work, I found the beds neatly made.

Wherever he'd spent the night, it hadn't been near me. After the revelation of Corinne's pregnancy, I was stunned that I'd been left on my own with no explanation. I felt like this huge bomb had exploded in front of me and I was left standing in the rumble, alone and confused.

Angus and the Bentley were waiting for me downstairs when I stepped outside. Irritation simmered. Every time Gideon pulled away from me, he sent Angus in as a surrogate.

"I should've married *you*, Angus," I muttered, as I slid into the backseat. "You're always there for me."

"Gideon makes sure of it," he said, before shutting the door.

Always loyal, I thought bitterly.

When I got to work and learned that Megumi was still out sick, I was equally concerned about her and relieved for me. It wasn't like her to miss work—she was always at her desk early—so the repeated absences told me something was really wrong with her. But not having her there meant she couldn't catch my mood and ask questions I didn't want to answer. Couldn't answer, actually. I had no idea where my husband was, what he was doing or feeling.

And I was angry and hurt about it. The one thing I *wasn't* was scared. Gideon was right about marriage fostering a settled feeling. I had a grip on him he'd have to work to break. He couldn't just disappear or ignore me forever. No matter what, he would have to deal with me at some point. The only question was: When?

Focusing on work, I willed the hours to rush by. When I got off at five, I still hadn't heard from Gideon and I hadn't reached out to him, either. As far as I was concerned, *he* needed to bridge the gap he'd created between us.

I headed to my Krav Maga class after work, where Parker worked one-on-one with me for an hour.

"You're on fire tonight," he said, when I threw him to the mat for the sixth or seventh time.

I didn't tell him I was imagining Gideon in his place.

When I got home, I found Cary and Trey hanging out in the living room. They were eating torpedo sandwiches and watching a comedy show.

"We've got plenty," Trey said, pushing half of his sandwich toward me. "There's beer in the fridge, too."

He was a great guy, with an awesome personality to match. And he loved my best friend. I looked at Cary and for a second, he let me see his confusion and pain. Then he hid it behind his bright, gorgeous smile. He patted the cushion next to him. "Come sit, baby girl."

"Sure," I agreed, partly because I couldn't bear the thought of being alone in my room with my thoughts driving me crazy. "Just let me take a shower first."

Once I was freshly scrubbed and cozy in worn sweats, I joined the two men on the couch. I brooded over getting a "not found" error when I tried to track Gideon's smartphone with the instructions he'd given me.

I ended up sleeping in the living room, preferring the couch to a bed that might smell like my missing husband.

I woke up to the smell of him anyway, and the feel of his arms around me as he lifted me. Weary, I rested my head against Gideon's chest and listened to the sound of his heart beating strong and sure. He carried me to my bedroom.

"Where have you been?" I muttered.

"California."

I jolted. "What?"

He shook his head. "We'll talk in the morning."

"Gideon . . ."

"In the morning, Eva," he said sternly, putting me to bed and pressed a rough kiss to my forehead.

I caught his wrist as he straightened. "Don't you dare leave me."

"I haven't slept in damn near two days." There was an edge to his voice that set off alarms.

Pushing onto my elbows, I tried to see his face in the semidarkness, but it was too hard and I was still trying to shrug off sleep. I could tell he was wearing jeans and a long-sleeved shirt, and that was about it. "So? Got a bed right here."

He heaved out an exasperated, weary breath. "Lie down. I'll get my prescription."

It wasn't until he'd been gone too long that I remembered he kept a bottle of his pills in my bathroom. He'd left for no other reason than to leave. I shoved the blankets off me and stumbled out of the room, making my way through my darkened living room to find my keys. I went to Gideon's apartment and let myself in, nearly tripping over a suitcase left carelessly by the door.

He must have taken just enough time to drop it off before coming to me. And yet he hadn't intended to spend the night in my bed. Why had he come? Just to see me sleep? To check up on me?

Fuck. Would I ever understand him?

I searched for him and found him sprawled facedown on the master bed, his head on my pillow and his clothes still on. His boots lay a few feet apart from each other at the end of the bed, as if he'd kicked them off in a rush, and his smartphone and wallet were tossed on the nightstand.

The phone was irresistible.

I picked it up, typed in *angel* as the password, and scrolled through it without shame. If he caught me doing it, I wouldn't care. If he wasn't going to give me answers, I had every right to search for them myself.

The last thing I expected to find were so many pictures of me in his photo album. There were dozens: some of us together taken by paparazzi, others that he'd taken with his phone when I was unaware. Candid shots that afforded me the opportunity to see myself through his eyes.

I stopped worrying. He loved me. Adored me. No man could take the pictures he did of me otherwise, with messy hair and no makeup, doing nothing more interesting than reading something or standing in front of an open refrigerator contemplating what I wanted. Pictures of me sleeping and eating and frowning in concentration . . . Boring, commonplace things.

His phone log showed mostly calls placed between him and Angus, Raúl, or Scott. There were voice mails from Corinne I refused to torture myself by listening to, but I could see he hadn't answered her or called her in a while. There were calls between him and business associates—a couple with Arnoldo, and several with his attorneys.

And three calls exchanged between him and Deanna Johnson.

My gaze narrowed. Those ranged from several minutes long to a quarter of an hour.

I checked his text messages and found the one he'd sent to Angus when we were at the hospital.

I need her out of here.

Sinking into the armchair in the corner of the room, I stared at the message. *Need*, not *want*. For some reason, the word choice changed my perception of what happened. I still didn't get it completely, but I didn't feel quite so . . . pushed aside.

There were also texts between him and Ireland, which made me happy. I didn't read them but could see that the last one had come in on Monday.

Returning the phone to its former spot, I watched the man I loved sink into the deep sleep of exhaustion. Sprawled as he was, dressed as he was, he looked his age. He carried so much responsibility and he made it look so effortless . . . so innately artless, that it was easy to forget he was as vulnerable to being overworked and stressed out as anyone.

It was my job as his wife to help him deal with it. But that was impossible for me to do if he shut me out. In saving me worry, he took more onto himself.

We'd be talking about that as soon as he caught some sleep.

I woke with a crick in my neck and the lingering sense that something was wrong. Moving gingerly so as not to pull something, I unfolded from my curled-up position in the armchair and noted that the dawn was well on its way. Pinkish-orange light was visible through the windows, and a quick glance at the bedside clock told me it was creeping into morning.

Gideon groaned and I stilled, dread sliding through me at the sound.

It was a terrible noise, the sound of a creature wounded in both body and soul. A chill swept over me as he moaned again, everything in me reacting violently to his torment.

Rushing to the bed, I climbed on it, kneeling as I pushed at his shoulder. "Gideon. Wake up."

He flinched away from me, curling around my pillow and squeezing it. His body jerked as a sob escaped him.

I spooned behind him, wrapping one arm around his waist. "Shh, baby," I whispered. "I've got you. I'm here."

I rocked him as he cried in his sleep, my tears wetting his shirt.

"WAKE up, angel mine," Gideon murmured, his lips brushing over my jaw. "I need you."

I stretched, feeling lingering aches from the last two nights of hard training and the few hours I'd spent sleeping in the armchair before moving to the bed and joining him.

My T-shirt was pushed up, exposing my breasts to his avid, hungry mouth. A hand pushed beneath the waistband of my sweats and then my panties, finding my cleft and expertly coaxing me to a swift arousal.

"Gideon . . ." I could feel the need in his touch, the desire that was far more than skin deep.

He took my mouth, hushing me with a kiss. My hips arched as his fingers pushed into me, fucking me gently. Eager to answer his silent demand for more, I pushed at my sweats, kicking restlessly until I got them off.

I reached for the button fly of his jeans, yanking it open and shoving the denim and cotton boxer briefs out of the way.

"Put me inside you," he whispered against my lips.

I circled his thick erection with my fingers, positioning him and then lifting to take the first inch of him inside me.

Burying his face in my neck, he thrust, sinking into me, moaning with pleasure as I closed tight around him. "Christ, Eva. I need you so much."

My arms and legs caged him, holding him tight.

Time and everything else in the world ceased to matter. Gideon renewed all the promises he'd made to me on the sands of a Caribbean beach, and I tried to heal him, hoping to give him the strength he needed to face another day.

I was putting on my makeup when Gideon joined me in the bathroom, setting a steaming mug of creamy sweet coffee on the marble counter next to me. He wore nothing but pajama pants, so I guessed he wasn't going into the office or at least not right away.

Eyeing him in the mirror, I searched for signs that he remembered his dreams. I'd never seen him so deeply troubled, as if his heart were breaking.

"Eva," he said quietly, "we need to talk."

"I'm on board with that."

Leaning back against the counter, he held his mug in both hands. He stared down into his coffee for a long minute before asking, "Did you make a sex tape with Brett Kline?"

"What?" I faced him, my hand tightening on the handle of my makeup brush. "No. Fuck no. Why would you ask me that?"

He held my gaze. "When I came back from the hospital the other night, Deanna caught up with me in the lobby. After the situation with Corinne, I knew brushing her off was the wrong approach."

"I told you that."

"I know. You were right. So I took her to the bar up the street, bought her a glass of wine, and apologized."

"You took her out for wine," I repeated.

"No, I took her out to tell her I'm sorry for how I treated her. I bought her the wine so we had a reason to be sitting in the damn bar," he said irritably. "I figured you'd prefer a public place over bringing her up to the apartment, which would have been more convenient and private."

He was right, and I appreciated his thinking of how I'd react and making accommodations for it. But I was still annoyed that Deanna had snagged a pseudo date with him.

Gideon must have known what I was feeling because his lips tilted up on one side. "So possessive, angel. You're lucky I like it so much."

"Shut up. What does Deanna have to do with a sex tape? Did she tell you there was one? It's a lie. She's lying."

"She's not. My apology smoothed things over enough for her to throw me a bone. She told me about the tape and that an auction for it was imminent."

"I'm telling you, she's full of shit," I argued.

"You know a guy named Sam Yimara?"

Everything stopped. Anxiety pooled in the pit of my stomach. "Yes, he was the band's wannabe videographer."

"Right." He took a sip of his coffee, his eyes hard as they looked at me over the rim of his mug. "He apparently set up remote cameras at some of the band's shows to gather backstage material. He claims to have re-created the 'Golden' video with actual explicit footage."

"Oh my God." I covered my mouth, feeling sick.

It was bad enough thinking about strangers watching Brett and me fucking, but it was a million times worse imagining Gideon seeing it. I could still picture the look on his face when he'd watched the music video, and *that* had been terrible. He and I would never be the same if he viewed the real deal. I knew I'd never be able to scrub images of him and another woman out of my mind. And over time, they'd eat at me like acid.

"That's why you went to California," I whispered, horrified.

"Deanna gave me what information she had, and I secured a temporary injunction barring Yimara from licensing or selling the video."

I couldn't get a clue about what he was thinking or feeling from his body language. He was closed tight and restrained, rigidly in control. While I felt like I was coming apart at the seams. "You can't stop it from getting out," I whispered.

"We have a temporary seal on the court proceedings."

"That video hits one of those file-sharing sites and it'll spread like the plague."

He shook his head, the ends of his inky hair brushing over his shoulders. "I've got an IT team dedicated to nothing but looking twenty-four-seven for that file on the Internet, but Yimara won't make any money giving the footage away. It's only worth something as an exclusive. He's not going to fuck that up before he exhausts all other options—including selling it to me."

"Deanna will tell. It's her job to expose secrets, not keep them."

"I offered her a forty-eight-hour exclusive on our wedding photos, if she keeps a lid on this."

"And she was okay with that?" I asked skeptically. "That woman's hot for you. She can't have been happy about you being off the market. Permanently."

"There is a point at which it becomes clear there's no hope," he said dryly. "I think I managed to make that point. Trust me, she was happy enough with the money to be made on the wedding exclusive."

I moved to the toilet, dropped the lid down, and sat. The reality of what he'd told me sank in. "I'm sick over this, Gideon."

He set his coffee down next to mine and came to crouch in front of me. "Look at me."

I did as he ordered, but it was hard.

"I will *never* let anyone hurt you," he said. "Do you understand? I *will* take care of this."

"I'm sorry," I breathed. "I'm so sorry you have to deal with this. And with everything else you have going on—"

Gideon caught my hands. "Someone violated your privacy, Eva. Don't apologize for that. As for dealing with this . . . that's my right. My honor. You'll always come first."

"It didn't seem like I came first at the hospital," I argued, needing to get the resentment out before it festered. And needing him to explain why he was always pushing me away when he was trying to protect me. "Everything went to hell and you shoved me at Angus when I wanted to be there for you. You took off to *another state* and didn't call . . . didn't say anything."

His jaw tightened. "And I didn't sleep. It took every minute I had and too many favors to count to get that injunction done in the time I had to work with. You have to trust me, Eva. Even if you don't understand what I'm doing, trust that I'm always thinking of you and doing what's best for you. For us."

I looked away, hating that answer. "Corinne's pregnant."

He exhaled harshly. "She was, yes. Four months along."

One word chilled me. "Was?"

"She miscarried as the doctors were treating the overdose. I'm choosing to believe she didn't know about the baby."

I searched his face and tried to hide the pitiful relief on my own. "Four months? The baby was Giroux's, then."

"I would hope so," he said curtly. "He seems to think it was his, and that I'm responsible for her losing it."

"Jesus."

Gideon's head dropped to my lap, his cheek resting on my thigh. "She *had* to be clueless. She couldn't risk a baby over something so stupid."

"I won't let you blame yourself for this, Gideon," I told him sternly.

He wrapped his arms around my waist. "Christ. Am I cursed?"

I hated Corinne so much in that moment I felt violent. She'd known

Gideon's father had committed suicide. If she knew Gideon at all, she would know how much her attempt would devastate him.

"You are not responsible for this." I ran my fingers through his hair, offering comfort. "Do you hear me? Only Corinne is responsible for what happened. *She'll* have to live with what she's done, not you and me."

"Eva." He hugged me, his breath warm through the silk of my robe.

A quarter hour after Gideon left me in the bathroom to take a call from Raúl, I was still standing at the vanity, staring into the sink.

"You'll be late for work," he said gently, joining me and hugging me from behind.

"I'm thinking about just calling in." I never did that, but I was tired and feeling worn out. I couldn't imagine pulling it together enough to give my job the focus it deserved.

"You could, but it won't look good when you're photographed at the gala tonight."

I looked at him in the mirror. "We're not going!"

"Yes, we are."

"Gideon, if that footage of me and Brett gets out, you don't want your name linked to mine."

His body went stiff, and then he turned me around to face him. "Say that again."

"You heard me. The Cross name has been through enough, don't you think?"

"Angel, I'm as close as I've ever been to taking you across my knee. Luckily for you, I don't play rough when I'm mad."

His gruff teasing didn't distract me from the fact that he was determined to protect the girl I'd been, the girl I was ashamed of. He was willing to stand between me and scandal, shielding me as best he could and taking the hit alongside me, if it came to that.

I didn't think it was possible to love him more than I did, but he kept proving me wrong.

He cupped my face in his hands. "Whatever we face, we face together. And you'll do it with my name."

"Gideon—"

"I can't tell you how proud I am for you to have it." He brushed his mouth across my brow. "How much it means to me that you've taken it and made it yours."

"Oh, Gideon." I pushed onto my tiptoes and surged into him. "I love you so much."

I was a half hour late to work and found a temp at Megumi's desk. I smiled and said hi, but worry ate at me. I popped my head into Mark's office and apologized profusely for being late. Then I called Megumi's cell when I got to my cubicle, but she didn't answer. I headed over to Will's.

"Got a question for you," I said, when I reached him.

"Let's hope I have the answer," he shot back, swiveling in his chair to look up at me through his stylish glasses.

"Who does Megumi call to say she's sick?"

"She reports to Daphne for everything. Why?"

"I'm just worried. She hasn't called me back. I'm wondering if I pissed her off somehow." I shifted on my feet. "I hate not knowing or being able to help."

"Well, for what it's worth, Daphne said she sounds horrible."

"That sucks. But thanks."

I headed back to my cubicle. Mark gestured me into his office as I walked by.

"They're hanging the six-story banner for Tungsten scarves today."

"Yeah?"

He grinned. "Want to go check it out?"

"Really?" As scattered as I was feeling, getting out in the muggy August heat was preferable to sitting at my cool desk. "That'd be awesome!"

He grabbed his jacket off the back of his chair. "Let's go."

WHEN I got home shortly after five o'clock, I found my living room taken over by a team of white-coated beauty technicians. Cary and Trey were kicked back on the couch with green goop on their faces and towels under their heads to protect the white upholstery. My mother was chatting away while her hair was styled in a sexy cap of waves and curls.

I took a quick shower, then joined them. In an hour, they managed to take me from bedraggled to glamorous, affording me the time to think about everything I'd ruthlessly suppressed all day—the video, Corinne, Giroux, Deanna, and Brett.

Someone was going to have to tell Brett. That someone was me.

When the beautician came toward me with a lip brush, I held up my hand. "Red, please."

She paused a minute, her head canting as she examined me. "Yes, you're right."

I was holding my breath through a finishing blast of hair spray when my smartphone vibrated in the pocket of my robe. Seeing Gideon's name on the screen, I answered. "Hi, ace."

"What color are you wearing?" he asked, without a hello.

"Silver."

"Really?" His voice took on a warm purr that made my toes flex. "I can't wait to see you in it. And out of it."

"You won't be waiting," I admonished. "You'd better have your fine ass over here in about ten minutes."

"Yes, ma'am."

My eyes narrowed. "Hurry up or we won't have any limo time."

"Umm . . . I'll be there in five."

He hung up and I held my phone for a minute, smiling.

"Who was that?" my mom asked, coming up beside me.

"Gideon."

Her eyes lit up. "He's escorting you tonight?"

"Yes."

"Oh, Eva." She hugged me. "I'm so glad."

With my arms around her, I figured it was as good a time as any to start spreading the engagement news. I knew Gideon wasn't going to wait long before insisting on sharing our marriage with the world.

I said quietly, "He asked Dad for permission to marry me."

"Did he?" When she pulled back, she was smiling. "He talked to Richard, too, which I think is such a nice touch, don't you? I've already started planning. I was thinking June, at the Pierre, of course. We'll—"

"I suggest December, at the latest."

My mother gasped, her eyes widening. "Don't be ridiculous. There's no way to pull off a wedding in that amount of time. It's impossible."

I shrugged. "Tell Gideon you're thinking of June next year. See what he says."

"Well, I have to wait until he actually proposes first!"

"Right." I kissed her cheek. "I'm going to get dressed."

23

I WAS IN my room, sliding the strapless gown up over my matching bustier, when Gideon came in. I literally stopped breathing, my gaze drinking in his reflection in my cheval mirror. Standing behind me in a tuxedo tailored just for him, with a lovely gray tie that matched my dress so well, he was dazzling. I'd never seen him look so gorgeous.

"Wow," I breathed, entranced. "You are *so* getting laid tonight."

His mouth quirked. "Does that mean I can skip zipping you up?"

"Does that mean we can skip going to this thing?"

"Not a chance, angel. I'm showing off my wife tonight."

"No one knows I'm your wife."

"*I* know it." He came up behind me and secured my zipper. "And soon—really soon—the world will know it."

I leaned back into him, admiring our joint reflection. We took great pictures together.

Which made me think of other pictures . . .

"Promise me," I said, "that you'll never watch the video."

When he didn't answer me, I turned to look at him directly. When I saw the closed-off look on his face, I started freaking out. "Gideon. Did you watch it already?"

His jaw tightened. "A minute or two. Nothing explicit. Just enough to prove validity."

"Oh my God. Promise me you won't watch it." My voice rose and grew sharp as panic spread through me. "Promise me!"

His hands encircled my wrists and squeezed hard enough to make my breath catch. I stared at him, wide-eyed, confused by the sudden aggression.

"Calm down," he said quietly.

The oddest rush of warmth spread outward from where he touched me. My heart beat faster, but also steadier. I stared at our hands, my attention catching on his ruby ring. Red. Like the cuffs he'd bought for me. I felt similarly captured and bound now. And it soothed me in a way I didn't understand.

But Gideon obviously did.

That was why I'd been afraid to marry him so quickly, I realized. He was taking me on a journey that had an unknown destination and I had agreed to follow him blindfolded. It wasn't about where we'd end up as a couple, because that was never in question. We were obsessed, dependent on each other in the unrelenting way of addicts. Where *I* would end up, who I'd be at the end, was what I didn't know.

Gideon's transformation had been almost violent, happening in a moment of sharp clarity when he'd comprehended that he wouldn't—couldn't—live without me. My change was more gradual, so painstakingly measured that I'd believed I wouldn't have to change at all.

I was wrong.

Swallowing past the lump in my throat, I spoke more steadily. "Gideon, listen. Whatever's on that video, it's nothing compared to what you and I have. The only memories I want in your head are ones *we* make. What we've got together . . . that's the only thing that's real. The only thing that matters. So please . . . promise me."

He closed his eyes briefly, then nodded. "All right. I promise."

I breathed out a sigh of relief. "Thank you."

Lifting my hands to his mouth, he kissed them. "You're mine, Eva."

BY silent, mutual agreement, we refrained from mussing each other up in the limo before our first public appearance as a married couple. I was nervous, and while an orgasm or two would help alleviate that, looking less than perfect would only make it worse. And people would notice. Not only was my silver gown eye-catching, with its brilliant sheen and short train, but my arm-candy husband was an impossible-to-miss accessory.

Attention would be on us, and Gideon seemed determined to keep it that way. He helped me out of the limo when we arrived at Fifth Avenue and Central Park South, taking a moment to slide his lips across my temple. "That dress is going to look amazing on my bedroom floor."

I laughed at the cheesy line, which I knew he'd intended, and camera flashes went off in a storm of blinding light. Once he turned away from me, all warmth left his face, the beautiful planes settling into a closed expression that gave nothing away. He set his hand at the small of my back and led me across the red carpet and into Cipriani's.

Once inside, he found a spot he approved of and we stayed there for an hour as business associates and acquaintances circled around us. He wanted me at his side and he wanted to be at mine as well, something he proved a short while later when we were headed to the dance floor.

"Introduce me," he said simply and I followed his gaze to where Christine Field and Walter Leaman, of Waters Field & Leaman, were laughing along with the group of people they were standing with. Christine looked restrained and elegant in a black beaded dress that covered her from throat to wrists to ankles except for the plunging back, and Walter, who was a large man, looked successful and confident in a nicely cut tuxedo and bow tie.

"They know who you are," I pointed out.

"Do they know who I am *to you*?"

I wrinkled my nose a little, knowing my world was going to change drastically once my single-girl self was subsumed by my identity as Eva Cross. "Come on, ace."

We headed over there, weaving through round tables covered in white linens and decorated with candelabras wrapped in floral garlands that lent a wonderful fragrance to the room.

My bosses spotted Gideon first, of course. I don't think they even recognized me until Gideon quite obviously deferred to me by letting me speak first.

"Good evening," I said, shaking Christine's and Walter's hands. "I know you're both familiar with Gideon Cross, my . . ."

I paused, my brain grinding to a halt.

"Fiancé," Gideon finished, shaking hands.

Congratulations were exchanged; smiles got bigger, eyes brighter.

"This doesn't mean we're losing you, does it?" Christine asked, diamond drop earrings glinting in the soft light of the chandeliers.

"No. I'm not going anywhere."

That earned me a sharp pinch on my butt from Gideon.

We were going to have to deal with the work issue at some point, but I figured I could hold him off at least until our next wedding.

We talked a bit about the Kingsman Vodka campaign, which was mostly a way to emphasize what a good job Waters Field & Leaman had done so the agency could hook more Cross Industries business. Gideon knew the game, of course, and played it well. He was polite, charming, and clearly not a man who could be easily influenced.

After that, we ran out of things to talk about. Gideon made our excuses.

"Let's dance," he murmured in my ear. "I want to hold you."

We moved onto the dance floor, where Cary was drawing attention with a stunning redhead. Flashes of a pale, shapely leg could be seen through the risqué slit in her emerald green dress. He moved her into a spin, then a dip. Undeniably suave.

Trey hadn't been able to come because of an evening class, and I was sorry about that. I was sorry, too, that I was glad Cary hadn't brought Tatiana instead. Thinking that way made me feel bitchy, and I seriously disliked catty bitches.

"Look at me."

I tilted my head at Gideon's command and found his eyes on me. "Hi, ace."

With his hand at my back and my hand in his, we swept casually around the dance floor.

"Crossfire," he whispered, his gaze hot on my face.

I touched his cheek with my fingertips. "We're learning from our mistakes."

"You read my mind."

"It feels good."

He smiled, his eyes so blue and his hair so damn sexy I wanted to run my fingers through it right then and there. He pulled me closer. "Not as good as you feel."

We stayed on the dance floor through two songs. Then the music ended when the bandleader turned to the mic and made an announcement: Dinner was about to be served. Seated at our table were my mother and Richard, Cary, a plastic surgeon and his wife, and a guy who said he'd just wrapped up shooting the pilot episode to a new television show he hoped would be picked up for a full-season run.

The meal was some sort of Asian fusion and I ate everything, because it was good and the portions weren't that big. Gideon had his hand on my thigh beneath the table, his thumb rubbing lightly in small circles that made me squirm.

He leaned over. "Sit still."

"Stop it," I whispered back.

"Keep wiggling and I'll put my fingers inside you."

"You wouldn't dare."

He smirked. "Try me and see."

Because I wouldn't put it past him, I sat still, even though it killed me.

"Excuse me," Cary said abruptly, pushing back from the table.

I watched him walk away and caught his gaze lingering on a nearby table. When the redhead in green followed him out of the room a few moments later, I wasn't too surprised, but I was very disappointed. I knew the situation with Tatiana was stressing him out and I knew mindless sex was Cary's cure-all, but it also fucked with his self-esteem and led to more problems than it fixed.

It was good that we were only a couple days away from seeing Dr. Travis.

Leaning into Gideon, I whispered, "Cary and I are going to San Diego this weekend."

His head swiveled toward me. "You're telling me this *now*?"

"Well, between your exes and my ex, my parents, Cary, and everything else, it keeps slipping my mind! I figured I'd better tell you before I forgot again."

"Angel . . ." He shook his head.

"Hang on." I pushed to my feet. I needed to remind him that Brett had a tour stop in San Diego at the same time, but I had to catch Cary first.

He looked at me quizzically as he stood.

"Be right back," I told him, adding very quietly, "Got some cock-blocking to do."

"Eva—"

I heard the warning in his tone and ignored it, lifting my skirt and hurrying after Cary. I'd just made it past the ballroom entrance, when I ran into a familiar face.

"Magdalene," I said in surprise, stopping. "I didn't know you were here."

"Gage was wrapped up in a project, so we ran a little late. Missed dinner entirely, but at least I got my hands on one of those chocolate mousse things they served for dessert."

"Kick-ass," I agreed.

"Totally." Magdalene smiled.

I thought to myself that she looked really good. Softer, sweeter. Still stunning and sultry in a one-shouldered red lace dress, her dark hair framing a delicate face and crimson lips. Getting away from Christopher Vidal had done her a lot of good. And having a new man in her life surely helped. I remembered her mentioning a guy named Gage when she'd visited me at work a couple weeks before.

"I saw you with Gideon," she said. "And I noticed your ring."

"You should've come over and said hi."

"I was eating that dessert."

I laughed. "A girl's got to have her priorities."

Magdalene reached out and touched my arm briefly. "I'm happy for you, Eva. Happy for Gideon."

"Thank you. You should stop by our table and tell him that."

"I will. Catch you later."

She walked off and I stared after her for a minute, still wary but thinking she might not be so bad after all.

The one negative about running into Magdalene was losing Cary. By the time I resumed chasing after him, he'd already ducked out of sight somewhere.

I headed back to Gideon, mentally preparing the ass-chewing I was going to give Cary. Elizabeth Vidal halted me in my tracks.

"Excuse me," I said, when I nearly bumped into her.

She grabbed me by the elbow and pulled me over to a dark corner. Then she caught my hand and looked at my gorgeous Asscher diamond. "That's my ring."

I tugged free. "It *was* your ring. It's mine now. Your son gave it to me around the time he asked me to marry him."

She looked at me with those blue eyes that were so like her son's. So like Ireland's. She was a beautiful woman, glamorous and elegant. As much a head-turner as my mother, really, but she had Gideon's iciness.

"I won't let you take him away from me," she bit out between brilliantly white teeth.

"You've got it all wrong." I crossed my arms. "I want to get you two together, so we can put everything out in the open."

"You're filling his head with lies."

"Oh my God. Seriously? The next time he tells you what happened—and I'll make sure he does—you're going to believe him. And you're going to apologize, and find some fucking way to make it easier for him to bear. Because I want him healed and healthy and whole."

Elizabeth stared at me, clearly fuming. She obviously wasn't on board with that plan.

"Are we done?" I asked, disgusted with her deliberate blindness.

"Not even close," she hissed, leaning into me. "I know about you and that lead singer. I'm on to you."

I shook my head. Had Christopher talked to her? What would he have said? Knowing what he'd done to Magdalene, I believed him capable of pretty much anything. "Unbelievable. You believe the lies and ignore the truth."

I started walking away but stopped. "What I think is really interesting is that after I confronted you last time, you didn't ask Gideon about what happened. 'Hey, son, your crazy girlfriend told me this crazy story.' I can't figure out why you didn't ask him. I don't suppose you'd want to explain?"

"Fuck you."

"Yeah, I didn't think you would."

I left her behind before she opened her mouth again and ruined my night.

Unfortunately, when I started heading toward my table, I saw Deanna Johnson sitting in my seat, talking to Gideon.

"Are you kidding me?" I muttered, my gaze narrowing at the way the reporter kept putting her hand on his forearm as she talked. Cary was off doing what he shouldn't be doing; my mom and Stanton were on the dance floor. And Deanna had slid in like a snake.

Whatever Gideon thought, it was obvious to me that her interest in him was as hot as ever. And while he offered no encouragement aside from listening to whatever she was saying, just the fact that he was giving her attention was watering that weed.

"She must be great in bed. He fucks her a lot."

I stiffened and turned toward the woman talking to me. It was Cary's redhead, who had the flushed, bright-eyed look of a woman who'd just had a very nice orgasm. Still, she was older than I'd first thought from a distance.

"You should watch out for him," she said, looking at Gideon. "He uses women. I've seen it happen. More than it should."

"I can handle myself."

"They all say that." Her sympathetic smile rubbed me the wrong way. "I know of two women who've experienced severe depression over him. Certainly, they won't be the last."

"You shouldn't listen to gossip," I snapped.

She walked away with an irritatingly serene smile, reaching up to pat her hair as she skirted tables on the way to her own.

It wasn't until she was halfway across the room that I placed her face.

"Crap."

I hurried back to Gideon. He stood when I reached him.

"I need you real quick," I said briskly, before shooting a look at the brunette in my chair. "Deanna, always a pleasure."

She ignored the dig. "Hi, Eva. I was just leaving—"

But I'd already tuned her out. I caught Gideon's hand and tugged. "Come on."

"All right, hang on." He said something to Deanna, but I didn't catch it, pulling him along instead. "Christ, Eva. What the hell is the rush?"

I stopped by the wall and looked out over the room, searching for green and red. Seemed to me he would have noticed his former lover—unless she'd been deliberately avoiding him. Of course she looked so different without her former pixie haircut, and I hadn't seen her white-haired husband, which would have made it easier to identify her sooner. "Do you know if Anne Lucas is here?"

His hand tightened on mine. "I haven't seen her. Why?"

"Emerald green dress, long red hair. Seen that woman?"

"No."

"She was dancing with Cary earlier."

"I wasn't paying attention."

I looked at him, getting aggravated. "Jesus, Gideon. It was hard to miss her."

"Forgive me for having eyes only for my wife," he said dryly.

I squeezed his hand. "I'm sorry. I just need to know if it was her."

"Explain why. Did she come up to you?"

"Yeah, she did. Shoveled some shit my way, then wandered off. I think Cary sneaked off with her, too. You know, for a quickie."

Gideon's face turned hard. He turned his attention to the room, sweeping it from one side to the other, with a slow searching glance. "I don't see her. Or anyone like you described."

"Isn't Anne a therapist?"

"Psychiatrist."

A sense of foreboding made me restless. "Can we go now?"

He studied me. "Tell me what she said to you."

"Nothing I haven't heard before."

"That's reassuring," he muttered. "Yes, let's go."

We went back to our table for my clutch and to say good-bye to everyone.

"Can I hitch a ride with you?" Cary asked, after I hugged my mom good-bye.

Gideon nodded. "Come on."

ANGUS shut the door of the limo.

Cary, Gideon, and I settled back into the bench seats, and just a couple of minutes later we pulled away from Cipriani's and into traffic.

My best friend shot me a look. "Don't start."

He hated when I laid into him about his behavior, and I didn't blame him. I wasn't his mother. But I was someone who loved him and wanted good things for him. I knew how self-destructive he could be when left unchecked.

But that wasn't my biggest concern at that moment.

"What was her name?" I asked, praying he knew so I could identify the redhead once and for all.

"Who cares?"

"Jesus." My hands flexed restlessly around my clutch. "Do you know it or not?"

"I didn't ask," he retorted. "Drop it."

"Watch the tone, Cary," Gideon admonished quietly. "You've got a problem, fine. Don't take it out on Eva for giving a shit about you."

Cary's jaw tightened and he looked out the window.

I sat back and Gideon drew me into the curve of his shoulder, his hand running up and down my bare arm.

No one said another word on the ride home.

WHEN we reached my apartment, Gideon headed into the kitchen to grab a bottle of water and ended up on the phone, his gaze meeting mine across the breakfast bar and the several feet separating us.

Cary stalked off to his bedroom, then turned abruptly at the hallway and came back to hug me. *Hard.*

With his face in the curve of my shoulder, he whispered, "Sorry, baby girl."

I hugged him back. "You deserve better than the way you treat yourself."

"I didn't do her," he said quietly, pulling back to look at me. "I was going to. I thought I wanted to. But when it came down to it, it hit me that I have a kid coming. A *kid*, Eva. And I don't want him—or her—growing up thinking of me the way I do my mom. I gotta get my shit straight."

I hugged him again. "I'm proud of you."

"Yeah, well." He pulled back, looking sheepish. "I still rubbed her off, since I'd taken it that far, but my dick stayed tucked in my pants."

"TMI, Cary," I said. "Totally TMI."

"We still heading out to San Diego tomorrow?" His hopeful look twisted my heart.

"Hell, yeah. I'm looking forward to it."

His grin was tinged with relief. "Good. I've got us flying out at eight thirty."

Gideon rejoined us just then, and the look he gave me told me we weren't done talking about my going away for the weekend. But when Cary headed down the hallway to his room, I grabbed Gideon and kissed him hard, delaying that conversation. As I'd hoped, he didn't hesitate to pull me in and take over, his mouth eating at mine with lush, deep licks.

Moaning, I let him sweep me away. The world could go crazy by itself for a night. Tomorrow was soon enough to face it and everything we had to deal with.

I grabbed him by the tie. "Tonight, you're mine."

"I'm yours every night," he said in that warm, raspy voice that stirred the hottest fantasies.

"Start now." I walked backward, pulling him toward my room. "And don't stop."

He didn't. Not 'til morning.

AUTHOR'S NOTE

Yes, dear reader, you're right. This can't possibly be the end.

Gideon and Eva's journey isn't quite finished yet. I look forward to seeing where they'll take us next.

All my best,
Sylvia

SYLVIA DAY

BARED TO YOU

Our journey began in fire...

Gideon Cross came into my life like lightning in the darkness – beautiful and brilliant, jagged and white hot. I was drawn to him as I'd never been to anything or anyone in my life. I craved his touch like a drug, even knowing it would weaken me. I was flawed and damaged, and he opened those cracks in me so easily . . .

Gideon *knew.* He had demons of his own. And we would become the mirrors that reflected each other's most private wounds . . . and desires.

The bonds of his love transformed me, even as I prayed that the torment of our pasts didn't tear us apart . . .

'A hundred degrees hotter than anything you've read before' *Reveal*

'Move over Danielle Steel and Jackie Collins, this is the dawn of a new Day' *Amuse*

Sylvia Day

REFLECTED IN YOU

Gideon Cross. As beautiful and flawless on the outside as he was damaged and tormented on the inside. He was a bright, scorching flame that singed me with the darkest of pleasures. I couldn't stay away. I didn't want to. He was my addiction . . . my every desire . . . *mine.*

My past was as violent as his, and I was just as broken. We'd never work. It was too hard, too painful . . . except when it was perfect. Those moments when the driving hunger and desperate love were the most exquisite insanity.

We were bound by our need. And our passion would take us beyond our limits to the sweetest, sharpest edge of obsession . . .

Intensely romantic, darkly sensual and completely addictive, *Reflected in You* will take you to the very limits of obsession – and beyond.

Sylvia Day

SEVEN YEARS TO SIN

The novel that inspired Sylvia Day to write bestselling novel, *Bared to You, Seven Years to Sin* is a smart, sensual story of a young woman's sexual awakening at the hands of a handsome rogue in Regency England.

Seven years ago, on the eve of her wedding, young Lady Jessica Sheffield witnessed a scandalous seduction by the roguish Alistair Caulfield. But after years of serene but unfulfilling marriage, she still cannot free her dreams of this illicit liaison. So when newly widowed Jessica steps aboard Caulfield's ship for a transatlantic passage, years of denied pleasure and passion will be unleashed in the most provocative way . . .